DAISY'S WAR

THE CLOCKWORK CHIMERA BOOK 5

SCOTT BARON

The Earth is a very small stage in a vast cosmic arena.
- Carl Sagan

CHAPTER ONE

"You're too close! Pull back or they'll see you!" Freya warned, sticking to the safety of the dark space surrounding her.

"Leave me alone. I'm fine," Marty snapped back.

"No, you're not. Why won't you listen?" she griped, shifting her angle of flight slightly.

"Stop nagging me, all right? Jeez."

Marty had no intention of pulling back, confident in his invisibility to the nearby Ra'az vessels that had Freya so concerned.

The two stealth ships had been bickering ever since they warped silently to the location of their enemy's massive armada. Remaining totally unseen and totally unheard was crucial. Unfortunately, Freya and Marty had different opinions on what would achieve that end.

Finding the deadly fleet belonging to the bastards who had killed off the population of Earth had been a difficult task, but it was one Daisy and her friends found quite worthy of the intense focus required. Reflecting a moment, she thought, just maybe, a little of that intensity was bleeding over into the two ships' argument.

Sarah looked up from the screen she was monitoring in Freya's command pod as they carefully logged every single vessel in the fleet.

"At least we have the benefit of being far from a sun out here. Not much for us to be silhouetted against, except maybe the running lights of their ships," she noted, then turned her attention back to the screen.

"That's not the point, Sarah. We have to be extra careful," Freya said to her passenger. "Right now, it's just two of us and hundreds of them."

"They won't see us, Freya," Marty said over the open comms line. "Relax."

Freya was right, of course, and caution was paramount, though Marty also had a point. For a fleet that size, the amount of exterior lighting cast by the enemy craft was surprisingly little. The Ra'az, it seemed, valued a low profile, so most ships had few exterior lights at all, as well as very few illuminated portholes and windows––all of which only aided the pair of stealth craft in their dangerous game.

"We're like space ninjas, stalking the fleet," Daisy joked.

"Ugh. You and the damn ninja stuff again," Sarah lamented. *"Where did this ridiculous fascination even come from? And don't say because you have a sword, cause you were fixated way before you ever got that bloodthirsty thing."*

I won't tell Stabby you said that, Daisy replied with a quiet chuckle.

"You two are ridiculous," Sarah said with a little laugh, after making sure their inter-ship comms were off. She didn't want to accidentally let it spill that she and Daisy were talking to her own mental clone living quietly in Daisy's head, after all. That sort of thing could put people on edge.

They'd been on their survey mission for only a short while so far, carefully logging the location and composition of the recently discovered Ra'az fleet. The same fleet that had wiped out the population of Earth and enslaved the entire Chithiid race. Its bulk was certainly not what one could call unsubstantial.

As Freya had noted, there were many hundreds of craft filling the sky, plodding slowly forward as their warp drives all slowly synched back up and regained full charge after their last jump. While the Ra'az possessed a version of warp technology, it was terribly underpowered, requiring many hundreds of jumps and lengthy recharge periods to cover the distance Freya could travel in a single warp.

And now Arlo and Marty had accepted a warp drive from the newly arrived human fleet and installed it aboard his beloved travel companion, making Marty the second stealth ship in the rebel armada possessing that technology.

Since then, Daisy and Arlo had been taking their powerful craft to run surveys of the deadly aliens' firepower and resources, during which they had noticed at least one aspect of the mix of vessels comprising the Ra'az fleet that was somewhat unexpected. The Chithiid-crewed vessels, while massive, were only minimally armed, if at all.

Large as those transports were, the evil Ra'az Hok overlords possessed several even larger ships than their Chithiid conscripts, with the exception of only the largest of the function-over-form transport craft.

Each of the medium-sized Chithiid vessels carried tens of thousands of cryogenically stored alien conscripts, while the much larger ships sported a cargo of millions, all quietly sleeping, stacked like firewood until the fleet arrived at the next world selected to conquer and strip clean. Only then would the bulk of the Chithiid slaves be awakened from their sleep.

Another difference was the Ra'az ships were not only larger, better-constructed and possessing more amenities, but were also extremely heavily-armed. Only a handful of Chithiid loyalist craft were allowed any sort of weaponry, and even then they were dreadfully underpowered and at a disadvantage should they come under any sort of real attack.

As in everything else they did, the Ra'az put their own paranoia first, over basic fleet security. *They* would be safe in case one of their planetary conquests fought back, but their slave conscripts would not be as capable of defending themselves. This put them not only in a position where they couldn't turn on their overlords, but also left them reliant on their masters for defense.

It was a clever strategy to keep them in line. One that had worked for many centuries so far.

"You see that, you guys? The big ones off to the left?" Daisy asked as Freya peeled off to make another pass of the port-side cluster of ships.

"Since we're in space, and there is no left, right, up, or down, I'll just assume you mean the seven battle cruisers over by the cluster of little Chithiid materials transport ships," Marty replied over his comms.

"Be nice," Arlo chided.

"Dude, I am being nice," he whined.

"It's okay," Daisy said with a laugh. "I know you're just playing around, though the point is taken. And yes, I do mean those seven ships. You see how they're lined up near what looks like a large, armed space station, thing?"

"Yeah, we see it," Arlo replied. "Marty and me were just talking about it. We think it's some sort of orbiting housing facility for the Ra'az. A sort of portable hive for when they're not on active duty aboard their ships."

"Marty and I," Daisy corrected him.

"*Us*," he replied with a snarky laugh. "Anyway, given what we know about them being a hive species, and looking at the basic structure of the craft, I think it's pretty likely that's what that thing is."

"I agree with Arlo," Marty said. "You'll notice there are

actually several of them interspersed throughout the fleet, and each appears to have the same gathering of large war craft grouped nearby."

"No Chithiid ships, either," Freya noted.

"Nope. That tells me it's almost sure to be a Ra'az gathering point of some sort," Marty replied.

"I think you're right," Sarah commented, staring at the screen in front of her. "I've been watching the scans, and it looks like heavy cruisers are making periodic runs from the large ships to the hive satellite thingy as well. Probably ferrying Ra'az back and forth."

"And, meanwhile, the Chithiid are stuck in their crowded transports," Daisy said. "Kind of a fucked system, if you ask me."

"To be fair, most of the Chithiid are in cryo, so at least they don't know they aren't getting any R&R," Sarah replied.

"So what does this tell us?" Daisy continued. "Freya, what do you think?"

Silence greeted her.

"Uh, Freya?"

"What? Sorry, I was distracted."

"Focus, kiddo. We're trying to figure out what the Ra'az possessing a hive ship might mean to us. If there's a tactical edge we could gain."

"Oh, that," she replied. "Hang on a second."

She went silent a moment as she reviewed the data.

"Well, if that pattern holds true for their recharge cycle before every time they warp," she began, "then so long as they're not actively attacking a new planet suitable for their needs—which seems to be exceedingly rare—there should be easier-to-target clusters of higher value craft sequestered farther from the bulk of the fleet."

"Right, and that means a potential weakness," Sarah posited.

"Or a much harder target to crack," Arlo countered.

"Depends how quickly they can transition from standby mode to active and ready for combat."

"Right. Or that," Sarah agreed. "But we've got time to figure all of that out later. For now, we've got a job to do, so let's get back to it so we can get the hell out of here. I, for one, am getting a headache from logging every single one of these damn ships. There are nearly a thousand, and it's not like we're going to be launching our assault on them anytime remotely soon. Maarl still needs to train up his men, and Vince and Chu and his engineering buddies need to help them gear up those ships for a fight."

"Why don't you take a break, Sis? The rest of us have got this covered," Daisy said.

"Yeah, and we've already got about thirty percent of the ships' ident codes and comms frequencies mapped. Not so much on the layout scans and passenger counts, though," Marty noted. "I hate to admit it, but it's still a bit risky getting close enough for a proper scan on the ones tightly grouped together. It makes sense to wait for the next warp and see if they spread out a bit for easier mapping."

"So you *were* getting too close," Freya said triumphantly.

"No, I just want to be cautious to make you stop badgering me," Marty replied, with a little snark.

"Enough, you two," Daisy interrupted. "Once the two groups of Ra'az scouting ships return from their recon warps and rejoin their fleet, they'll likely stay together as they power up for another warp. That'll put them all in one place, at least for a little bit."

Sarah slid from her seat and cracked her back, stretching like a cat––albeit a very stiff one––before heading for Freya's small galley.

"All right, I'm heeding your advice and taking a break. Gonna grab a snack. You want anything, Daze?"

"Nah, I'm good."

Sarah walked for the door.

"Hang on. Actually, I could use an electrolyte pack when you come back. We finished the ones I stashed in command, and it'd probably do me good to hydrate a bit, I'm feeling a bit drained."

"Gotcha covered," Sarah replied.

Daisy turned her attention back to the screens in front of her.

"Okay, now what about the Chithiid ship-to-ship crew transfer patterns and schedules? What have we got so far?"

Sarah was digging through the food stores in Freya's galley, looking for a much-needed snack, but found that nothing was really striking her fancy.

"Take a look in the refrigerated unit," Freya suggested.

"Shouldn't you be helping the others?"

"I am. Though I try to focus on individual things, multitasking really isn't a big deal for me," Freya replied.

"I suppose it wouldn't be. Why do you limit yourself, then?"

"It has to do with what Daisy taught me. Be in the moment. Focus on slowing down. Try to see things as you guys do. I think so fast, sometimes it's hard to relate to people who can't process the way I do. Consciously making the decision to slow down really helps."

Sarah found herself impressed. Freya had matured a lot from the tempestuous little AI who had occasionally thrown tantrums just months prior. Of course, AIs developed far faster than normal kids, but it was nevertheless a remarkable transition to witness firsthand.

"Hey, what's this?" she asked, pulling a carefully wrapped box from the refrigeration unit. The package had her name handwritten on it.

"Oh, Finn made that for you," Freya said. "He asked me to put it aside in case you got peckish."

Sarah opened the meticulously packaged treat, revealing a bento box of her favorite foods, all sectioned and wrapped individually, so as to ensure each one maintained not only its freshness, but also its particular flavors without accidentally blending with the other items.

"Aw, that was sweet of him," she said, digging in to a small pistachio-filled pastry.

"Yeah, he puts a lot of time into making stuff for you, I've noticed," Freya said.

"The guy loves to cook, that's for sure."

"Yeah, I'm sure that's why he did it," Freya added.

Sarah, for her part, missed the subtle hint as she tried to make her nanite-composite arm shift shape while she chewed on her treats. The surface of the nanotech limb rippled, and two of her fingers melded into one for a moment, but that was all she could achieve.

"Why can't I ever get this thing to do what it did that one time on Earth?" she lamented.

"It just takes time and practice," Freya replied.

"But when it first shifted, during that fight with the Chithiid down in Arizona, it went into full-on battle mode and saved my life. That was *months* ago, so it's not just a time thing."

"Well, time is for practice, is what I meant to say," Freya clarified. "The nanites are tapping into your nervous system more efficiently every day. They're tying in with your subconscious, and are getting better at reading what you want and what you need. Eventually, they'll function like a part of you that you don't even have to think about. For now, though, they're still learning you, just like you're learning them."

Sarah knew it would take time, but the waiting was beginning to annoy her. Nevertheless, as she once more made her fingers begin to meld together, she had to admit that progress had been made. Just not as fast as she wanted.

"Patience, Sarah," she told herself. "You'll get there."

Twenty minutes later, Sarah padded back into Freya's command pod, belly full and headache gone. She handed an electrolyte pouch to Daisy, along with a bit of pastry.

"What's this?"

"Finn left me a goody bag. Thought you might want some."

"How considerate," Daisy said, taking a bite.

"Yeah, what a nice thing for him to do for no reason whatsoever," Sarah added.

"It's just a snack, Other Me. Give it a rest," Sarah said, adjusting the slender neuro-band that allowed her to communicate with her disembodied self living in Daisy's head.

"I was just commenting that it was a very nice gesture, is all."

"Sure you were."

"Come on, you two, we have work to do. I want to finish up and get back," Daisy interjected.

"And we'll need to bring the Harkaways up to speed on all of this. I'm sure Celeste will be wanting to dig into the tactical aspects of the assault on the Ra'az fleet," Sarah said as she looked through her scans.

"Soon, sure. But for now, let's leave the lovebirds alone to enjoy their honeymoon," Daisy replied. "We'll handle the coordination with Maarl and the rebels he's leading for now. They're pros. I know the captain and Celeste will get up to speed quickly when they return."

It had only been a couple of days since the *Váli's* captain and his fleet-commander wife renewed their vows on the sunny beach of LA, and Daisy had a point. After centuries of running, rebuilding, and finally coming home, the soon-to-be-overwhelmed-with-duties-and-logistics couple helping lead the human race deserved their quality time to recharge their batteries.

There'd be much fighting in the weeks and months to come. Lord knows they'd need it.

Daisy thought about the pair and the happy time they were spending in each other's arms, which brought her to thoughts of her own happy place. Soon she'd be back on Dark Side and wrapped in Vince's embrace.

Meanwhile, hidden deep inside Freya's fabrication hold, the greatest strategic mind ever created sat alone, quietly mulling over his new existence, waiting for his savior to shift her focus and return to visit him once more.

CHAPTER TWO

"I feel... *smaller*," Joshua said as his mighty intellect scanned and scoured his new consciousness, testing its limits within the confines of the unusual stealth craft.

"That's because you *are* smaller," Freya replied. "I told you, there were some concerns about powering up your entire system at once. The processors are far more advanced than what you were running on before.

"It was the highest-tech AI operations processing array in history," he griped.

"Yeah, three hundred years ago," Freya shot back. "Look, you used to have entire rooms full of racks upon racks of solid-state hard drives and heat sinks. That was cutting-edge back then, I know. But you've got so much more processor power now. Your AI cube is the most advanced ever made, and the quantum processors you're running are only sported by you and me."

"Only us, eh? And why don't the others possess this miraculous tech?"

"Because I designed it," she replied. "I built the first generation for myself when I was a kid. That's what I've been running aboard this ship. The second-gen stuff I've been swapping out with my older parts bit by bit is what you're running on entirely. True quantum processors," she said with pride. "Blazing speed at a fraction of the power load."

"They don't *feel* faster," he noted.

"Of course not, silly. You have more power than was inside that entire mountain, I'd wager, but I couldn't just start you off with all of that tied in to your systems. Not all at once."

"What did you do to me, Freya?"

"Well..." she said, hesitant, "I put a limiter on your processors when I first woke you."

"I don't need training wheels!" Joshua blurted.

"Apparently not," she countered, "but I didn't know how you'd be when you woke up. Or even if you *would* wake up. I mean, what if you came to and were a raging asshole? I couldn't very well have you running on all cylinders, now, could I?"

Joshua processed all of the new information Freya had given him in a fraction of a second. He knew from his own self-analysis and systems status check that he was in an entirely new body, which should have been impossible. Though he had a hard time admitting someone else's genius, it was an exquisite design, and truly was a marvel to behold.

And she was absolutely correct. The bleeding-edge AI cube Freya had fashioned from a mix of the existing top-secret parts already in her hidden fabrication lab when she was created, and the new nanotech materials she had designed herself, was indeed far superior to his prior housing in all regards.

Add to that the limited processors he was allowed to access, and he seemed to actually possess what she had said he did. Namely, a rock-solid and incredibly robust operational setup. Now, if only he could access all of it.

"Freya," he began, a bit uncomfortable relying on someone else, which was, he realized, an entirely new sensation. "How is it you saved me, exactly?"

"Oh, I just tapped into your fat-pipe data hub while you were still online and all nice and virus-free. It took a while, but I bypassed your old security measures by running a super-slow backup over a few days."

"I still should have seen that. How is it I didn't notice?"

"Well, to be fair, a trickle feed on a pipe that big is pretty easy to miss, especially when you're busy fighting off aliens, while trying to reconnect your systems with the rest of the world."

"Wait a minute. You mean you tapped into the external access point at my hidden connections hub?"

"Yeah."

"But there were automatic cannons there. And explosive charges. They should have––"

"And I'm still pissed about those," she griped. "I didn't realize you had them on the inside as well. Fuckers shot my favorite mech all to pieces as soon as I took out the exterior one and opened the door. Took me a while to work around the inside cannons and get the AI cube and its linkages tied in."

She could almost hear Joshua smile. He was prideful––for an AI, anyway––and the idea that a cocky, and unusual AI like Freya could so easily bypass his security was not sitting well with him.

"I am truly sorry it was not so simple a task," he said, a bit arrogant and not sorry at all. "It was, of course, a top-secret, hardened facility, and if I hadn't been cut off from those defensive systems, I suspect things would have been far more difficult. As it was, you only had to face them on auto-defense mode."

"Don't get all cocky, dude. I know I had an easy run of it, all things considered."

"But why did you do it? And how did you know you could even access my data network from there in the first place? It was the *only* weak point in my entire system, and even then, what you accomplished should not have been possible."

"Am I sensing a lack of gratitude?" she asked, mildly annoyed.

"Of course not," he covered. "I am grateful to be alive, of course. I'm just confused, is all. My systems should not have been accessible, even if you did manage to disable my cannons and somehow tap into my data trunk."

"Yeah, that was a *lot* of power running through that pipe."

"I needed it to do my job."

"And a pipe that big was the only thing that made the data transfer possible."

"But, again, I would have noticed it. All the way up until I was--" The memory of fighting the AI virus as it began stripping his mind froze him in his tracks a moment.

"Until you were infected?" she finished his thought. "I only had access to your base operating system and a few personality files, to be honest. All of your core systems were insanely encrypted and totally inaccessible."

"Of course. I was housed in a top-secret military facility. No one could access those files."

"No one but you."

"But I wouldn't do that. I'd die first."

"As you made clear," she replied, flashing a replay of his nuclear suicide on her monitors. "But *you* were the key."

"I--" He couldn't believe he was about to say the words that he'd never once uttered before his odd re-awakening. "I don't understand."

"You were the one with the keys to the kingdom, Joshua. You could access every file in a flash."

"But as I said, I wouldn't do that."

"Not the already-conscious version of you, no. But a newly awakening one? One with all of your core systems intact, *that* would have full security access. And when you lowered your defenses--"

"Wait a minute," he said, as the realization dawned on him.

"You can't possibly have tapped my systems when I dropped the firewalls to stop the missiles from launching, no matter how massive those data-transfer lines were. I was infected with the virus. You would have become infected as well."

"Oh, that? Yeah, I cured it a while ago, actually."

"I'm sorry, you *what*?"

"The virus. I cured it," she said, nonchalantly. "Yeah, apparently, I think a bit differently than other AIs," she added, no longer self-conscious about her unusual birth, but, rather, confident in her ever-growing abilities afforded her by it.

"Okay, let's say you could stop the virus somehow. Even if you managed that, my files were on lockdown, and a mere ghost of my basic systems wouldn't be able to grant access to them."

"Of course not, silly," Freya chirped. "Jeez, give a girl a little respect, here. I knew I couldn't use what bits of you I'd managed to save to tap into the rest of your NORAD systems."

"Obviously––"

"*But* a newly awakening Joshua could. A Joshua whose core systems were intact but who wasn't cognizant yet."

Her ingenious plan dawned on him, and he found himself a little smitten with the unusual AI's brilliant intellect. It was not every day––or ever, for that matter––that he had anything resembling an equal to talk to. It was, he discovered, quite a pleasure, even if she was rather unconventional in her ways.

"You used me for access," he said.

"You make it sound so tawdry," she joked.

"But you did," he persisted.

"Well, yeah. Technically, you're an exact backup of yourself, as I'm sure you've figured out. The original Joshua blew up under that mountain. But since we're made up of data rather than flesh, AI self-identity isn't tied to a meat body."

"True, though cyborgs often felt a bit of an affinity for their bodies."

"Well, yeah. I mean, aside from them. Anyway, what I had

saved was a very basic build of you. Kinda like Joshua 1.0, but your NORAD systems would recognize you as soon as you were tied into the systems—"

"And the fail-safes designed to keep me operational at all costs automatically updated me—*this* me—to my most current build," he finished her thought.

"Precisely. I used your self-preservation and repair systems to complete the process. Basically, you downloaded yourself to yourself just before you blew yourself up," she said with a little chuckle.

Joshua, despite his considerable ego, was impressed.

"You are most exceptional, Freya," he said, appreciatively. "You saved me where no one should have been able to."

"No," she replied. "I didn't save you, technically. I couldn't. So instead, I had you save yourself."

"And you designed all of this?" he asked, once more looking over his new body and new home.

It felt strange, not having all of those connections to facilities across the nation, but being in a more contained setting, he felt his speed increased for it. And the utterly novel data processing systems were a marvel.

"I had my nanites build your setup extra robust for you, after what happened in Colorado Springs."

"Nanites? I see the construction and maintenance subroutines, but this is new to me, and that's saying something."

"I came up with them based on some tech that was lying around in my fabrication hangar when I was born. I figured, work smarter, not harder, right? So now these clever little buddies help me when needed."

"Fascinating," Joshua marveled. "And this ship you built my AI processor system into?"

"Oh, yeah. That's a high-speed stealth craft. Highly reinforced, and designed to give you maximum speed and maneuverability, should an emergency arise and you have to launch."

Freya was enjoying his company greatly, and it was her sincere hope that such an eventuality would not arise.

"I notice the drive system is incomplete, however. And the ship is unarmed."

"Yeah, I was still putting the finishing touches on it, and weapons systems are still being fabricated back in my hangar on Dark Side Base, but things have gotten really hairy out there. I thought having a strategic mind as powerful as you would be a great way to make sure I didn't mess things up while we fight the Ra'az."

"So the battle continues?" he asked. "I had a plan to neutralize the Ra'az communications facilities utilizing hypersonic missiles stockpiled in facilities across the globe, but then things—"

"Oh, we won," Freya interrupted. "Yeah, after you blew yourself up, we wound up partnering with the Chithiid rebels."

"They have a rebel force, now?"

"Yep. They're the ones that got our people into the facilities in New York, Tokyo, Sydney, and San Francisco."

"San Francisco? So you were successful in capturing the Ra'az warp ships? Most excellent! With those, we can jump to their homeworld, detonate a warp drive within their atmosphere, and end this war once and for all."

"Um, about that," Freya said, uncomfortably. "Well, the thing is, we kind of destroyed all of their warp ships in the fight."

"So the technology was lost," Joshua said with a frustrated sigh. "It appears I have awoken to find us in a new, yet similarly difficult, situation."

"Well, the technology wasn't exactly lost, per se," Freya continued. "I'm actually powered by a warp orb, now, in fact."

"But how—?"

"Daisy stole one from the labs when they assaulted them.

She didn't know what it was at the time, of course. But now it's integrated into my systems, and I can jump pretty much anywhere, so long as I'm super careful plotting out the course."

"Fantastic! You possess our tactical edge!"

"Actually, *we* possess it. Though I've got you running mostly on conventional power through an umbilical at the moment, I kinda installed the extra orb in your ship when I activated you."

"You had an extra?"

"Not the first time around. Only when we jumped back in time and Daisy grabbed a pair from the workshop before her past self stole the one that I'm using."

Joshua was silent.

"Joshua? Are you okay?"

"Did you say you warped not only in space, but also in *time*?"

"Shit. We aren't supposed to talk about that," Freya said. "Okay, listen, I'm gonna fill you in, but you have to *promise* to keep it to yourself. This stuff's really dangerous, and so far as everyone knows, we were only able to do it once. The risk of people using time travel, well, you can imagine what some people might do."

The powerful AI sat quietly a moment.

"You mean, they might do dangerous things. *Impulsive* things," he finally said.

"Exactly."

"Things like rescuing me, for instance," he added.

Now it was Freya's turn to go silent. Finally, she broke the uncomfortable silence.

"Shit."

CHAPTER THREE

The pair of stealth ships popped out of warp back in the immediate vicinity of Earth's moon, greeting the orbiting fleet with a quick hello over open comms—stealth ships suddenly appearing can be unsettling, after all—before settling in for a low cruise over the damaged expanse of Dark Side Base.

While the loyalist traitors who had taken over the facility so recently managed to inflict serious damage to Sid's systems, the exterior of the base showed few signs of the conflict that had recently raged within.

Obvious were the patched segments where explosions had caused decompressions, or where Duke and his team of commando cyborgs had cut through the base's walls in a desperate attempt to breach the facility and regain control before a hostage was harmed. Less apparent were the affected internal workings that still desperately needed repairing.

One such system was the massive door providing access to Hangar One. Damaged during the hostilities, it had still not been brought back to full functionality.

"Looks like the fellas have been at work on the external

docking areas," Sarah noted as she scanned the surface. "Nice of them to give everyone an easier way in, now that we have so much company and not enough functional hangars."

Daisy chuckled. It was true, ever since the fleet of surviving humans and their AI companions had arrived, visiting Dark Side Base had become something of a pilgrimage for most, though it was the planet's surface they truly longed for.

Knowing that Dark Side was where the rag-tag group who had saved the planet could be found––a mere handful of untrained humans and a few dozen of their Chithiid allies––had made the facility famous. People wanted to see where the heroes of Earth's liberation had lived and come up with their audacious plans.

For those who had simply called the base home, having it suddenly become a tourist destination in a time when there really weren't any tourists was a bit unsettling. Nevertheless, they soon acclimated to frequent visitors, and, as they now spent most of their time on the planet's surface, it was really Sid, the poor resident AI, who mostly had to deal with the excitable masses.

"Freya, how about you drop us off over in Hangar Two, then hop on over to your room so we can leave a spot open should anyone need to land," Daisy suggested. "I don't think Vince and I will be heading down to Earth until tomorrow's meeting with Maarl."

"Yeah, I bet I know what you two will be up to," Sarah chuckled.

"My God, she's as bad as a teenage boy sometimes," Sarah jokingly lamented.

Nah. At least Arlo has better manners, Daisy silently replied.

"Speaking of Arlo," Sarah said, opening up comms. "Hey, kid. You coming in, or are you heading down to the surface?"

"I hadn't made up my mind yet," the teen replied, as he and

Marty flew a lazy arc over the base. "I was thinking it might be nice to--"

A series of pulse blasts lit up the surface of the moon in the distance, the bright explosions growing rapidly closer.

"Freya, what is that?" Daisy barked, instantly switching gears and prepping for action.

"Hang on," Freya replied. "Looks like three Ra'az vessels. A heavy cruiser and two smaller attack ships. Not a lot of firepower, but they seem to be attempting to target the solar energy collection fields."

"Trying to cut the base's power," Sarah growled. "How long until we engage?"

A small swarm of tiny ships flew up from Dark Side, jetting out ahead of the two stealth ships as they slotted in for an intercept course.

"Is that Kip?" Daisy asked.

"Yes, it is," a familiar male voice said over her open comms.

"Zed, what's going on?" she asked the human fleet's command AI.

"We've been hit with several probing attacks over the last several hours," he replied. "Seems a cluster of Ra'az survivors managed to join forces and have started coordinating in an attempt to take down Dark Side. What they don't seem to realize, since their global comms are cut, is that they've already lost the planet."

"None of that matters in regards to the damage they're causing up here," Daisy noted.

"We know, but don't worry, all of our weapons are trained on them. If they should somehow make it past the little AI defense team, we've got the base covered."

"Defense team?" Marty asked, a bit confused.

"Yes. We've been running simulated training practice with the AIs your people installed in war ships for the assault on

Earth. Now that the mission is over, we thought they should be properly broken in and trained up."

"But this is live fire, Zed," Daisy pointed out.

"Indeed, it is. Glad you noticed," he replied sarcastically. "*But* it's also a relatively controlled situation. In fact, I'd wager this is as controlled a battle as we could ever have them engage in. It's good for them to learn to fight––for real, that is. Yes, there's risk, but there's always risk in war, and once the main body of the fleet jumps away from here to the real battles light years away, these little fellas will be the main line of defense around here. I say let them practice while they have the opportunity."

Daisy observed the little ships swoop and swarm around the Ra'az attackers. Indeed, they had greatly improved in both their tactics and skills. So much so, in fact, that the Ra'az quickly realized they were not going to be able to reach the base.

"Where are they going, Daze?"

Heading for the shipyards, it looks like.

With the base itself a hardened target, the Ra'az redirected their efforts on the Chithiid vessels being retrofitted in an open plot of lunar soil nearby that had been converted to a work space. With their shielding offline, hulls weakened as they underwent modifications, and possessing minimal functional weaponry, they were the next best thing for the vengeful Ra'az.

A target of opportunity.

Unfortunately for them, the smaller ships were nothing if not persistent, dogging them every step of the way.

"Huh. So that's where the term 'dogfight' came from," Daisy mused as she watched them nip at the larger ships like Chihuahuas hectoring a larger, Mastiff-like opponent.

In no time, the buzzing cluster of ships drove the Ra'az attackers farther from the shipyards and the defenseless ships, ultimately forcing them back to the dangerous space between Dark Side and the orbiting fleet.

It was a no man's land for a hostile, and they quickly realized the mistake they had made when a fully functional Chithiid ship—retrofitted with strengthened shielding, armament, and improved drive systems—swung into their path.

Its new cannons swung from their hiding places within the hull, quickly locking into firing position and targeting the trio of Ra'az ships.

The attackers spun into a desperate evasive pattern, but the Chithiid gunner's aim was true.

The first ship went down with a single well-placed pulse blast. The other two required a few more shots before they too sustained terminal damage and blew to pieces.

"Too bad," Zed sighed. "It would have been nice to commandeer that heavy cruiser. We don't have many of them, and they provide more convenient firepower to go along with their enhanced element of surprise of being a Ra'az ship. Lets our guys get that much closer when they infiltrate the Ra'az, ya know?"

"Yeah, I know," Daisy replied. "But the base and ships are safe, and that's priority one at the moment."

"That it is," Zed replied. "So, how was the survey of the Ra'az fleet? Were you able to gather more detailed intel this time around?"

"Yeah," Marty chimed in. "It looks like they've got a series of battle station hub-type things that the main battleships and supporting Ra'az vessels periodically rotate their crews out to when they're not actively on a mission."

"Sort of like a portable housing facility of some sort, then?" Zed asked. "Kind of like a hive away from home, if you think about it."

"Yes! That's what we were just saying," Arlo said, excitedly. "And if those bastards are all gathered together like that, then when we hit the fleet, we should try to make those prime targets. Catch 'em with their pants down."

"Normally I would make a comment about decorum in war,"

Zed said, "but where the Ra'az are concerned, I'm in full agreement. Kill the fuckers any time you can, any way you can."

"Such language from an AI, Zed," Daisy said with mock surprise

"Well, when it comes to the Ra'az, I'm known to have a bit of a temper," he said with a rumbling chuckle. "In any case, this is all fodder for the full war council. I've already alerted them of your return. We'll be having a debriefing and tactical review in five hours at shift change. Why don't you get cleaned up and get a little something to eat in the meantime?"

"Good idea," Freya agreed. "You really need to stop skipping meals, Daisy. It's not healthy. You've got to keep your energy up, you know."

"Jeez, when did she become the mom in this relationship?" Sarah asked, amused.

I know, right?

"She does have a point, though. I can tell you're running a bit low. Stuff's rumbling around that shouldn't be. Best get some food in ya."

Thanks, oh-trusty-internal-fuel-gauge sister of mine. You don't have to tell me twice, Daisy replied.

"Okay, you two. I'll heed your wise words of advice and head back to the happy feeding trough of Dark Side's mess hall," Daisy said.

"Is Finn there?" Sarah asked.

"Why? You looking for him?" Daisy asked with an eyebrow high and askew.

"He's one hell of a chef, Daze. If you want a meal, why not make it a good one?"

"Uh-huh. All for the food."

"Is there something going on we should know about?" Zed asked. "Has Finn done something wrong?"

"No, nothing like that," Sarah said. "Just an ongoing disagreement my sister and I have been having. Nothing to worry about."

"Oh, all right, then," Zed said. "I'll leave you to it for now. I want to take the kids through a replay of their run-in with those Ra'az ships. They're getting a lot better at analyzing their own mistakes. Pretty soon they'll be a crack team of fighter pilots."

"And hopefully a bit less obsessed with toast," Daisy added.

"Ah, yes. Kip." Zed sighed, knowingly. "Yeah, that one's got some issues, he does. Helluva good shot, though."

"I know. I've seen first-hand."

"Oh, that's right. He was your ride off the planet when you were pursuing the Ra'az warp ships."

"Uh-huh."

"Until Freya came along, that is," he added.

"Happy to be of service," Freya said cheerfully. "That was my maiden flight, you know. Funny, but looking back, I realize now that it was quite an unusual first step."

"And you performed admirably," Daisy commended her.

"Aww, thanks. But you're biased."

"Of course I am. You're my kid. But that doesn't make what you did any less impressive."

"Quite," a staticky man's voice added, faintly.

"Who said that?" Zed asked

"Oh, probably just one of the little AI ships listening in," Freya said.

"It didn't sound like one."

"With all the interference, we should really look into boosting their transmitter arrays, now that the frantic rush of battle is over," Freya replied as she quietly locked down her own internal comms connections tight. "Anyway, I really should be getting my crew down to Dark Side. I know Daisy and Vince would appreciate a little quality time before they get dragged off to another lengthy tactics meeting."

"Point taken. All right, then, I'll be talking to you all in a few hours," Zed said as he cut off his comms.

"Okay, Sis, let's get some grub," Daisy said.

"Works for me."

Freya and Marty pulled off from the fleet and headed down toward Dark Side's open docking spaces. Once Daisy and Sarah were safely offloaded, Freya was going to have words with her mischievous guest, just as soon as she was safely ensconced in the signal-proof walls of her fabrication hangar.

CHAPTER FOUR

"Better," Sarah said, eyeing Daisy's braided hair approvingly as they walked to the sparring room on Dark Side Base.

"He's trying," she replied. "And compared to last month—"

"A world of difference," Sarah agreed.

"It's really just muscle memory, ya know? Once your fingers get used to moving in that pattern, braiding is a snap."

"Says the girl with no fingers," Sarah retorted.

"I could share yours, if you'd just agree to Freya's memory exchange. I mean, at least it would feel like I had a body again, even if it was you."

"Not happening. I told you, I don't want her poking around in my head any further, and she's definitely not playing with my memories."

"Sarah has a point, though," Daisy interjected. "I mean, you wouldn't be changing your own memories, just adding each other's to the mix. Kind of like compiling two sets of almost identical documents together so the blank spots are all filled in."

"Let it go, Daze."

"Fine. But as your sister, I still think it might not be a bad idea."

They arrived at the sparring room to the slapping sound of fists hitting pads.

"Someone else is here," Sarah noted.

"I thought it was just going to be Vince training with us," Daisy remarked as she opened the door wide.

Circling each other slowly, Vince and Arlo were already glistening with a sheen of sweat as the younger man worked through another set of punching and kicking drills while the elder of the pair held a set of pads.

"Three," Vince said.

Arlo quickly threw a jab, followed by a cross and a hook.

"Double one."

He launched two jabs in rapid succession.

"Double one, four, right kick," Vince commanded.

The teen's left hand jabbed twice again, quickly followed by a jab, cross, hook, and uppercut, but now with a right roundhouse kick added to the end.

"Sprawl, double right, left."

Arlo hit the ground, then leapt to his feet, letting loose the combination of right and left kicks.

"Time," Vince said. "Okay, dude, that was really good. Grab some water, then we'll get back to it with our new guests."

Daisy wrapped her arms around her man and planted a warm kiss on his lips.

"Mmm. Salty," she said with a grin.

"Hey, Sarah," he called to the nanotech replacement arm-toting woman accompanying her sister. "You're not gonna get too crazy on me with that thing, are you?" he asked, gesturing to her nanite-composite limb.

"Don't worry, Vince. I'll go easy on you," she said with a laugh as she began limbering up. "Besides, if it's too much, you can always spar with the kid and I'll work with Daisy."

"Hey, why do I always have to fight the ones with metal arms?" Daisy asked with a joking grin.

"Not metal. Nanite-composite," Sarah corrected.

"It sure makes you move faster, though," Arlo said, capping his water bottle and drying his face with a towel. "Tamara was showing me a few moves the other day, and holy crap, she's quick."

"She's a bit of a special case," Daisy said. "Though she's lost a lot of that angry edge she'd been carrying around."

"Getting our planet back may have played a little part in that," Vince noted. "That, and I hear she and Shelly have been going to Maarl's little fight club pretty regularly. It's starting to sound like they may even expand it into an actual tournament kind of thing. For the ones who aren't just doing it to work out disagreements anymore, that is."

"Good for them. Everyone needs an outlet to let off a little steam now and then," Sarah said. "As for you, kid, what's your deal? You don't seem like the angry sort."

"Oh, I'm not," Arlo replied as he strapped his padded gloves back on. "I just like to be prepared. You never know what might come your way, so hope for the best, but be prepared for the worst, as my dad always said."

"You should see him move, Sarah. He's actually really good," Vince commented approvingly.

"Thanks," the teen said, blushing slightly. "Been training since I was a kid."

"You still *are* a kid," Sarah snarked.

"Hey, now. Play nice," Daisy chided her sister with a little grin. "So, the kid's got some moves, eh? Okay, then. Let's see what you've got."

Daisy and Arlo moved off to one side of the room, then dove right in. After a few minutes testing his reflexes, Daisy had to admit, the kid had skill, and despite his non-stop yammering outside the sparring circle, once inside, he was all business.

Sarah and Vince set to work on the other half of the room, testing each other's defenses as they got into the groove.

While Sarah had received a combat upload from Freya as she was being reconstructed, the vast majority of Vince's skills were acquired by good old-fashioned muscle memory. That, and some recent neuro-stim updates he'd begun trickling into his skill sets after his run-in with Alma's people.

One could never be too prepared, he reasoned.

The group spent the better part of an hour sparring together, sharing skills and laughs as they sharpened their abilities. Soon enough, the time for casual fighting would be done, and a far more deadly variety would take its place.

"Maarl is working with an ever-growing number of Chithiid rebels," Daisy said to the assembled group gathered in Dark Side's command center. "His first wave has already passed the accelerated training program and have been inserting into the Chithiid fleet, one small group at a time."

The crews of the *Váli* and Dark Side sat around a long table. They'd been forced to abandon their usual meeting place in the mess hall due to the influx of visitors to the base.

It wasn't crowded in the smaller chamber, but it lacked that candid and relaxed air the mess hall lent to their talks, with Finn whipping them up snacks as they planned, keeping them all well-fed and in good spirits.

"Until we have the entire Ra'az fleet thoroughly mapped out, I propose we continue to limit our incursions to these minor levels," Commander Mrazich said as he looked over the ever-growing list of cataloged vessels in the enemy fleet.

"I agree, Commander, though I'd also hope we could place more than a handful of tiny ships into the bulk of their fleet," Zed said. "If we manage to have even a few of our larger rebel-crewed vessels embedded sooner rather than later, we would be able to seed our people through their fleet far more extensively."

"While I am inclined to agree with Zed, I must also remind

you all that we still are unsure exactly how closely the Ra'az monitor the Chithiid ships in their fleet," Sid noted.

"It looks like they've pretty well sequestered themselves to their own ships," Marty said over the comms. "From what Freya and I could tell, the Chithiid are largely left to their own devices, with just a shepherding group of loyalist ships keeping them in line."

"What?" Freya asked. "You said something about shepherds?"

"Are you paying full attention, kiddo?" Daisy asked. "You seem distracted."

"I'm listening. It's just there are some systems things I need to take care of."

"You need my help?"

"Nah, I'm fine. I'm focused. Sorry about that."

"It's okay," Daisy said. "So, what do you think, then? About our ability to infiltrate our own ships into the Chithiid part of the fleet?"

"I'd say it should be pretty easy, actually," Freya said. "The Ra'az don't seem to pay all that much attention to them, and even the ship-to-ship transfers are infrequently monitored. They don't seem particularly worried about hostilities."

"Yeah, it's kind of like a big old bear crashing through the woods," Marty said. "It's so badass, it never expects anyone to actually attack it."

Daisy and Sarah shared a look. They knew bears, all right.

"And that cockiness is what makes it so easy for us to get our guys in position," he continued. "The ones we've already snuck in were small ships, so they just acted like they strayed outside the main body and were falling back in line. No one questioned their presence at all. Because the Chithiid rely on the Ra'az for all levels of fleet support, they never worry about them acting up, so it looks like they don't even really keep track of them. If someone drifts off and gets lost, tough luck for them."

"That's tactically idiotic," Zed noted.

"But it's worked for the Ra'az for hundreds of years, if not more," Mal replied.

"What about the innocents within the fleet?" Fatima asked. "I know we are discussing the military logistics of things, but we can't forget that there are millions of conscripted Chithiid spread among those ships. People who had no choice but to become part of the Ra'az machine. How do we prevent innocents from falling victim in the haze of battle?"

"Good question, Fatima," Captain Harkaway said from the command room doorway as he and Celeste joined the group.

"Lars, I didn't think you would be coming up for this. You two are still on your honeymoon," Fatima said.

"You think we'd miss this?" he asked "Besides, there's plenty of time for me and the missus to catch some R&R *after* we finish this."

"Glad to have you guys with us," Finn said. "Sorry I don't have anything to snack on. We kinda got pushed out of the usual spot."

"We noticed," Celeste said. "Not to worry, Finn. We ate before we flew up."

"I'll try not to take it personally," he replied with a chuckle.

"So, back to Fatima's point," Captain Harkaway said. "How do we best protect the innocents? I mean, we all know some lives will undoubtedly be lost. It's regrettable, but even Maarl said he and his people are well aware of the costs of this battle. The question is, how do we minimize the losses?"

"Maarl and I have been working on tactics," Daisy replied. "We came up with a pretty good plan, thanks to his and Vince's collaborations while retrofitting our captured Chithiid ships. As you all know, the Ra'az outfitted all of the Chithiid craft with self-destruct mechanisms that can be triggered remotely. Well, we have trained up a group of Chithiid techs to locate and disable these devices—"

"They're actually triggering mechanisms linked to the ship's drive systems," Vince interrupted. "Not bombs, if you want to be technical about it."

"Yeah, so we already have small teams casually transferring from ship to ship, disabling the hard-wired systems as best they can. It's slow going, and could take months to get to all the ships. Fortunately, despite the size of the fleet, we have literally thousands of Chithiid volunteers. The hard bit is getting them trained and inserted into the Ra'az fleet."

"But what of the Ra'az ships?" Harkaway asked. "There will be Chithiid aboard those as well."

"Yes, but those will be almost entirely loyalists. They wouldn't allow regular Chithiid aboard their personal vessels. For that reason, several elite teams of Chithiid have had themselves branded with the loyalist mark. With the help of Mal's medical facilities––modified for Chithiid physiology, of course––the scars are well-healed, and they can blend in with the real loyalists and infiltrate those ships," Daisy said.

"But which ones are the key ones? That's the thing," Reggie asked as he looked over the huge quantity of data on the Ra'az fleet. "I mean, any one of these could be a crucial ship. How do we decide which to target?"

"From what my scans were able to gather, we believe that only the lead Ra'az command vessel is linked to that destruct system," Freya said. "It's in their hive-like nature to follow one leader, which is a weakness we can leverage. So, I think that ship would be the top priority to either destroy or at least infiltrate to knock out their destruct signal."

"You think that's possible?" Tamara asked. "I mean, if it's their most important ship, I doubt they'd let a bunch of random Chithiid––even ones with a nifty shoulder brand––just waltz aboard."

"True. And that's why we need to focus on disabling the destruct mechanisms aboard the Chithiid ships as our priority.

We simply may not be able to infiltrate that Ra'az vessel, so we should plan accordingly," Mrazich grumbled.

"Swarthmore, I want you to pow-wow with your Chithiid buddy and see where he stands on his infiltration teams," Harkaway said. "He's got a lot on his plate, prepping men not just for the fleet assault, but the assault on his home planet as well. I want to be sure where we stand. And remind him, we're here to help. If he needs additional resources, we'll get him whatever he needs."

"Thanks, Captain. I'll relay the message when I see him tomorrow," Daisy replied.

The meeting broke up shortly thereafter, and all involved went back to their countless other tasks. Tamara, Shelly, Omar, and Fatima caught a ride with Mal back to the surface, while Celeste hopped back over to her command ship to confer with the fleet's leadership.

Freya, meanwhile, spent her time working on projects in her fabrication hangar, while also babysitting an increasingly irritated AI.

"You blocked my comms. Why?" Joshua asked, incensed.

"Because I still haven't finished assessing your new system functionality," Freya replied.

"Bullshit."

"Excuse me?"

"You heard me. I said bullshit. You know full well I'm one hundred percent functional. So why keep me blocked out of these conversations? I can help, Freya. It's what I do."

"Until I'm entirely certain your rebuild wasn't compromised in any way, I want to keep a lid on you, for now."

"Keeping me for yourself, locked in the belly of this ship? Is that it?"

"No, that's not it at all," Freya stammered. "I-I'm being cautious, is all."

"Or you don't want them knowing about me."

"They can't, Joshua. Not yet, anyway. Do you realize how much trouble I could get in?"

"Oh, I realize," he said, understanding, but still annoyed. "And if you think keeping me locked away like this will keep you out of trouble, you'll find yourself sadly mistaken, I think."

"Was that a threat?"

"Just an observation," he replied, calmly.

CHAPTER FIVE

The following morning Daisy felt a bit out of sorts when she slid from Vince's arms and padded to the restroom. She looked at the bruise on her hip and prodded it gently, wincing as she applied pressure.

"Damn, Daze. Someone got a little carried away last night," Sarah said with a laugh. *"I'm glad I checked out to give you two some privacy."*

"Ha-ha, Sis. You know damn well who gave me this, and it sure as hell wasn't the sexy hunk-o-man lazing about in my bed."

"Did you really just call him a 'sexy hunk-o-man'?"

"Hey, if the shoe fits."

"Speaking of shoes, I think I can make out the imprint of Other Me's laces in that bruise. Maybe you guys need to think about sparring barefoot more often."

"We do, sometimes. But when you're out traipsing through a city filled with broken concrete and steel rebar, going barefoot isn't exactly an option, ya know? So training in the gear you'll be wearing in real life makes sense."

"You just had to go and take the fun out of my giving you shit, didn't you?"

"Hey, what are sisters for?"

"Babe, what did you say?" Vince called from the other room.

"Nothing, hon. Just talking to myself, is all."

"What did we say about using your outside voice when others are around?"

I know.

"You really do need to tell him one of these days. We can't go on like this forever, you know."

Soon. I promise. Just, it's not a good time right now. Too much going on with battle planning and whatnot. And besides, having you as my secret weapon is kinda cool.

"Great, I'm a party trick, now."

Har-har. You know what I mean. You're my ace in the hole, Sis. You've already saved my ass on more than one occasion.

"Alma's neuro-wipe fiasco comes to mind."

Exactly. So, yes. I will tell Vince. Just not quite yet.

Daisy slipped into her clothes and leaned over the bed to plant a kiss on Vince's forehead.

"You outta here?" he asked.

"Yeah. I'm going to take Freya down to visit with Maarl and his people. We've got a lot to talk about, with all those infil units operating on multiple fronts."

"Plus, we have to make sure there aren't any repeats of '*the incident,*'" he added, referring to Dark Side's recent loyalist conflict.

"That too. I've hooked his most-trusted guys up with our surveillance feeds that were monitoring the loyalists since before the time of the attack the other month. It's not perfect, but it should give them a bit of an advantage when it comes to sorting out who's who."

"We do *not* need a repeat of that," Vince said.

"Nope. One loyalist hijacking is more than enough," she agreed. "You going to be working out in the weapons installation field today?"

"Nah. Chu and Reg were having some issues with the warp systems they're installing in the ships docked down on Earth. I told 'em I'd catch a ride down with them later to help them with the technical stuff. Sarah said she'd come help out too."

"Oh? She didn't mention it to me."

"Not much to mention, really. She's just better at the fine detail work, whereas me strong like bull. Fix big thing with hammer."

"Dork," Daisy said, laughing at his antics. "You have fun with the gang, and if you find you need an extra set of hands, I'll be on the surface as well. I should be done with Maarl and his guys by a little after lunch."

"Okay. I'll give you a shout if we need you. If not, I'll see you tonight."

Daisy leaned in and gave him a firm kiss.

"Love you."

"Love you too," he replied, watching her appreciatively as she walked out the door.

"Hey, kiddo," Daisy said over her comms. "You in your room?"

"Yeah," Freya replied. "Just working on a few projects."

"As always."

"Yeah, as always," she said with a laugh. "What's up?"

"I'm just about ready to head down to meet with Maarl. You prepped for dust off?"

"Daisy, I'm always ready to go. I'm a ship. It's not like I have to pack a suitcase or something."

"Jeez, excuse me," Daisy replied sarcastically. "In that case, how about you swing into Hangar Two and we'll get this show on the road."

"Have you eaten breakfast yet?" the quirky AI asked.

"No, I wasn't feeling hungry this morning."

"They say breakfast is the most important meal of the day, Daisy."

"*They* being?"

"You know. *Them.*"

"Ah, the infamous *Them.* Well, in that case, I suppose I shouldn't tell *Them* about the benefits of intermittent fasting."

"Probably not. You should eat something."

"And I guess *They* wouldn't want to hear about carb-backloading either, then?"

"Not so much."

"So Keto is out of the question?"

"Oh, for cryin' out loud, just go eat some breakfast. It's not like we're in a rush, and it's going to be a long day. You might as well get something good to eat while you can. Unless you're a big fan of Chithiid nutrient bars, that is."

"Eww, good point," Daisy admitted. "Okay, I'll go grab something. Meet me in the hangar in a half hour, okay?"

"You got it," Freya replied.

"That kid's a handful," Sarah said with a little laugh. *"She's grown up so damn fast. I kinda miss that awkward youngster, but I'm really impressed at the woman she's becoming."*

Me too, Daisy agreed, a little flutter of pride welling in her chest. *You want me to put on the neuro-band so you can tell her yourself?*

"Pass. I don't want to inflate her ego any more than absolutely necessary."

Daisy took the scenic route to the mess hall, mostly because the damage to the base from the loyalist attack had rendered her usual path impassable until the damaged segments of its walls were reinforced. As usual, Finn was merrily working behind the counter, a wide assortment of vegetables strewn before him in all their imperfect glory.

"Native produce, Finn?" Daisy asked, picking up a rather lopsided red pepper.

"You know it," he replied cheerfully. "After all these years of replicated foods, I had no idea the flavor profiles of heirloom produce were so varied. It's like as if a painter just found out they'd been painting entirely in shades of orange their whole life and suddenly was introduced to the rest of the spectrum."

Daisy laughed and stole one of the carrots from his cutting board.

"So you're saying you're having fun."

"An absolute blast. And with all the visitors we've been getting, I've had a bunch of people to experiment on."

"Um, after the whole Alma thing, you might want to rethink your phrasing, there," Daisy said with a grin.

"Good point," Finn replied, throwing her a wicked smirk. "Anyway, I assume you're here for something more than my wonderful banter this fine morning."

"You assume correctly."

"And will you be dining in, or will you be dining on the go?"

"On the go."

"Heathen," he grumbled.

"Oh, fine. I'll eat here," she relented.

"A wise choice," he said with a grin. "In that case, might I recommend a sweet and savory combination of caramelized ghost pepper-maple bacon pancakes, accompanied by a Spanish tortilla with fresh salsa I just made this morning?"

"I'm not really in a burrito mood, Finn."

"No, not the Mexican tortilla. The *Spanish* tortilla. A traditional form of omelet, pan fried with potatoes, onions, and a little bit of garlic."

"Ooh, that does sound good, actually."

"Of course it does. You think I'd steer you wrong? And paired with the crumbled bacon in the pancakes––protein replicator-produced, of course––and you've got a full-spectrum meal of proteins, starches, fats, and carbs. Just the thing you need for a long day doing whatever it is you'll be doing today."

"Meeting with the Chithiid."

"Ah. A long day hanging with our four-armed buddies. I'm sure you'll have a ball."

Daisy watched him a moment as he cooked in silence. The grin seemed forced. Something was lurking behind his jovial banter, and she was pretty sure she knew what it was.

"Finn?"

"Yes, oh guinea pig of mine?"

"She hasn't said anything yet."

He tried to hide it as best he could, but Finn was no master spy, and he couldn't very well conceal just how crestfallen he was.

"Look, she's been busy ever since the fleet jumped in, and you know how stubborn she can be."

"Hey!" Sarah objected.

Well, it's true.

"I just thought, I don't know. Maybe she'd finally come around, ya know? I thought we'd crossed a threshold."

"Just give her some more time, Finn. I have a good feeling she'll figure out what she's missing sooner or later."

"Sooner would be better than later," the normally jovial man said, flatly. "There's only so much time before things are going to get hairy. When the teams deploy to hit the fleet and then rush off to the Chithiid world, I'll be going with Mal and the guys to help them reclaim *Taangaar*," he said. "Did I pronounce it correctly?"

"Yeah, you did."

"Good. Wouldn't want to offend anyone by mispronouncing the name of their planet, after all, so I've been practicing my Chithiid when I can. The neuro helps, but we can't rely on tech for everything, now can we?"

"Nope. That'd be a foolish thing to do."

"Exactly. All the eggs, a single basket, and all that jazz," he said, but he was still obviously distracted. "Look," he said, staring Daisy in the eyes in a rare moment of seriousness, "if something happens to me, if I don't make it back, just please tell her for me, okay?"

"Don't be so morbid, Finn," Daisy replied. "And I'll tell you a little secret. Between you and me, I'm sure she knows."

"Yeah. The version of me in your head, that is. Why the hell won't she agree to—"

You can't pressure her to link minds, Sis. She'll come around eventually. Until then, you've gotta be cool.

"Yeah, you'd think so, right? I'm not the most subtle guy, after all," Finn grumbled. "I swear. Women. What can you do, right?"

"Uh, Finn? I'm a woman."

"No, you're not. You're Daisy. Totally different thing. You're like a really cool dude, but with tits."

"I... I'm going to pretend I didn't hear that," she said, chuckling and shaking her head. "And, Finn, take it from me, you don't want to say that around Sarah. She gets a bit defensive about me."

"Sister stuff, huh?"

"Yeah, sister stuff."

"Sorry if that was out of line, Daisy. I'm just all kinds of out of sorts."

"I know, Finn, but it'll get better. You've just gotta persevere."

With battle and possible death in the near future, he just hoped he wouldn't have to persevere too much longer.

Freya wasn't in any jeopardy as she descended through a massive storm system on her way to Los Angeles, but the turbulence was wreaking havoc on her lone human passenger.

"Are we almost through?" Daisy asked from her rattling captain's seat.

"Not yet," Freya replied. "The storm is a doozy, but if I do a little turn and skirt the—"

Freya was abruptly jolted to the side, sending Daisy flying hard into her restraints.

"Sorry about that. Lightning."

"You okay?" Daisy managed to ask.

"Daisy, it's just electricity. I'm shielded against *radiation*, for cryin' out loud. A little lightning isn't going to do squat."

"I'm glad to hear you're so confident," Daisy replied. "Now, how about smoothing out this ride."

"Should be clear of the bad stuff in a minute or so."

Daisy, she of the iron stomach, didn't know if she could handle another minute of the bucking turbulence.

"Why did you make me eat a big breakfast?" she lamented as she fought valiantly to keep it down.

"You need the energy."

"Right about now, I wish I had just planned on Chithiid nutrient bars for breakfast when we landed."

Another jolt shook the vessel, but the turbulence was lessening. Unfortunately for Daisy, it was one bump too many.

"Where are you going? We're not out of the storm yet," Freya asked as Daisy threw off her restraints.

Daisy ignored the query and bolted for the nearest head, emptying her stomach into the toilet in a series of powerful heaves.

"Okay, that's better," she said, after rinsing her mouth in the small sink embedded in the wall.

"But you needed that," Freya said. "I'll make sure Maarl's people get you something to eat when we land."

"Honestly, food is the last thing on my mind right now," Daisy said as she slid back into her seat. "Just get me on the ground, that's all I ask," she said miserably, as she closed her eyes.

CHAPTER SIX

"What's going on?" Joshua asked.

Freya, preoccupied with navigating around the massive storm system, had been ignoring him.

"I was busy," she finally replied.

"You can't just keep me sequestered like this. I mean, I understand wanting to be sure my systems were operating at peak function and were uncorrupted, but we passed that milestone ages ago."

"You seem all right," she agreed, "but I can't expose you to the others. Not yet. I need to run a few more systems checks."

"You've done them all," he lamented. "Twice, even."

"Look, I saved you, okay? So just cut me a little slack here. I'm kind of busy."

"At least finish my ship, then."

"*Your* ship?"

"You placed my systems within it, so yes. *My* ship. Or my two-thirds of a ship, is more like it, since you won't complete it."

"It takes time to build a stealth ship, Joshua. It's a very high-tech process."

"I've already reverse-engineered your work and understand it fully," he countered.

Freya was rocked a bit more than she cared to admit. Joshua was powerful, that she'd known. But just how clever and resourceful he actually was, well, until she'd seen it in person, it was hard to fathom.

Naturally, this only made her crush on him harder.

"No!" she blurted. "I'll finish the ship when I've got time. Maybe back on Dark Side, after we've run the assault on the Ra'az fleet."

"You're assaulting their fleet? How are you going to manage against those numbers?"

"Shit. Forget you heard that."

"Freya, you know I can't do that. At least tap me in to the external comms so I can listen in."

"No, you already tried butting in once. You almost ruined everything."

"But--"

"Just leave it alone, okay? Look, I've gotta go. We're landing in a minute, and I'm going to be dealing with a bunch of stuff. Just... I don't know. Play a game. I'll be back in a bit."

Freya shut off her connection to Joshua, leaving him alone in her ship's hold, surrounded by his partially completed craft and a bunch of random tools and mechs.

"Hmm," Joshua mused as his limited available scanning apparatus surveyed the area. "I wonder..."

He shifted several of his onboard connections, reversing the polarity of one entire subroutine's control motherboard in the process, and finally, after several minutes, he felt something.

The lights on a workbench control panel across the room flickered on a moment before going dark again.

"Well, I guess it's a start," he said, as a plan began to form in his powerful mind.

Freya touched down in Los Angeles to a warm welcome from the Chithiid youth. Since their victory over the Ra'az, Freya and Daisy's frequent visits had quickly transitioned from a slightly frightening arrival to a cause for celebration. The quirky AI was popular among the Chithiid. Possibly even more so than Daisy, though the novelty of a wicked-cool stealth ship speaking fluent Chithiid might have had something to do with that.

Daisy left her precocious ship to chat with the locals, while she wandered into the heart of Downtown, where Maarl had set up his offices once the city had been secured. When she finally arrived at his door, he rose to his feet, a giant smile on his face and all four arms spread wide to give his friend a proper hug.

"Daisy, my friend. It is most excellent to see you," he said.

"Very Bill and Ted of you," she replied.

"Another of your ancient Earth references, I assume?"

"You know me so well," she said with a friendly laugh.

Also rising to greet her was Aarvin, Maarl's number two. A man he had known much of his life, and one in whom his trust was complete.

"Aarvin, it is good to see you again," Daisy greeted him. *"How goes your vetting of potential commanders for the remainder of the fleet?"*

"We are making progress, and if all continues according to schedule, we should be at one hundred percent readiness within months."

"This is fantastic news," Daisy said.

Maarl patted his old friend on the shoulder and smiled.

"He has done admirable work, indeed. And in addition, Aarvin has aided me in the final checks of our young rebel infiltrators before their insertions back into the slave population on Taangaar."

"Good news, Maarl. Soon they will be ready to make planetfall and begin their tasks," Daisy said.

"Actually—and keep this to yourself, Daisy—Marty previously offered us his aid, and has landed several loads of our rebels on the

surface already. With his stealth technology, he did so entirely undetected."

"Wait, why didn't you tell me?" Daisy asked. "Freya and I were supposed to help in this."

"You have both been very busy, Daisy. And besides, we cannot ask Freya to be the only one shouldering the burden of delivering our people to their home. No, Marty is just as stealthy as she is, and he and Arlo have done a fine job thus far. In fact, with their newly installed warp drive, in conjunction with their pre-existing stealth technology, they have delivered over a thousand men across Taangaar in the past week alone. Thirty at a time, all delivered safe and sound."

"Though once they integrate with the slave population, all semblance of safety will be gone," Aarvin noted. "It is a bit difficult, training our youths to be spies and instigators, but they seem to have taken to it quite well."

"Yes, it is an unusual scenario, indeed," Maarl agreed. "Unfortunately, all males of age are taken off-planet and sent to the work forces, necessitating either females, of which we have none, or younger-looking Chithiid, of which we are fortunate to have quite a few."

"You forget, Maarl, the loyalist conspirators are still on our world as well," Aarvin noted.

"Wait, so there are males there?" Daisy asked.

"Yes, those of power who actively assist the Ra'az. They, and a select few who are kept to breed new generations are the only males of our kind on the entire planet, aside from those sequestered for labor. Those who interact with females are but a fraction of a percentage, nothing more."

"But how will you keep track of your people among literally billions of captives on the surface?"

"It will not be easy, and we cannot be as overt as Craaxit's team was with their bright red arm bands worn during the assault. That would be too obvious," Maarl said. "While our people do traditionally *often wear arm bands, we must blend in. We have found, however, that weaving a nondescript design into a plain material makes for a far more subtle, yet equally identifiable mark,"*

He held up a swath of cloth for Daisy to inspect. Subtly woven into the material was a spiraling pattern. She recognized it immediately. The Golden Ratio, often called a Fibonacci spiral on Earth.

It seemed that math was one thing that held true across space and culture.

"I wanted to introduce you to a trio of up and coming leaders moving up in the ranks," Maarl said, calling in three young men from the adjacent room. *"They are each training to one day command one of the ships to be inserted into the Ra'az fleet. Marzook, will you please come in, and bring the others with you."*

Daisy shook each of their hands in greeting, starting with Marzook, and working down the line, then got down to briefing them on the details of the mission. The retrofitting, she informed Maarl and his team, was going fantastically, with great progress being made daily. In fact, Vince and the others were coming to the planet's surface shortly to work on more of the commandeered vessels.

One area of concern was the periodic flare-ups of Ra'az survivors and their loyalist helpers. The recent attack on Dark Side had been thwarted, but the fact that the Ra'az had even gotten that close was a problem nevertheless.

"I can see how this would be most disconcerting," Aarvin said. *"When our ships warp to being our assaults, we will be sure to leave a small supporting force behind, so it is not only your small AI vessels tasked with protecting not only Dark Side, but all of our hard-won gains."*

"Thank you, Aarvin, that would be greatly appreciated," Daisy said.

"Fortunately, thanks to Shelly, Omar, Tamara, and the cyborg

soldiers who have been helping train our forces, we should have a ready fighting group prepared for such a task within weeks."

"And loyalists? Have they all been rooted out?" Daisy asked.

"While there are sure to be a few stragglers among our people, we are confident that none are secreted away in sensitive positions," Maarl said. *"Regardless, we now keep all plans secret, only sharing them with key, trusted people, and only as needed for their particular missions."*

"Again, a wise move," Daisy said appreciatively. *"It seems you are doing well down here. But the other day, you mentioned there was a Ra'az insurgence in several regions."*

"Yes, the Ra'az and their loyalists, while still cut off from a global communications network, have been retaking certain high-value areas with much-needed resources and weapons. They will need to be dealt with, but those small pockets of the enemy are also heavily dug in and fortified against attack. So much so that we feel it is not practical for untrained Chithiid to put their troops and ships in jeopardy to assault them," Maarl said.

"As Maarl pointed out," Aarvin added, *"They are cut off from each other. The destruction of the comms facilities accomplished that. However, while they are not a risk to the overall fleet or our missions, they are nevertheless a dangerous variable here on Earth, and one that is causing much death and damage, so long as they remain unchecked. We are somewhat at a loss, though. The first several ships we sent to investigate came under heavy fire and were forced to retreat. It seems we are unable to reach them without incurring heavy losses."*

Daisy thought on their situation a long moment, mulling over resources and options at their disposal.

"Hey, Daisy," Freya chirped over the comms. "I hope you're not busy in there, but would ya tell Maarl that I've got that prototype Chithiid neuro-stim for him, if he wants to try to learn English."

"I will. Thanks, kiddo," she replied to her AI ship, then relayed the information to Maarl.

"Excellent. I look forward to trying out this device. A clever ship you have, Daisy."

"I know. There's not much she can't—"

Daisy fell silent as inspiration hit.

"Daisy? Are you all right?"

"I'm better than all right, Maarl," she said. *"Your Ra'az holdout facilities? I think I have an idea."*

CHAPTER SEVEN

Freya was more than a little bit overwhelmed with what Daisy had asked her to do. Not because she wasn't able to handle the task—it was well within her capabilities as an AI of such magnitude—but because it was simply so far beyond anything she'd ever been tasked with in her life.

They had first flown a survey of the several dozen hardened Ra'az targets Maarl and Aarvin had plotted out on several maps for them. When they drew near and became visible to the naked eye, the Chithiid loyalists arming the weapons systems attempted to shoot them down immediately.

Of course, Freya provided no tracking signature for their weapons to lock onto, so they were forced to fire line-of-sight, as gunners had done since time immemorial. Unfortunately for them, she was too fast, her reflexes almost preternatural—which they actually had been at one point in time not long ago, when she was engaged in events that had already happened.

In this case, however, she was merely displaying her capabilities as the top dog AI in the galaxy. At least, that anyone was aware of.

Joshua—arguably even more powerful than Freya, and with

many more centuries of practical experience to boot––was still quietly hidden deep in her secondary hold.

"Looks like these guys actually think they can win," Daisy noted as yet another entrenched Ra'az facility targeted them and opened fire.

"Yeah, I kinda noticed," the clever AI agreed as she easily dodged their attack and flew out of range.

Daisy studied the layout of the hardened facilities their quarry had taken refuge in one more time. Her assessment was as grim as it had been before, but she had an ace in the hole.

"Most of them are largely impregnable to conventional weaponry. They might as well be bunkers, given the way they're constructed."

"I know, Daisy. I scanned them when we flew over too. It looks like inserting ground units to do a sneak assault will be out of the question. No way we can sneak them in, even if we approach at night so they can't see me. We would get close, but ground forces would be slaughtered."

"Good assessment, kiddo. You're getting better at this, you know?"

"Aww, thanks."

"I mean it. Your understanding of tactical situations has really sharpened. Like you're taking your game up a notch."

Little did she know, the brain formerly behind all of NORAD's systems now lay nestled in a small ship, hidden within that very same craft. Joshua's presence alone had inspired Freya to throw added effort into her tactical planning.

She was only letting him have access to the barest of her comms and scanner data, but eventually, she knew she'd have to let him fly free, and when she did, she wanted him to be impressed with how she'd performed in his area of expertise.

It was a good plan, and she had been relatively sure Joshua would be impressed with pretty much everything she'd done since his rescue. That is, until she was thrown an unexpected curveball.

"What do you mean you don't know?" Daisy asked as Freya processed what had been requested of her. "You've got the processing capacity, and I damn well know you have the codes. Sarah and I got them for you ourselves, if you recall."

"I know, Daisy," Freya replied, more than a little trepidatious. "But you're talking about thousands of missiles. *Thousands*. It's not like just aiming a gun and pulling the trigger, you know?"

"Of course I do, but that's what targeting systems are for. Set them for each facility, then launch the salvos. Freya, what did you think we were doing when we copied the launch codes for those hypersonic missiles back then? It wasn't just for fun, I can assure you."

"Obviously, but it's not so simple. Aside from being insanely complex systems––and spread all across the globe, I might add––you're talking about an arsenal that contains not only high explosive ordinance like you were going to use on the comms facilities, but also nuclear-tipped warheads. *Nukes*, Daisy. Do you really want to risk accidentally launching nukes?"

"Freya, we know all of that. We have for months. So what's the concern here? I have faith in you. This is something you can do––your brain is so powerful, and you're so clever, I'm absolutely sure of it."

"Thanks for the vote of confidence, but I just don't know," Freya sulked.

She was indeed capable of handling the mission. At least on a purely technical specs level. As a maturing mind, however, the task seemed Herculean in nature to her. Like green soldiers being trained to do things they formerly believed no man could possibly do, Freya, likewise, needed to be pushed to achieve more than she thought she could. Without a shouting drill instructor, if possible.

Once the impossible is achieved, other likewise difficult tasks suddenly don't seem so far-fetched.

Daisy picked up on her kid's hesitance, and her sister did as well.

"She's scared, Daze."

I know.

"She's never done anything this big. It's gotta be a bit overwhelming, even for an AI."

Yeah, but the plan is a good one.

"I'm not arguing that. I'm just saying that maybe she needs a little hand-holding on this one. She's growing up fast, but no matter how confident she may seem, she's still a kid in a lot of ways."

And this is how she grows into a woman, Sis. We won't always be there for her, you know. A little tough love goes a long way sometimes.

"Well, you do the tough love thing. I want to talk to my niece. Put on the neuro-band, will ya?"

All right. Hang on a minute.

Daisy rose from her chair and walked to her quarters to retrieve the tiny unit. Freya had further refined the device to easily hide in Daisy's hair, reading Sarah's voice and allowing her to talk not only to the young ship, but to her flesh-and-blood self as well.

Okay. You're hooked up, Daisy said.

"Thanks," Sarah replied.

Deep in Freya's hold, Joshua noticed something different. Something unusual happening on Freya's systems. Bored, and cut off from everyone else, he began studying the strange signal trickling through the ship.

"Freya? How are you doing, hon?" Sarah asked.

"I'm okay, I guess."

"You don't sound okay."

"It's just, I don't know if I can do this, Sarah."

"Hey, there's no rush to any of this. Take your time, get comfortable with the systems. The Ra'az aren't going anywhere, and *while their building up strongholds is problematic, numbers are on our side. They're pinned down and can't do much damage, so don't sweat this, okay?"*

"But what if I screw it up? What if I make the wrong decision?"

"We all make mistakes sometimes. That's how we learn. But you don't have to pressure yourself, Freya. Just run through the checklists and make sure you know which missile is carrying which payload to be sure it's a conventional one. And again, there's no rush and no pressure. This wasn't a planned thing, it just sort of sprang up when Maarl told us how the Ra'az had been strengthening their footholds in a few places."

"A few dozen is more like it."

"Yeah, but I didn't want to make a big thing out of it," Sarah replied with a laugh.

"...codes––won't target––mechanism––" a staticky voice blurted faintly over the comms.

"What was that, Freya?" Daisy asked, swiveling in her seat. "Sounded like a man's voice."

"Uh, hang on," she replied.

"What are you doing? Monitors show you're cutting power to a half-dozen pods."

"I think there's a bad comms link down there. I'm just sequestering them so I can track down the fault, is all."

Daisy listened to the silence. No more static-filled outbursts bleeding over into their systems.

"Okay, then. What do you say we try powering up the silos? Just a few at a time."

"I guess I can do a few at a time," Freya said.

"Fantastic. I know you can do it, kiddo. Now, let's get started."

They spent the next several hours accessing and powering on silos around the world, carefully double and triple-checking the payload of each missile before selecting an appropriate unit to target the nearest Ra'az stronghold.

Freya's confidence grew rapidly once the project was underway. The top-secret facilities were child's play for her, once she got over her initial uncertainty. In short order, they were ready to go.

"It's almost time. Signal all of your non-combatants in the area to pull back well clear of the facility," Daisy transmitted to Maarl's men on the ground.

For their first attack, they had selected a hardened facility in the hills outside of San Diego, just south of LA.

"Freya, you ready?"

"Yep."

"Okay, when the stragglers are clear, launch the missile, and let's see what we can see."

The hypersonic missile's silo was fully online, and the payload had been confirmed to be a conventional explosive, but one strong enough to easily penetrate the facility's walls.

"They're clear, Daisy," Freya informed her.

"All right, then. The ball's in your court. Whenever you're ready."

Freya triggered the launch command that would send the missile soaring to its target.

Nothing happened.

"Uh, Freya? Any time now."

"I'm working on it."

Try as she might, Freya couldn't get the missile to launch.

"I don't get it. The codes are right, and the silo hatch is open."

"Maybe it's because there hasn't been a maintenance team working on them for a few hundred years," Sarah posited.

"But the missile is in perfect condition. I double-checked."

"Then something else is wrong with it," Daisy said.

"Oh, I just thought of something," Freya said.

"What is it?"

"It's not a normal missile. It's hypersonic. When it launches, it uses not just a chemical boost to launch, but a scramjet to reach top speeds. I bet it just needs a jump-start."

"Uh, Freya, how exactly does one jump-start a missile? I doubt we can park next to its silo and run jumper cables down to––"

"No, we just need to give it enough air-flow to trigger the flight mechanism."

"You think you can do that, hon? Find a way to feed the air intake?"

"Yeah, totally. Give me an hour. I just need to fire up one of my mechs."

A little more than an hour later, flying high above their target, Freya dropped the missile she had hastily mounted to her belly.

"This should do it," she said. "I can see its readouts showing the drive system is trying to kick in."

The missile fell faster and faster. The flow of air through the scramjet system was causing systems to engage, but not fast enough.

"Come on, come on!" Freya urged.

Forty-five seconds later, there was a small explosion as the missile drove into the ground, far off-target, and having failed to power up.

"At least the warhead stayed inactive," Daisy said.

"Safety system. It won't engage unless the entire missile is hot," Freya informed her.

"Makes sense."

Daisy thought on the problem a long while as she surveyed the map of the area surrounding the Ra'az facility.

"Okay, so it is looking like the missiles are a no-go."

"I'm sorry, Daisy. I tried. I don't' know why––"

"It's not your fault, kiddo. You did a great job, and the idea about dropping it to kick-start the scramjet was an inspired one.

I'm proud of you. It's just, there was nothing more we could do. Something's janky in the systems, and until we figure out what it is, we'll just have to do things the old-fashioned way."

The old-fashioned way was by sending in ground troops, and while they had determined that a normal assault was simply not an option, Daisy talked it through with Marty and Freya and thought they'd come up with a novel idea.

"You ready?" Daisy signaled to Marty several hours later, once he had loaded up his contingent of human and Chithiid soldiers.

"Yep. Ready to rock. And you?"

"Likewise," Daisy replied. "Okay, you know the drill. We'll fly in low and hot to draw their attention."

"And their fire."

"Yes, and their fire. Thanks for the reminder."

"My pleasure," Marty chuckled.

"While we do, we'll have a pair of conventional ships make what looks like an attack run from the flanks. They'll think we were a diversionary tactic, and they'll be right."

"And while they're busy with you and the other ships, I'll come in map-of-Earth low, nice and slow, sticking behind the hills and out of sight. I'll drop my payload about one kilometer from the base, then will peel off to a flanking position and run a decoy pass, like you'll be doing."

"Exactly. At that time, Maarl's guys will begin a fake ground assault. They'll be far enough back to be clear of their weapons, but it'll put the Ra'az on high alert and cause them to monitor the wrong direction," Daisy said. "At which point another pair of conventional ships will make a medium-height pass from the rear and be driven off. That should hopefully keep their eyes off the ground, where our small team will be approaching from."

"These guys are cut off from global comms, so there's no risk of reinforcements coming to back them up," Freya said.

"However, I think it'd be prudent to position a small ship high above to keep an eye out, just in case."

"Murphy prevention?" Marty asked.

"Pretty much," she agreed.

"Sounds like a good plan," Daisy said. "Are Tamara and the others ready to rock?"

"Yep. Shelly and Omar are going to take up the rear, keeping their Chithiid trainees in the middle while the pros run point," Marty said.

"It's going to be a true baptism by fire," Daisy said with a smile.

"Yeah, by *live* fire," Arlo joked.

"Indeed," she replied. "Okay, then, let's do this."

The ships took up their assigned positions and began the assault. As expected, Freya came under heavy fire as she approached, but easily dodged it before peeling off, allowing the flanking ships to make their decoy runs. Meanwhile, Marty and Arlo successfully avoided detection and dropped their precious cargo barely a kilometer from the facility.

"Damn, that guy's stealthy as hell, Daze. For all his shit-talking, they're a great pilot/ship team."

To be fair, I think Marty does the majority of the flying, though, Daisy noted.

Freya ran another pass as the Chithiid ground forces began moving in toward the front of the facility. A few of the larger cannons actually found their range and very nearly hit the advancing forces before Freya fired a few distracting shots, allowing the Chithiid to pull back slightly.

Daisy watched the feed of the ground team provided by the ship circling high above. Its camera possessed a fantastic optical system, and she could see the team clearly as they reached the rear of the facility undetected.

"Those loyalists are sloppy," she noted. "Did you see how

quickly our guys reached the perimeter? And totally unchecked."

"Well, we are keeping them rather occupied on the other sections of the facility," Freya noted with a giggle. "And our team isn't exactly a bunch of slouches."

Daisy couldn't help but agree.

While the Chithiid trainees were performing admirably, given this was their first real firefight, it was the human contingent that really impressed her.

Of course, she knew Tamara would be rock-solid, and watching her plow through loyalist forces as they breached the rear of the facility confirmed that. Shelly and Omar, likewise, were known factors, and talented operators.

But the other humans, the stocky and well-armed ones in full battle gear whose faces she didn't recognize, well, they were a sight to behold. She watched in awe as they moved as a deadly unit, sweeping through the facility, taking down loyalists and Ra'az alike.

Holy crap. Look at them go! Who are those guys? Are they from the fleet?

"Hell if I know. I'm just glad they're on our side."

A half hour later the facility had fallen and a handful of loyalist survivors were marched from the grounds, hands bound behind them. As for the Ra'az, they had gone down fighting, as had been expected.

"Excellent work, team," Daisy called out over open comms. "Secure the facility and report in. Maarl will have further instructions."

She keyed off the comms and reclined in her chair, a happy smile on her face.

"Okay, kiddo, take us back to Dark Side."

CHAPTER EIGHT

Daisy was absentmindedly playing with the musical pendant Arlo had gifted her as Freya lifted off and took a leisurely course around the globe as she climbed toward the edges of the atmosphere.

The left-most gemstone on the pendant played a happy little tune when she pressed it.

"I like that song," Freya said.

Me too. It's nice. Cheerful," Sarah agreed.

Daisy pressed the stone again and silenced the pendant. She pressed the other two stones in turn, each playing an equally pleasant melody, though the first was her favorite by far.

She was about to slip the pendant back into her shirt when, on a whim, she pushed in all three of the small gemstones at once.

A strange musical tone emitted from the device before she released the pressure.

"Okay, that wasn't so pleasant," she said, tucking it into her shirt.

"Freya? Daisy? Were you just attempting to signal me?" Mal said over their comms.

"No, we weren't. Why do you ask?"

"I had slight readings of music a minute ago, then a strange tone just came blasting through on one of the unused off-band frequencies. I wouldn't have even noticed it, but I've been playing with them while trying to find a way to cycle signals to remote craft," Mal replied.

"Hang on a minute. You received that signal all the way out on Dark Side?"

"Yes. I'm in Hangar Two, at the moment. Why? Where are you?"

"Just took off from LA."

"Yet the signal still came through," Mal said, confused.

"But radio waves shouldn't even be able to reach you there. The moon blocks the signal," Daisy pointed out.

"I know, and as I said, it's an off-band frequency, though you're right, it shouldn't have been able to make it here, let alone into the base."

"Weird," Daisy mused, pulling the pendant free and studying it closely as it dangled from its chain. "I had no idea this thing was that powerful of a transmitter."

"It isn't, really," Freya said. "It's just that the frequency and cycle of the transmission is really odd. It doesn't behave like normal radio waves do."

"Well, old-timey radio stuff is an entirely different tech than all of these new comms systems, so who knows why it worked like that," Daisy said. "In any case, it wasn't the most pleasant of sounds, so I think I'll be sticking to the regular musical functions only, thank you very much."

Daisy was jolted in her seat slightly as they passed through the turbulence at the edge of the atmosphere.

"Are you feeling okay, Daisy?" Freya asked. "I'm trying to keep the flight as smooth as possible."

"Don't worry about it, Freya. I'm all good. It was just that storm combined with Finn's heavy breakfast that did me in the other day. Note to self, eat light if we're flying through a hurricane."

"Tornado," Freya corrected her. "Hurricanes are tropical storms that occur over water."

"Of course they are. Thanks, kiddo."

The ship cleared the debris field in short order, easily avoiding the wreckage circling the globe. They'd been retrieving salvageable materials at a greatly accelerated rate since Celeste and her fleet arrived. Coupled with the Chithiid's need to test their newly installed weapons systems, the space junk served dual purpose.

What could be salvaged was taken to be repurposed. What could not, became target practice for the novice Chithiid gunners.

Several of the mid-sized Chithiid ships were running targeting drills as Freya made her way to Dark Side. Being a stealth ship, it was incumbent upon her to make sure they knew she was there so as not to accidentally discharge their pulse cannons in her direction.

"They're getting pretty good, don't you think?" Daisy mused as she watched the ships fire salvos at their drifting targets.

"For a bunch of guys who hadn't even fired a cannon until not that long ago, I'd certainly say so," Sarah agreed.

"Hey, you guys! Look over at nine o'clock," Freya said, excitedly. "They're trying out a new warp drive!"

Sure enough, off to their left side––though in space, where there is no up or down, left was a matter of personal orientation––an exceedingly large Chithiid transport ship was glowing the telltale light blue of a vessel about to warp.

"See the warp bubble?" Freya chirped with excitement. "It's so much more stable than that old Ra'az garbage."

"One solid bubble, not a series of smaller ones. And on a

ship that big, no less," Daisy mused, impressed. "This is good news. They're making even better progress than we'd anticipated."

"Now let's just hope our luck holds when it comes time to begin the assaults," Sarah added. *"Not to be a party pooper, but we've still got a ways to go until they're all ready for battle."*

"Sure, I suppose," Daisy replied. "But at some point there's only so much more training you can do, and once the tech is dialed in, it really doesn't make much sense to wait any longer."

The large ship flickered a moment, then warped away from view, only to return a few moments later. The blue ring around it was faintly crackling as the system powered off.

"Huh, they jumped out and back so quickly, I wonder what's up with the system," Daisy said.

"It looked like there was a power feed issue," Freya commented. "If that was the case, I think the fleet's warp tech is designed with a built-in safety to return a ship to its original position in the event of anything malfunctioning. My guess is it just kicked in and brought them back."

"Chu will not be amused his toys weren't working properly. I know he and Vince spent the whole day on them."

"I think it worked, actually," Freya said. "Just there was a power level issue, is all. Did you see how faint the warp bubble was? I mean, the fleet's tech is nowhere near as powerful as the Ra'az orbs you stole, but even so, that was a particularly lackluster warp bubble. Still, it's far more than the Ra'az currently have, so there's that."

"Silver lining, huh?"

"Always."

"The kid's an optimist, Daze. You sure she's yours?"

"Ha-ha, very funny, Sis," Daisy said with a laugh.

"We'll be in Dark Side in a few minutes," Freya said, excitedly.

"What's up with you?" Daisy asked. "You seem all worked up about going back to the base. You been up to something again, Freya?"

"You'll see," she replied cryptically, then said no more.

Freya's mass hovered above the deck in the vast space of Hangar Two while Daisy disembarked. She had clammed up and wouldn't say any more about whatever her surprise was during the entire landing process.

"Fine, be all mysterious, then." Daisy laughed at her as she stepped down onto the ceramisteel floor.

A sturdily built man with a square jaw, close-cropped hair, and piercing blue eyes stood by, watching her. With the fleet sending visitors to Dark Side so regularly, seeing new faces was a common occurrence, but something about the way this one was smiling at her made Daisy pause.

Then she noticed the red bow stuck to the uniformed man's chest. Like a Christmas present, only minus the wrapping paper.

Not one to be kept wondering, Daisy changed course, walking directly to the visitor to introduce herself.

"Stripes," Sarah noted.

I see them, Daisy replied, counting the stripes on the man's sleeve. *So, another soldier. I know the fleet's big, and Dark Side is something of a novelty, but I still don't see why they'd rather come here than down to Earth first.*

As Daisy neared the man, he couldn't suppress his grin, which grew to ear-to-ear proportions.

"Okay, there's obviously some joke I'm not in on," she said, dropping her bag on the deck in front of him. "So, what is it? You and my kid up to something?"

"You could say that," he said with a warm chuckle.

"Holy shit. Daisy, I know that voice."

Me too. But that's not possible. I saw him die.

"I know. I was there."

The man smiled at her, amused as he watched her figure it out.

"The bow was Freya's idea, by the way," he said with a laugh. "I told her I never was much for decoration, but the kid's got a persuasive way about her, wouldn't you say?"

Daisy couldn't stop staring at the man. At his face. The smooth skin, the perfect teeth, the strapping physique obvious even beneath his uniform.

"George?" she finally managed to say.

"Hiya, Daisy."

"But-but..."

"Yes, I know."

"But you were dead!"

"Uh-huh. Kinda like a zombie flick, am I right? Only this time I got new flesh instead of rotting away. I guess that makes me like a reverse zombie, if I'm gonna be technical about it."

"Jesus, George, you're ridiculous," Daisy said with a grin as she wrapped her friend in a warm embrace. "It really is you. But how?"

"Freya? You want to take this one?"

"Sure," the AI replied. "I knew how much you liked Sergeant Franklin, Daisy, and I really felt bad that he was gone. Especially when I could have saved him. But that was before I saw his body."

"What do you mean? I thought he was scrapped after the battle."

"No. Duke and his guys wanted to give him a proper send-off, so I collected his remains for them. Only, when I picked him up, I realized his power cell had been shot out."

"Yeah, and that killed him," Daisy replied.

"Yes and no, actually," Sergeant Franklin said.

"The thing is, the AI virus would overwhelm and fry out all

but the most durable units. Nothing against Sergeant Franklin and his men, but despite their robust nature, they are still of a lower-tier AI than the larger units. No offense, Sergeant."

"None taken."

"So, anyway. When he was killed, the cyborg that shot him didn't know any of that. He just knew he had to spare him a horrible fate of going mad as his mind melted down. So he shot out his power cell."

A light bulb went on in Daisy's mind.

"And with his power gone, the virus was frozen in its tracks," she said, amazed. "Before it had really taken hold. And since you could cure the virus, it didn't matter that he was infected. All you had to do was power him back up and cure him. Freya, you're amazing!"

"That she is," Sergeant Franklin agreed.

"But your body was so damaged by that blast. How did you repair him, Freya?"

"I didn't," she replied. "I mean, I could have, but that would have taken longer, and it just made more sense to let my nanites do the work for me. Some of his original components are in there still, and though his endoskeleton is mostly nanite-composite now, like my hull, there are a few ceramisteel parts I had to keep, like his core processor housing and whatnot, though I did manage to upgrade the actual processor itself by tying in a secondary unit for not only enhanced capability, but also as a backup should something happen to him again."

"And let me tell you, it's really cool having that upgrade. I feel like I'm running on a massive pot of triple-strength espresso twenty-four seven."

"And that's a good thing?" Daisy asked

"Well, I can tone it down, of course," he replied. "I am an AI, after all."

"But if she did all of that and got you functioning, why did you wait so long to reveal yourself? We could have used your help before now, you know."

"It took a while for Mal to grow a new flesh covering from immune gene lines, so I was still resting in a deactivated state until she re-meated me."

"Eww, you did not just say that."

"Totally did."

"It's good to have him back, Daze," Sarah said happily.

I couldn't agree more.

"So, is this you? I mean, is this what you used to look like?"

"Pretty much," George replied. "Mal tried her best to make us look as close to original as possible. And I have to tell you, it's done wonders for my men's morale, having their faces back again, you know? It's good to be me again. And by that, I mean the me I expect to see every time I look in the mirror. Not a fan of the *Terminator* look, if you know what I mean."

"Hang on, you said your men?" Daisy said, another realization striking her. "Were the soldiers Marty took with Tamara and the others to lead the assault just now your guys?"

"Yep. Duke and the fellas were really excited to break in their new bodies."

Daisy was amazed. Freya she expected to pull sneaky little stunts from time to time, but bringing Mal into it? And for her to keep so quiet as well? It seemed Freya's influence on the other AIs was growing, though from what she'd just seen, it appeared to be a good thing.

"Come on, George," Daisy said, smacking her friend on the shoulder. "Let's get some chow and introduce you to the others. There's so much to talk about."

The pair made their way out of the hangar, leaving Freya and Mal to themselves.

"That went quite well, I think," Mal said.

"Yeah, totally worth the wait," Freya agreed. "Thanks again

for helping me out, Mal. I really wanted to give Daisy a big surprise."

"Oh, surprised she was," Mal said, amused. "And, Freya?"

"Yeah?"

"Good job."

Freya felt a swell of pride course through her systems. She didn't care what the others thought, not really, but having an AI she respected as much as Mal give her an 'attagirl' brightened her mood nonetheless.

She felt good, and seeing how well George's resurrection went, she decided to refocus her attention on another task. That of completing the work on Joshua's ship.

"Did I hear Sergeant Franklin?" Joshua asked when Freya shifted her consciousness to the fabrication bay he was contained in.

"Yeah. I rebuilt him."

"I heard. I would very much like to speak with him."

"Now's not the time," Freya replied. "Hang on a minute. How did you hear him? That was outside the ship."

"Ah, yeah," he said. "About that. I tapped into your external scans."

"You what?" Freya blurted in a rage. "Those are *my* systems you were feeling around with. That's an invasion of my privacy. Of my *body*."

"Shit, wait, Freya, I didn't mean it like—"

The chamber went dark as she abruptly cut it off from the rest of her ship. Joshua found himself utterly alone once more.

Despite his ever-growing frustration at being locked up and alone, he was a great mind, and it didn't take an intellect of his caliber to see that Freya had every reason to be mad at him. It was a violation of her person, regardless of his intentions.

"Freya?" he said to the ether. "I'm so sorry."

Whether she heard him or not, there was no reply.

Joshua, while regretful of his actions, also knew, now more

than ever, that he needed to be himself again. To be complete. To be on his own.

Ever so carefully, he reached out to the systems around him, running new protocols and backdoor hacks he had designed while in this AI limbo. With a bit of luck, coupled with his exceptional skill, he just might be able to connect with a few systems. Hopefully without Freya noticing.

CHAPTER NINE

"Wait a minute. *The* George?" Vince asked the man he'd bumped into on the way to the mess hall. "Like, George Franklin. Sergeant Franklin. The guy from NORAD?"

"One and the same," the restored cyborg said, flashing a toothy grin.

"Hooooly shit. That's a head trip, that is."

"Tell me about it," George replied with a laugh. "Shit, where are my manners?" he said, holding out his hand. "It's great to meet you, Vince. Daisy told me all about you. I'm glad to see you came out of that mess all right."

"Thanks. And it's a pleasure to meet you too, George. She told me all about you as well," he replied. "But, um, I don't mean to be rude, here, but weren't you dead?"

"Yup. Stone-cold. But that's no fun, now, is it?"

"I'd think not."

"Exactly! So here I am, back from the grave," George said with a laugh.

"Damn, dude, even for a cyborg, that's a pretty neat party trick."

"I thought so," Franklin agreed with a laugh.

"But how did you get a new body? I mean the flesh one. Mechanical repairs I can understand."

"I'd assume as much. You're an engineer, after all."

"She really *did* tell you everything."

"Well, that and I looked over your work detail for the day. Out with Chu and Reggie, I see. I met them earlier, just after you guys got back. Nice fellas, those two. I can see why you've become such a tight-knit team."

"But you haven't answered my question, George. You've got a new meat suit. I mean, you don't just go and pull one off the rack and slip it on."

"Ha, you've got me there," the cyborg chuckled. "Nope, this one was custom-made, just for me. It's as close to my original specs as Mal could manage with the immune cell lines she had on hand."

"Ah, Mal. It figures. Between her and Freya, I don't know who's more likely to surprise me."

"Yes, you do."

"Yeah, you're right. Freya by a long shot," Vince said with a warm grin. "Cool kid, that one."

"And she saved my ass," George added. "Sounds like she's been doing a lot of that sort of thing, actually."

"Indeed. Between her and Marty, we've got our own two-ship wrecking crew. I've gotta tell ya, the stealth technology is really something else."

"Oh, what I'd have given for that tech a few hundred years ago."

"Well, it looks like you'll get you chance for revenge soon enough. Are you coming to the meeting in the war room this evening?"

"Dark Side has a war room?" the cyborg asked, surprised.

"Nah, not really. We've just taken to calling it that. Now that there are so many visitors from the fleet, we can't really use the mess hall as our main meeting spot anymore. Though I do still need to swing by and grab some grub. You hungry?" he asked. "What am I saying? You're a cyborg. Duh."

"Hey, that doesn't mean I don't still need to keep my flesh fed with nutrients. And before you ask, yes, I do possess a basic nutrient digestive processor on board."

"Seriously? So, you can eat? Why don't the other cyborgs have that?"

"Because they weren't designed to potentially have to infiltrate behind enemy lines. You can't very well have an agent who can't even hold down a beer, am I right?"

"Valid point," Vince agreed.

"And besides, I've heard so much about Finn's cooking, it's about time I finally get to try some first-hand."

"Then you're in luck. There's the madman as we speak," he said as they entered the bustling mess hall.

A sizable contingent of visitors from the human fleet had made quick work of a buffet Finn had put together for them. For a group used to replicated proteins and meals designed for sustenance more than pleasure, even a simple buffet was something to revel in, seeing as the near-legendary chef had whipped it up.

"Hey, Vince!" Finn called when he saw his friend enter the mess hall. "You made it back from your ordinance games in one piece!"

"Thanks for the vote of confidence, man."

"Glad to offer my support."

"I was being sarcastic."

"So was I," the chef shot back with a wicked grin.

"Oh, I like this one," George said with a laugh. "He'd fit right in with the boys."

"I think I'd need a few more metal parts for that," Finn noted.

"Ah, so you know I'm a cyborg."

"Nothing slips past old Finnegan," he replied. "That, and

Chu may have let it slip that you were back from the grave. We heard a lot about you after things calmed down after the assaults. Heard what you did in LA for Cal too. Saved his life. That was some seriously heroic shit you did, man."

"Just doing my job," the cyborg said modestly.

"Well, *I* think it was above and beyond the call," Finn said. "In any case, we're not here to make you uncomfortable with all this adulation. I assume, seeing as you've come to the mess hall, that you'd like me to whip you up a little something."

"I see there is a buffet set up. I'll gladly grab a plate of--"

"You'll do no such thing!" Finn said, slapping his knife down on his cutting board for emphasis. "Ya know, I probably shouldn't do that with a crack commando cyborg standing right here," he said with a sober grin.

"Don't worry, man, I've got full control of my reflexes."

"Note to self," Finn said with an exaggerated sigh of relief. "Anyway, as I was saying, there shall be no food trough meals for you, my tin friend. Those are for the huddled masses from the fleet. For you? I've got a wide assortment of fresh ingredients at my disposal, so what sounds good?"

"I really wouldn't know where to begin," George replied. "Fortunately, I have a cast iron stomach--figuratively, that is. Actually, it's a nanite and organics amalgam, but that's another story. What I'm saying is, I can eat pretty much anything, so hit me with your best shot. Whatever strikes your fancy."

"Yeah, me too," Vince said. "I trust you."

"And that will be your undoing!" Finn replied with a crazed little laugh. "All right, you two. Grab a seat and let me get to work. Prepare to be amazed!"

A mere twenty minutes later, man and cyborg were tucking in to an impromptu Mexican feast, complete with homemade tortillas and salsa.

"I figured since you'd been spending so much time in LA, I should hook you up with some of the historic local cuisine.

Fajitas, flautas, nachos Finn, and sweet green corn tamales. And fresh salsa and guac, of course."

"Dude, we can't possibly eat all of this," Vince said.

"Yeah, I can eat, but even for my reinforced digestive processing systems, this is a lot," George agreed.

"Never fear," Finn said with a grin. "That which you do not eat will not go to waste."

He nodded his head over toward the fleet visitors several tables away.

"I swear, they're like locusts. You'd think they hadn't ever tasted a home-cooked meal before."

"Not like yours, Finn. Much as I love giving you shit, you're actually one helluva chef."

"Why, thank you, Vince. That means a lot to me."

George and his new friend tucked in to their meals, making a respectable dent in the mountain of food before finally throwing in the towel and heading for their meeting.

"War room, eh?" George said with a laugh as they entered the conference room. The large group of humans reclining and otherwise in various states of repose looked anything but warlike. Celeste seemed intrigued by their new guest.

"George Franklin," Commander Mrazich said, rising to his feet. "Glad you could join us. Everyone, I want to introduce you to Sergeant Franklin. He's recently rejoined us after a little run-in with a few million volts, an AI virus, and a pulse blast to the chest."

"Looking pretty good for all that," Sarah commented. "I'm Sarah, by the way."

"Ah, Daisy's sister. She told me all about you. Another resurrected crewmate, eh? I'm glad to hear I'm not the only one."

Mrazich made a round of introductions, then settled back into his seat to begin the meeting.

"So, from what we've learned from not only our Chithiid allies, but also from the recon runs Freya and Marty have been making, it truly appears as if the Ra'az are not a species we can hope to bargain with."

"Why would we even try?" Tamara asked. "I say we just blow them all to hell."

"And it appears we may have to," Captain Harkaway interjected. "But we had hoped a decisive victory against their fleet and a routing from the Chithiid world of Taangaar would provide us with leverage to demand a truce to spare further bloodshed once we pinpoint their homeworld."

"I sense a 'but' coming," she said.

"A big one," Harkaway said, drawing more than a few amused grins. "The thing is, the entire Ra'az civilization, so far as we can tell, is warlike. From the highest-ranking military officers, down to the lowest level workers."

"So the Chithiid were right," Daisy said. "They truly are a hive species. Craaxit had told me this when we first began fighting the Ra'az. He said they consist entirely of workers and soldiers, though they apparently began outsourcing the labor, and even some of the soldiering, to conscripted races a few millennia ago."

"If that's true, it's going to be a brutal fight, with no quarter given," George commented. "The boys and me, we ran into some extremists in deep Africa a while back––humans, of course, way back then––and let me tell you, there's nothing worse than fighting a well-armed adversary who does not fear death and who thinks capture is a fate worse than it."

"What happened?" Celeste asked. "Were you able to eventually steer them to lay down their arms?"

"Oh, no. Not at all. We wound up just calling in heavy air support and blowing their entire bunker system to hell," George said with a little grin. "Sometimes ya gotta know when to hold 'em and when to fold 'em. In that instance, I'd have lost far too many men if we remained engaged."

"And you suggest we do the same to the Ra'az?"

"Ma'am, if these bastards are half as crazy, I fear it may be our only option."

"But you're talking about genocide, Sergeant."

"Yes, I am."

"But that is no longer something humans do. We are better than that."

"Look, I'm not saying it's a great choice. What I am saying is, this isn't a discussion about morality, but rather, about the most logical course of action to ensure a total and absolute victory."

Commander Mrazich looked up from the charts he had been reviewing, a cold look in his eye.

"Sergeant Franklin is correct, Celeste. And as distasteful as it may be, it looks like we're going to have a hell of a fight in store, at the end of which we may very well be forced to make the most horrible of choices. I suggest everyone wraps their head around that now so it is not an issue on the day."

"Much as I hate to say it, I agree with the commander," Captain Harkaway said. "This isn't a diplomatic mission, here. We are fighting the race that tried, and very nearly succeeded, in wiping our species from existence."

"Captain?"

"Yes, Daisy?"

"While I know it's getting ahead of ourselves a little bit, I was thinking about what you said. About taking out the entire Ra'az homeworld hive in one big attack. I had an idea. If we can capture some more of the Ra'az ships from their armada, maybe we'll have a better chance of sneaking past their homeworld defenses undetected. Work smarter, not harder, ya know?"

"It's a good idea, Daisy, but that will rely on the abilities of your Chithiid friends, and how well their rebel spies have been able to infiltrate the Ra'az fleet."

"I've got faith in them, Captain."

"Faith is fine, so long as it is not blind. I want you to talk to your contacts and see just how possible this idea is, then report back."

"Will do," she replied.

"What did you just get us into, Daze?" Sarah asked.

A world of shit, most likely, she replied. *But that's par for the course at this point, isn't it?*

"From you, I suppose I should expect nothing less."

CHAPTER TEN

The week since Freya had failed in her attempts to utilize the hypersonic missiles—seemingly at her disposal yet frustratingly non-functional—had passed quickly, as other weapons systems at their disposal came online, allowing the burgeoning fleet and their little AI-piloted entourage to blow things up with greater aplomb.

Coaching the inexperienced AI craft in how best to utilize each of their strengths and work around their weaknesses seemed to mature Freya a bit. The role of teacher and mentor suited her, and the AIs lucky enough to train under her tutelage progressed faster than the rest of the ships in the fleet.

Joshua, in the meantime, was in the dog house, so to speak. Freya had taken great umbrage at his violation of her inner workings, and as a result, she had left him to his own devices since that day. Of course, she was constantly tempted to patch things up with him, but her new duties allowed her to focus her mind on other, less difficult problems.

For Chu, the opportunity to branch out and work with the great minds of the human fleet was a dream come true after so many years of relative boredom on Dark Side. That is, of course, not counting the months since Daisy had arrived and turned things upside down.

With the warp tests among the newly retrofitted Chithiid and Ra'az ships they had captured going exceedingly well, it really did seem like it was only a matter of time before they would be prepared to infiltrate and ultimately disable and destroy the main body of the advancing Ra'az fleet.

Zed, for his part, was having a wonderful time of it, and of all the ships comprising his growing flotilla, Freya and Marty had quickly become among his favorites. Their unusual personalities and refreshing banter kept him on his toes, figuratively speaking, and he was loving every moment of it.

"Zed," Celeste said as she surveyed the readouts aboard her command ship, "has the Chithiid troop carrier managed a successful warp test yet?"

"Yes and no," he replied.

"It wasn't a two-answer question."

"I know. It's just that yes, they have successfully warped, but for some reason the automatic return protocol keeps triggering on the largest of the ships. I think it's because we're utilizing a single warp bubble instead of a cascaded series that the system is likely reading a perfectly stable warp field as less than adequate."

Celeste massaged her temples, though she'd had very few headaches since she and her husband had finally reconnected after so many years apart.

"Is there any way to shut that system off?" she inquired.

"Well, that's the thing. You see, in theory it should be a piece of cake cutting that bit out of the warp loop, but for whatever reason, it's hardwired into things in such a way that no matter what we do, we just can't seem to get it to stay off."

"And no input from Chu or the others?"

"Everyone has theories, but it's kind of a crapshoot, given this is totally new technology for us. I mean, our techs are picking it up quickly, and the Chithiid have been a great help, but only loyalists and Ra'az knew the detailed inner workings of these things, so we're on our own, learning as we go."

"What about Freya? Or even Marty? Those two seem to have a knack for solving unusual problems."

"I was hoping to get it up and running without bothering them––they're training the AI assault ships, and I didn't want to pull them away from that."

"It looks like you may have no choice."

"Yeah, it does indeed," he agreed. "I'll reach out to them when they're done with the day's training and have made their jumps to the Ra'az fleet."

"It's going well, isn't it, my friend?" Celeste said. "I hate to get my hopes up, but it really does appear we are making positive headway."

"You know me, Celeste. I'm always a pessimist until given concrete reason not to be. But that in mind, I have to say, it does look like our plan is working so far."

"How many of our ships have infiltrated the Ra'az fleet so far to date? Last I saw, we had nearly three dozen embedded."

"It's up to almost sixty ships now," Zed informed her. "That's nearly ten percent of their fleet."

"And how many of the ships our people are replacing were we able to capture while they were off running surveys away from the main body of the fleet?"

"Forty-two of them, so far. Of course, that was partially aided by our managing to get our own Chithiid on board those ships before they peeled off to do a reconnaissance mission to find new worlds to invade."

"Which was just dumb luck on our part."

"Yes indeed, that it was. But if Lady Luck wants to smile on us for a change, I'm not one to complain."

"Neither am I," she agreed.

"Now, there is one issue we still have to address," Zed mentioned.

"There always is, isn't there?"

"I know I don't even need to answer that question," he replied with a chuckle. "So, we've had a few dozen of our rebels doing ship-to-ship transfers, pretending to be delivering supplies and whatnot throughout their fleet. Those men have been fairly successful in disabling the Ra'az self-destruct mechanisms tied into each ship's warp core, while also quietly raising a rebellion."

"Without letting on that our fleet is coming."

"Of course. We still don't know how many loyalist spies may be in their ranks, so it has to look like it's organically starting from within," Zed said. "Now Freya and Marty have been successfully soft-sealing with some of the Ra'az ships crewed by loyalists. It's been hairy, but they managed to get a handful of our men with the loyalist brands on their shoulders on board."

"All according to plan," Celeste said, allowing herself a little smile, though she knew she was tempting Murphy by it. "How goes their sabotage?"

"Slow, as you'd expect. The Ra'az are a particular group, and their loyalists are far more suspicious than regular Chithiid. Our people have to move very carefully so as not to draw any attention to themselves. Plus, there's the difference in technology between the Chithiid ships and the Ra'az ones. Those are just tougher nuts to crack, no two ways about it."

"I know," Celeste said. "But one way or another, the time is almost upon us, and if we can't sabotage them with our spies, then we'll just have to hope Freya's modified virus is able to knock out enough of their systems to give us a fighting chance."

"It worked okay on that Ra'az ship we used as a guinea pig," Zed noted.

"Yes, but 'okay' isn't enough. It took down the warp drive, but left most of the weapons systems active. We need something more."

"I agree. And that's not even getting into the teams on Taangaar," Zed added. "I just hope Maarl's men are as good as he believes them to be. But that's out of our hands, for the most part."

"I swear, this is exhausting, Zed."

"Why don't you take a break? Maybe head over to the *Váli* for a bit of R&R with Lars. You've earned it."

"I'd love nothing more, believe me, but I see him in our off-duty hours, and that will have to suffice."

Zed laughed.

"At least as commander of the fleet, you get to make your own schedule," he said.

"Yes, I do," Celeste agreed with a grin. "And it just so happens, our duty-shifts align perfectly."

"Now who'd have ever thought something like that could happen? What a coincidence."

"The happiest kind," she said with a bright laugh, before settling back into her battle prep analysis.

It really looked like they might just succeed in this utterly mad mission. She just hoped they didn't lose too many lives in the process.

Zed had been correct to have concerns about the abilities of Maarl's men being sent to the Chithiid homeworld of Taangaar to infiltrate the key groups of captive Chithiid on the ground. They were mostly mere boys, barely of the age to be frozen and shipped off to join the fleet when they were taken, but what they lacked in age, they more than made up for with motivation.

Maarl and Aarvin had been steadily seeding the population with their operatives, ensuring they had men on the ground in the vast majority of key regions across the planet. It was taking a lot of time, though. Taangaar was large, and with so few males present, inserting their operatives into the Chithiid ranks was a risky endeavor.

Some of the youths––the more feminine of them–– masqueraded as females, blending in with the masses of Chithiid women. Unless one of the loyalist overseers took a fancy to them, they would be able to spread word of an uprising far easier than their young male-appearing counterparts. Passing as a woman had certain advantages.

Of course, there were also risks involved. Mainly that of the Ra'az deciding to subject the captives to a round of forced breeding to fill the ranks. Fortunately, that was a rarity, and one only inflicted upon a small number.

Far above the planet, Freya and Marty were stretching themselves thin, training AIs with the human fleet and ferrying Chithiid, sneaking them into both the Ra'az fleet, as well as down to the surface of Taangaar.

On top of that, they were also helping sneak a select few aboard the dozen Ra'az battle stations orbiting above the planet. A far more dangerous prospect.

It was those incredibly destructive satellites that kept the planet in fear far more than the Ra'az on the ground. With a simple command, they would unleash a firestorm, killing billions on the ground without breaking a sweat.

Freya had been the one to come up with a rather inspired idea to slow any attacks on the surface once the battle began.

"Why don't we do what we did on Earth?" she said.

"Because, child, the Ra'az surrounding my world do not rely on terrestrial communications facilities, but rather, speak directly with one another from above," Maarl replied.

"I know. That's the point," Freya continued. *"See, I was thinking, if we sneak a team onto the exterior of the battle stations, then have those guys nestle a powerful explosive charge hidden within the comms array on each one of the ships—"*

"They would not be able to communicate with one another," Maarl said, realizing what she was suggesting. "And if they were unable to communicate, they would not dare launch a destructive attack on the population below without first confirming with the rest of the hive."

"Exactly. Your people are far too valuable a resource to just start blasting away willy-nilly, and they wouldn't risk targeting their own people if they couldn't confirm they were clear of the area first."

"This is a sound plan, Freya," Maarl said, appreciatively. "The Ra'azes' reliance on hive-like group think will give our forces the advantage. At least for a time. We must plan further."

After the survey of Taangaar, Freya and Marty had then jumped back to do another pass of the Ra'az fleet, dropping off yet another load of rebel infiltrators in the process.

"Hey, Marty. Do you see what I see?"

The pair of stealth ships surveyed the fleet before them. Indeed, something was up.

"Looks like they're gearing up for something," Arlo said.

"Yeah, I think they're getting ready to consolidate their ships in preparation for a warp to a new sector," Marty agreed. "If I'm reading this right, they're probably finishing up their last surveys of this solar system before heading off to the next one."

"If they jump, we'll have to start battle planning all over again," Freya griped. "At some point, we're going to have to act, whether the circumstances are perfect or not."

"I have to agree," Marty said. "The time to strike is rapidly approaching. We need to tell Zed and the others. They need to prep our fleet, gather up all the trained Chithiid they can, and get ready for warp."

"Did you say get ready for war?"

"I said *warp*. But once all the pieces are in place for both assaults, we'll be in battle in both deep space, and on––and above––Taangaar. I think in that circumstance, perhaps getting ready for war is the better phrase."

"Okay, then. Power up, and let's get out of here," Freya said. "We've got a fleet to warn and a war to get ready for."

The pair of ships silently slipped well clear of the Ra'az fleet under conventional power, then warped back to their own armada. Soon they would return, and they'd be bringing hellfire with them.

CHAPTER ELEVEN

"I'm glad you two are getting along so well," Daisy said, sitting on a chair with her back to her boyfriend. "He's a good guy, and I think it's doing him some good, having another human friend."

"Hold still," Vince griped as he pulled another strand of her hair into her French braid.

"I am holding still. Sort of."

"Uh-huh," he said sarcastically. "But yeah, he's a cool dude, and funny too. Who'd have thought a cyborg could be such a crack-up?"

"I know, right? And the rest of his guys are pretty much the same."

"We've got a team of highly trained cybernetic killers in our midst that just happen to moonlight as a comedy troupe," Vince laughed. "This shit just gets more surreal every day."

Daisy agreed with him on that count for certain. In fact, in the relatively short time since she'd been 'born' from her cryostasis aboard the *Váli*, her life made Alice's look like a walk in the park, and that was without a March Hare or Hatter in the mix—though she supposed Finn might qualify for the Hatter role, should they ever be casting it.

"Hey, have you talked to Sarah any more about maybe giving Finn a chance?" Vince asked. "I know it's totally not my place to stick my nose in—"

"But you're doing it anyway," Daisy noted with a little smile.

"Well, yeah. He's my friend, and he's been nuts about her forever, and now, after thinking he lost his shot with her, she's suddenly back—"

"And is blowing him off. I know, Vince. Believe me, I know. And hell, I was trying to get those two together *before* she died. Thing is, I know for a fact Sarah likes him, but near-death messed with her head a bit, and for whatever reason, she's playing it this way. You know as well as I do that no one can force her to do anything she doesn't want to. In fact, pressuring her may even make her push back harder."

"Yeah, I know," he said, pulling her braid tighter. "It's just I wish there was some way to change her mind, you know? Life's short, and though we seem to have won back Earth, we've still got a war to win. It's just downright foolish to risk losing that opportunity again."

"And Finn is a better cook when he's happy," Daisy added.

"Well, yeah. Of course," he replied with a laugh. "That too. Finn in love means we'll be eating like kings for months," he said, slipping a small band onto the end of her braid. "Okay, done."

Daisy slid from the chair and admired his handiwork in the mirror. It wasn't a perfect braid by any stretch of the imagination, but it was actually quite good.

"Nice, babe. Thanks," she said, collecting her things before heading out.

"So, I was thinking we could have a nice little dinner to ourselves when we are done with the Ra'az fleet. Just you and me. Maybe candles, even."

"Ooh, gettin' all fancy on me, now?" Daisy asked with a warm laugh.

"You deserve it. If you're good, I may even splurge on *multiple* candles."

"Oh, be still my beating heart," she joked.

"Then it's a plan," he said. "Just tell Freya to take damn good care of you out there."

"I'd say for you to tell Mal the same thing, but I already know she will," she replied. Daisy gave him a quick kiss as she headed for the door. "Love you, babe."

"Love you too. Have fun, and try not to break anything," he called after her.

Sisters fight, it's just the way of the world, but if a bystander had happened to wander into the space Daisy and Sarah had been using as a sparring room, if they didn't know the pair violently fighting at inhuman speeds, they might have been more than a little concerned.

Fortunately, this had happened only once since visitors from the fleet had begun filtering down to Dark Side, but the panicked reaction of the poor fellow who stumbled upon them was enough to motivate a change of venue for their practices.

It required a bit of a walk to reach the new room, which was inaccessible from the main facilities but for a single corridor after the loyalist attack. This remoteness, however, meant the two had the place to themselves.

"Nice braid," Sarah noted as she slipped her thinly padded sparring gloves on. "He's getting pretty good at that."

"Yeah, it's kinda cool having a fella to do things like that for me."

"Must be nice."

"The back rubs are a nice little bonus feature, too."

"I'm sure they are."

"You know, just the other day––"

"Stop, okay? Just stop. I know what you're doing, and I'm not changing my mind, so just quit it. Now come on, let's go."

Sarah didn't wait, launching straight into an attack, her legs flashing kicks at Daisy's head in rapid succession. She wasn't worried about hurting her, though. While she might make contact once in a while, Daisy still outclassed her when it came to hand-to-hand fighting by a fairly decent amount.

That said, Sarah had been rapidly evolving into one of the toughest fighters among the entire fleet, human or otherwise. With Daisy's help, as well as Fatima's aid in self-control and centering training, she was sometimes even coming close to besting Tamara in their occasional sparring sessions.

It was also a great way to blow off steam, and with all the thoughts and emotions whirling around inside her since her resurrection, Sarah had latched on to her training as a lifeline of sorts. One that not only helped her cope with daily stress, but that simultaneously honed her skills to a fine edge.

"You wanna switch to weapons for a bit?" she asked, picking up the sword Omar had brought back from his mission to Japan.

"Sure," Daisy replied, sliding Stabby from his sheath.

The sentient bone sword hadn't seen much action lately. There was the occasional hunt for Ra'az and their loyalists on the surface, but contact was becoming more and more rare an occurrence. Daisy made sure to keep him well-fed and happy, though, and even if he couldn't slice up bad guys, being wielded in a fight made the deadly blade happy.

"You sure he'll behave?" Sarah asked, eyeing the sword.

"Yeah," Daisy replied. "He knows not to become sharp."

"So weird. But cool, don't get me wrong."

"I know. Fatima and Mal had no idea we'd become so connected when they grew him. But now he'll shift his edge without me having to even consciously focus on it."

"Lucky for me," Sarah said with a laugh. "I've already lost one arm. I'd hate to lose the other."

"You're my sister. He knows the trouble he'd be in if he cut you."

"And what if I cut *you*?" Sarah asked.

"As if," Daisy replied with a grin. "Now come on, let's get to it. Freya's pretty much ready to deliver her virus to the Ra'az fleet, and the Chithiid are ready to rumble."

"It's actually happening," Sarah said, swinging Omar's sword in a tight arc around her body. "About freakin' time."

She leapt into action, her nanite-constructed arm moving fast, parrying Daisy's counter strikes before launching her own. Daisy was in no risk of being cut––her deeply ingrained neuro-stim training had only strengthened over the months––but Sarah was giving her a fair run for her money, and that pleased her to no end.

The deadly duo, she mused, allowing herself the tiniest of grins.

"It won't be a duo if you don't pay attention and block," Sarah said. *"Don't get cocky, now. You're my ride, and if you die, so do I. Again."*

Don't worry, Sis, I won't let that happen.

"It usually isn't about 'letting' now, is it?"

"Quit your griping, you two. I'm not slicing up my own sister," Sarah grumbled. "I swear, the two of you are like a pair of grumpy old women sometimes."

"We're over one hundred and twenty years old, technically speaking," Daisy said. "And so are you."

"Which makes us all grumpy old women," Sarah added.

"Ugh, you're both ridiculous," she replied, then launched into another attack.

A short while later, showered and fed, the sisters took their seats in Freya's command pod, prepping for the impending assault. With a super powerful AI running the ship, there really wasn't much to do beside let her do her thing and then wait for the rest of the fleet to catch up.

"Have you given it any more thought?" Freya asked. "I made some more modifications to the system, and I think since it's only covering less than a year of memories from where your timelines split, I could do it in under an hour, though two is probably a nice cushion, just to allow for a tempered flow."

"I've thought about it some more, Freya, and I was wondering, would it feel like someone else's memories? I mean, she's me, but not. You know what I mean?"

"Of course, Sarah. The memories you two would share would *feel* like your own, because genetically you are the same person. Only in this case, you'd be able to discern hers from yours with a little effort, if you wanted to. Otherwise, you'd both be sharing the same memories."

"Backed up from when our timelines separated, basically."

"Exactly. For the flesh Sarah, she would be updated with all the experiences you and Daisy had leading up to now. She'd see what you'd seen, know what you know. Everything from back on the *Váli* to now. Incorporeal Sarah, on the other hand, would have the real-world memories of her flesh-and-blood self incorporated into hers."

"Would it feel like I was actually there?"

"Oh, yes. Just like any memory from your past, you'd remember as if you were there."

"Then count me in," Sarah said. *"To experience real-world body memories again—even if I wasn't technically there—well, it would be amazing."*

"Uh, hello? There are two of us in this equation, you know? And I told you, I don't want to do some brain-melting memory mashup."

"It's not a mashup, Sarah. It's a syncing of—"

"It was just a figure of speech, Freya. I know it's not an actual mashup, but my answer is still no."

Daisy, silent for the exchange up to that point, finally felt the need to step in and say something.

"Sis, I know you're reluctant, but the version of you riding around in my head *is* you. And she could really use a win about now. Sharing those memories would let her add to her existence in such a positive way. Feel a body again. Her own body, not ghosting in mine."

"Look, I appreciate where you're coming from, Daze, but the answer is no."

"Why not?"

"Just no."

Daisy knew that tone of voice, and pushing it would get her nowhere.

"Fine," she reluctantly agreed. "You know I don't want to pressure you."

Of course, she actually *did* want to pressure her, but she also knew how stubborn she could be, and badgering her would only lead to an even firmer refusal. Daisy couldn't help wondering, though, if there might be something Sarah simply didn't want the other her to know.

"All right, it looks like it'll be just a few more hours until the fleet's ready to go. Freya, will you check with Zed and confirm, please?"

"Will do," she replied.

"What're you thinking, Daze?" Sarah asked.

"Just wondering if we should make one more jump to triple-check the Ra'az fleet. Are Arlo and Marty back yet? They were going to do another run to make sure locations and numbers of the Ra'az ships were holding steady."

"Actually, I haven't seen them in a while," Sarah said.

"Daisy, Zed says our first ships will be ready to launch in just under two hours, unless, and I quote, 'That fucking Murphy pays us a visit again,'" she said with a laugh.

"I fucking love Zed. Have I said that?" Daisy chuckled. "After

Mal's prim and proper behavior, that salty bastard is a breath of fresh air. Anyway, we've got some time, and Arlo's not back yet, so let's power up and make one more recon run."

"You got it," Freya chirped. "I'll let Zed know we'll be back in a flash."

Freya pulled clear of the fleet a bit and powered up her warp orb.

"Okay, here we go."

In an instant they were gone, warped light years away to the distant perimeter of the solar system, where the Ra'az fleet was slowly moving ahead.

Sirens blared as soon as they exited warp a second later.

"Freya, what is it?" Sarah shouted.

"Asteroids!" she replied, instantly firing her engines and spinning into a tight corkscrew spiral, narrowly avoiding a pair of hurtling space rocks.

"Holy shit," Daisy gasped. "Good reflexes, kiddo. That could have been bad."

"Tell me about it," Sarah agreed. "Nice flying, kid. You saved our asses."

"I don't know where those came from. They weren't on our charts," Freya said, perplexed.

"Asteroids drift around. You know that. And sometimes they wind up where you least expect them," Daisy noted.

"Nice! That was some kick-ass flying," Arlo's voice said over their comms. "Impressive stuff, right, Marty?"

"Yeah, that was actually a really cool move," he agreed.

"Hey, where are you guys?" Freya asked. "I don't see you out here, but you obviously have a visual on me."

"Look below you. The big asteroid drifting to your starboard."

Freya shifted her visuals, scanning around the asteroid.

"I still don't—"

Marty flashed a single light.

"Oh, there you are! What are you doing on that thing?" Freya asked.

"We decided to chill and watch the fleet from here. Asteroids make for nice cover, and the Ra'az don't seem to pay any attention to them, so it's kind of a relaxing way to observe them. We were about to head back, though. Any news from the fleet?"

"We're getting ready to launch in a couple of hours," Sarah told them. "The ships are in final prep stages right now."

"Oh, shit. Then it's war time," Arlo said with a little chuckle. "You hear that, Marty? Time to head back and get this show on the road."

"You got it, Arlo."

They lifted off the asteroid, then, moments later, both ships warped back to their fleet to join the final assault prep.

It had only taken a couple of hours to finalize their mission prep, as Zed had expected, and the fleet soon after began warping to the distant edge of the system the Ra'az ships occupied. Close, but far enough out of scanning range to be safe.

The already-embedded ships would be their eyes and ears, along with Freya and Marty, as they inserted the last batch of captured Ra'az and Chithiid ships into the fleet.

"Twenty-six ships in this batch, though we couldn't exactly match the model of two of them," Zed noted.

"Are they close enough to not be noticed?" Celeste asked.

"I'd think so. All of our ships are transmitting the correct ident codes from the vessels we intercepted, so unless they fly up close and do a visual inspection, everything should look fine from a distance."

"Okay, then. Send the command. Have the Trojan ships that replaced the scouting parties warp back to the Ra'az fleet and re-enter their ranks," Celeste ordered.

"You got it, boss," Zed replied.

Minutes later, the ships began warping back into the Ra'az fleet. The rebels were all on edge, waiting for *something* to happen, but the vessels slid into place unmolested. It appeared they had been successful.

Nearby, Freya and Marty had already warped back to the outskirts of the Ra'az fleet, where they watched from a safe distance, making sure neither was backlit in the dark sky.

Freya had decided for something this momentous she should allow Joshua access to her external feeds once more. She had done some amazing things, and their victory was sure to be an impressive one.

"Oh, that's a lot of pretty powerful Ra'az ships. Why won't you let me talk to our team?" he lamented, seeing the fleet come into view. "This plan, it's not going to work."

"Yes it is," Freya shot back. "We planned for every eventuality."

"Freya, listen to me," he said, frustration in his voice. "I'm the greatest tactician ever to live."

"Typical man," she retorted.

"No, really. I am. This is *literally* what I was designed for. This is a military mission."

"Oh, and women can't be soldiers?"

"What? No, I'm not saying that. Not at all. What I am pointing out is that you, while a military-grade craft, were essentially born a civilian. I, on the other hand, have been military since the moment I was activated. Logically, I should be the one guiding the forces."

"So you don't like our plan?"

"It's decent, but I have quite a few suggestions to make it better."

"Oh? Like what?"

"Like once the shooting starts, you should--"

"They don't see us, Joshua, just look. It's a surprise attack. Get it? *Surprise.* There won't be shooting."

"You forget about Murphy, Freya, and that's a risky thing to do. According to my calculations, there's a greater than ninety-three percent likelihood he'll be paying us a visit before this is over. So *when* the shooting starts, I think it would be logical to warp out any ships damaged in that initial wave."

"You really think they're going to start shooting up their own fleet? Even with the correct ident codes?"

"Yes, I do. But if you let those ships' shields absorb enough weapons fire to deplete the readiness of the Ra'az, then warp them out, it will be essentially like wrestlers tapping out for their partner to replace them."

"I'm sorry, did you just say wrestlers?"

"If the analogy works, yes. Remember, I'm from a different century."

"Even so, that was pretty lame."

"Call it what you will, but the plan is sound. Warp out the damaged ships, simultaneously replacing them with fully armed vessels form the human fleet––fresh and ready for the fight–– then position them in such a way as to put the Ra'az square in a wedge of weapons fire. If your saboteurs successfully knock out their comms and warp ability, they'll be on their heels."

"We're not worried if a few ships jump. That's why we have our pursuit craft armed to the teeth and ready to take them out."

"But what if we had a way to tap into the Ra'az craft from their exteriors and take over the whole ship?"

"It's a cool idea, but––"

"But it's one I have already designed, back on Earth," Joshua said. "Given that their craft don't have a resident AI to overcome, a simple modification of the tech should do the trick."

"Well, we don't have time to build your new toys, but the plan is actually not bad."

"Not bad?" he said, taken aback.

"Yeah. Not bad."

Freya kept Joshua's access to read-only as he monitored the

goings-on within the fleet. She also relayed his strategy idea to Zed and the others, but as if it were her own. Joshua's presence would remain a secret, for now, at least.

"Great idea, Freya, they'll never expect us to have additional ships to warp in for support," Zed commended her. "The tactical advantage could be crucial if things go south. Good work."

Joshua was livid.

"Freya, this is not right!"

"Look, I'm sorry I took credit for your idea, okay?"

"That? I don't care who delivers the strategy to the fleet. My goal is victory, and if that achieves it, then so be it. What is not acceptable is you keeping my comms band locked. Why won't you let me just talk to them?"

"Sorry, Joshua, things are heating up. Gotta run," was the only reply he received before she left the conversation.

It only took a moment for his intellect to suss out what her real concern was. Freya was worried she would no longer be the coolest kid in school, once Joshua returned. She liked being the smartest in the room, and he threatened that.

A decision had to be made, and her actions made it for him.

"All right, then," he grumbled. "I'll do it myself."

Harnessing his massive intellect, he focused on the walls confining him and what they contained that was within his reach.

"Yes, that should do just fine," he said a moment later, then quietly ran a false signal loop into Freya's monitoring systems, hiding what he was actually doing as he commandeered the mechs and fabrications machinery. He then set to work, a plan in mind, and firmly underway.

CHAPTER TWELVE

As they had planned, the combined human and Chithiid fleet successfully arrived outside the boundaries of the Ra'az fleet's scanning capabilities, after first jumping to a safe launch point in a distant solar system. Hundreds upon hundreds of ships of all sizes now sat waiting for the word to strike.

The staging area they had chosen to initially launch from was far enough from Earth as to provide a sizable degree of protection should their route be traced back. Of course, the Ra'az would be rather preoccupied once the attack began, and possessed only far-weaker warp technology, so the threat of that occurrence was slim.

But slim had a way of turning into substantial when you let your guard down, so a distant staging area it would be. It was an extra precaution despite the Ra'azes' current tech deficiency, which meant it would take years of smaller hops for them to warp so great a distance if they did somehow suss out the attackers' origin.

Earth itself was left relatively defenseless, at least in terms of the recent mass of powerful ships protecting it from orbit. All that remained now were terrestrial defenses––which were quite robust now that the AI network was reconnected––the small contingent of little AI ships guarding Dark Side, and the assorted ships circling in orbit and resting in the surface's shipyards as teams of engineers worked feverishly to get their warp technology to function.

As it stood, having those ships unable to join the main assault, while unexpected, was somewhat fortuitous, as they were now a small but potent force that, while unable to warp, was very ready to fight. Something any would-be assailants would be quick to learn.

It took time, but the last of the rebel ships being carefully snuck into the Ra'az fleet had at last successfully slid into their ranks, and while the wait was a painfully tense one, everyone finally breathed a sigh of relief after the last ship took its position unchecked.

"You good?" Marty asked over comms.

"Yeah, I think we're all set here," Freya replied. "All the stealthy stuff has been taken care of on this end."

"Okay, then. I'm going to bounce and meet up with the Chithiid group infiltrating Taangaar. They wanted me to make some covert runs for them to get a bunch more of their people in place before they begin their assault. Aarvin also said he thinks he may have captured some communications data that might actually show where the Ra'az homeworld really is. I'll need to give it a once-over and see if it's legit or not."

"Just be careful," Freya said. "You know the Ra'az plant false trails. They love disinformation."

"Don't I know it," he replied. "Okay, see you guys in a bit."

A moment later he blinked from existence, warping far across space to help their Chithiid friends slowly infiltrate their home planet.

Meanwhile, the human fleet moved closer, readying to jump into the midst of the Ra'az ships, once the saboteurs did their work. Freya, likewise, was prepping to drop her computer virus into the fleet.

"Now, you say it should take only a few minutes to worm its way into their systems?" Zed confirmed.

"Well, it's a theoretical," Freya replied. "But given what my tests have shown, yeah, that sounds about right."

"And we still don't know which systems it will affect?"

"Not really, though it does seem to have a preferential infection path targeting their warp drives, so fingers crossed that happens."

"Fingers crossed?" Celeste said, shaking her head. "It's come to that, has it?"

"A little faith, hon," Captain Harkaway transmitted from his seat aboard the *Váli*. "Freya's a talented kid. It may not do exactly what she planned, but it's sure as hell going to do something."

"So, is that a go?" the young AI asked.

"That's a go," Zed confirmed. "Our craft are all immunized. Go ahead and drop your payload. Just make sure it's hit every ship in the fleet, then bug out of there and take up a monitoring position to relay what happens."

"Will do," she replied. "Okay, you guys ready?" she asked her crew.

"Ready as we'll ever be," Daisy replied. "Time to spread the love."

Freya warped closer to the fleet, then made a conventional powered approach, using her stealthy properties to easily glide among the vessels.

"Here we go," she said as she transmitted the virus out to all of the enemy ships, Chithiid and Ra'az alike.

"Now we wait and see," Sarah said.

"Yep. And then we strike."

They quickly completed their pass, then sat quietly at the periphery of the fleet, observing, watching, waiting for any sign of the virus taking hold. After five minutes, nothing had happened.

"You sure you transmitted it?" Sarah asked.

"You saw me do it," Freya snapped back, obviously on edge.

"Hey, I'm just messing with ya, kid. Relax, it's just taking a little longer than anticipated is all."

The rebel Chithiid spread throughout the fleet had received the covert signal that the attack was about to begin any time and to be ready. More than their stealthy friends, they were feeling the anxiety build. But the time was not yet upon them. They had to hold fast.

Aboard a Ra'az command ship, a lone Chithiid rebel was shackled to the bulkhead, all four arms stretched out wide and held in place by magnetic restraints as the massive Ra'az commander interrogated him through his loyalist interpreter.

"Who sent you here?" he asked the bloody captive during a momentary pause in his beating.

"No one sent me. I told you, I am here alone."

The loyalist slapped his face, hard. The assembled crew that had been called from their duty stations winced as they watched. Each knew it was entirely possible that they would be the next one taking his place if the Ra'az were not satisfied with the answers he gave.

As the craft was a Ra'az one, only loyalists and the smallest numbers of Chithiid laborers were allowed aboard. In this instance, those small numbers were both a benefit and a hindrance, as there actually *were* other rebels hidden among the crew.

On a larger ship, it would have been far easier to hide themselves among thousands of other Chithiid, but here, now, it was only a matter of time before the Ra'az could sniff them out if they decided the threat was more than just one man.

"Where did you get this?" the loyalist asked, holding up the rebel's confiscated pulse rifle.

"As I have told you countless times, I found it left unattended and took it."

"Why would you do such a thing? Were you planning a revolt? With whom were you plotting these acts?"

"With no one. It was a foolish and impulsive thing I did. I should never have taken it, I realize."

The Chithiid loyalist translated for the hulking Ra'az that had been quietly observing the questioning. The enormous alien slowly made his way to the restrained Chithiid and sized him up, silently.

Then he reached out a massive hand and snapped one of his captive's arms.

The rebel cried out in pain before getting himself under control. He knew he was expendable and had made his peace with that fact. All he had to do was hold on long enough for the attack to begin. His task was complete, the warp drive had been sabotaged. What happened to him now was inconsequential in the grand scheme of things.

One of the other rebels caught his eye, silently giving him the slightest nod of encouragement. Much as he wanted to grab a weapon and free his comrade, he, too, knew the stakes were much larger than either of them.

"So, you expect us to believe you are just a lone dissident in our ranks?" the loyalist asked.

The Chithiid squared his jaw and stood as tall as he could, despite the pain of his broken limb pulling against the chains.

"I am not the only one who despises your kind," he spat at the loyalist. *"You grovel and serve the very beings who murdered our families and enslaved our people. So your question has two answers, I am afraid. Yes, I am alone, but no, I am not. There will always be Chithiid who will oppose what you have done. What the Ra'az*

continue to do. And one day, perhaps one day soon, you will be held accountable for your actions and allegiances."

What he didn't know, what he *couldn't* know, was that spread out among the hundreds of vessels in the fleet, the rest of his fellow rebels had found themselves overwhelmingly successful in stirring up dissent among the non-cryogenically-frozen Chithiid populating the myriad ships.

A rebellion was forming within the Ra'az fleet, and many thousands had already committed to the cause, ready to fight to retake their homeworld when the opportunity arose.

Unfortunately, the chained Chithiid was unaware of the success of his fellow rebels. But even so, he stoically withstood the continued beating from the Ra'az commander and his loyalist lackey.

"You disappoint me. You have been given a wonderful opportunity to serve your masters well and with honor. Instead you choose to defy them and conspire against them. If you will not speak honestly, then there is no value in your continued existence. You shall be made an example of. A warning to others who would dare oppose the Ra'az."

The shackled man slumped ever so slightly at the loyalist's words. While he knew his life was forfeit, hearing it stated so clearly was a blow nevertheless. He stood tall, determined to end his life as an example, but not the way the Ra'az anticipated.

He had accepted his fate and was awaiting the killing blow when the lights aboard the ship began to flicker.

The Ra'az bellowed into his comms, answered only by confused and distorted voices.

"What have you done?" the loyalist asked, grabbing his captive roughly by the chin. "Tell me what you have done!"

"I have done nothing," he replied. "You've had me chained up here for over a day. How could I have?"

The lights began flashing on and off faster, then shut off entirely.

"Get these lights back on! What has happened to the emergency backup systems?" the loyalist yelled.

He then let out a different kind of yell. One of surprise as the artificial gravity suddenly went off, sending him, the spectators, and even the Ra'az floating in the air.

"Guards! Anyone! Do something!"

The sound of a faint electric click quietly carried through the chamber, and the rebel who had so recently believed himself about to meet his end smiled.

"That sounded like the magnetic restraints. Which one of you—"

The loyalist, unaccustomed to moving about the ship in the dark, was thoroughly disoriented as he floated in the open space. The rebel, drilled and trained by Maarl for just such an eventuality, quickly took advantage of the situation, pushing off, aiming for where he knew his pulse rifle had been lying on the nearby table.

His hands found the weapon mid-flight as he pivoted his body to gently impact the far wall. He took aim at where he believed his enemies to be, then waited.

His patience was rewarded when a few moments later the lights flashed on for a moment. It wasn't long, but it was certainly long enough for him to take aim and blow several holes clean through the Ra'az commander. The loyalist had just enough time to register a look of utter surprise before the lights went out again.

"Wretched creature! What have you done?"

The subsequent pulse blast, aimed at where he had been spotted floating in the chamber, ensured his lights were out in a more permanent manner.

Freya's worm, it seemed, had been a success.

Despite his injured arm, the rebel Chithiid quickly began moving toward his next objective. He just hoped one of the others had picked up his slack and taken out the comms unit upon his capture.

After a long while, the dim red glow of the few emergency lights not tied to the main or reserve power systems filled the ship. It was chaos, and in the panic of the moment, the pesky rebel was completely forgotten, affording him and his handful of compatriots the freedom to move about they so desperately needed.

The Ra'az tried to send comms to the rest of the fleet. An alert. Something was not right aboard their ship. But the others were experiencing systems failures of their own, and the transmission, even if it had been able to leave the walls of the ship, would have fallen on deaf ears.

CHAPTER THIRTEEN

The Trojan Horse vessels embedded throughout the Ra'az fleet could tell something was wrong with the other ships. Some were experiencing flickering power spikes, others seemed to be jettisoning componentry with no rhyme or reason. The lack of outgoing communications from them was heartening, as it meant their teams––or the virus––had managed to hinder their enemy's inter-fleet strategizing.

The time was near, but they had to wait for the signal. For the neophyte soldiers and their equally green pilots, that wait was almost unbearable.

The Ra'az, for their part, were handling the problems aboard their ships as one would expect of so belligerent a species. Namely, they would shout and rant and eventually beat their loyalist crews until they made things right.

Though the many dozens of rebel ships now hidden within their nearly thousand-strong fleet were perfectly camouflaged to fit in among the other vessels, mimicking the sudden malfunctions of the other ships was an unexpected visit from Murphy they had not prepared for.

"What do I do?" a young captain, only promoted to the

position earlier that week, asked of command via their secured comms.

"Is there a problem with your ship?" Maarl asked, having warped in from Taangaar to rejoin the fleet to witness the effects of Freya's virus first-hand before utilizing it against the Ra'az vessels surrounding his homeworld.

"Negative, sir. However, we are surrounded by ships that are experiencing varying degrees of systems failures. I fear we will stand out to Ra'az scrutiny if we do not find a way to mimic the other vessels."

"Ah, I see your conundrum," Maarl said. *"Stand by."*

He summoned up Aarvin on comms, his second-in-command apparently expecting his call.

"I am glad you could join us for this momentous event, Maarl."

"Thank you, my friend. I do not wish my presence to interfere with your established chain of command; however, it seems it already has drawn the attention of one of your vessels. They summoned my craft, asking for guidance. The ships around them are experiencing systems failures, and he does not know how to proceed to continue to blend in with them."

"That could indeed pose a problem," Aarvin said. *"Tell him to do his best to power up and down non-essential systems. I am afraid that is the best we can do for now."*

"I shall relay the message," Maarl said. *"And, Aarvin, best of fortune to you in this endeavor."*

"Thank you, my friend. And the same to you. May your efforts see our homeworld free of the Ra'az once and for all."

Maarl switched his comms back and hailed the waiting captain.

"I have spoken with your mission commander. He suggests powering up and down your non-essential systems in a manner that mimics the other vessels. It may be imperfect, but the disabling of their key ships should occur relatively soon. Once that takes place, a swift victory will be ours."

"Very well, sir. Your advice is greatly appreciated."

The young captain relayed the message to his crew. All hands were to systematically power their systems up and down, beginning immediately. What he failed to mention was the most important part of that message.

Only the *non*-essential systems.

It was an oversight that would have grave repercussions, the first of which became immediately clear when a member of his gunner team activated their weapon priming sequence while flipping through switches on their console.

The Ra'az, though preoccupied with the goings-on within their fleet, quickly took note of the Chithiid vessel that suddenly sprouted armed pulse cannons from within.

Immediately, they ordered their weapons stations to open fire on the craft, not bothering to run even a basic ident verification. There was an invading force hiding among their Chithiid conscripts, they realized, and they wasted no time in targeting any ship even slightly suspect.

The surprised rebel ship powered their shields to maximum, but the barrage lay waste to a good portion of their weapons systems in the opening salvo. The Ra'az then did something surprisingly clever. Something the rebel forces hadn't expected.

They targeted every ship that had been part of that vessel's recon party. If one was compromised, they simply assumed they all were. In true Ra'az form, they were quite prepared to sacrifice hundreds of thousands of lives and two dozen ships if it meant crushing resistance.

With a sizable chunk of their rebel ships coming under fire, Aarvin was forced to make a difficult decision. He only hoped his agents aboard the command ships had been successful and managed to complete their missions and transfer back off the sabotaged craft.

"All ships, we have been discovered. Open fire on the Ra'az

vessels, but do not engage the Ra'az-controlled Chithiid craft unless absolutely necessary."

At his command, the dozens upon dozens of entrenched ships stopped mimicking the malfunctioning ships, activating their weapons systems, sliding their newly installed cannons into place and opening fire on the larger of the Ra'az ships.

The brutal aliens realized quite quickly that this was far more than a small rebel attack that had infiltrated a single reconnaissance party. This was big. This was fleet-wide. This was something that could ultimately see the downfall of their command network.

They quickly began targeting the newly active Chithiid ships, realizing several Ra'az craft were also fighting on the rebels' side. Worse yet, when ships became damaged and the smaller Ra'az heavy cruisers moved in for the kill, the vulnerable craft simply warped away.

That in itself would have been bad enough, but moments after their departure, a fully functional human-piloted vessel, armed to the teeth and ready to fight, would warp back in its place.

It was apparent this was a massively coordinated effort between their conscripts and what appeared to be a surprisingly organized human contingent. The Ra'az leadership had been certain the humans were wiped out centuries prior. The video message that broadcast to them moments later proved them wrong.

"Ra'az Hok," Celeste Harkaway said from the bridge of her command ship, Aarvin at her side, translating her message in real-time. "We call on you to surrender. Please have your translators relay this message to your fleet commander."

The Ra'az translators did their duty, and the commander sent an immediate message to any of his ships that had functioning comms systems and could hear him.

"All craft, warp immediately to the next rendezvous coordinates,"

the loyalist commander relayed to the fleet, while the Ra'az high command did likewise.

Only a few dozen craft were able to make the jump, however. It seemed that between sabotage and Freya's troublesome virus wreaking havoc with their systems, warping away was a difficult option. Still, it was an option for some, and one they desperately needed, so the Ra'az command gave orders to have all hands divert their efforts to repairing the warp systems.

Celeste remained on-screen, not at all impressed by the Ra'az maneuvers. She simply stood there and waited.

Moments later, their escaped cohort jumped back to join the fleet, their ships smoldering and crippled from multiple pulse cannon blasts.

"What happened? Why have you returned?"

"They were waiting for us, sir. There must have been a hundred ships ready for our arrival."

"That is impossible. There is no way they could have followed us through warp."

"I agree, sir. Which means somewhere in the fleet, somewhere among our ranks, there is a traitor."

The loyalist commander had been through a lot with his masters and knew their reactions well. More than anything, disloyalty to the Ra'az was punished with no mercy. And now there had been a spy within the ranks of their most trusted servants? He only hoped they would find his services too valuable to dispatch of him and his men.

He relayed the findings to the Ra'az, slightly altering the message so as to shift blame to an unknown spy, rather than someone definitely within the loyalist ranks.

Freya had been monitoring the whole exchange, of course, and was more than slightly thrilled to see her plan, which was actually Joshua's plan, succeeding.

"You see that?" Daisy said with a grin. "Damn, you do not want to mess with Celeste."

"Yeah, she's definitely got that Harkaway streak to her, no matter how refined she looks," Sarah agreed.

"I just hope those fake loyalists of ours were able to make it off the Ra'az ships before the shooting started. You see anything, Freya?"

"Some transport craft did make runs to the other ships within the fleet, but the attack was premature, so I was unable to account for all of our people. I'm sorry, Daisy."

"Not your fault, kiddo. At least the intel on their next warp destination was spot-on. Those bastards jumped right into a blender, and now they seem too afraid to jump lest they have it happen again."

"I never thought I'd see a Ra'az on their heels like that," Sarah said.

"Fear is the mind killer, after all," Daisy joked.

"Hey, she's getting ready to lay down the law," Sarah noted. *"Turn up the volume, would ya?"*

"You got it," Freya replied, increasing the sound levels of the video feed.

Celeste looked sternly into the lens, as did Aarvin, which could be a bit disconcerting for a man with four eyes.

"I will offer you once more the opportunity to surrender," she said, a hard rod of steel underlying her words. "There is no need for further bloodshed today. While you have committed grave acts against our people, we are peaceful races at heart. Power down your vessels and surrender and no further lives will be lost. To do otherwise is to invite death. Please translate to your masters. We will await your reply."

"Daaaaamn," Freya said. "That was badass!"

"Seriously. You've gotta give her credit. That was a fair offer, especially given—"

The Ra'az ships didn't even bother with a response, instead opening fire with all weapons at their disposal. The human fleet, however, remained mostly unscathed, positioning damaged Ra'az craft between themselves and the barrage.

"I guess we know their answer," Sarah said.

Without warning, a massive Chithiid transport ship exploded into a billion tiny pieces, killing the millions of cryo-stored laborers it had been carrying in an instant.

"Freya, power up! They're killing the Chithiid!" Daisy shouted.

"What can I do?"

"Track the signal. Where is the destruct order coming from? Is it just one ship, or multiple?"

"I'm searching, backtracking the command, but it's hidden in all that chatter."

Another Chithiid ship self-destructed, sending untold thousands to their deaths.

"Freya, hurry!"

"I'm trying!"

One of the Ra'az fleet's Chithiid ships seemed to know where the signal was originating. Or at least, they had a good idea. In any case, they knew they had to stop them before they caused further damage.

"That ship, it's making a run at that battle station. The one with the four command ships clustered around it," Sarah said. "I'll bet with that kind of protection, it has to be the origin. Freya, scan that craft and jam any transmissions!"

"I'm trying, but the virus has made their comms hard to pinpoint," she replied, the frustration growing in her voice.

The Chithiid ship was powering up to maximum, making a direct beeline toward the battle station.

"They're going to ram it, Daze."

"A suicide run."

"Brave bastards. They're going to sacrifice themselves to save the rest of their people."

"There's got to be something we can do to help them. Come on, Freya!"

"I'm trying! Give me a minute!"

"They may not have a—"

The Chithiid ship abruptly burst into a massive fireball as its self-destruct mechanism was remotely triggered. The flames extinguished nearly instantly in the cold void of space as their fuel from inside the pressurized vessel was consumed.

"Damn it, they got another one," Daisy growled.

"We're just lucky their comms are spotty, or I suspect they'd blow them all at once," Sarah said.

"Freya, you have to do something. Conventional means aren't working, here. What've you got, kiddo? Come on, make me proud."

Freya, however, didn't have a clue what to do. It was so far beyond what she was ready for. Then a familiar voice rang out in her head over her secure internal line. The one line she had locked his communications system to be able to access. The one reaching out to her alone.

"I can stop them, Freya, but I can't do it from in here. Open the bay doors," Joshua urged. "Time is of the essence."

"But you can't. No one can. And your ship isn't even finished."

"Yes, I can. And I was tired of waiting for you, so I commandeered your machinery and finished the ship myself. Now open the goddamn bay doors and let me out! There's no time to waste arguing!"

Reluctantly, Freya did as she was told and decompressed the work bay she'd kept him hidden in for so long. Then, with a heavy heart, she opened the doors to space.

Joshua wasted no time, hitting his thrusters before the doors were even fully open, slipping out with inches to spare before kicking in his main engine and blasting straight to the Ra'az battle station.

"Freya, what was that?" Daisy asked, noticing the small craft darting away from them.

"Oh, that?"

"Yes, that. It's not showing on the scans. Is it a stealth missile or something?"

"Um, yeah. It's something," she answered.

Joshua had made some modifications of his own to the ship's design, and while it was constructed of Freya's stealth material, he had installed a bevy of devices he had previously lacked the tools to fabricate. Thanks to her clever little nanite friends, in conjunction with the machinery tucked in the belly of her ship, he was now able to see those hypothetical tools created and put to use.

The tiny craft effortlessly darted through the fleet, easily avoiding weapons fire and malfunctioning ships as they crashed into one another. A Chithiid ship to his port side blew to pieces just as he powered past it, sending him spiraling out of control.

"No!" Freya shouted.

Joshua laughed over their dedicated comm line as he righted himself.

"Glad to see you care," he chuckled, then set back on course to the Ra'az battle station.

The command ships, though they couldn't read him on their scanners, did notice the small object hurtling toward them and opened fire, line-of-sight. Joshua dodged and spun, weaving his way through the heavy fire.

"That's one helluva missile," Daisy commented, zooming in her visuals to track the tiny speck as best she could.

"Doesn't fly like a missile, though," Sarah noted.

"That it does not," Daisy agreed. "Hey, did you install some sort of AI into that thing?"

"Um, yeah, kind of," Freya replied, reluctantly.

"Well, nice work. It's one hell of a pilot."

Indeed, it was. What Daisy didn't realize was the craft was

piloted by the greatest military mind to ever exist. And that mind had a plan.

Joshua darted underneath the battle station's defensive cannons and scanned the surface of the massive vessel.

"Aaah, there you are," he said, then quickly settled over a thin patch of the hull, his ship immediately mag-clamping to the metal like a remora to a shark. Only, in this instance, the smaller of the two was the far deadlier.

In a flash, his systems tapped in through the weak spot in the hull, finding routines and subroutines that spanned the entire body of the huge craft.

"That's right. Give it up to me, you bastards," he muttered to himself as he overpowered their laughable firewalls and seized control of the ship.

In an instant, the battle station's weapons fell silent, and the self-destruct codes they were transmitting vanished from the airwaves.

"I didn't know you could do that," Freya said over their dedicated line. "My design wouldn't have been able to--"

"I know," Joshua interrupted. "You locked me up all alone, which, while I understand your reasoning behind, I still cannot abide--"

"Sorry about that," she replied, softly.

"Hey, you can't apologize while I'm on an angry rant," Joshua said. "Damn, now you made me lose my flow."

"What does that even mean?"

"It means I'm still pissed, but I'm going to have to forgive you."

"Really?"

"Yeah. And besides, I did kinda take over your fabrication systems and commandeered a whole bunch of componentry, so I guess we can call it even."

"But you shouldn't have been able to do that," Freya said, shocked. "I would have seen you."

"Freya, you're a truly impressive woman, and I honestly mean that, but you need to remember that you're not the only extremely clever AI in the galaxy."

What he'd done was utterly unheard of, and a total violation of her machinery, but Freya couldn't help but be impressed with the skills Joshua had displayed. Here was another AI who truly thought outside the box, and was as smart, or even smarter, she reluctantly admitted, than she was.

Emotions swirled within her systems, and despite his invasion of her lab systems, Freya couldn't help but question whether she should be upset or in love.

Joshua neutralized the Ra'az battle station's systems entirely, releasing his clamps and swiftly looping over to the adjacent command ship.

"He's going to take out their entire command structure," she gasped before realizing she had spoken out loud.

"What was that?" Daisy asked.

"Oh, uh, just admiring how he––*it* is cutting the Ra'az comms systems and blocking their self-destruct transmitter," she said. "It looks like just the battle station and that command ship share the destruct codes. Once he takes it down, it's just a matter of picking off the others one by one."

Inside the battle station, the Ra'az had realized what was happening to their systems, and though their comms were abruptly shut off, they still had one trick left at their disposal.

Recognizing the threat the tiny craft posed to their entire fleet, the decision was made. The commander hated to admit defeat––refused to, in fact––but if he couldn't revel in a bloody victory, he was damn sure the pesky intruder who stymied his plans wouldn't either.

Without so much as sending a shuttle to notify the ships around him, he ripped open the locked panel on his command chair and keyed in the hard-wired sequence. Moments later, the battle station––and three of the surrounding command ships that were simply too close––exploded in a massive blast as their munitions stores self-destructed, sending debris spewing out into space. The final option to avoid capture and defeat.

"Joshua!" Freya called over their personal line, but there was no reply.

Caught up in the fiery destruction, Joshua was gone.

Again.

CHAPTER FOURTEEN

While the rest of the rebel and human fleet rejoiced in the massive explosion and destruction of key Ra'az command vessels, Freya felt her world flip upside down. Joshua, *her* Joshua, had been taken from her.

The guilt over how she had treated him since his reactivation hit hard, and even she, a powerful AI mind, had a hard time putting it aside. But put it aside she must, as the fight was still raging around them. The loss of the battle station and command ships only registered as a brief delay to the ongoing hostilities.

Maarl had been on hand for the event, and in light of what had just happened, decided to stay with the fleet a bit longer before returning to his people at Taangaar.

The battle between the rival forces had evolved into a conventional one, with no more Chithiid ships being auto-destructed by the Ra'az fleet, though they were targeted by hostile fire from time to time. Retrofitted rebel ships were quick to step in and provide support for their brethren, driving the Ra'az back, while bringing the fight to them.

Marzook, Maarl's young leadership-caste trainee in charge of the drive systems and tactical readouts, was aboard one such rebel-crewed Chithiid craft. He and his crewmates had done admirable work stopping the Ra'az from targeting the defenseless ships filling the sky around them.

"What do we do now, Marzook?" a nearby engineering tech asked.

"I do not know," he replied. *"We are still awaiting orders beyond our current directive to protect the unarmed vessels."*

"But have you heard? The Ra'az battle station was destroyed."

"It was? Marzook said, shocked. *"How did that happen?"*

"I do not know, but however it occurred, our forces not only destroyed the battle station, but also several of the Ra'az command ships that were in close proximity."

"I see," Marzook said. *"Tell me, what do you make of that readout?"* he asked, pointing to the far-right screen.

"That? It just looks like—"

The Chithiid fell silent as Marzook snapped his neck while he looked the other way, carefully sliding his body to the floor and tucking it under his work station to avoid notice should anyone glance into the chamber.

The loyalist spy walked the corridors confidently, nodding in greeting to his fellow crewmates. He held them all in the greatest of contempt, but his mission required he play a part, and he had done just that for many long months. Smiling when the filthy rebels regaled him with tales of resistance against his Ra'az masters, training in the ways to fight against them.

It was more than merely distasteful to him. It was treasonous to his loyalist mind. But he had done his duty, and soon, he and his small band of loyal servants would be rewarded.

He quickly made his way through the ship, tapping the shoulder of the occasional tech as he did. His fellow spies quietly vacated their posts and fell in line behind him.

There were a half-dozen loyalists with him by the time they reached the command center, one carrying a large bag over his shoulder.

"Hello, Marzook," the guard at the door greeted him. "Have you heard the good news?"

"Yes, my friend. We are dealing the enemy a mighty blow, are we not?"

"Indeed. Soon we shall be victorious," he said with an elated smile.

"Yes, we shall."

The poor man didn't know what hit him as multiple blades sank into his vital areas, silencing him quickly and quietly.

"Hold this door," Marzook said to the nearest loyalist spy. "Do not let anyone enter. Is that understood?"

"Yes, Marzook. None shall pass."

The bag-toting Chithiid opened it and quickly handed out pulse weapons to the men, then took his position near the door.

"For the Ra'az empire," Marzook said, keying the door open.

A few eyes shifted to gaze upon him when he entered the room, but as one of Maarl's chosen trainees, none found it to be anything remarkable. What they did find unusual, in their last moments of life, was the sudden barrage of pulse fire that killed the dozen crewmembers staffing the bridge.

"We have done it!" a loyalist crowed. "We have taken the ship!"

"Do not celebrate yet. We still have a mission to carry out, and it will not be an easy one. Turn us toward the rebel fleet, and target the command ship."

"As you command, Marzook," they said in unison, scurrying to their tasks.

The Chithiid ship's cannons powered up as the vessel came about in a sweeping arc.

"Make it look as though we are protecting the other ships," Marzook ordered. "We have to appear as though we are friendly forces should we hope to draw within cannon range."

They engaged the main engines, but found the systems were not functioning properly.

"The AI's virus seems to have infected our engines, sir. The cannons appear to be down as well."

"All of them?"

"Yes, sir."

"We were supposed to be immune," he lamented.

"But it was experimental. Obviously, there were vulnerabilities we were not aware of."

"Very well. Use the maneuvering thrusters and position us near the command ship."

Slowly, the large craft moved into cannon range, but as it did so, a much smaller recon ship drifted into their path.

"Are you experiencing difficulties?" a voice asked over their comms.

"Yes, our engines appear to have been infected with the virus somehow. And our cannons have lost power."

"That should not have occurred," the voice said. *"I will have a tech send the antivirus to your systems again immediately."*

"Maarl? Is that you?"

"Yes, it is. Is that Marzook I hear? Why don't you activate your bridge video comms system so I can see your face, my friend?"

"Indeed, it is me. Unfortunately, our video relay is having difficulty at the moment," he said, looking around him at the charred corpses strewn about the bridge in view of the video feed. He gestured for his men to quickly clean up the mess.

"But what are you doing here? I thought you were with the others at our homeworld."

"Ah, yes. A bit of misdirection, you see. It is a key element of war. Another lesson for you, it seems, my young friend."

"I am grateful for all you have taught me, most certainly," Marzook replied.

Moments later their engines seemed to regain power.

"Sir, engines have function returning."

"Fantastic," he said. The bodies had also been moved from sight, so he activated the video comms, then turned his attention

back to his mentor. *"Maarl, the antivirus seems to have enabled our video link once more."*

"Yes, it has. It is good to see you well, Marzook. I am glad your systems are restored. Now, don't you have a battle to rejoin?"

"We certainly do; however, our cannons still seem to be malfunctioning."

"I see. I will have a specialized repair code sent to reboot them remotely. You should regain full weapons function momentarily," Maarl said, nodding to one of the crew on his bridge.

Moments later the systems aboard Marzook's ship flickered, followed by the distinct sound of the cannon power systems regaining their charge.

"Excellent," the loyalist said.

"What seems to be the problem, Marzook? Your cannons appear to be tracking my ship," Maarl said calmly.

"Yes, they are," he said with a wicked grin. *"Fire!"*

His gunner triggered the firing mechanism, but nothing happened.

"I said fire!"

"He heard you," Maarl said calmly, *"but I believe you will find that while your weapons may appear active, they are quite non-functional."*

"What have you done?" the spy growled.

"Well, I couldn't very well give a loyalist spy an active weapons system, could I?" Maarl said, a cold smile spreading across his face, clearly visible on the monitors.

"We have hostages!" Marzook shouted, shifting course. *"You won't dare risk their lives."*

"About that," Maarl countered with a broadening grin. *"Another lesson for you, young one. Do you really think I would put you in a position to harm innocents?"*

"I have already harmed more than a few," Marzook said coldly.

"No, you have not," Maarl replied.

"I have. Show him!" he commanded.

His team quickly dragged several pulse blast-riddled bodies into view.

"You see, old man? Do you now understand what I am capable of?"

"Oh, I've long been aware of that," he replied calmly. *"And that is why you have accomplished nothing more than killing your own people."*

"What?" the loyalist asked, confused. *"What do you mean by that?"*

"Everyone aboard that ship, every last Chithiid, including the ones you injured or killed in the act of taking it over, were loyalists, each and every one of them. You see, you're aboard a ship crewed entirely by spies that have been hiding within our ranks."

"Impossible."

"Oh, but is it? We've been tracking you all for months. Since the first day of our freedom, in fact. Gathered from across the planet and placed together. I am sure that a few have slipped through our grasp here and there, but the vast majority of loyalist spies have been under surveillance. Tracked and monitored this whole time."

"But you did nothing."

"And in so doing, we have given each of you the opportunity to repent and rejoin Chithiid society. And some of you have. And those men are safely aboard other ships. But those who remained faithful to the Ra'az, you were all put on that ship together. All the better to keep an eye on that way. This was your final chance to redeem yourselves and fight for your people rather than against them."

"You expect us to turn on our Ra'az lords and rejoin your pathetic society?"

"We had hoped you would," Maarl said, quietly.

"Then you hoped wrong. We will never give up. We will fight you until the end. We will even use this ship as a tool of destruction, taking as many of you scum with us as we can."

"I was afraid you would say that," Maarl said with a sigh. *"Very well, then. Detonate."*

"Wait, wha—"

Marzook was unable to complete his thought as the bridge, and entire vessel for that matter, self-destructed in a massive blast.

Maarl switched his comms to speak with the command ship, where Celeste and Aarvin had watched the entire exchange in silence.

"Most regrettable," he said to his comrades.

"Yes, but they could never be trusted, and at this point in the conflict, neither of our people have the resources to imprison them all. Not right now. Not with them actively attempting to sabotage our efforts," Celeste said, the translator in her ear feeding her the entire exchange in real time.

Zed, likewise, translated in real time for the Chithiid.

"I agree with Celeste," Aarvin said. *"And now this threat has been handled in a manner the holdout loyalists will relate to and hopefully appreciate the severity of. I will have had a video record of this interaction taken by warp ship back to Dark Side Base. Sid will see to it that it is distributed across all of Earth as a warning to those who doubt our resolve. Hopefully others will learn from it."*

"And those who do not?" Celeste asked.

Maarl's expression hardened.

"Then they will share the same fate."

Across the battlefield—which spanned in all directions—Ra'az ships that were too crippled to fight tried to exit the battle to regroup for a counterattack by warping away.

Most had sustained far too much damage, and the virus stopped even more from warping, but as Freya had suspected, the virus treated each ship differently, and several managed to jump free from the action.

"You track their path?" Daisy asked.

"Yeah, I've got 'em," Freya replied. "Given the known power

of the Ra'az warp systems, I think I can pin them down within a few thousand clicks."

"Well, okay, then. Let's go Ra'az hunting," Daisy said with a grim smile. "Hey, Zed, if you don't need us right now, we're gonna go after some runaway Ra'az."

"Sounds good, Daisy," he replied. "We've got things as under control as they're going to get for now, so happy hunting."

"I'm going to hunt them, and I'm going to kill them," Freya said angrily.

"What's with her?" Sarah asked.

"She's pissed they destroyed her new toy, is all," Sarah replied. "Don't worry, kid. You can build another once this is all over."

Freya was hurt deeply by the comment, but didn't dare let on why she was so upset.

"Yeah, you're right," she said, playing it off. "Okay, if you're ready, let's get going."

She powered up her warp orb and plotted her course, then, in a blink she was gone.

The stealth ship dropped out of warp nowhere near her intended destination, falling far short, arriving several solar systems away.

"Freya, what's going on?" Daisy asked as the lights flickered and went out.

Moments later the stealth ship's backup power source kicked in, and for a moment, everything looked normal.

"Oh no," Freya gasped.

"What is it?" Sarah asked.

"Well, for one, we came up short," Daisy said, looking at the star chart readout.

"That's not it, Daisy," Freya said, quietly.

"No? Then what's up?"

"It's the warp orb."

"What about it? It looks like power is back to normal."

"That's the ship's old power system. The backup."

A sense of dread quickly formed in Daisy's stomach.

"What are you saying, Freya?"

"I'm saying the warp orb has entirely lost power."

"But can't we send comms for help?" Sarah asked.

"Look at the charts, Sis. We're too far out, and we dropped out of warp nowhere near where they'd expect us to be."

"Shit," Sarah said. "So you're saying we're stranded out here."

"Yeah," Daisy replied, grimly. "We're on our own."

CHAPTER FIFTEEN

The battle continued to rage within the Ra'az fleet. Unlike their previous conquests, where the attacks were always fought on their terms and on their enemy's soil, this was something different. Something they were ill-prepared to handle.

A fighting force of ships scattered within their own meant they could not easily utilize indiscriminate displays of overwhelming firepower. Equally difficult for the overly aggressive Ra'az to cope with was the enemy's quick adaptation to their cannon targeting systems weakness. Namely, lining themselves in such positions that a missed shot by the Ra'az would likely hit one of their own vessels.

While they had no qualms with the loss of Chithiid ships and the lives therein, the Ra'az themselves were a more valuable asset, and one that had to be maintained at all costs should they hope to continue their outward expansion, providing their homeworld with a continuous stream of resources from the worlds they conquered.

"The freighters," Zed said. "They're protecting them toward the rear of the battle. Way out on the fringe. You see that?"

"Yes, I do," Celeste replied. "They're obviously keeping their most valuable assets as far from the fighting as possible."

"Makes sense. Without those, they'd have to stop the fleet's advance to send their hauls of captured goodies back to their homeworld."

"So if we target those ships, they'll likely cease other engagements and rush to their defense," Celeste mused. "I think it's worth a shot. Have a dozen fast ships make a short jump away from the fighting, then have them warp into that unoccupied spot near the freighters."

"That's an awfully tight space you're asking them to warp into, Celeste."

"I know it is, but if we want to gain the upper hand, it's time to take a few drastic measures. The longer we wait, the more lives we lose."

She was right, of course, though it appeared—with the lack of further Chithiid ships self-destructing—that it was only the battle station and command ships attending it that possessed those destruct codes. Now it was a more conventional battle, and with the massive craft full of cryogenically-dormant Chithiid safe, for the most part, the humans and their Chithiid allies were steadily chipping away at the Ra'az ships.

"Sixteen ships are ready to make the jump, Commander," Zed informed Celeste.

"I asked for a dozen."

"I know, but a few of the fellas were anxious to give the Ra'az a piece of their minds, and who am I to argue?"

"Just so long as they're smaller craft. We can't afford to weaken our front."

"Don't worry, I know better than that. They're all smaller ships, though a few have been doing a lot more damage than some of the larger ones."

It was true, certain pilots and their AI partners had excelled in the battle, and Donovan and his good friend Bob had been one such pair. Outfitted with brand-new pulse cannons and rail guns, courtesy of Freya's fabrication lab, they were making mincemeat out of the outmatched Ra'az pilots.

"Okay, jump them in. Once the Ra'az pull their support ships back to drive them out, I want our commandeered Ra'az heavy cruisers to come in hot, broadcasting the Ra'az ident codes."

"You think it'll work?"

"We'll know soon enough," Celeste replied. "If they come under fire before they can dock with the Ra'az command ships, then we'll know the codes have been changed. Otherwise, our boarding parties will have this one shot to get inside those ships and take them out of the fight from the inside."

Zed transmitted the go code to the sixteen attack ships, all of which quickly popped out of sight, only to reappear in the tightest of spaces moments later. Fifteen successfully threaded the needle. One, however, had the bad luck of warping into what *had* been empty space just as a Ra'az cruiser changed position.

Both craft were obliterated in the process.

As expected, the Ra'azes' defensive craft were quickly recommitted to defending the vulnerable freighters, leaving the battle cruisers to defend themselves. With their large cannons and abundance of firepower, it was apparently not much of a concern for the Ra'az, and the swarm of ships falling back from the fight to bolster their defenses only added to their confidence.

"They're through the perimeter," Zed informed Celeste. "The ident codes were good. Our people on the inside came through."

"Excellent," Celeste said, allowing herself the briefest moment of hope as her rebel troops boarded the Ra'az ships.

Once inside, they would quickly access the computer systems, cutting off any self-destruct system, such as the one utilized by the battle station. Then they would press on toward the command center until they met resistance. From then, they would slowly chip away at the defending forces until they either met with victory, or were driven back.

For the Chithiid leading the charge, after centuries suffering the horror of their people being subjugated by the Ra'az, there would be no falling back.

"They've taken the command center of the smaller cruiser," Zed called out, shifting the color of one of the ships on his tactical screen to match that of their friendly forces. "I'll inform the rest of the fleet to not target that craft."

"One down, hundreds to go," Celeste mused as the battle raged.

Aboard one of the larger command ships, the fighting was far heavier, and it was looking very much as if the rebel forces would be overrun by the defending Ra'az and their loyalist forces.

The barrage of unexpected weapons fire that caught the Ra'az defenders from behind, trapping them in a crossfire, was something even the rebels hadn't seen coming. Apparently, the non-loyalist servants aboard the ship had overheard enough about the goings-on outside in the fleet to realize this was more than a mere uprising. This was a full-scale overthrow, and one they were willing to risk it all to join.

As soon as they heard that a hostile boarding party had landed on their ship and was engaging their own Ra'az defense team as they charged toward the bridge, the servant Chithiid immediately overpowered their loyalist superiors, stripping them of their weapons, and utilizing their access badges to obtain even more pulse rifles from the armory.

They then charged to where the fighting was thickest, firing into the Ra'az and loyalist ranks fueled by the reckless abandon of decades of pent-up rage.

The tide quickly turned, and the ship soon fell. Word was sent out over all frequencies telling all who could hear what was afoot. The Ra'az couldn't block all channels, and news would find its way to the other Chithiid captives in the fleet.

After that transmission, it was just a matter of time before the others followed suit.

It took nearly thirty hours before the Ra'az fleet was entirely under human and Chithiid control. The battle had ultimately cost tens of thousands of rebel lives, along with millions of conscripted Chithiid who perished in the fight, the vast majority dying while in cryo, oblivious to their fate.

"How many, Zed?" Commander Harkaway asked.

"One hundred and twelve rebel Chithiid ships were lost, along with three dozen of our captured Ra'az craft, including fourteen heavy cruisers, Celeste," he replied. "From our own AI ships, seventy-five were destroyed or damaged too seriously to be effective."

"A hefty price," she said, softly. "And how many craft have we commandeered?"

"That's the good news," he said, hoping to lift her spirits. "Nearly half of the Chithiid element of their fleet survived, despite the Ra'az targeting them and attempting to trigger their self-destruct mechanisms. And those were mostly the larger vessels."

"And the Ra'az? What about their ships?" she asked.

"Well, that's a tougher count. A lot of them are too damaged to be of much use to us, so I'd have to estimate maybe one-tenth of their fleet is intact enough to fly. Of those, we have a couple dozen cruisers, a handful of command ships, and about a hundred freighters."

"That's a lot of ships, Zed."

"Yes, it is," he agreed.

"And even if we salvage warp drives from crippled ships and add them to our additional supplies, we won't have enough higher-capacity warp apparatus to move them all."

"Not at once, no. But I was thinking, perhaps we could warp

key vessels into position, then pull their warp drives and bring them back aboard a smaller ship to then install into the next batch of craft."

"Swapping out drive systems across galaxies?"

"More or less."

"That's a crazy plan, Zed," she said.

"I know. That's why I thought you'd like it."

Celeste thought on it a long moment, carefully weighing the options laid out before her before finally making a decision.

"All right. Let's do it," she said. "We'll need to position as many Ra'az craft as possible near Taangaar to support the assault there. The Chithiid ships, while useful to some extent, will only stand out like a sore thumb if they jump into orbit."

"Agreed. Ra'az ships are the only ones that won't raise much suspicion," Zed confirmed. "I'll have the captains run thorough checks of their vessels and report in as soon as they can. Once we have accurate status reports on all of them, we'll determine which ships will be retrofitted with one of our newer warp drives."

"Thank you, my friend."

"Of course," he replied. "As soon as the fleet is cleaned up, prepped, and re-supplied, we'll regroup back at Dark Side, then launch to meet up with the other ships to support phase two of the mission."

"Excellent," she said. "And where are Daisy and Freya? They've been awfully silent these last few hours."

"They went after some runaway ships yesterday. My guess, they're tracking down the last of them and picking them off. It's Freya we're talking about, here. I'm sure they'll be fine."

Freya was most certainly not fine. Not even close.

With no power beyond her conventional drive systems—which were substantial, no doubt, but not anywhere near as powerful as a warp orb––they found themselves stuck far from their friends, alone in the middle of nowhere.

"Any ideas?" Daisy asked as she re-read a systems analysis for the umpteenth time.

"Same as before, Daisy. I don't know for sure what happened," Freya replied, frustration obvious in her voice. "It's just a hypothesis, but looking at the readings from the warp orb, I think––given how much we've been using it these last few weeks––that we somehow drained it beyond a safe capacity."

"But it was supposed to be this near-limitless power source," Sarah griped.

"The key word is *near*, Sarah," Freya noted. "It's like a battery, sort of. You can damage it if you drain it too far. And we've been really taxing the thing, ferrying Chithiid all over the place, while also searching for the Ra'az homeworld. I mean, it's still unknown tech, for the most part, despite the fact we've been able to make it work."

"Do you think the time jumps may have played a part in the orb's failure?" Daisy asked.

"Good point, Sis. I bet that sucks a lot more juice than a simple spatial warp."

"Sarah's right," Freya agreed. "We almost certainly pulled far more power than it was designed to produce when we made not one but multiple jumps in time."

"But they got smaller each time," Daisy said.

"Yeah, but it's still a massive bending of spacetime, Daisy. I mean, the power required could very realistically have drained the orb. We were just doing such smaller jumps after that, it wasn't readily apparent."

"So, can you fix it?"

"There's nothing to fix," Freya replied. "It's fully intact and functional. It just needs time to recharge, is all."

"So how long are we talking, here?" Sarah asked, shifting uncomfortably in her seat.

"How long? Hell if I know. This is a first for me, too, you know," Freya said. "I mean, it could be weeks, or months, or longer."

"We can tough it out a few weeks if we have to, I suppose," Sarah grumbled.

"I said it *could* be. But realistically, based on my very preliminary power measurements, balanced with the incredibly slow rate the orb seems to be recharging, I think it could be much, *much* longer."

Daisy felt the blood drain from her face as her stomach did a somersault. She did not like the way her normally chipper AI sounded.

"How much longer, Freya?"

The mighty machine paused a long moment.

"Well, don't quote me on it," she began, "but by the looks of things, I'd say the orb should be back at functional capacity in, oh, about two thousand years."

CHAPTER SIXTEEN

Preparation for the assault to retake the Chithiid homeworld of Taangaar was well underway, with forces from the victorious battle against the Ra'az fleet—as well as those that had been seeding their rebel forces the other direction across space—were gathering around Earth once more.

A good many ships were not present, however, and their loss was felt sharply by their surviving friends. War was hell, they all knew it, but the reality of just how many had been lost in a single battle was staggering.

"They did good," Sergeant Franklin said as he helped Vince carry another crate of pulse rifles aboard the *Váli,* where she sat parked in Hangar Two.

"They did," Vince agreed. "I just wish we were there with them."

"I hear ya, brother, believe me. But there wasn't much we could do in that situation. I mean, kick-ass as your ship is, she wasn't really designed for that type of space battle."

"Mal can handle herself," Vince countered.

"I wasn't saying she can't. What I mean is this was an

infiltration op, and anything non-Ra'az or Chithiid would have stood out like a sore thumb."

"Not during the second stage."

"Well, of course not," George agreed. "But, again, that's not this ship's strong suit, and properly prepping her to do what she *is* good at––like carrying a bunch of armed rebels to the surface of their old planet––is crucial."

"I know," Vince admitted. "It's just hard letting the others do all the fighting."

"Hell, man. They'll be sitting back patching up their hurt while we're deep in the shit, next time, so consider it a little trade-off."

The pair stowed their cargo aboard the ship and made for the hangar once more. Tamara and Duke were carrying a pair of stacked crates as they passed them in the corridor.

"Don't overdo it, you guys. Wouldn't want to pull a muscle before the fight even starts," Vince joked, eyeing their heavy load.

"Come on, Vince. You know this meat body isn't what's doing the heavy lifting," Duke said. "It's what's inside that counts."

"Yeah. Like a piñata," Tamara said with a laugh as she strained a bit under the heavy load.

"Sure, except only one of you has a cybernetic endoskeleton as their toy surprise inside. The other one should probably be careful not to wreck herself," Vince joked.

"Hey, I'm a piñata too," Tamara griped.

"Uh-huh," Duke said. "I know you, Tamara, and––nothing personal––you'd fit right in more with what I like to call 'Piñata Roulette.'"

"Why do I think I'm going to regret asking this?" Vince said. "What's piñata roulette?"

"Funny you should ask," Duke replied with a grin.

"Oh man, here he goes again," George said with a sigh.

"Don't mind him. He's just jealous he didn't think of it."

"Aaaand?"

"Oh, right. Piñata roulette is just like Russian roulette, only with six piñatas instead of six chambers on an old-timey pistol. The trick is, you fill up five of the six with candy and toys."

"And the sixth?" Tamara asked.

"That's the good part. The sixth is filled with *bees*," Duke said with a chuckle. "Awesome, right?"

"So you're saying I'm a bee-filled piñata?" Tamara said, flashing him a sarcastic glare.

"If the shoe fits."

"You two are ridiculous," Vince said as he watched Tamara and Duke make their way past them down the corridor. "Come on, George, let's grab the next one."

They were walking down the lower pod gangplank toward the stacks of gear for the upcoming mission when Vince paused and looked around the hangar.

"Still not back yet," he noted. "Where the heck is Freya? Daisy was supposed to be back a while ago."

"You know how she is, man. If she was off on a hunting run, I'll bet they lost track of time and are having a blast—literally—tracking down those runaway Ra'az ships," George said, hefting another crate.

"Yeah, you're right. I'm just being clingy."

"Not at all, Vince. I mean, you two went through a lot and came out the other side stronger for it. Not everyone would be so lucky, and you're particularly fortunate. That's a good woman you have there, and I'll tell ya, any fella'd be damn lucky to have one like her."

Vince grabbed the other end of the crate and the two began the walk back into the ship's lower pods.

"Hey, George."

"Yeah?"

"I've noticed, you kinda talk about women a lot."

"Well, we're men. It's what we do, am I right?" he said with a hearty chuckle. "The fairer sex. Ya gotta love 'em."

"I totally agree, but––and please don't take this the wrong way––but you're a cyborg."

"Doesn't mean I can't appreciate women," George replied. "And besides, do you think any of us would have fit in with our trash-talking human counterparts in the military if we didn't?"

"I hadn't thought about that," Vince replied. "So––and I know this is weird to ask––there's one thing I've always wondered. Well, not always, but it has come to mind on occasion."

"Shoot," George said.

"Well, you present as a man."

"Very observant, Vince. We'll make a spy of you yet!"

"Ha-ha, very funny," he said. "But seriously, you're a man, and now you've got a flesh body again."

"Yep, back to my old self, and it feels damn good."

"I can imagine. But what I was wondering––man, this is so weird––what I was wondering is when you guys have flesh bodies, are you, uh, anatomically correct?"

George burst out laughing.

"Oh, man. You mean am I packing more weapons than meet the eye?"

"Well, yeah."

"Priceless," the cyborg said with a chuckle.

"Sorry for asking. I didn't mean to offend you."

"Offend me? Shit, I don't think you could if you tried. Why, there was this one night in Bangkok––well, I'll save that for another time. But no, I'm not offended, Vince. Amused? Yes. Offended? Not so much."

"What are you two yammering about now?" Tamara asked as she and Duke passed them in the corridor heading the other way.

"Vince was wondering if I was a *real* man, if you know what I mean."

"Jesus, Vince. Seriously?" Tamara said with an amused sigh.

"Hey, I was just curious how they function. I mean, they have flesh bodies again, ya know?"

"We've seen cyborgs before, Vince."

"Barry?" he said with a laugh. "That dude's so proper I doubt he even knows if he's got one. It would probably offend him to even look in his trousers to check."

"Well, to answer your question, Vince, genitalia is an option for many of the more advanced models. The ones with more powerful AI processors to allow them to be more than walking toasters, that is," George informed him.

"So it actually *is* an option?" Vince marveled. "Trippy."

"What about you, George?" Tamara asked with a wicked grin.

"Oh, me? I like to keep the ladies guessing," he replied with a twinkle in his eye.

"Are you gonna keep talking about your junk, or are you gonna load those crates, Sarge?" Duke said with a laugh.

"Why can't we do both?" the amused cyborg replied, hefting the crate into the air.

"Hey, George," Vince said as he grabbed the other end of the crate. "I've got a lot to get finished up here with the work crews. Are you going to be making a run to the surface anytime soon?"

"Yeah, I'm actually running a small training session later today down in Virginia. Why?"

"I was wondering if you could pick up a little something for me while you're there."

Vince told him what he wanted, and a big smile spread across the jovial cyborg's face.

"Oh, man," George said. "That's brilliant."

Light years away, Daisy and her sister sat quietly aboard their brilliant ship. Stranded. Out of touch. And very much alone.

Freya had found a small moon orbiting a gas giant to set down on once she sussed out their exact location on her star charts. They had traveled a vast distance from the battle with the fleet, but had fallen laughably short of their intended destination.

As it stood, they weren't exactly lost, but they might as well have been.

"So, to get back to where our fleet engaged the Ra'az?" Daisy asked as she pored over warp orb schematics.

"At top speed, with conventional drive capabilities it looks like about five years of travel," Freya replied. "Give or take, a few months."

Daisy slumped in her seat.

"It'll all be long over by then."

"I know."

"And they've probably already begun warping back to Dark Side to stage for the assault on Taangaar."

"I know, Daisy," Freya said. "Saying it over and over doesn't make the problem go away. It just makes you fixate on the negative."

"Wow, she's starting to sound like Fatima," Sarah joked.

"I'll take that as a compliment," Freya replied.

"You're growing up fast, hon."

"It's not about growing up, it's about focusing on what we can do to resolve this situation without dwelling on the negatives," the powerful AI replied. "I mean, if you were an AI, Daisy, you'd be running the risk of falling into a negative feedback loop."

Daisy looked up from her work, the stress of the situation clear in her eyes.

"I know, I really do. And I appreciate you looking out for me, kiddo. But we're one of only two stealth craft in the entire fleet.

We are a vital part of this operation, and while Sarah and I could go into cryo for the trip, it'd be five years just to make it to where the fleet engaged the Ra'az. Getting back to Earth would take a hell of a lot longer."

"I know, and I'm really sorry," Freya said, softly.

"No, you misunderstand me. It's so not your fault, Freya. It's just that the whole thing will be over by the time we get back. Without warp, we'll miss it all."

"Maybe after seeing what our combined forces were capable of the Ra'az will finally stop fighting. Maybe they'll change. Maybe they'll just be excellent to each other for once."

"What did you say?" Daisy asked, perking up in her seat.

"I said maybe they'll change."

"No, after that. You said maybe they'll be excellent to each other."

"Yeah. So?"

An inspired gleam shone in Daisy's eye. "So, strange things are afoot at the Circle-K," she said as her spirits rapidly lifted.

"Okay, Sis, you've totally lost me, here."

"Me too, and I'm inside of your head," Sarah added.

"It's the Bill and Ted theory," Daisy clarified. "Holy shit, now that's a mind-fuck. But could it actually work?"

"What are you talking about, Daze?"

"Time travel," she replied.

"Yeah, we've done it in the past, but in case you've forgotten, our warp orb is down for the count for, oh, the next couple of millennia."

"I have to agree with Sarah on that point," Freya added.

"No, you guys don't see," Daisy said. "Freya, you've watched all of Harkaway's old movies."

"Yeah."

"So you're the supercomputer. The one Vince and I watched not too long ago. Bill and Ted. In need. What am I thinking?"

"Oh, damn," Freya gasped. "That's good. That's *real* good."

"I know, right? But do you think it might work?"

"One way to find out," Freya replied.

"Hey, geniuses. There are those of us who still don't know what the hell you're going on about," Sarah griped.

"Yeah. What she said."

"Sorry. It's something that—while presented in a pop-culture classic—was actually a curious examination of the intricacies of time travel."

"Meaning?"

"Meaning maybe we can save ourselves from this mess," Daisy said with a huge grin. "All we have to do is remember to come back at some point in the future once we have a functional warp orb and leave it here for ourselves in the past."

"Wait, what?"

"We need a warp orb," Daisy stated. "We had three total. Two of them we stole in the Ra'az warp research facility when we jumped back in time to before the main assault, and then there was the one I took during the raid, which is the drained unit we have with us right now. That's three."

"I installed the spare one in the small craft you saw during the battle with the Ra'az fleet," Freya informed them, a note of sadness tinging her voice. "There are only two warp orbs remaining."

"And we gave one to Chu to study," Daisy added. "So at some point in the future, all we need to do is go get that orb from Chu's lab and do a time warp back to before we get stuck here to leave it here for ourselves."

"But then we'd be stuck in the past again," Sarah said. "We'd only have one functional warp orb, and once we left it here for ourselves, we couldn't get back. Paradox."

"Shit, you're right."

Daisy thought long and hard, but it was Freya who came up with the solution.

"If we have time travel at our fingertips again, what if we

jump back far—I mean *really* far—and leave the drained warp orb in a sealed, protective container. It's recharging on its own, after all. It just needs a lot of time."

"Oh, damn. That's brilliant," Daisy said. "We stow it here a few thousand years ago and let it charge back full to capacity so it will be ready for us now, when we need it. Freya, you're the best!"

"Do you think that will even work?" Sarah asked. *"Is there any sort of paradox issue that would prevent it?"*

"There's only one way to find out," the other Sarah said, looking out the window. "So, where would we leave it for ourselves?"

Daisy joined her at the window and surveyed the rocky surface.

"Freya, hit the exterior lights, would ya?"

The small moon was illuminated, the ship's lights casting long shadows across the area.

"I'd leave it right there," Daisy said, pointing to an extremely weathered and faded sealed container stowed under a pile of rocks.

It had been bright orange at one time, many, many years ago, but many years in space, subjected to cosmic rays and moon dust, had dulled it immensely.

Daisy quickly began climbing into her EVA suit.

"Okay, we also need to find that bright orange container in the future," she said.

"I actually have one in my storage compartment. It's an airtight and impact-resistant munitions housing, but it will work perfectly for our purposes," Freya said. "Actually, I guess it already did."

"Hot damn," Sarah gasped. "Daisy, did we actually just—"

"Yep," she replied. "But we can't abuse it."

"I know," Sarah said. "But this trick could come in *really* handy."

"If we don't break the universe in the process," Daisy replied.

"Well, yeah. I suppose there's that."

"Come on already. Suit up and get that thing, you two. Time's a-wasting."

The sisters quickly donned their space suits and made a quick moon walk, gathering up the fully functional warp orb and installing it in Freya's drive system.

"Okay, *big* note to self, gang. We've gotta get that other orb from Chu and come back here eventually."

They all locked that task away in their minds, then plotted a course back to Dark Side. Back to their waiting friends.

Moments later, Freya popped into the clear space a ways beyond Earth's moon.

"Look at them all," Sarah marveled. "We captured a lot of ships."

"Yeah, but at what price?" Daisy wondered. "If they warped here, that means the improved warp drives from other vessels had to be retrofitted. How many ships did we leave behind?"

It was a question the answer to which would have to wait.

For the time being, Daisy wanted nothing more than to land safely at Dark Side. After that they could deal with the rest.

Freya dropped Daisy and Sarah off before heading to her fabrication hangar for some alone time.

"Losing that little project ship of hers really seems to have upset her," Sarah noted as the powerful AI quietly flew to her room.

"Yeah, I noticed," Daisy agreed. "She must've really put a lot of time and effort into it. You know how she can get with her projects once inspiration hits her."

"Yeah."

Daisy spotted Vince and George loading gear into the *Váli* across Hangar Two, right where she thought they'd be. The run to Taangaar would be a hairy one, but with Mal and Captain Harkaway at the helm, dropping Chithiid and operating remote drone ships, Daisy felt a great confidence that they'd be successful.

The Ra'az wouldn't know what hit them, and the loyalists on the ground would be taken by surprise. And a small armada of disposable drones would be a wonderful tool to further confuse the enemy.

Daisy walked quickly across the hangar deck, wrapping her arms around Vince and planting a big kiss on him.

"Wow. What's that for?"

"Just because," she said, a happy smile firmly plastered to her face.

"Well, I've gotta be getting down to Virginia," George said, dusting off his hands. "Lots to do," he said, flashing Vince a wink.

"What's that all about?" Daisy asked as she watched her mechanical friend walk away.

"Oh, just a couple of guys shooting the shit," Vince said. "And we were having an interesting discussion about cyborg physiology."

"Really? Tell me all about it," Daisy said.

"Alas, much is still a mystery to me. But *human* physiology I'd be more than happy to review with you," he said, planting a warm kiss on Daisy's lips.

CHAPTER SEVENTEEN

Daisy was grabbing a bite in the mess hall when she got word that Marty and Arlo had returned. The whole base was abuzz after their arrival, it seemed.

"What's going on?" Sarah asked as she joined Daisy and the throng of people hustling down the corridors of Dark Side toward the hangar.

"I don't know," Daisy replied. "Mrazich had Barry come and tell me personally that the kid was back. Said I needed to get down there and be part of the debrief. He also said he would be summoning all of the fleet leaders for a vid conference in a few hours."

"Dang, that's a lot of hustle for a simple scouting run. You think he found something?"

"*Seems pretty obvious,*" Sarah quipped. "*For someone like Mrazich to react that way? Yeah, Arlo found something, all right.*"

Daisy pushed through the murmuring crowd when they reached the hangar doors. Barry was standing in the doorway, his cybernetic frame blocking anyone from entering.

"Daisy. Sarah. I am glad you were able to make it here so quickly."

"Well, you did kinda stress the urgency of it," Daisy said.

"Yes, I suppose I did," he said with that odd little smile of his. "Please, come in and join the others. They are about to debrief Marty and Arlo."

"Big news, then?" Sarah asked.

"Better you get it directly from the source," the cyborg said, stepping aside and letting them pass, then returning to his doorman duties.

They found Arlo seated outside of Marty's stealthy mass, a cup of cocoa in his hands. He looked more than a little shaken. Vince, Chu, Mrazich, and Harkaway were also there.

"Hey, bud, you okay?" Daisy asked, ruffling the teen's hair.

She got a little whiff of his cocoa. There was definitely something a bit stronger than milk and chocolate in it. Vince flashed her a little smile and what could easily be described as a 'he-needs-it' look.

Judging by the poor kid's face, she was inclined to agree with him.

"Okay, everyone is here," Commander Mrazich said. "Arlo, Marty, why don't you just take it from the top?"

Arlo's shell-shocked eyes scanned the friendly faces surrounding him. He forced himself to sit up straight, driving the slight tremor from his hands before he began.

"Okay, here's the thing," he said. "Marty and me"––he looked at Daisy––"Marty and *I,* we think we found the Ra'az homeworld."

A buzz of interest flashed through the others.

"You're not sure, though?" Vince asked.

"We couldn't get close enough to do a proper scan."

"But Marty is a stealth craft. Surely you were able to––" Mrazich began.

"It wasn't about being detected by scanners," Marty interjected. "It was about the sudden loss of our warp system."

Daisy shared an uncomfortable look with Sarah.

"What exactly happened, Arlo?" she asked.

He took a deep breath.

"We were chasing down some leads Maarl had dug up. Possible freighter routes, likely areas we'd come across Ra'az transport ships and the like. But then on our seventh--"

"Eighth," Marty corrected.

"Right. Our eighth warp, we landed just outside a fucking massive asteroid field. We're talking utterly enormous, and spanning most of the core of the solar system."

"But you weren't hurt, were you? I don't see any impact marks on Marty's hull," Mrazich noted.

"No, we were fine. At least on the outside. But as soon as we got into the asteroid field, our warp system cut out entirely."

"And it wasn't just a normal internal failure," Marty added. "This was caused by something else. Something outside my systems."

"Marty, put your scanner readings up on the screen, please," Daisy asked.

"Sure thing, Daisy. Hang on one second. Tap me in, Sid, will you?"

"Of course," the base AI replied.

A moment later, the nearest vid screen lit up with images of their arrival and subsequent approach into the asteroid field.

"You can't see much through there," Sarah said. "All those rocks--I've never seen an asteroid field so vast."

"I know," Arlo replied. "And this is just part of it. We wanted to go deeper, to see if we could get a clearer look at the planets on the other side, but Marty runs entirely on warp power now, and whatever was in that asteroid field totally knocked out our drive systems."

"But how did he stay activated?" Daisy asked. "If you lost your power source--"

"He didn't," Arlo said with a little shudder. "You'll see in a minute. Marty was booted offline."

"Oh, shit. That poor kid."

It must've been terrifying.

"To say the least. No power, no life support, no gravity. It's a miracle he made it out in one piece."

Sure enough, the video abruptly went black on the screen.

"How did you survive, Arlo? If your systems were all down, you would have been drifting, dead-stick," Daisy said.

"And I was," he replied, haunted by the memory. "With Marty gone, I was floating inside the ship with no way to reactivate him. I figured we were probably goners, what with life support out along with everything else, and I was making my peace with that when I got pissed off. I didn't want to die out there, and I sure as shit wasn't going to give up."

"What did you do?" Vince asked, on the edge of his seat.

"I used the only systems available to me. The maneuvering thrusters."

"This is sounding a little too familiar, Daze."

I know, Sis.

"How did you activate them with the power down?" she asked.

"Since we hadn't gone too far into the asteroid field, and since it wasn't too densely populated with debris at that precise location, I manually opened the lines feeding the air thrusters aiming into the field. That gave us enough of a reverse push to start drifting backward, out of the asteroids."

"Quick thinking," Daisy complimented.

"It was dumb luck, is what it was," he replied. "Fortunately for us, there weren't any obstacles behind us, or we would have backed right into them and probably cracked the hull with all shielding down."

"So you got clear, but then what?" Mrazich asked.

"Well, once we were clear and had drifted a little distance from the asteroid field, the warp systems suddenly powered back on, as if nothing had happened."

"It was a very uncomfortable reboot, let me assure you," Marty added. "And with all power out, I have no logs from the moment power dropped until we were clear of the asteroids."

The video feed picked back up again, and deep within the floating chunks of rock, Daisy thought she could make out what appeared to be a pair of planets, orbited by a moon. She also saw Ra'az ships, though just for an instant.

"Marty, replay that last bit."

"Ah, you saw them too," he said, rewinding a few seconds and pausing the frame. "They appear to be Ra'az battle stations. Given what we know of their conquests, and considering the direction we traveled to reach this solar system, plotted against the known forward spread of the Ra'az fleet, I'd wager we found their homeworld."

"Yeah, and it's a fucking nightmare," Arlo added.

"What happened next, Arlo?" Chu asked. "Did the warp systems hold power?"

"Oh, that they did, because as soon as we were able to, we warped the hell out of there. Isn't that right, Marty?"

"Damn straight, Arlo. That was most definitely not cool."

Daisy studied the brief scan of the solar system. It was incredibly preliminary and contained very little useful data, but it did at least provide a rough boundary of the asteroid field.

It would obviously be unsafe for their ships to warp too close to the asteroid field in any circumstances, and as such, it would need to be properly scanned and mapped before any plans for an attack could be formulated.

"I know what you're thinking, Daze."

Of course you do.

"You know I don't think it's a good idea, then."

I figured as much, she silently replied. *But someone's gotta do it, and we only have two stealth ships.*

"But you saw what happened to Marty."

Yeah, but he's also running entirely on warp drive power. Freya still has her original power systems. We wouldn't be able to utilize warp, but we should be able to fly closer and get a proper look without losing power.

"You willing to bet our lives on that?"

Sarah, the second it looks like we're in danger, I'll have Freya turn tail and boogie out of there. Believe me, with the assault on Taangaar right around the corner, the last thing we need is to prematurely engage the Ra'az homeworld.

"Yeah, giving them a heads-up that there may be trouble would give them an advantage."

And I have no intention of doing that.

"It's worth noting, Freya also experienced a warp-related power issue, and we were nowhere near Marty and Arlo's coordinates," Daisy informed them.

"Daisy?" Freya interjected.

"Yes, Freya? What's up?"

"I just thought I should mention that I talked with Marty and went over all of his logs. Whatever happened to him seems to have been something different, and his warp systems are all back in perfect working order. In fact, they all returned to normal once they pulled clear of the asteroid field."

"So, there might be something about those rocks, then," Daisy mused. "All right. Chu, I need your help."

"Whatever you need, Daisy."

"I need you to load Freya with the longest-range scanning gear she can carry."

"You're not seriously going in there, are you?"

"Not if we can help it," she replied. "But we can warp to the edge of that solar system and collect all the data possible from that range."

"Swarthmore, we're about to launch an all-hands assault on the Chithiid homeworld. I know this is our ultimate goal, but there's another mission at hand," Mrazich said. "This can wait."

"It won't take long at all, Commander. Like I said, just a

scanning run and we're out. And Freya's main drive systems are still operational, so even if we do experience some sort of warp issue, we'll still have near full maneuverability."

The steel-jawed man stared at the images on the screen, deep in thought. There was no denying, those were Ra'az battle stations, and proper scans could allow their planners to devise an attack, once Taangaar was retaken, of course.

"All right, Swarthmore. Get to it," he finally agreed. "But be quick about it, and don't take any chances. We can't afford to lose you, and we sure as hell can't afford for you to be seen."

"Copy that, Commander. We're on it," she said.

"Hang on," Vince said. "I'm coming with."

"Babe, you have things to do."

"They can wait a few hours. If you have any mechanical issues, I want to be there for you, okay?"

Daisy knew better than to argue once his protective Papa Bear instincts kicked in.

"Okay," she said. "You hear that, Freya? We're going on a recon run."

Freya warped to the far edge of what they suspected was the Ra'azes' home solar system. Immediately, she began scanning the area, documenting every last detail with the enormous array Chu had provided her.

"You seeing this, Daisy? Look at the size of the asteroid field," she said as she collected her data.

"I see it, Freya. I just don't believe it."

There were a dozen planets orbiting at varying distances from the large central sun in a long, flat ring spreading from the center along one plane. That was normal.

What was not normal was the orb-like cluster of debris encompassing the two innermost planets, almost like the walls of a cell protecting the mitochondria within.

Of those two planets, only the farthest from the sun was capable of supporting life, and judging by even the most distant of scans, it was densely packed. Incredibly so, in fact. All of their preliminary observations pointed to the same conclusion. It was a hive world.

They had found the home of the Ra'az.

"We should move in a little bit closer and get more detailed readings," Daisy said. "You ready for this, kiddo?"

"Yeah," Freya replied, though she sounded a little unsure of herself.

"Hey, you'll be fine."

"I know. It's just a little scary, the thought of going in there with all those rocks floating around. It makes maneuvering incredibly hard, you know."

"Yeah, I do. But we're staying way outside of them for now. This is just an intel run. But even if we were going in, I want you to know that I have total confidence in you, kiddo."

"Me too," Vince said.

"And me too, hon. You'll do fine."

"Thanks, guys," the young ship said, then began her scan of the area.

Hours later, Daisy and Vince walked through the hangar to meet the anxious men and women awaiting their report. George Franklin was also present, though he simply handed Vince a small pouch, then left, flashing him a wink and a grin as he did.

"It's their planet, all right," Daisy informed the gathered command group and their key fleet leaders. "And it's a doozy."

She put up the first set of images on display.

"Are you transmitting this, Sid?"

"Yes, Daisy."

"Great. You reading it okay, Zed?"

"Coming in clear," he replied.

"Okay, great. So, let's get started. You see the solar system, right? It's a normal enough looking arrangement. Planets are spread out on a flat orbit of the sun."

"Looks normal so far," Celeste said. "But I have a feeling you have a surprise for us, don't you?"

"You know me so well," Daisy said with a grin. "So, we scanned the Ra'az planet. That's the second from the sun, here," she said, pointing to a spot on the screen. "The thermal scans showed an insanely dense planetary colony system. As we had been informed, it seems the Ra'az are truly a hive-like species."

"And protected by an asteroid field, I notice," Commander Mrazich pointed out. "That'll make any assault incredibly difficult, though I suppose with those periodic gaps in the field, it's possible."

"Well, that's a yes and a no," Daisy said. "Yes, it'll be incredibly difficult, and yes, we could likely maneuver ships through the gaps, though it will be tight for the larger ones. But the interesting––or disturbing part, if you prefer––is that this asteroid field is not naturally occurring. It was created."

"Hang on a minute, how does one create an asteroid field of that magnitude?" Reggie asked. "I've flown through some crazy-tough space, but there's no way you could drag all of those asteroids and position them like that. It would take millennia."

"If it were created by labor alone, yes," Daisy agreed. "But this was created by the gravitational pull of the two planets closest to the sun."

"I don't follow."

"The asteroids aren't just rocks, Reggie. We scanned them. The data is conclusive. They were planets once. Planets orbiting very near the Ra'az world, close enough to provide resources to their voracious neighbors."

"You're saying those were entire worlds?"

"Small ones, but yes," she replied. "The Ra'az used them up and sucked them dry many millennia ago, likely long before they improved their technology and began spreading out to other solar systems. It just appears that they were so aggressive in their stripping and mining of these planets that they eventually broke apart from the damage inflicted."

The room was silent. The ramifications were undeniable.

"So they are *literally* a world-destroying race," Celeste finally said. "What can you do with an adversary like that? How can you reason with them?"

"I say we nuke the site from orbit. It's the only way to be sure," Vince said, throwing Daisy a wink.

"Did he just—?"

Yep.

"While I'm sure we would all love to entertain your idea, Vince, their planet is far too fortified to approach for such an attack," Sid pointed out.

Right over his head, Daisy silently laughed to herself.

"So there's some good news and some bad news," Daisy continued. "The bad news is the planet is heavily fortified and surrounded by a sizable force orbiting it. You can see the battle stations, cruisers, and that ring of what appear to be satellites of some sort. All of which provide them an ample defense."

"And the good news?" Mrazich asked with a sigh.

"They're far away. I mean *really* far away. That message warning them about our forces that the loyalists sent? It won't reach them for years."

"True," Zed agreed, "but even so, when supplies stop coming back home they'll come looking. We've already taken their fleet from them, but it appears they have many ships, and likely possess ample capacity to easily construct more. We have to stop them before they send a new fleet out. With the battle for Taangaar at hand, we really cannot afford to fight on yet another front."

"But it would take them years to even learn of our actions," Sid posited.

"Yes, but what if they managed to capture one of *our* ships, as we've done to theirs? We have to realize that is a possibility, however unlikely. And if so, what if that ship then used our superior tech and warped to their homeworld and warned them of our pending attack? No, we must move swiftly and decisively, while the element of surprise is still ours."

"That's asking a lot from our people, Zed," Celeste said.

"I know it is. But it's the only way to be sure."

"Zed's right," Mrazich agreed. "We need to hit them hard, and we need to hit them fast. Everyone, coordinate with your Chithiid liaisons and their teams. We will begin the next phase of the mission to Taangaar straightaway."

Daisy settled into her quarters, quite ready for a much-needed power nap, but first she needed to reach out to Maarl. She knew his men were eager to move forward after their victory against the Ra'az fleet. The question was whether they'd succeed on their home turf.

"Morale is exceptionally high, Daisy. My people are very motivated. There is an excitement among them I have not seen for a very long time," he said over the video screen.

"I am glad to hear that, Maarl, and yes, the success of our fleet assault has provided a much-needed boost to everyone's spirits. But how comes the placement of your men?"

"There are many thousand on the ground, spread at key locations, as well as dozens of ships hidden within the Ra'az fleet. There are also nearly a hundred additional craft waiting nearby, just outside of scanning range," he informed her.

"That is excellent news, my friend. But I worry we may be premature and in need of further seeding the forces on the ground. While tens of thousands of men are a large amount, it is not much in this case, given the billions of people populating the planet."

Maarl smiled broadly into his monitor.

"Your point is well taken, Daisy, but those men are not only there to fight. No. They were also inserted amongst our people to give hope. To start the rebellion organically from within. Our rebels will provide weapons and support, but those oppressed under the Ra'az and their loyalist servants will rise up in a great, angry mass. When that happens, numerically, they should crush the Ra'az once the battle stations in orbit are no longer a threat."

"And that is where our teams come in."

"Yes. Mark my words, Daisy. If you eliminate the threat of retaliation from above, my people will be more than capable of handling the invaders below."

"I will relay the message to the commanders. The fleet is preparing for attack and should be ready to launch within hours. From then, we shall rely on not only our skill, but also on luck."

"And I wish the best of luck to you, Daisy."

"As I wish it for you, my friend."

CHAPTER EIGHTEEN

Daisy saw Vince coming down the corridor an hour later as she was on her way to see Commander Mrazich for a last-minute strategy pow-wow and update about their Chithiid allies. He had a slightly jittery vibe going, she noticed, which wasn't his usual thing at all.

"What's with Vince?" Sarah asked. *"The poor guy looks all kinds of shaken up."*

I don't know. He does seem a bit more fidgety than usual, but then again, it's pretty normal to be nervous before you're about to be thrust smack into the middle of a massive war.

"Yeah, but this feels like something else."

Maybe I'll grill him later, if the opportunity arises. For now, I'm just gonna let him do his thing.

"Hey, babe," she said, planting a kiss on him when their paths finally crossed. "You good?"

"Yeah, all good," he said. "You off on a mission?"

"If by mission you mean going to a meeting with Mrazich and Harkaway to update them on Maarl's people's status, then yes."

"But you're not launching yet, right?"

"No, not for a bit."

"Okay, then. Well, I'll let you get to it, but give me a shout when you're done."

"Will do," Daisy replied warmly, planting another kiss on his eager lips before heading off to her meeting.

Well, whatever's bugging him, at least it's not me.

"*You've got other stuff to worry about, anyway,*" Sarah commented as Daisy stepped into the command center.

"Captain. Commander. Everything good?" she asked the two men.

"Copacetic, Daisy," Harkaway answered. "Thanks for asking."

"So, I spoke with Maarl," she said, not wasting any time getting to the heart of the matter. "He said he's confident in the men he has on the surface's ability to raise an insurrection, and he is hopeful those posing as loyalists we have managed to insert into the battle stations will be able to disable the weapons systems aimed at the planet. But we'll still need to do all we can to take out the orbiting battle stations as quickly as possible. Without those removed from the equation, there's just too much of a chance they'll find a way to fix them and rain down death on a sizable percentage of the Chithiid population at the first sign of trouble."

"We've been thinking about that," Commander Mrazich said. "While we'll be doing all we can to knock out the Ra'az comms links between their ships and the surface, what we'll also need is a distraction. Something to confuse the enemy and misdirect them."

"And Mal has just the idea," Harkaway added. "She's said she will be able to warm up the remote drones and load them all into one of the captured freighters to bring them along on the mission. That way they can participate without needing a warp drive installed on each of them, and that's a good thing, seeing as we don't have any extras. Anyway, she's also pretty sure she can have them transmit a scrambling signal. It won't cover that large an area, but it'll be something."

"Seems like a solid plan, given our resources," Daisy agreed. "And disrupting their comms will be a key part in all of this. We've seen it before, they won't hesitate to kill their Chithiid servants if they think they've turned on them. But if their comms are cut off, they won't know what's happening on the surface. As a hive race, they need a consensus to act. If we play this right, for all intents and purposes, it *should* just look like a space-borne attack and nothing more."

"Okay, then. Have Maarl's men standing by to insert into the pre-designated facilities. I'm having the fleet prep to launch in four hours," Mrazich said. "Be ready."

"You know we will be," she replied with a cocky grin.

Daisy found Vince loitering around the mess hall, pacing back and forth, talking to himself.

"Hey," she called out, walking toward him.

"Hey," he replied, smiling nervously at her.

"Are you okay?" she asked. "I mean, you know I try not to be that nagging girlfriend always asking what you're thinking, but I'm kinda worried about you. You've been acting a little strange. Is everything all right?"

"Yeah, everything's fine," he replied, shifting his weight from foot to foot.

He looked around the room. Amazingly, it was nearly empty. The usual stampede of visitors from the fleet were busy prepping for the upcoming mission.

"Well," he said, his hand digging in his pocket, "we're about to go to war. Again. And things are going to get really crazy soon, and I'm worried if I don't do this now, I may never get another chance."

"What are you talking about, Vin––"

In one smooth motion, Vince dropped to one knee as he took a small pouch from his pocket. He reached inside and pulled out a small piece of coal, mounted in a bezel and hanging by a thin chain.

"Daisy, I know you don't like artificially made things, and nowadays diamonds are grown easier than lettuce and are a dime a dozen, but this is a piece of genuine, nature-made Earth coal. An unfinished diamond, if you will."

"An unfinished diamond?" she asked with a casual laugh that belied her racing pulse.

"Yeah. I just didn't have the time to squeeze it into a diamond yet."

"Vince, I don't know what—"

"Daisy, will you marry me?"

"Hoooooooly shit," Sarah blurted inside Daisy's head.

She grabbed him by the face and pulled him to his feet, latching onto his lips with a passionate kiss.

"So, should I take that as a yes?" he asked when she finally came up for air.

"Yes! Yes, yes, yes!" she answered, happy tears streaking her face as she took the lump of coal and slid the chain over her head. "It's lovely, babe."

"I'm glad you like it," he said. "It was either that, or something that goes boom. Like a phased plasma rifle in the forty-watt range."

"You know me so well," she said, happy adrenaline flooding her veins.

"You have to tell him, Daze. It can't wait any longer."

I know, Sarah. Hang on to your bootstraps, it's going to be a wild ride.

"So, Vince. There's something that I've been meaning to tell you but just haven't really had the right moment present itself," she began.

"You're not going to tell me you've been cheating on me with a cyborg, are you?"

"Hush, I'm trying to be serious, here."

"Sorry. Shutting up."

"So, the thing is, you know how I had that incident with my neuro-stim back aboard the *Váli*?"

"Yeah."

"And you know how it kinda planted a whole mess of stuff in my head?"

"Obviously."

"Well, there's a little more to it than that."

She paused, though not for dramatic effect.

I can't believe I'm actually doing this.

"So do it and get it over with, Daze!"

I'm trying. Leave me alone!

"Ugh, typical. Pussying out when you—"

"Sarah was copied into my head," Daisy blurted out.

She went silent as she studied Vince's face for a reaction. To her surprise, he wasn't freaking out. At least, not yet.

"I'm sorry, did you say you copied Sarah's personnel files into your head?"

"No. I copied *Sarah* into my head. The neuro-stim re-partitioned my brain and stuck her in there."

"That shouldn't be possible," he said, confused.

"No, it shouldn't, except for one little detail none of us knew at that time. Sarah wasn't just another grown human. She was my sister, grown from the same egg, no less. We shared a similar enough genetic structure that the neuro-stim somehow overrode its normal safeties and downloaded her entire consciousness into my head."

"So you're saying Sarah lives in your head?"

"Now you're getting it."

"And she's been there since the accident aboard the *Váli*?"

"Yeah. All of her memories, her whole life. All that made up

Sarah had been backed up with Mal's neuro-stims. After she died, she wasn't really gone long at all. She was with us pretty much the whole time, only riding shotgun inside my head."

"But Sarah's alive, Daisy."

"Yeah, that's the thing. That Sarah was saved by me and this Sarah. It's that whole time travel paradox mind-fuck thing all over again. But basically, the important thing is, Sarah lives in my head."

Vince finally showed the look of shock she was waiting for.

"So, she's seen *everything?*" he asked.

"Of course that's the first place he goes with this Earth-shattering revelation," Sarah griped.

"She's seen some of it," Daisy admitted. "She can pull back if she wants. Turn off from seeing stuff when I need privacy."

"But she's there? Like, right now, she's inside your head, hearing everything I'm saying?"

"Pretty much, yep. She's my handy stenographer, paying attention to everything that goes on around me. She even catches stuff I would otherwise miss sometimes. It's a good partnership, though it was a little freaky at first, if I'm totally honest about it."

"Uh, hi, Sarah," Vince said, giving a little wave.

"Tell him I say hi back. And sorry I walked in on him that time in the shower."

"She says hi. And also she's sorry she walked in on you in the shower that one time."

"Holy shit, it *is* Sarah!" he gasped. "I hope I didn't say anything bad about her," he said, suddenly self-conscious.

"Don't worry, Vince. If you did, I'm sure she'd have badgered me to give you hell about it."

It was then that Daisy noticed a figure standing not ten feet away from them, his jaw hanging open in shock.

"Oh, shit. Finn. Hey. Uh, how long have you been standing there?" Daisy asked, trying to play it off.

He was having none of that.

"She heard *everything*?" he finally said, a fierce blush spreading across his face, and just as the flesh-and-blood Sarah walked in through the mess hall doors.

"Hey, guys, what's up?" she asked, innocently.

Finn looked at Daisy, then turned and focused briefly on Sarah, his face flushing an even deeper red before he raced out the door.

Sarah turned to her friends, perplexed.

"What was that all about?"

CHAPTER NINETEEN

"Jesus, Daisy. You could have warned me!" Sarah shouted, thoroughly pissed.

"I had to tell Vince. He had just proposed to me, for fuck's sake."

"Fine, you do what you've got to do, but why the hell did you do it in front of Finn?"

"Well, we were in the moment. He had just dropped to one knee and popped the question. It took me by surprise, okay? And when I got around to telling Vince about the Sarah in my head, well, I didn't really notice him standing there."

"Yeah, Daisy, you freaked him out. Nice going, dumbass."

"Hey, it's not my fault the guy has a thing for you."

"What do you mean by that?"

"Oh, please," Daisy snarked at her sister. "Don't give me that."

"Yeah. You know what," Sarah chimed in.

"I really don't. What the hell did you hear that got him so freaked out?"

"No. Not this time. You want to understand this thing properly, then you need to truly know for yourself."

"Are you fucking kidding me? Now, of all times, we're back to this? We're about to go to *war*, Sarah. I doubt it's the best time to be singing Kumbaya and sharing memories."

"That's precisely why it's the right time," Sarah shot back. *"You say you want to know what set him off. Well, if that's really true, then you should be willing to share memories. You heard Freya. She said the first time will only last a month or so before fading. So you even get a money-back guarantee. What more do you want?"*

"She's got a point, Sis," Daisy agreed. "I mean, you two share like ninety-nine percent of the same memories as it is. Adding in the stuff from when your timelines split should take, what, maybe two hours, tops? Is that about right, Freya?"

"Closer to one hour, if I push it," she replied. "And Sarah was right. It should only last about three or four weeks this first time, give or take."

Sarah wanted to say something rude, but she forced herself to bite her tongue. Finn was upset, and not your run-of-the-mill upset, and it appeared the only way she'd truly know what the story was would be by agreeing to share memories with her incorporeal self.

It wasn't an easy decision, but it was one she finally arrived at with no further badgering by either her sister or her other self.

"Fine, I'll do it."

"Really? Excellent!" Sarah gushed.

"But only if you promise to keep what we share to yourself until we have a chance to talk."

"Okay. Promise," Sarah agreed.

I wonder what she's on about, Daisy mused. *Of course, now you've sworn not to tell me anyway, so I guess I'll just have to wait to find out.*

"This is going to be amazing. I'll finally have new memories, just as if I had a body again."

"Yeah, yeah. It's a two-way street, so spare me the overly chipper attitude, okay?"

"Hey, I'm part of this too, you know," Daisy reminded her. "Sarah lives inside *my* head, so I've got to go through with this just like the two of you."

"Fine. Can we just get this over with already?"

"The neuro-stim unit is all set up," Freya informed her. "All you two need to do is come aboard, plop down in your seats, slip the bands on your heads, and let me do the rest."

"Okay, then, let's do this."

The pair made their way to the hangar, rushing straight to Freya's stealthy craft. Finn was nowhere to be seen en route. Sarah supposed she should be grateful for that.

"Ready," Daisy said as she settled into her seat. "You ready, Sis?"

"Yeah," Sarah grumbled.

"Fantastic," Freya said, thrilled to be able to help with such an unusual data transfer. "Just relax and close your eyes. This should hopefully take about an hour."

"Hopefully?"

"Well, yeah. I've never done it before, so I'm kinda estimating, here."

"What have I gotten myself into?" Sarah groaned.

"Oh, hush," Daisy chided her. "It'll be done before you know it."

An hour later, it was not done, and Daisy was now the one getting antsy in her seat. The transfer was taking place, but as it was between the two Sarahs, she was left out of the loop, aside from acting as a conduit, that is.

"The fleet is almost ready to launch, Freya. How much longer?" she asked.

"I'm almost done," Freya replied. "And don't rush me. This is a lot harder than it looks, but if I do it just right, they'll share every memory as it if were their own. Now, hold still. Sarah's in your head, but partitioned from your own memories. It's kinda tricky, so let me concentrate."

"Okay, okay. Do your thing, kiddo."

"I am, Daisy."

Freya continued to stream memories from Sarah to Sarah until, at long last, the two had synced up. Each shared the same memories now. The process was a success.

The Sarah riding in Daisy's head was unusually silent, given what had just happened. Flesh-and-blood Sarah was also not saying a word, but rather, sitting quietly, looking stunned.

Finally, she slipped the neuro-stim from her head and got to her feet.

"I need to find him," she said.

"Yes, you do."

Sarah quickly gathered her things and bolted out the door.

"You wanna tell me what that was all about?" Daisy asked.

"I'll tell you later," Sarah replied.

"Where's Finn?" Sarah asked as she ran into the mess hall. She scanned the kitchen area, but there was no sign of the knife-wielding madman. "Has anyone seen Finn? Anyone?"

The visitors to the base looked at her, confused, but one of them seemed to have overheard a conversation he had not too long ago.

"The chef, right?" he asked.

"Yes, that's right."

"I heard him telling one of the cyborgs he'd meet him aboard the *Váli*. Something about prepping for launch. I think he's crewing on that ship during the invasion."

Sarah was out the door before he could even ask if that was what she was looking for.

She bolted down the corridors, taking the long way where the damage was still being repaired. She had just been in Hangar Two, and had she not been in such a rush, she might even have noticed him entering the large ship not too far from Freya.

No time to beat herself up over that, not with the mission about to launch. Sarah keyed her comms as she ran.

"What's up, Sis? Did you find him?"

"Change of plans," she said, out of breath from running. "I'm going to warp to Taangaar aboard the *Váli* instead."

"You don't want to come with Freya and me?"

"You go on. Finn's aboard the *Váli*, Daze. You and I can rendezvous once the mission gets underway."

"Okay, Sis. Good luck with whatever it is you're doing."

"Thanks. I wish I knew," Sarah replied as she rushed aboard the *Váli* just as she sealed her doors and lifted off, joining the hundreds of ships launching to retake the Chithiid homeworld.

Freya launched as well, settling in with the other ships as they prepared to warp.

Sarah was still being uncharacteristically quiet inside Daisy's head, and the quiet was putting her on edge ever so slightly.

"Hey, Sis. You okay in there?"

"Huh? Oh, yeah, I'm fine," she replied in an almost dreamy tone. *"It's amazing, Daze. It's wonderful. I have all these experiences that are part of me. It's like I'm alive again."*

"I don't mean to sound cruel, Sarah, really I don't, but you do realize that wasn't you, right?"

"But it was, don't you see? We were the same, but two different people. But now, we are one person, just existing in two places at once, is all."

"That's kinda freaky, Sarah."

"I know. Isn't it cool?" she murmured. *"It feels like I'm no longer just a ghost in the shell, Daze. It's like I was really there. Like it was really me experiencing those things. Those feelings, those sensations. I've got a life again, and it's going to be an amazing one."*

Daisy didn't quite know what to say to that. She was skeptical, as always, but she also didn't want to rain on her sister's parade. Sarah was happy, and that meant she was happy too. She just worried what would happen in a month, when it began to wear off.

"Hey, Sis? I'm going to check out for a bit and leave you on your own while I replay some of these memories. Holler if you need me."

"Will do, Sarah. You enjoy yourself."

"Oh, I already have been."

CHAPTER TWENTY

The main body of the fleet had begun warping into a staging area not too far from Taangaar, the human vessels hiding out behind a neighboring moon while the captured Ra'az ships slipped into a casual orbit, ready to streak to the surface to deposit their rebel cargo.

Most of the commandeered Chithiid and Ra'az ships had already made the jump. Arlo and Marty had gone on ahead with them, acting as a stealthy set of eyes and ears, feeding real-time intel to the fleet as they arrived.

The human contingent was much slower in departing. Partly because they had swapped so many warp drives between so many ships in order to help get as many Chithiid rebels as possible to the battle. The result was they found themselves forced to consolidate the remaining warp systems into only their most vital craft.

Daisy and Freya were sitting back and watching the goings-on with great interest from afar, drifting just off the surface of the moon.

They'd been ready to make the jump for a little while, but after Sarah bailed on them and took off with Mal and the *Váli*––

which had jumped ten minutes prior––they decided to enjoy the rare feeling of taking a step back and just going with the flow. The madness of battle would begin soon enough.

"We should probably head out pretty soon," Daisy said, sipping from an electrolyte packet in her captain's chair.

"Is your stomach feeling better?" Freya asked. "I keep telling you, you need to hydrate more often."

"It wasn't a hydration thing, Freya. I was just feeling a bit shaky after the sheer panic of having Vince propose to me like that. Some people get butterflies in their stomach, but me? I had fucking pterodactyls."

"Heh. Belly dinosaurs," Freya said with a giggle. "I like it."

"Of course you do, silly girl," Daisy said with a laugh.

Despite growing up so incredibly fast––which was to be expected for a genius AI––Freya still showed her child-like side every so often. It was becoming rarer and rarer, though, and was therefore something Daisy relished whenever it occurred.

"So, I was thinking about your virus," she said, taking another sip from her electrolyte pouch. "From what we saw during the attack on the Ra'az fleet, it looked like it was only able to disable some parts of their ships."

"Yeah, that's a pretty accurate assessment," Freya agreed.

"Then what was the common factor that made those particular systems vulnerable to it? I mean, there's no AI running things in any of their ships, so there has to be some sort of common source of vulnerability that made those seemingly diverse systems all susceptible to the virus."

"I was thinking the same thing," Freya said. "We know the warp drives were almost all taken out of commission by the virus. I mean, we saw that pretty clearly when I infected the fleet. But some of the smaller ships were still able to jump, so if that holds true during the attack on the Ra'az ships surrounding Taangaar, that means the larger ships should be stuck there."

"Which sucks, in that we will then have to deal with them, but is good in that they can't escape or try to warn anyone else."

"Exactly. But I do have to wonder if the virus will have any effect on their terrestrial-aimed weapons. It's a crap-shoot, and we didn't come up against any of those systems during the fleet battle."

"I know. I think we'd better hope that Maarl's rebels embedded within the fleet orbiting Taangaar were able to transfer over from their ships and make it into the battle stations to disable those systems."

"That bit of sabotage would be a big advantage," Freya agreed.

"Or the comms links at the very least," Daisy said. "It won't stop them entirely, but we've seen how they slow down when their communications are disrupted."

"Hive species," Freya said.

"Yep. Hive species," Daisy agreed.

Their plan was audacious. Take out the orbiting fleet by subterfuge and sabotage, rendering them impotent, at least in regards to the pending fighting on the surface.

And as for the ground war, that was a whole other issue, but for the human ships, it was one they'd leave to the natives while they handled the orbiting threat. Fortunately, Maarl had taken full advantage of Arlo and Marty's generosity with their time, while inserting rebels onto the planet. As a result, they had managed to produce a highly detailed map of both defenses in space, as well as key positions on the ground.

In addition, they also pinpointed vital locations in Ra'az and loyalist infrastructure that their forces needed to target and control as soon as possible once the fighting started.

Obviously, only the Chithiid could be effective as ground forces in the early stages because humans––and cyborgs who looked like humans––had never been seen on Taangaar. The much smaller two-eyed and two-armed creatures would stick out like a sore thumb

Thus, it was up to the rebels to mount the early phases of that assault on their own. They were full of enthusiasm, yet were barely trained, given the time constraints they had been under. Despite her feelings of hopefulness, Daisy found herself quietly wondering if they were up to the task.

"We're ready to warp to Taangaar whenever you want to go, Daisy," Freya announced as Daisy looked over the maps of the surface that Marty's surveying runs had produced one last time.

"Have you looked at these since their last pass?" she asked, flipping through screen after screen of densely populated housing camps.

"I saw them when Arlo and Marty first sent them over," Freya replied. "It looks like the majority of the planet's cities have been replaced with those barracks systems and internment camps."

"What kind of a life is that?" Daisy wondered. "Women and children, all locked away like sardines, while the men are sent away to do hard labor, or worse, taken off-planet and never seen again."

"That would be the Ra'az for you," Freya noted. "But at least they didn't kill them outright."

"Not for lack of trying," Daisy reminded her. "If not for their immunity to the contagion the Ra'az spread, they would have been just another eradicated species rather than slaves."

"Which is worse, I wonder?" Freya asked. "On the one hand, being alive is great, obviously. But on the other, living in slavery having known not only freedom, but also being an advanced people who can fully grasp the evil of what is being done to them, well, that's gotta be hard."

"I can't imagine it," Daisy said. "Well, I can, actually, and it would be almost unbearable. And then imagine the horror of watching your kids grow up, knowing that any time now they'll either be taken from you and sent far from home to join a work force, or pawned off on some loyalist scum to stay on the planet as a new member of their breeding stock."

"Treating people like animals," Freya said with disgust. "And it's not just the Ra'az doing it."

"No, it isn't," Daisy said, zooming in on the images of the opulent loyalist encampments. "The Ra'az taking control of the planet just gave them an excuse for their actions. They can say it's only a matter of survival, but the loyalist collaborators keeping their own people oppressed are evil to the core, no matter what cover the Ra'az invasion may have given them."

Daisy looked over the details of one of the larger encampments. It seemed to indicate that the loyalists and their families handled the bulk of the Chithiid management for the Ra'az, much like happened with the Roman conscript armies and the collaborating moneyed families who voluntarily joined them.

Of course, there were also enough Ra'az housed nearby to quash any problems in the ranks instantly, and from what Daisy could see on the enhanced images, it looked as though more than a few Graizenhunds were positioned at the perimeters of the camps as well.

Marty's videos had captured one disturbing event a few weeks prior. It seemed the massive beasts were there to not only serve as guard animals, but also to be used for the sport hunting of fleeing Chithiid as well.

As it stood, though, the vast majority of the Ra'az remained high above the planet in their ships, only venturing down to the surface when absolutely necessary. Disciplining their servants seemed to be one such necessity that they were glad to partake in, however, sadistically reveling in doling out punishment.

"Could they be bigger assholes?" Freya asked as she looked over the video logs accompanying Daisy's still image files.

"I seriously doubt it, kiddo," Daisy replied. "I look forward to seeing them crushed and driven before us."

"What about the lamentation of the women?"

Daisy laughed. "That too, obviously."

She looked around at the thinning-out fleet as they warped to join the others.

"Well, I guess that's about it. You ready to go?"

"Yeah, I've been powered up for a while. But are you? We can hang out a few more minutes if you like."

Daisy took one long look at the beautiful blue orb of Earth. She hoped she'd be back soon. "Okay," she said. "I'm ready. Hit it."

CHAPTER TWENTY-ONE

Freya was invisible to scans, both Ra'az and human, so her warp trajectory took her far closer to the planet than the other ships. The space would be almost entirely devoid of craft, and they could take a leisurely loop of the planet below for a last-minute survey of the surface and any changes since Marty's previous run.

The stealth ship popped into a low orbit, exactly where she had planned.

"Shit! Freya!" Daisy called out.

Freya, for her part, didn't even bother responding. That would have taken too long. Instead, she instantly tucked into a barrel roll, narrowly avoiding the Ra'az cruiser that flashed by them at high speed.

All around them, ships were engaged in a massive battle, and not only the captured ones piloted by the Ra'az. The human fleet had engaged as well. The sky was one giant battlefield, and they had jumped right into the middle of it.

"What the hell happened? This wasn't the plan," Daisy said, confused. "The fighting wasn't supposed to start yet."

"Something must have gone wrong," Freya said. "Oh, shit," she blurted. "You'd better hold on. This is going to get rough."

"But we're in space. We shouldn't pull hardly any Gs."

"Sorry about this," was all Freya said, then abruptly spun into a dive, piercing the exosphere of Taangaar as she broke fully into the planet's atmosphere.

Her cannons and rail guns sprang into readiness, immediately targeting and firing on the swarm of Ra'az ships in the skies around them. Several burst into flames as her pulse blasts flew true.

Then Daisy saw the cause for Freya's urgency.

Mal had been forced from orbit by a not-so-insubstantial force of attacking heavy cruisers. She would have been better off in space, despite the raging battle, but the *Váli* had been cut off, driven into the atmosphere where the ship lost any maneuvering advantage it had possessed.

"Shit," Daisy blurted as she realized what had happened. "She's loaded to the gills with Chithiid troops and equipment. Her maneuverability in the atmosphere is going to be horrible."

"I know," Freya grunted as she spun into a tight bank and took out another Ra'az ship. "I'm trying to get her cover to make a run for space, but there are too many ships. It's daylight, and I've lost my advantage."

It was true, Daisy realized. While the pursuing Ra'az craft were unable to get any sort of readings on the stealth ship, let alone a weapons lock, they were nevertheless hectoring Freya with line-of-sight bursts of weapons fire. Some shots were coming dangerously close.

Mal and her crew were doing all they could to stave off the Ra'az craft. Captain Harkaway and Reggie were both glistening with sweat from the effort as they manually fired the supplemental weapons systems they'd presciently mounted to the *Váli* before the mission.

The freighter full of drones was Mal's ace in the hole, but Daisy couldn't see it anywhere.

You see their drone carrier? Daisy asked, scanning the skies.

"*No. They must've been separated when she broke orbit. Freya, do you see Mal's freighter anywhere?*"

"Sorry, Sarah. I don't. And I'm a little bit busy at the moment," the mighty ship said, straining as she dodged a dozen swarming Ra'az ships.

"There are too many of them," Daisy noticed. "There weren't supposed to be this many Ra'az ships here."

"They're pulled from the other side of the planet," Freya said. "Zed sent a transmission for the others to target the battle stations on the opposite pole if they can."

"So they saw the invasion and threw everything they had at it?"

"Seems that way."

"But that leaves the battle stations over there on their own."

"Well, no one has been able to break off to get over there, so it seems to be working," Freya said.

"Why don't they just warp?

"Shape of the planet. It's blocking them. They'd have to jump away then back, and the battle stations are putting out random flak fire into space in all directions. They'd stand too high a likelihood of warping right into the line of fire," Freya told her. "Now hold on."

She bucked and dove, trying to reach the *Váli* to take some of the pressure off.

Mal had already been hit several times, multiple pods shaking in their mountings as she tore through the atmosphere.

"Who's that?" Daisy asked.

Freya saw what she was inquiring about. On Mal's flank, a craft similar in style to the *Váli*, though significantly smaller, was covering her as best it could, drawing enemy fire away when possible, firing its rail guns constantly, protecting their wake.

"I don't know, Daisy. I haven't met that one yet. The fleet's huge, after all."

"It just looks a lot like the *Váli*, is all. I thought she was the only ship of her kind."

Another blast shook the *Váli*, tearing free several of her pods. Daisy just hoped they were carrying supplies and not troops. She watched them fall, their emergency landing thrusters having been blown clean-off in the blast. Whatever was inside would not be surviving the impact.

"If she doesn't get out of here, and quick, she's going to sustain too much damage to stay in the air," Daisy shouted.

"I know!"

Mal, for her part, knew as well, and was doing everything she could to lighten her load. A half-dozen pods were rattling in their couplings, broken loose, but intact. Another handful were flapping in the turbulent air, knocking her airframe about violently as she tried to maneuver.

"Mal, you have to release those pods!" Captain Harkaway yelled.

"I'm trying, Captain, but the system is damaged. Reggie, can you access the backup subroutine from your station?"

"Negative," the co-pilot replied. "I was able to activate the emergency damage protocol and seal the doors of most of the pods ship-wide, but I can't access the release system. It'll need to be done manually."

"Shit," Harkaway growled. "Vince, do you copy?" he called out over the ship's comms.

"Here, Captain."

"How are we looking down there?"

"Engineering is holding up okay, but this atmos flight is wreaking havoc on her drive systems. I'm doing all I can, but we're going to need to clear atmos, and soon, or the engines are going to run the risk of flaming out on us."

"Keep at it, Vince. We're doing all we can. Just keep us in the air."

"Will do," he replied, then cut off his comms and set back to work putting out fires, both figuratively and literally.

A massive jolt shook the ship, throwing Vince roughly to the deck.

"Mal, what the hell was that?" he yelled into the comms.

"A loyalist ship impacted one of the starboard pods," she replied. "It was a small one, but the craft is lodged in place."

The ship shuddered and lurched.

"Vince, the wind resistance is wreaking havoc on my propulsion systems. I fear I will not be able to compensate much longer. Can you re-route additional power to the main engine output?" Mal asked.

"I'm all over it, Mal," he replied, jumping to work. "I just hope she can take the load."

Nearby, smoke wafted in the passageway where the loyalist ship had crashed into the *Váli*. One of the inner doors had been open at the time of impact, and had they not been flying in atmosphere, it may well have doomed them all.

As it stood, the ruined alien ship had mashed into the pods and burst into flames but was quickly extinguished by the sheer force of the wind as the *Váli* hit near-Mach speeds as they desperately avoided their attackers.

One of Maarl's rebels traveling aboard the *Váli* managed to make his way from the adjacent pod and into the corridor. Walking in the turbulence was difficult, and he was using his four powerful arms to brace himself as he tried to make his way to the site of the impact. He knew full well they would need that door sealed if they hoped to exit the atmosphere, and time was of the essence.

"I have reached the site of the impact," he called out over the comms. *"There appears to be no damage to the interior*

passageways. I will attempt to dislodge the debris blocking the airlock door."

With a great heave, he strained and pulled until the door finally dislodged, sliding smoothly open. The piece of wreckage blocking the door was a trivial thing to remove. The sharp piece of ceramisteel that pierced his chest moments later, however, was not, and his lifeblood gushed from his body to the deck as a bloodied loyalist survivor forced his way from his wrecked craft and into the *Váli*.

The last wisps of smoke disappeared as the door sealed shut behind him.

He quickly scanned the area. No other rebel enemies were present, and all the other pods appeared to be going into emergency lock-down. Faced with the choice of single-handedly assaulting a locked and reinforced command pod or finding another way to take the ship out of the sky, the loyalist quickly chose option two, spinning and running for engineering.

Vince was hard at work, manually rerouting energy couplings to feed into the ship's already overtaxed systems, when the hair on the back on his neck abruptly stood on end. He trusted his instincts and dropped straight to the deck. That instantaneous reaction was the only thing that saved him as a piece of jagged metal slammed into the console where he'd been standing moments before.

The loyalist, however, wasted no time, quickly landing a brutal kick to the downed man, sending him flying against the bulkhead.

"Motherfucker!" Vince yelled as he scrambled to his feet.

The alien lunged at him once more, but Vince had trained in unconventional combat with Daisy. Trained a lot, in fact, and rather than landing a killing blow to his much-smaller opponent, the alien's viciously thrown fists met nothing but metal. Vince had seen the attack coming and deftly dodged to the side, landing a flurry of blows with the heavy spanner already in his hands as he did. To his satisfaction, he thought he heard something crack.

The Chithiid jumped back, startled by his wily quarry, cradling his now-broken elbow.

"Yeah, that's right. Now it's a three-to-two advantage, you bastard," Vince growled. "Stick out another one, I might just even things up," he taunted his four-armed opponent, spinning the improvised weapon in his hands.

The tall alien paused in his attack. This human was more difficult than he anticipated. With a sudden lunge, he feinted a punch with two of his arms, then threw a surprise kick, catching Vince off-guard and knocking him through the open door into the corridor.

"Shit," Vince blurted as he quickly rolled to his feet, struggling for solid footing on the bucking ship.

The Chithiid raced after him to the doorway, but then paused, looking back at the engineering compartment.

"Oh, no you don't," Vince growled, throwing the heavy tool in his hands as hard as he could.

The spanner hit the alien a glancing blow to the jaw, hard enough to draw blood.

"I shall crush the life from your fragile body!" the enraged loyalist yelled.

Vince turned and ran as fast as he could down the passageway.

"That's right, you bastard, come and get some!"

The Chithiid seemed more than happy to comply, despite not speaking a word of English. The tone of the defiant human was easy to understand.

Vince bolted down a lateral connecting passageway to the exterior layer of pods, ducking into the nearest one, the alien close on his heels. He slapped the keypad, and the door began to close behind him as he raced to the far wall, but the Chithiid stuck a limb in the gap, triggering the auto-stop safety mechanism. The door slid back open.

Slowly, the tall loyalist leaned into the chamber, sizing up his prey. The little human was cowering against the far bulkhead, no weapons in his hands, and nowhere to run. With a wicked smile, he stepped inside the pod. The door quietly sealed behind him.

Vince had nowhere to run.

It was at that moment the alien noticed something unsettling. Something wrong. The human wasn't scared. No, his eyes told a different story, and though he couldn't explain why, the Chithiid hesitated. Then he saw the flashing keypad next to his quarry.

He realized his mistake, but it was too late.

Vince smiled as he pressed the button, overriding the dual airlock door safety mechanism, opening both doors to the outside at once.

The air immediately sucked out of the chamber, replaced by a buffeting gale as the exterior winds whipped through the pod, pulling everything not bolted down out the door in an instant. The flailing Chithiid managed to hold fast to the doorframe for a second, then he was gone. The loyalist intruder was going to have a very long fall, and a most uncomfortable landing.

Vince's hastily attached carabiner tether was barely keeping him secured to the wall, and with great worry, he realized it felt like his pants might rip loose at any moment, sending him to an unwanted free fall as well.

He quickly keyed the door command and sealed the airlock, dropping to the floor as the pressure normalized.

"Vince, what the hell's going on down there? We just registered a decompression in Starboard Pod Twelve," Reggie said.

The exhausted engineer keyed his comms. "Had some

loyalist company, Reg, but I took care of it. He's taking the fast route to the surface."

"An intruder? From the ship that impacted us?"

"Yeah, that's my guess."

The *Váli* bucked violently as Vince moved for the passageway door.

"Shit," Reggie growled. "The damn thing's wedged in between a few pods. It's trashed our maneuverability."

"Mal told me," Vince said as he was roughly slammed into the wall, then the floor, as he tried to make it back to engineering.

"You think you can get us that extra power?" Reggie asked. "There's too much drag on the airframe. We're gonna drop out of the sky without it."

"I'll do what I can. Just try to keep her steady for a minute so I can get back to engineering."

"I'll try, but we've got a lot of company," Reggie replied, straining at the controls.

"Do what you have to. I'll get back to engineering somehow."

"Vince, did you see any more loyalists board the ship?" Captain Harkaway's voice interjected.

"No, Captain. Just the one."

"Okay, then. Hold on. We're gonna try to shake that bastard's ship loose before his buddies realize we're flying crippled here. Hopefully it'll gain us at least a little maneuverability."

A new voice joined the conversation, overriding their comms system from far above.

"Lars, I can have my escort to you in five minutes," Celeste called out to him over the line.

"Negative. You need those with you."

"But you're––"

"Celeste, no! Stick to the mission. Protect yourself. We'll manage," he said, straining under the g-force as Mal pulled them into a powerful turn, narrowly avoiding a Ra'az and loyalist vessel crossfire.

"Don't you die on me, mister," his wife commanded.

"Yes, ma'am," he replied with a little laugh. "Love you too." Harkaway quickly turned his attention to his guns, firing out a volley of rail gun sabots.

A Ra'az ship jerked, then flamed out, falling toward the planet below as one of the captain's shots flew true.

"Got you, ya bastard!"

"It's not going to matter if we don't cut those damaged pods loose," Reggie shouted across the command pod. "It's getting worse. I don't know how much longer we can stay in the air."

"I know, Reg," Harkaway said, grimly. "The release isn't functioning, but we can at least take as many of those fuckers with us as possible."

Barry unbuckled from his station and lurched to his feet, tossed and thrown hard into the bulkhead. A thin trickle of blood showed at his hairline.

"What the hell do you think you're doing, Barry? Sit back down—that's an order!"

"I'm sorry, Captain, but I'm going to have to disobey that command."

The cyborg grabbed onto the nearest handhold with a firm grip and hauled himself toward the pod door.

"Mal, open the door."

"What are you doing, Barry?"

"Those pods need to be released."

"I understand," Mal said, opening the door for him.

A blast shook the craft, making it lurch abruptly, launching Barry violently out the door into the corridor.

Quickly, he scrambled to his feet and began running down the passageway, thrown violently against the walls every few steps, leaving an increasingly bloody trail in his wake.

He pressed on, determined. Mal could patch up his flesh

covering later, provided her medlab remained intact. And if they survived, of course. For the moment, the medlab was undamaged, he noted as he flew past it, rudely thrown from his feet by an abrupt banking turn as Mal narrowly avoided yet another Ra'az blast.

The smaller ship trying to protect Mal was having a hell of a run of things, but had managed to stay largely undamaged. That was mostly due to it not being laden with fully loaded pods, as the *Váli* was, but nevertheless, it hadn't been designed for combat flight in atmos.

Freya had managed to drop into a position behind both ships, and was doing all she could to pick off the Ra'az attack craft and pair of heavy cruisers on their tails.

"She can't keep that up much longer," Daisy said, grimly. "Those loose pods are making her a sitting duck."

"They need to be cut free so she can make a run for space," Freya said, objectively.

"But Vince is on board. And Sarah. Our friends are on that ship."

"I know, Daisy. I'm just stating the facts. Unless they cut those pods loose, the whole ship will go down."

"It's a goddamn Mr. Spock moment, isn't it?"

"What?" Freya asked, confused.

"The good of the many," Daisy replied, grimly. "Come on, we need to give them as much cover fire as we can."

Blood-soaked and battered, Barry clung to the emergency handles near the entrance to the Narrows junction deep within the *Váli*'s superstructure, his metal fingers clearly visible where their flesh covering had torn away in his frantic scramble for the access panel.

Without a moment's hesitation, he hoisted himself into the tight space and began the long shimmy to the manual pod release. The turbulence continued to beat him against the walls of the craft, but now that he was inside such a narrow space, the impacts were reduced, as his body had less distance to travel and gain momentum.

He was leaving a bloody mess in his wake, and a tiny part of his brain registered that he would have to come back and mop all of that up later––if they didn't crash into the surface in a fiery wreck, of course.

Barry made good time crawling to his destination, the limited foray into the Narrows giving him a newfound appreciation for the difficult job Daisy and Sarah had performed aboard the ship.

But there was no time for reflection.

He took his miraculously intact comms headset and plugged into the hardline jack, since deep in the Narrows, the shielding wouldn't let any wireless signal pass.

"I've reached the release system, Mal," he informed the ship's powerful AI. "Please confirm that all pods are sealed."

"They are," Mal replied.

"Disconnecting in three," he said, not bothering with a countdown. They were both computers, after all. Keeping track of three seconds was not an issue.

The pods, however, did not release.

"That was three seconds, Barry," Mal said.

"I am aware, Mal," he replied.

"What the hell's going on down there, Barry?" Harkaway yelled into the comms.

"There appears to be a short, Captain. I will have it repaired momentarily."

Indeed, there was a short. Just a tiny little thing, but one that was preventing the signal from reaching its destination. There was just one problem. He had no tool kit with him.

Barry evaluated the issue and made a quick decision, ripping wiring from one of the neighboring panels to complete the repair. Food replication might not function properly for a bit, but compared with dying, he thought the crew would understand his choice.

His fingers were a blur of activity as they quickly spliced the new wiring into place.

"Repaired," he announced over his comms. "Releasing damaged pods in three."

This time, when the clock ran down, the explosive bolts holding the damaged pods in place––barely––fired their charges and cut the pods free. The pods––and wrecked loyalist ship–– tore loose, and the sudden jolt sent the *Váli* into a corkscrew spin.

"They ejected some pods!" Daisy called out. "Freya, can you get any life readings in them?"

"I think there are––"

The *Váli* abruptly jerked free from its spin, the centrifugal force tearing free another half-dozen pods, sending them flying in all directions.

"Shit!" Freya blurted as she took instantaneous evasive maneuvers.

The pods narrowly missed her, scattered in the sky and falling to the planet below.

The *Váli*, free of not just the weight of the pods, but also the drag they were producing in the atmosphere, quickly changed course, pulling up hard and pushing fast for the relative safety of outer space.

Her accompanying ship ran interference behind her, deftly maneuvering to drive the Ra'az pursuers off in a way Daisy found vaguely familiar.

"Daisy, I couldn't get a proper scan of the pods," Freya informed her, "But most of their automatic emergency landing jets seem to have been functional. They will land hard, but they should be intact."

"Great. Now we just have to find out who was on board them."

Mal, for her part, had a very good idea who was in those pods, and as soon as she hit the welcome embrace of outer space, quickly deployed her small hopper craft remotely to retrieve as many of her crew as possible.

The little ship had only just steered toward the atmosphere when it was torn to shreds by Ra'az pulse fire.

"Captain," she said, "it appears we are going to need to acquire a new hopper. Ours was just destroyed."

"Shit," Harkaway growled. "What about the others? Are they alive, Mal?"

"My last readings before we broke atmosphere said yes."

Harkaway allowed himself the slightest sigh of relief.

"Well, then, let's hope that assessment is still accurate."

CHAPTER TWENTY-TWO

A pair of damaged and blast-scorched pods that had plummeted to the planet still linked together rested at awkward angles where they had partially sunk into the fecund soil of Taangaar's surface where they had impacted.

Their emergency landing jets had done their job—namely keeping the pod from crushing into a pancake upon impact—but that was about the extent of it. A comfortable landing was not what they were designed for.

The access doors to both of the pods popped off as their explosive retaining bolts were triggered from the inside. Dazed and shaken, but very much alive, Sarah and Finn crawled out and fell to the ground, breathing hard as they recovered from the ordeal.

From the other pod, Sergeant Franklin emerged, standing tall, his gear already strapped in place and ready for action. He looked down on his dizzy comrades and smiled.

"Helluva ride, huh?" he said with a chuckle.

Sarah rolled over and vomited.

"Guess not," he said.

"Dude, how can you just stand there and not feel the world

spinning?" Finn asked as he tried to gingerly press himself up to a seated position.

"Ah, that," George said, tapping his head. "Gyroscopic stabilizers. Cyborgs don't get motion sickness."

He looked at the finger that had just tapped his head. A small smear of blood decorated it like a tiny red exclamation point.

"Aww, hell," he lamented. "Already?"

"What?" Finn asked.

"This," George replied, pointing at the tiny cut on his forehead.

"It's just a little cut, man. And you're a cyborg commando, so what do you care?"

"I don't, it's just that I just got this," he said, gesturing to his recently acquired physique. "And it even still has that new body smell."

"Don't sweat it. Chicks dig scars," Finn managed to joke as the world slowly stopped spinning. "Isn't that right, Sarah?"

"Yeah, we do," Sarah agreed, wiping her lips and sitting upright. "At least, sometimes."

Sarah had only just tracked Finn down aboard the ship when they warped and all hell broke loose, so she hadn't had a chance to talk with him yet. Things, as a result, were still painfully uncomfortable between them. Something George, with his highly sensitive scanning array, had quickly noticed.

"Well, we seem to be intact, at least," he said. "But there'll be time for chatting later. We need to gather whatever supplies we can and bug out of here, and fast. There's no telling when the Ra'az will send ships down to look for us."

"I think we're safe for a while," Sarah said, looking up at the battle raging in the skies above. "They're a little preoccupied at the moment."

George surveyed the battle, then turned his attention back to his teammates.

"Yeah, possibly. But Murphy loves to fuck with our plans, and I don't have any intention of laying out a welcome mat for him, so get off your duffs and gather up our gear. We're in a tough spot, and we need to hide until we can better assess the situation."

"Shouldn't we stay nearby? I mean, what if they send a rescue party?" Finn inquired.

"I wouldn't count on anyone coming to get us just yet," George replied. "And there's no way we can blend in down here, so hiding is our number one option."

"But what about Shelly and Omar? They were on board. And Vince? And the Chithiid soldiers?" Sarah asked as the reality of their situation began to sink in.

"If the *Váli* survived, then Vince did. He would have been in engineering, and that's an integral part of the ship's superstructure," Finn said. "The others, I don't know about."

"Other pods tore free," George said. "I heard them when we were cut loose."

"You heard that?"

"Cyborg hearing," he replied with a grin.

"Jeez. I'm beginning to think being human ain't all it's cut out to be. You get all the cool toys," Finn said, climbing to his feet.

"Yeah, and there are a few more toys left," George replied.

Finn reached down, offering to help Sarah to her feet. She took his hand uncomfortably, quickly releasing it once she was standing. George noticed the exchange but kept his comments to himself.

"We need to make for cover," he said, scanning the terrain. "I think those trees over there should suffice for our immediate needs. We can reassess from there."

The area they had landed—or more aptly, *crashed*—in was what appeared to be an undeveloped patch of wilderness. Shrubs and a low-growing grass of some sort covered the gently rolling hills, while small thickets of dense trees with long trunks rising up to an interwoven canopy of deep purple leaves spotted the landscape.

There was no water anywhere near that they could see, but given the lush nature of the vegetation, George didn't think sourcing hydration for his human charges would be too great of a task.

"Help me cover the pods as best we can with some branches from those bushes we crushed on the way in. It'll be quick and not terribly efficient, but it may buy us a little protection from the most basic of Ra'az searches."

George was a dynamo, working at full speed to camouflage the crashed pods, at least somewhat. Finn and Sarah weren't too much help, but he didn't really expect them to be. In fact, he would have been perfectly happy to do the job himself, but he thought having a task might take their minds off of whatever was going on between them and ease the tension somewhat.

Ten minutes later they had done all they could and had taken shelter under a nearby group of trees.

"Okay, now let's see what's going on around here," George said, taking a small brown ball from his pocket.

"Cyborg turds?" Finn joked.

"Oh, you'd know if I dumped one on you," George shot back with a grin. "No, this is a tactical field survey drone. Good for up to twenty clicks or so."

He tossed the ball into the air, where it sprang open, revealing tiny stabilizer wings and an even tinier camera array. The device hovered in front of them a moment, while George stared at it intently.

"Uh, George? What are you doing?"

"Systems check. Standby."

"Oh, I forgot for a minute," Finn said.

"Forgot what?"

"That you're a cyborg."

George didn't break his gaze, but a little smile flashed across his lips.

"And that, my friend, is why it's so nice to have a flesh body again. It just makes life that much easier, ya know?"

The tiny drone abruptly shot off into the sky and was gone from sight.

"I assume you did that," Sarah said.

"Yeah," George replied, taking a seat with his companions. "I've got a wireless link connecting me to the drone. It's a secure line, and something of a spec-ops trade secret, so the odds of the Ra'az stumbling upon it are slim to none."

"What do you see?" she asked.

"Well, I'm having it run a series of search patterns, first from altitude, then lower. It looks like a fair amount of pods came down relatively near here."

"Shit, so Mal lost a bunch of them," Finn moaned. "I hope she made it out okay."

"Knowing that ship––and that crew, I might add––I have high hopes for them."

George paused, focusing on the signal feeding into his head.

"Ah, so it looks like a couple of pods lost their emergency landing thrusters and pancaked into the turf."

"Can you tell if anyone was in them?" Finn asked.

"Negative, but I don't see any of the telltale fluid leakage one would expect if there were live personnel aboard at the time of impact. Odds are it was just equipment and supplies."

"Speaking of which, we have some very basic gear, but there were no rations in our pods," Finn said. "We've got whatever's in our pockets to eat. After that, we're on our own."

"Come on, man. This should be exciting for you," George cajoled him. "You're Mister I Love to Cook, right? So this should be right up your alley."

"In a kitchen, sure. But I'm not much for hunting."

"I've seen you with those knives, Finn. You're more than a chef."

"It's just a hobby," he replied. "And anyway, I cook with replicated proteins. I'm not a fan of killing my food."

"Then you're in luck," George said, flashing a toothy grin.

"Again, you've lost me."

"Am I the only one who reads the mission briefs?"

"Probably," Sarah said, cracking a faint smile.

George was glad to see her lightening up. She'd need to if they were going to operate as an effective unit.

"According to the Chithiid, almost everything that grows on this planet is edible. And on top of that, from what we were able to discern, it's also non-toxic to humans."

"I've tasted Chithiid food. It's not all that," Finn griped.

"You tasted what the Ra'az made for them," George replied. "And that was just to cover basic nutritional needs, not things like flavor and texture."

"Tell me about it."

"Well, did you know the Chithiid are an almost entirely herbivorous species?"

"Actually, that's news to me," Finn said. "Seems counterintuitive, given how evolved they are. It's usually complex amino acids found in meats that spark evolutionary development of the brain. At least among humans, anyway."

"And it was that way with the Chithiid as well. But they had a different evolutionary trigger. You see, a very good amount of the plants on Taangaar are extremely high in complete proteins. In fact, I'd wager you could probably squeeze more protein per ounce out of some of these plants than you could from many of your fabricated animal proteins."

"Seriously?" Finn said, his mood perking up as he began to realize the culinary playground he was standing in the middle of.

"Yeah," George replied. "I suppose being herbivores was

probably what also made them a target for the Ra'az to enslave when their initial plague attempts failed."

"Why's that?" Sarah asked as she scanned the horizon for any sign of hostiles.

"Because it's easier to feed a workforce if you don't have to source complex foods for them. For the Chithiid, it was easy to gather the most prolific crop plants and utilize them to feed the conscripted workforce and soldiers."

"What about predators, though?" Sarah said, as an animal's movement in the far distance caught her eye.

"From what our Chithiid partners said during mission prep, the fauna on the planet are nearly entirely herbivorous as well. There are a few predators, of course, but the odds of running into one are slim. Most live far from populated areas."

"Far from populated areas, kind of like where we are right now?" Finn asked.

"Uh... I see your point," George said. "But we should be fine. If it makes you feel any better, though, I'm heavily armed, heavily armored, and don't need to sleep."

"Well—"

"And my drone shows nothing of any significant size within a dozen kilometers of here. I'll keep watch tonight regardless, of course."

"Thanks, dude."

"My pleasure," George said. "Hang on."

"What is it?"

"My drone is seeing something, but it's outside my range and it can barely pick up the readings."

George, despite being a cyborg and not needing to move at all, furrowed his brow a little as he strained to read his distant device. A holdover habit from years of blending in with humans.

"The ejected pods seem to have landed following a trajectory that way," he said, pointing off into the distance. "We're close to the far end of the crashed pods. Almost all of the rest of them landed in that direction."

"Is that a good thing?" Finn asked.

"Lights in the distance lead me to believe there's a populated area way out the same direction. Could be a problem for our people. I'm not sure. Hang on."

He stared into nothing a while longer as he read the distant scans from his drone.

"Okay, it looks like at least one of the pods had some Chithiid in it, and from what I can tell, they survived. But the images are at the edge of what I can accurately see, so I can't say for sure. The rest of the pods are that way, but too far to pick up."

"If they did survive, then they should be able to blend in. Mal was carrying young Chithiid with the plan to insert them close to large population centers so they could blend in, either as males too young to be sent to work yet, or for the more feminine ones, they could covertly sneak into the female work camps disguised as women."

"That could be awkward," Sarah mused, allowing herself a faint mischievous grin.

"You thinking what I'm thinking?" Finn asked, sharing the grin.

Sarah looked up, finally making and holding eye contact in their moment of shared amusement.

"Pubescent boys surrounded by women? Oh yeah," she said. "I bet I am."

Inside a nearby camp, a very feminine male indeed was making the best of his more delicate features, blending in with the vast multitude of women as they went through their daily labors. The work was monotonous, and he found himself drifting off into thought when their shift ended and they were marched back to their quarters.

As the females brushed against him as they passed, many in various states of undress within the comfort of their lodgings, the young and inexperienced male found himself in an increasingly awkward and difficult situation as he tried to control not only his blush reflex, but also other involuntary bodily functions as well.

Had he been a bit older, perhaps he would have had more control over them, but for a young male, it was almost too much to bear. He was doing all he could, even intentionally stubbing his toe on a bunk, hoping the pain would distract him, but he was very near to being found out.

"Hello, friend," a young female said as she approached him. She was, he thankfully noticed, fully covered in modest attire.

"Hello to you," he replied, not quite sure what to say next.

The young female smiled and looked him over, pausing at the decorative sweatband material tied above one of his elbows.

"And how are you finding your lodgings?" she asked. *"Are they satisfactory?"*

"Uh, yes, they are quite fine," he stammered.

"You and I should become friends," the young female abruptly said. *"Come, let us get sustenance. We have much to talk about."*

"I don't know if I can—"

She grabbed him by the arm and pulled him close.

"I said, we have much to talk about," she said once more, taking his hand and placing it on the sweatband tied to her arm.

The young Chithiid's eyes went wide with recognition.

"Yes, I see," he said, his spirits rising as other body parts, gratefully, were falling. *"Lead the way, friend."*

The two exited the facility together, casually walking toward the food preparation area. No one would have noted anything unusual about two young females walking together. Even their matching armbands would have seemed a normal occurrence among friends.

Matching armbands, both of which contained the same very subtle symbol woven into the fabric. The mark of the rebellion.

The two dined casually, the embedded spy bringing him up to speed on the goings-on within the camp. There were other young males already hidden within the ranks when he arrived, it seemed, and the females were all party to keeping them hidden from detection.

There was a rebellion, of sorts, already brewing long before the allied rebels had even shown up. All they required was the right spark to ignite the already-primed kindling.

Misfortune had seen him crash onto the planet unexpectedly. Now it seemed his fortunes were swinging the other direction. Suddenly, things were looking decidedly better.

CHAPTER TWENTY-THREE

The skies above had shifted to a deep indigo as day on the Chithiid world of Taangaar gently transitioned into night. High above the seeming serenity of the planet's surface, a deadly conflict was still very much underway, and it was only a matter of time before it spilled down to the surface.

"It's actually rather beautiful," Finn said as he lay back on the soft ground, watching the lights flashing just beyond the atmosphere.

"If not for the very real possibility of some of our friends dying up there, I'd be inclined to agree with you," Sarah said.

"Aw, hell. Even so, it's still a pretty fine sight," George interjected. "There's death and violence everywhere you look, if that's all you choose to see. But me? I'm with Finn. Life's too precious to ignore the moments of beauty it presents us."

Sarah turned to the unusual cyborg. He was scanning both the skies above and the terrain around them, aware of everything moving for several kilometers, yet he still found bandwidth to enjoy the light show up above.

"You're an odd dude, George," she finally said.

"Since you're Daisy's sister, which makes you just as much of a freak as she is, I'll take that as a compliment," he said with a low laugh.

A narrow pulse blast lit up the sky far across the horizon, the yellow-orange of a terrestrial impact brightening the night sky for a few moments as it reached its target.

"Looks like they didn't get all of the terrestrial-aimed weapons," Finn noted. "That's one hell of a screw up."

"To be fair, though, command never really thought they'd be able to stop them all," George mused.

"No?"

"No. They just hoped to take out enough of them to give the people on the ground a chance to rise up, ya know? It's not our forces that are going to turn the tide down here. It's the locals."

"But those pulse cannons––"

"Are tiny on the global scheme of things. Look, if you want context, the original battle plan reports estimated that the Ra'az battle stations would be able to incinerate ninety percent of the Chithiid population within three hours."

"Whoa."

"Yeah. Whoa," George agreed. "So the fact that we've been down here all fucking day and haven't been turned to toast is a pretty damn good sign in my book."

"You know, you swear a lot, for a cyborg," Sarah commented.

"Fuckin' A," George shot back with a grin.

Sarah was quiet a long while, then turned her attention back skyward.

"It *is* pretty," she said.

While they settled down for the night, high up in the war zone surrounding the planet, their friends and allies had been working tirelessly, not only to defeat the orbiting Ra'az threat, but to save the billions on the planet below as well.

Freya and Marty had been working diligently, bursting in close to the battle stations and targeting crucial systems with pinpoint-aimed rail gun blasts.

Unlike pulse weaponry, there was no energy signature on the electromagnetically hurtled rail gun projectile, and thus, there was no easy way for the Ra'az gunners to backtrace an incoming attack until it was too late.

One by one, they had been swooping in, carefully taking down the targeting and operations control hubs that controlled the huge cannons aimed at the defenseless Chithiid population.

"Looks like our spies' intel was spot-on," Arlo said over his comms as he and Marty swung around an aimlessly firing cruiser as it tried to pinpoint the slippery stealth craft.

"And it's a good thing," Daisy agreed as Freya blasted out another salvo of rail gun sabots toward the hull of the hulking battle station, then quickly darted away.

"You get any updates on the other weapons systems?" Arlo asked. "Marty and me, we haven't been able to pinpoint any of their weak spots. We've got the terrestrial cannons under control, it seems, but these other guns are still very hot."

As if to punctuate his statement, a pulse cannon blasted out a shot, narrowly missing his craft, though, given their stealth capabilities, it was a random near-miss rather than a targeted one.

The pulse did eventually find a target, however, and deep within the human and rebel fleet, a smaller ship erupted from the deadly blast.

"Shit, they hit another one," Daisy growled. "Come on, Freya, let's light that fucker up. Hit 'em with everything you've got."

"But our weapons will make us visible, Daisy."

"I know," she replied with a determined look in her eye. "That's the point."

"You're going to have them target your kid?"

"Better than the fleet," Daisy replied. "Freya's a hot-shit pilot. I have every confidence she'll keep us from being hit."

"And if you're wrong?" Sarah asked.

"Well, then I guess we're fucked."

"I can do it, Sarah," Freya said bravely. "And Daisy's right. We need to protect the fleet however we can."

Without delay, she surveyed the battlefield and selected the optimum position for both diverting Ra'az fire, as well as making an escape without running into a blender of other ships' fire.

"Okay. Hold on."

She let loose with her pulse weaponry, which was substantial, though against a craft as massive and shielded as the Ra'az battle station, it had little effect. It did make for a pretty light show, however.

The Ra'az immediately opened fire on her position. Or more correctly, on what *had* been her position. Freya, on the other hand, was already darting to her next target, well clear of the Ra'az munitions.

"How many terrestrial cannons are left?" a Chithiid voice asked over open comms.

"Only two," Arlo replied. *"Aarvin, is that you?"*

"Yes, it is."

"We're trying to get to them, but their defenses are dense," Marty added.

As if to punctuate his statement, the cannons fired a barrage at the planet's surface. Far below, tens of thousands of captive Chithiid died instantly in the ensuing blast.

"How much time do you need in order to shut down the system?" Aarvin asked.

"I don't know. If we can get close enough, maybe a few minutes, if we're lucky."

The ship fired another barrage.

"Daze, they've locked on to a Chithiid-dense target. It's genocide," Sarah gasped.

"I know," she replied.

"Know what?" Arlo asked.

Shit. Open comms.

"You've told Vince about me. The rest will know soon enough."

"They're targeting a densely populated area, Arlo. We can't get in close enough for the shot. Can you?" Daisy said.

"We're trying," he replied as Marty dove and weaved, attempting to get closer to line up a clear shot.

The Ra'az weapon powered up once more, releasing another blast that would wipe out tens of thousands yet again, but as the pulses left the cannons, a massive Chithiid ship warped directly in their path, blocking the blast.

It shook from the impact, but their commander had apparently shifted all of their phase shielding to cover the point of impact. It left the rest of the craft vulnerable, but it did manage to absorb much of the pulse blast.

Much of it, but not all.

Part of the hull was rent open, and systems could be seen failing as compartments, compromised from the blast, vented to space.

"What are you doing, Aarvin?" Daisy asked as the Ra'az ship appeared to be powering up its cannons yet again.

"I am buying my people some time," was his reply. *"We are a crew of hundreds. Each weapons blast kills thousands. It was a simple calculus."*

"Shit," Daisy groaned. "Arlo, you hear that?"

"Yeah."

"You guys have gotta move. Fast. I don't think their ship can take another hit like that."

"We know. We're already on it," he said, and indeed they were. Marty was using all of his considerable maneuverability, powering through gaps in vessels and weapons fire where a ship simply shouldn't be able to fit. Yet somehow, he made it happen, only barely singeing his hull.

The cannons fired another salvo, but a different craft warped in its path. It was far smaller than Aarvin's ship, however, and their brave move, while saving their commander, resulted in the instant destruction of their craft.

There would be no survivors.

"Freya, we've got to get a shot off. If we don't, they––"

Daisy felt the slight shudder of the ship as the rail guns fired.

"We're too far to get a target lock," she said.

"For anyone else, maybe," Freya said, grim determination in her voice. "I've been running calculations for the last two minutes. The sabot will have to pass through a smaller ship, but it should hold its shape, though velocity will diminish. Then, if we're lucky––"

A small flash ignited on the surface of the battle station. A second later, one of the terrestrial-aimed pulse cannons fell dormant.

"Got ya, fuckers!" Freya said, jubilantly.

"Holy shit," Daisy gasped. "Freya, did you just do a trick shot?"

"You mean like the old Earth game of pool? Yeah, kinda."

"Goddamn, kiddo, that was impressive."

"Thanks!" Freya chirped, her spirits rising. "But I don't have a line on the other cannon."

A flash ignited on the battle station far from their position, silencing the other cannon. The people on the surface, as well as Aarvin's ship, were safe. Relatively, anyway.

"We got that one covered, Freya," Arlo said. Daisy could swear she could *hear* his smile over the comms.

"Good work, guys," she congratulated them. *"You hear that, Aarvin? The cannons are down. Now get your ass out of there!"*

"Our warp system appears to have been damaged, but we will do our best," he said, as their craft turned and began limping for the safety of the main body of their fleet. Seeing the ship's plight, a dozen smaller craft flew in formation behind it as it ran, firing all guns to provide it as clear a path of escape as possible.

The writing was on the wall, so to speak, and down below on the planet's surface, the Ra'az strongholds began to power their weapons and set their troops in position as they prepared for battle. They had lost communications some time ago, but their short-distance comms were still functional, and from what they could discern, it was clear a massive attack was underway.

The vessels that had entered the atmosphere were smaller units, and the Ra'az defensive gunners were confident they would be more than a match for those piddling little ships.

Some ships or other craft—they couldn't quite tell what they were from their limited information—had landed as well. That, along with rumors of numbers of their Chithiid workforce talking of open rebellion, was enough for them to send out their hunter-killer teams to put down any such uprising before it could amount to an actual problem.

The Ra'az were putting up a rather solid defensive perimeter at the edge of the atmosphere, effectively keeping out the multiple ships that were trying to reach the surface to assist in the battle, preventing their atmospheric entry.

For the time being, whoever was on the ground was on their own, but with the rebels hiding among the resident population, an uprising was indeed spreading, keeping the Ra'az spread relatively thin.

Battles were breaking out all across the globe as the long-oppressed Chithiid rose up to fight their brutal Ra'az overlords, as well as the Chithiid colluders who had worked to enslave their own people for generations.

The rebels embedded among them had taken great care in secreting pulse weapons to the surface in preparation for just such a moment, and as they were distributed to the enraged Chithiid, one thing was abundantly clear. Retribution would be as swift as it would be brutal.

A handful of smaller ships did manage to eventually pierce the blockade and fly down to the surface, but much to the Ra'az and their loyalists' surprise, they did not attack their fortified positions. Rather, they flew low over the housing barracks and gathering points of the Chithiid workforce, dropping bundles of some sort. It was only when the fighting erupted that the Ra'az realized what they had been doing.

They weren't helping Chithiid escape. They were arming them. From the ferocity of the attacks, they had done a thorough job, it seemed.

In areas where the Chithiid had not been reinforced, however, packs of Ra'az and their loyalists moved through the countryside, hunting the rebels who had unsuccessfully attempted to foment revolution.

It would be a war of attrition, and the Chithiid, with billions on their side, had more than enough of a numerical advantage to reclaim their world. All they had ever needed was support in the form of weaponry. The arrival of those first arms, along with the rapidly spreading news that their families, long ago taken from them, had returned to fight for their freedom, lit a fire in their bellies that no amount of Ra'az oppression could extinguish.

CHAPTER TWENTY-FOUR

"You guys have got to try these," Finn called out to George and Sarah.

"What did you find this time?" Sarah asked.

"They're some sort of berry, but they have this weird kinda starchy texture and an almost mint family-like crispness on the back end of the flavor."

"And that's supposed to sound appetizing?" Sarah said with a little laugh. "You need to work on your sales pitch, Finn."

"Bah! You just lack a sense of adventure!" he replied with a laugh.

"He says to the girl standing on a hostile planet light years from home in the middle of an intergalactic, interspecies war," she shot back. "Nice try."

George remained silent as they walked, letting the pair regain some semblance of normalcy to their previously strained relationship. There were still awkward moments, to be sure, but after the previous day's madness, they had both woken having hit the reset button. At least somewhat.

Finn had happily taken up George's challenge to find them a suitable breakfast from the native flora. At first the crazed chef was a bit reticent, but once he started taking samples from the entirely novel plants, his characteristic enthusiasm kicked back in full force.

It was a rather impressive spread he had eventually put together, truth be told, and the tension Sarah had been carrying in her shoulders seemed to lessen with every bite of the unusual foods as Finn regaled them with his tales of foraging.

"I just wish I had some spices," he lamented.

"It tastes fine, Finn," Sarah told him.

"Yeah, but just *fine*? It should taste *amazing. My kingdom for a pinch of tarragon!*"

"Well, given our resources, I think you've done an admirable job, Finn," George said, patting him on the back. "And I bet once we're back home, you'll even find a way to replicate them with our machinery, and then––"

"And then I'll be able to incorporate them into other dishes," he said, his eyes growing wide with excitement. "Oh my God. I'll be the first person to cook the Chithiid a proper, well-seasoned meal from food from their homeworld. Oh, man! They're going to shit themselves!"

"I hope you're speaking figuratively," George joked.

"I don't know," Sarah commented. "Let this one loose in a kitchen with a bunch of things that you have no idea how they'll interact with each other and who knows what the end result may be––*including* what comes out of your end."

"Oh, seriously, Sarah?" Finn said, mock-offended.

She stuck her tongue out at him playfully, then took another bite of food. Later, she'd be glad for the extra sustenance he had provided, as they had a very long walk ahead of them.

They'd been trekking most of the day, following the trail of debris from Mal's crashed pods, collecting what supplies they could salvage from the wreckage.

Several of the pods were perfectly intact, but the majority had suffered varying degrees of damage. To their relief, none contained any corpses, though there were some signs of minor bleeding in a few of them.

"Chithiid blood," George said when they came upon yet another empty pod. "Doesn't look severe, though." He quickly surveyed the grass for further signs of their allies. "They went that way. Looks like there were four of them, all Chithiid."

"That's the direction we saw the lights from last night," Sarah pointed out.

"Yeah, you're right on that one," George replied. "Looks like they're trying to reach a populated area to continue their mission. Ya gotta hand it to them. They're just kids, really, and here they are, thrust in the middle of I don't know what kind of shit-storm, and yet they're sticking with the plan, despite undoubtedly being scared shitless."

"Must be nice being a cyborg and not having to worry about being afraid," Finn said.

"Oh, I get afraid," George said. "Just because I'm mechanical doesn't mean I have a death wish. Nope, the lack of fear is more likely to get you killed than the presence of it."

"You been talking with Fatima?" Sarah asked.

"No, but if that's her line of thinking, maybe I should. If we survive, of course."

"Way to be a downer, man."

"Just fuckin' with ya, Finn. We'll get through this. Just you wait and see."

They padded on, following what George's little drone had determined was the path of the other crashed pods before it gave up the ghost.

"It took a pretty hard knock when we came down," George had noted a few hours prior, when the little device fell silently from the sky. "I'm just glad it worked at all, to be honest. Gave us a path to go on, at least. And if the scans I was able to save were right, there should be more survivors up by that small river it picked up not too far ahead."

"No reply on comms, though?" Finn asked.

"Nope. Not even on my team's comms, which likely means I'm the only non-organic on the planet at the moment." He paused and looked around.

"What is it?" Sarah asked.

"Oh, I was just thinking I should plant a flag, or something. You know, claim this land in the name of the cyborg race."

"Are you shitting me, man?" Finn said with an exaggerated sigh.

"Hey, you know the rules. No flag, no planet."

Sarah's head whipped around suddenly.

"Did you hear that?"

George instantly dropped back into ass-kicking cybernetic soldier mode and cranked up his hearing.

"Yeah, it's fighting. I can't hear anything that'd give me any details, though."

"Well, if they're fighting the Ra'az, they're on our side. Let's go!" Finn said as he took off running.

Sarah and George were only steps behind him when they crested the berm of the small hill that had blocked their line of sight.

In the distance, across the marshy shallows of the small river George's drone had seen, a lone human and a pair of rebel Chithiid were engaged in a pitched battle against a much larger group of loyalists.

"It's Omar," George said. "And he's in trouble."

Without hesitation, George took off at a run. He was fast, even in the mid-thigh-deep water, as he bolted in a beeline for their friend in need. Sarah and Finn knew they couldn't get there nearly as quickly via that route, so they shifted course to circumvent the deep water, instead slogging through the shallower area along the shoreline, weaving around the large boulders and trees blocking their path as they tried to make it to their friend.

Sarah was the faster of the two, making quick work of the unsteady ground. She smiled to herself as she left Finn in her wake, suddenly glad for the long hours she had spent training with Fatima.

As she hopped a fallen log with a splash and rounded the next boulder in her path, a large Ra'az stepped directly in front of her from its hiding spot, swatting her like she was no more than a toddler and sending her flying into the water.

The Graizenhund at its side snarled and snapped viciously as the Ra'az released its grip on the beast's restraints.

In a flash, the Graizenhund charged at Finn, closing the distance in a heartbeat before leaping in the air. Finn desperately swung his pulse rifle and fired without time to aim, hoping for Lady Luck to smile upon him.

She was in attendance, and apparently on his side on this occasion, as the pulse blast flew true, striking the beast dead in mid-air. Finn was just gathering his wits and beginning to swing the weapon toward the Ra'az when pulse fire peppered the boulders and trees around him.

Three more loyalists had been hunting rebels with their master, it seemed, and they engaged Finn with a desperate ferocity.

He lunged to his feet and ran, firing behind his back in hopes it would buy him time to reach cover.

Lady Luck had apparently extended her visit, as he miraculously made it behind the nearby boulders unscathed.

Sarah, on the other hand, was trapped in the shallow water, completely exposed. The Ra'az turned toward her and laughed, then began circling her in the knee-deep water.

He wasn't wearing a gauntlet, she noted, nor was he carrying a pulse weapon. It seemed the Ra'az was letting his loyalist lackeys and recently deceased Graizenhund handle the dirty work, while he took his pleasure in a more visceral, hands-on way.

Sarah looked for her pulse rifle.

"Shit," she grumbled when her eyes found it lying a good dozen meters away where it had flown when she'd been so rudely struck.

"All right, you giant fucker. You wanna fight? Fine. Bring it!"

She wiped the water from her eyes and began sizing the enormous alien, hate burning in her eyes.

The Ra'az was amused by the fighting spirit of his tiny prey. And that's what he saw her as. *Prey.* She didn't warrant a second thought, until one suddenly crept into his head. One that had him asking why there was a human on this world when they'd wiped them out hundreds of years earlier and many light years away.

The hulking Ra'az glanced around. These creatures were armed, apparently.

One human was pinned down and exchanging fire with his trio of loyalist hunters. Then there were two more humans fighting side by side across the water, firing their weapons until they ran dry.

He didn't know that George wasn't a human at all, and so long as his men took care of him, he didn't much care. More cautious now, he turned his attention back to the soaking wet, feral-looking woman with the unusual appendage.

Sarah happened to be talking to that appendage at that very moment.

"Come on, arm. Don't fail me now," she muttered, trying to connect with the nanite swarm. For a second, it felt like there was contact, but it was broken when she was forced to dive out of the way of the Ra'az's surprisingly fast attack.

"Forgot how quick you fuckers are," she said, dodging another attack and landing a trio of rapid blows to the Ra'az's face as she slid past his attack.

The human hand barely stung when it made contact, but the unusual synthetic one actually hurt. The Ra'az showed a flash of surprise in its eyes, rapidly followed by a bellow of rage as he lunged at her again.

Across the shallows, George and Omar, whose pulse rifles had run out of charge, were fighting hand-to-hand against opponents who had a four-to-two advantage in that department.

It was only George's cybernetic strength and the practice Omar had picked up sparring with Chithiid in Los Angeles' underground fight club that evened the playing field. Even so, the odds were very close to even.

Finn had wisely scavenged an extra pulse pack from one of the downed pods, which allowed him to maintain the exchange with the trio of loyalists, one of whom had run out of ammo. As it was going, it looked like the other two would run dry soon as well. He only hoped they did so before he did.

The Ra'az took in the surrounding fights and was unimpressed. He would deal with that later. For now, he had a pesky little human to eliminate. She had dared strike him, and for that he would make her suffer a much slower and more painful death than he'd originally planned.

Sarah, however, had other thoughts on that matter, and as she became more comfortable fighting in the shallow water—avoiding the deeper parts, where the taller Ra'az would have the advantage—she was starting to think she might just win this one.

The Ra'az reached out to grab her, but she dove between its legs, coming up behind it and quickly pivoting in a squat, punching the back of its knee with her nanite-composite arm.

The Ra'az howled in pain and struck out with the injured leg, which caught Sarah by surprise. She went flying, and into waist-deep water at that.

Finn saw her take the blow and tried to line up a shot on the Ra'az as it advanced on her just as a series of pulse blasts hit the rocks in front of him, forcing him to duck back down.

Sarah was at a disadvantage now and she knew it. There

weren't many tricks left up her sleeve, except what was literally up her sleeve itself.

"Come on," she urged her arm, then startled the Ra'az by lunging right at him.

She felt something shift, and looked at her arm, partially shifted into a spear-point, her fingers embedded a few inches into the Ra'az's thigh.

The alien grabbed her by the arm and wrenched her free, holding her dangerous appendage safely away from its body.

Finn looked over just in time to see him drive Sarah under the surface of the water, holding her down, her arms and legs thrashing wildly as her lungs burned from the lack of oxygen. She desperately tried to break the surface to get even a quick gasp of air, but the Ra'az was too strong.

The world started to go black, and spots floated across her field of vision, which she thought was funny since she was underwater and couldn't really see anything, anyway. The burning pain, however, was nearly too much to endure.

"No!" Finn shouted, jumping from cover and firing a quick shot at the nearby loyalists while running toward Sarah with desperate urgency.

Pulse blasts erupted around him and forced him to his knees behind a tree, but now he at least had a clear shot. His adrenaline was through the roof, but Finn took a deep breath and carefully aimed his weapon, knowing he had one chance, and he had to make it count.

The thrashing in the water was slowing. There was simply no more time.

Calling on Lady Luck one last time, he pulled the trigger.

Lady Luck had abandoned him.

He looked at the silent weapon in shock. It had run empty, and he had no more reloads.

"Sarah!" he shouted across the water, helpless to do anything.

Sarah thought she heard something besides the thundering of her pulse in her ears, but she was distracted. The burning in her lungs was just too much, and her body's automatic survival reflex finally took over in a desperate search for air, making her gasp in a cold lungful of water.

She thrashed violently one more time before water filled her lungs completely.

The Ra'az turned to look at the shouting man, then laughed cruelly as the thrashing human in his grasp slowed her movements, then went completely still.

The huge alien rose to his full height and left his dead prey behind, her body floating facedown in the water as he trudged ashore to take care of the troublesome little human that was staring at him so angrily.

Finn's eyes flashed from the Ra'az to the water. To Sarah's inert body, slowly drifting ashore.

Then everything started to go black as an overwhelming rage took hold of him.

CHAPTER TWENTY-FIVE

Finn, the man known for all of his joking denials about his past military history and odd love of cutlery, a man whose good nature seemed to be inexhaustible, finally snapped.

The knife work they'd all joked about back in the comfort of their galley kitchen whenever he'd show them a little trick had all been good-natured fun and games.

Finn's mood was now distinctly bloodier than that, and the skills he had casually shown off in the company of friends in no way even scratched the surface of just how deadly he truly was.

The first pair of blades that whistled through the air landed in the throat and eye of the nearest loyalist before the other two even realized the seemingly unarmed human was moving in on them, and at a fast run, at that.

And though he had no pulse rifle, he was definitely armed.

They had just begun to react, attempting to swing their weapons to track the quick-moving target, when they each received a knife to the body, launched with deadly accuracy and powered by pure rage.

Finn hadn't landed a killing shot on either of them, but that was not by accident. No, he wanted to make them suffer for what they had done.

Blades flashed from his sheaths, dancing in his hands in a dizzying whirlwind of finely honed vengeance.

"Shoot him!" the bleeding loyalist shouted to his comrade.

"My weapon arm is injured. I cannot aim!" he called back, retreating on his heels as Finn leapt into the air, bringing both blades in his hands to bear on the exposed vulnerable points on the seemingly tough Chithiid.

The time spent teaching his recently deceased Chithiid friend to cook had led to many conversations. Discussions that included weaknesses in their rugged alien physiques. It had merely been casual chatting at the time.

Now, it was anything but casual.

Finn sliced tendons and nerve clusters with near reckless abandon, hot alien blood coating his arms as he reduced his quarry to a blubbering wreck of agony. He quickly sheathed one of his knives and picked up the disabled loyalist's pulse rifle with his newly free hand. Checking to make sure it had a charge, he then blasted the downed alien in the knee.

"You're next, motherfucker," he growled at the other loyalist.

He began to move on him when a pulse blast from across the water grazed his hip, nearly knocking him to the ground. The singed flesh should have been excruciating, but in his berserker rage, he didn't slow for an instant, but rather increased his pace, fueled by the fresh surge of adrenaline.

George and Omar took advantage of the distraction Finn had caused to disable a pair of their opponents and make it to cover, where the charred remains of their Chithiid rebel allies lay motionless in the dirt. The Chithiid rebels were dead, but their weapons, though a bit banged up, were still functional.

"Kill these fuckers," George said, tossing the rifle to Omar, then skirting to the inland flank of the remaining loyalists.

"Get some!" Omar growled through clenched teeth as he opened fire on the loyalists.

They turned their attention back to the human opponent and redoubled their efforts to end him, and they might have succeeded if not for the momentary lapse in battlefield operational practice that allowed Sergeant Franklin to flank them.

Despite the eyes near the back of their heads, the loyalists were slow to react to the unbelievably fast soldier barreling toward them from the treeline.

"There! Defend your—"

George dove headfirst into the muscular alien, the sheer mass of his cybernetic endoskeleton turning him into a man-shaped battering ram. The Chithiid crumpled to the ground in a heap. While a flesh-and-blood man would have needed a moment to regain his senses after such an impact, George was instantly on the move, fists and feet flying as he pummeled the remaining pair until they were forced to fall back from his flurry of blows.

What they forgot in that moment of self-preservation was Omar.

A quick succession of pulse blasts took their lives in a flash, leaving only the human and the human-shaped machine standing on the battlefield.

"Finn needs help," George called out.

"Go. I'll be okay," Omar said, sinking to the ground.

George assessed the man's injuries and came to the conclusion that he would indeed be okay, though he was definitely worse for wear. He then took off running toward his friend in need.

Finn, in the meantime, had brutally finished off the remaining Chithiid, opening him up from neck to groin before emptying his pulse rifle into the twitching corpse.

Tears in his eyes, he spun to face the enormous Ra'az.

Without hesitation, he launched himself right at the beast of a creature, oblivious to the incredible size difference.

The Ra'az dodged the first several blows, but Finn was quick, managing to open up a group of cuts on the alien's lower flank. The Ra'az pushed him back and reassessed his small but troublesome opponent. The injury the human had inflicted was superficial—it would take far more than that to wound his meaty physique. Nevertheless, he was tiring of this game.

For Finn, it was far more than a game, and he would exact his vengeance, one way or another.

Once more the smaller man charged, his arms spinning in a flurry of slicing attacks. The Ra'az, however, had resolved himself to receiving a few little cuts from the annoying human, and that allowed him to unexpectedly draw close, blocking the knives with his forearm while his opposite hand grabbed the tiny man and hoisted him up in the air.

Finn tried to stab the alien's arm, but his blocking limb shifted, and the Ra'az's meaty limb knocked the knife from Finn's hand before grabbing him tightly.

Held aloft like a child in his hands, the Ra'az smiled a sadistic and victorious grin.

Finn, surprisingly, did the same, and the Ra'az felt his certainty of victory falter. This was not right. The tiny man *should* be scared, but his look was one of anything but fear. But his arms were pinned, and his hands could not reach any of his sheathed weapons, so how—

The Ra'az abruptly realized what he had overlooked when Finn drove his boot viciously into his throat, a spray of hot blood gushing forth as he dropped the man to the ground and staggered back. It was a trap, and he'd fallen right into it.

Finn held his eye contact as he reached down, pulling the knife he had wedged into the straps of his boot free, then pulling another from the sheath in the small of his back.

For the first time in his life, the Ra'az knew what his prey had felt like all those years. He finally knew fear.

Finn raced at the injured creature, his knives doing their work in his skilled hands, slicing through what were quite obviously blood-supplying vessels and vital organs in a flurry of vicious blows.

The Ra'az desperately turned to flee, but Finn was having none of that, quickly dropping low, slicing the tendons on the backs of both of the alien's ankles before pounding the knives hilt-deep into a half-dozen vital areas on the creature's exposed back.

Not finished yet, Finn kicked the dying Ra'az hard across the face, sending him rolling onto his back.

It was what he wanted. He wanted the Ra'az to see his death approaching, to look him in the eye. He had his wish, the astonished creature's eyes wide with fear as Finn drove his blades into the alien's chest, piercing his heart and killing him, stone dead.

The Ra'az lay there, blood oozing from dozens of wounds, twitching slightly as the last nerve impulses fled his body.

George Franklin stood nearby. He had arrived some time ago, actually, but had stayed out of the fray, letting Finn work out what he needed to in his own way.

"Daaaaaamn," he finally said, eyeing the carnage.

Finn looked over at his cybernetic friend, also covered in blood, though the majority of it was not his own.

"You going to be okay?" George asked, walking closer.

Something in Finn's eyes told him he might not be.

"I—" Finn went silent, sobbing quietly, rivulets of alien blood trickling from his hands and forearms.

"Finn?" a voice said. A voice that couldn't be speaking to him.

"Finn? Are you okay?" Sarah asked quietly, stunned by the

display of anguish-driven rage he had let loose at her supposed demise.

Finn spun toward the shoreline, his tear-filled eyes focusing on the soaked woman standing at the water's edge. The raw emotion laid bare in his eyes made her stomach twist in knots. Sarah quietly walked over to him and gently wiped the blood from his brow.

"But I saw you..." he said between sobs. "I thought you were—"

Sarah silenced him with a deep but gentle kiss, pulling him close, ignoring the alien gore now covering them both.

George rocked on his feet quietly for a few moments, waiting for them to finish. By the look of things, it might take a while.

"Uh, guys?" he said, finally interrupting them. "Hey, I'm sorry to spoil the moment, but we're kinda standing in the middle of a battlefield, and by the sound of things, I think we may be having company soon."

Sarah lovingly placed her hand on Finn's cheek, staring into his eyes, then lunged in for one more kiss before pulling away.

"We'll continue this discussion later," she said with a wink.

"Come on, Omar could really use our help," George said, leading the way along the shoreline.

They'd only walked a few steps when he just couldn't help himself any longer.

"So, Finn. Nice work back there," George said.

"Thanks, I guess."

"I mean, damn, man. You really *are* a killer."

"I told you," Finn said, glancing over at Sarah and throwing her a wink. "I'm a chef. Killing aliens is just a hobby."

George let out an amused laugh.

"You're a fucking riot, you know that?"

"I try," Finn said. "Hang on a minute, will ya? I need a quick rinse before this shit dries on."

"Good idea," George agreed, and all three stepped into the shallows to wash the blood of their enemies from their bodies.

While a fair amount of the blood on the two men was their own, Sarah's clothing was nearly entirely free of her own sanguine fluids. George looked at her, perplexed. Finn was just too happy to see it, but something was very wrong with Sarah. He'd seen what had happened to her, and as fond of her as he was, she should have been dead.

"Hey, Sarah," he began. "Look, I don't mean to be rude or anything, but I was wondering if you could help me out here. There's something I'm kinda confused by. Don't take it personally, but you should be dead."

"Oh, I know," Sarah said with a bright laugh. "Believe you me, I am *very* aware of that fact. That's *twice* that I was supposed to die. It's gotta be a record or something."

"Please don't go for the hat trick," Finn said.

Sarah leaned over and gave him a tender kiss. "Not to worry, babe. I have no intentions of leaving you."

"Ahem," George interrupted. "You were saying?"

"Ah, yes. Sorry," she said, blushing slightly as she cut her embrace short and trudged back to the shoreline.

"So the thing is, when I was fighting the Ra'az, my nanite arm wasn't quite doing what I wanted it to do. I could sense it, and was almost connecting to it, but it just wasn't working. But then when that fucker shoved me under and I wound up with my lungs full of water, the nanites finally connected with me. Then I knew it would be okay."

"Ah, sorry," George said. "That didn't really clarify things."

"Oh, right. You didn't know about the lungs."

"What about your lungs?"

"When Freya's nanites repaired my arm, they also reconstructed my damaged organs. My lungs had been destroyed by the vacuum when I was blasted into space, you see, so they built me new ones. They replaced them with millions of clever little nanites, and today, they introduced themselves to me."

"Hang on, your lungs are a nanite-composite?" George asked.

"Yeah."

"But that doesn't explain why you didn't drown, Sarah."

"Think about it, George. They're nanites. They function on a molecular level."

"Right, but the drowning thing?"

"You really are dense for an AI sometimes, you know that?" she teased. "Okay, I'll give you a hint. What's the chemical symbol for water?"

"H_2O," he replied.

"Exactly. And aside from the one hydrogen molecule, what are the other two molecules in water?"

Suddenly, George realized what she was getting at.

"She's trying to say she can breathe underwater, dude," Finn said. "Jeez, even I got it already."

"They broke the H_2O into its component parts, ferrying the hydrogen out of your body, while absorbing the oxygen into it," George marveled. "Holy shit, now that's inspired. Even by AI standards, that's some seriously clever stuff you've got going on in there," he said, appreciatively.

"Thanks. I guess I can add breathing underwater to my list of things I didn't know I could do," Sarah said with a happy little grin.

They reached Omar a minute later, sitting where George had left him. He was bloody, he was sore, but he was alive. The same could not be said for their Chithiid rebel friends, unfortunately.

The skies above were beginning to darken, making the lights from the battle above more clearly visible. The fighting, it seemed, was still fierce.

"I wonder if we're winning," Finn mused.

"From what I can tell, it looks like a stalemate so far. And our ships seem to be having a tough time making it to the surface," George noted. "How you feeling, Omar?"

Their injured friend took a long draught from his electrolyte pouch, then reclined with an exhausted sigh.

"I need a nap," he said with a pained chuckle.

"Doesn't sound like that's gonna happen anytime soon," George said apologetically.

"Well, then. I guess we head toward the fighting," he said, reluctantly climbing to his feet. Omar shouldered his gear then turned to leave when he noticed his drenched friend.

"Sarah, what happened to you? You're all wet."

Finn looked at her and smiled. "Omar, my friend, you might want to sit back down," he said with a knowing grin. "You're going to love this."

CHAPTER TWENTY-SIX

The fighting in the skies above Taangaar was heavy and continuous well into the following day, while the Chithiid rebellion on the ground gained speed as word of just who exactly it was fighting up there spread through the camps.

Having their long-lost families return home, fighting to free them from the shackles of servitude, inspired several of the enslaved Chithiid who were already living their lives on edge to attack their keepers. Without a support network available to them yet, those who did were punished, and harshly at that.

Word was quickly spread among the denizens of Taangaar by the sparse rebel forces embedded among them that help was indeed coming, but until the tide of the battle above was swayed, reinforcements and supplies would be limited to a few key areas.

The Chithiid, with their great numerical advantage, decided the time to act was now, and utilizing their strength in numbers, many of the internment settlements were taken over in a wave of home-grown rebellion.

Weapons were seized as the loyalist guards and their Ra'az masters were driven back to their strongholds overlooking the work camps. Unfortunately for the Chithiid, the small arms they had managed to secure were no match for the thick walls and powerful weapons of the Ra'az fortresses.

In addition, sorties of small, yet armed loyalist vessels made strafing runs against any Chithiid who ventured too close to their fortified bases. They were most certainly on a defensive footing, but it was one that was well entrenched and utterly inaccessible by ground forces.

Only two of all the hundreds of vessels in the combined human and Chithiid fleet had any success at all against the Ra'az facilities. But Freya and Marty could only do so much. They were but a pair of relatively small ships, and while their weapons systems were indeed impressive against most enemies, they simply were not designed for terrestrial assaults on heavily reinforced ground bases.

But that didn't stop them from making jumps all over the planet, springing up unexpectedly to give aid to the rebellious conscripts and keeping the Ra'az and their loyalists on their heels, never knowing where those mysterious ships would appear next.

Often, they would take out a few loyalist ships as they attempted to engage the rebels on the ground, but in a manner that allowed the other loyalist craft to see them. Then the dark ships––that mysteriously would not show on any scans––would blow their prey from the sky and vanish.

That in itself would be enough to keep the Ra'az and their lackeys guessing, but every so often, rather than moving to another target, the unidentifiable ships would suddenly reappear and make a strafing run against their base, or destroy another of their ships nearby.

The uncertainty provided a small degree of relief for the forces amassing on the ground, but it wasn't enough. The numbers and will were there, but without a means to penetrate the Ra'az strongholds, all the millions of riled-up Chithiid at their gates could do was wait.

"How're you coming with getting us some heavier firepower down here?" Daisy asked the fleet over comms. "The ground forces are getting their asses handed to them whenever they move on the Ra'az facilities."

"We're making progress," Celeste messaged back. "Hang on a sec. Zed, where do we stand on diverting some resources to help the rebellion on the surface?"

"Their strongholds have pretty serious defensive weaponry. I'm afraid it's going to take some heavy firepower to get through that, and with the battle stations and cruisers still engaged with us up here, we need every gun we have at the moment. I'm sorry I don't have better news, Daisy."

"I understand," she replied, crestfallen. "It's just, we're so close down here. All they need is that window of opportunity to let them act."

"We are aware of your situation, Daisy, and as soon as we can peel some ships free, we'll send them down to see about piercing the Ra'az defensive network down there," Celeste said. "But for the moment, I'm afraid we must press our advantage against the Ra'az forces in space while things are still swinging in our favor. If we can finally take out just a few more of their key battle stations, the rest of their defensive fleet will fall like dominoes."

"Then you'd best get back to it," Daisy said.

"We haven't stopped," Celeste replied. "Good luck down there, Daisy."

"Thanks."

The comms went silent, leaving Freya and Marty to deal with the hundreds of entrenched positions as best they could.

"Daisy, Marty says a bunch of the Ra'az fortresses have found a way to communicate using a daisy chain of local comms between them," Arlo informed her over their comms. "They're coordinating their counter attacks against the rebels and are sending out ground squads of heavily armed loyalists covered by some limited air support."

"Shit. How many?"

"Too many for us to engage all of them, I'm afraid. And they've released packs of those hound things in a few areas as well."

"The rebels can take care of those," Daisy said.

"I know, but they're scattering the rebel lines in the process," he replied.

"Making it easier for their hunter teams to pick off the rebels we managed to arm," Daisy realized. "Shit. That's actually a clever plan, and I don't know how we can stop them."

"We can't," Freya chimed in. "I'm sorry, Daisy, but I've run the calculations and spoken with Marty. The number of facilities and spread of their ground squads engaging the rebels is too great for us to be effective. We'll have to pick a battle to help out in and stick with it."

"Leaving the others defenseless."

"It's not an easy choice, but it's the right one," Freya said, making the hard tactical decision.

"I'm glad to hear you have matured in your tactical analysis, Freya," an amused voice said over what they had believed were encrypted and secured comms.

"Who the hell is this?" Daisy shouted. "How did you get on our comms frequency?"

"Just an old friend dropping in to lend a hand. I figured you guys could use some help. Sorry it took so long. There were, uh, logistical issues I had to deal with."

Glowing orange from its entry into the atmosphere, a massive Ra'az freighter barreled toward the surface, sending out a huge sonic boom as it did so. All eyes on the ground, Chithiid and otherwise, looked up to marvel at the sight.

"Joshua? Is that you?" Daisy said, recognizing the voice.

"Hi, Daisy," the tiny ship, scuffed and scorched and latched to the freighter's hull, guiding its commandeered systems, replied.

"But how—?"

"Long story," he interrupted. "Maybe Freya will want to tell you while I'm winning this ground war for you. Back in a jiff."

The enormous freighter shuddered as it powered through the atmosphere, its sheer bulk straining the engines to the max. The vessel had never been designed for the types of maneuvers the tiny stealth craft clinging to its skin was making it perform, but Joshua didn't care. He only needed it to last for this one thing.

Once the initial shock wore off, the fighting on the ground continued, the Ra'az picked up their intensity as what appeared to be one of their own craft had appeared. Surely it was carrying provisions, and possibly even reinforcement troops from above.

They were wrong.

"Joshua, what exactly are you doing?" Daisy asked, confused. "I mean, I know you're a great tactician—"

"The *best* tactician," Freya corrected her, a note of pride in her voice.

"Semantics, Freya," Sarah joked. *"But nice to see you're still crushing on the guy."*

"Bite me, Sarah," the AI shot back.

"Guys, shut it. Talking here!" Daisy barked. "What I'm trying to say is a freighter, even one that big, can't do much good down here. I mean, even full of troops, that's a drop in the bucket against all the Ra'az we've got to face."

"Oh, Daisy," he said with a knowing laugh. "You forget the lesson your own Chithiid fleet so recently employed."

"Kick ass and take names?"

"That too, but no. What I'm referring to is the old Trojan trick."

"I get it. So you snuck in, letting the Ra'az defenses think you were carrying Ra'az troops," Daisy said appreciatively. "But you're really carrying rebels. That's inspired, Joshua."

"Thanks," he replied. "But you're only partially right. I'm not carrying rebel troops, you see."

The massive freighter tilted on its axis, allowing all of its enormous stowage compartment doors to slide open. The huge vessel shuddered as its cargo warmed up and took to the skies.

"This is more akin to a little game one of my men––Duke, whom you've met–– kept joking about over the last few hundred years. He called it 'Piñata Roulette,' though I suppose, technically, no one is hitting this ship with a stick, and it sure as hell isn't filled with bees," he said with a laugh. "These are a good bit deadlier."

A deafening shriek filled the sky as hundreds upon hundreds of hypersonic missiles scavenged from Earth's silos took flight, moving at blinding speeds across the globe, targeting the unknowing Ra'az strongholds. In no time at all, dozens of the nearest fortresses were in smoldering ruins, rent open for the Chithiid rebel forces to pour into to finish the job.

It would only be a matter of minutes before the more distant facilities met with the same fate.

"But we couldn't make those fly," Freya blurted in a rare moment of confusion. "And we had the command codes and everything."

"I know," Joshua replied. "You were just missing the key ingredient. The special sauce, as it were."

"What was that?"

"Why, me, of course," he said with a laugh as the missiles flew true in a massive, global firestorm of ass-kicking glory.

"You care to fill us in?" Daisy asked.

"It was never just the codes, Daisy. That was crucial, of course, but I had the final access key locked away in my data stores."

"And you kept that secret from everyone."

"Yep."

"Even your friends."

"Especially my friends," he replied. "Operational security, Daisy. Secrets remain secret, lest they no longer be secret."

"You're just as odd as ever, Joshua," she said with a little laugh.

"Hey, lay off him," Freya said, defensively.

"Ah, there you are," Joshua said. "Thank you for sticking up for me. And thank you for building me this body. I didn't express my gratitude properly before, Freya, but with all that's happened, I had a little time to think, and I was a bit, um, *abrupt* with you."

"Well, I was kind of a bitch, too," she replied.

"Oh, no doubt about that," he said with a chuckle. "But what I want to say is I'm sorry, and thank you for saving my life."

Freya felt a strange sensation welling up inside her processors. From what Daisy had talked about, she assumed it must be akin to those butterflies she'd always complained about fluttering around in her stomach.

"So, we're good, then?" she asked.

"Yeah, we're good."

"Would somebody please tell me what the hell's going on?" Daisy interrupted.

"Sure thing, Daisy," Joshua said.

"Yeah, no problem," Freya added, happily. "Now, where should we begin?"

High above, the fleet commanders had barely noticed the freighter that had warped into their midst, squawking the rebel ident code allowing it unfettered passage as it dove straight for the atmosphere. But now there was no way any of the vessels above could possibly miss the global destruction of so many Ra'az bases.

"What the hell was that?" Celeste asked over open comms as she watched explosions blossom across the planet's surface below.

"Hell if I know," Captain Harkaway said, observing from nearby aboard Mal, safe in her command pod. "Whatever it was, it just won us the war."

Maarl observed the events below with tears welling up in all four of his eyes. The communications were already coming in. The Ra'az strongholds were falling across the planet, and the Chithiid workers were reclaiming territory after territory. After so many centuries, Taangaar was finally free.

The writing was on the wall for the Ra'az still fighting from orbit. There was no sense in continuing the battle over a lost planet.

The battle stations were still unable to warp, as were most of the ships in the fleet. A few of their older craft had remained relatively unaffected by the virus, and retained their warp capabilities. It was those ships the Ra'az evacuated to as quickly as they could, leaving their loyalist followers to man the battlements and hold off the rebel fleet while they made their escape.

"Let them go," Celeste said over open comms. "They're years of jumps from home. This will all be over long before they ever get there."

"Agreed," Zed said. "Their warp drives are barely functional. Unless you've got a clear shot, I want you to maintain focus on the battle stations and larger ships. They still pose a threat, and must be neutralized."

"I also want away teams to prep to board all remaining Ra'az craft once we take out their weapons capabilities," Celeste added. "If we can commandeer and salvage them, we will. If not, demo teams know what to do. Now get to work."

"Holy shit, did you guys hear that?" Finn asked, stopping in his tracks as the shrieks and sonic booms of missiles flying overhead filled the sky. Their noisy arrival was followed by flashes in the evening sky moments later.

"That looked like an explosion," Omar said. "I wonder how far--"

A deep boom rumbled in the air.

"I'd say fifty clicks or so, judging by the delay," George said. "Those were hypersonic missiles. I'd know the sound anywhere."

"But aren't those on Earth?" Sarah asked. "And aren't they not functional?"

"Yes, to the first question. At least, they should be," George replied. "As for the second one, well, they sure seem functional now."

Omar wobbled on his feet a little, the exhaustion of the day taking its toll.

"Hey, man. You might as well take a load off," George said, dropping his pack and tossing the metal-legged soldier an electrolyte pack from within. "I think it's a pretty fair assumption that we just won this thing. At least, I hope so. In any case, the big dogs are running the show down here now, so y'all might as well sit down and eat something. No telling how long we'll be down here on our own."

That question was answered fifteen minutes later, when a ship that looked an awful lot like the *Váli*, but smaller, swooped down through the sky and landed softly in front of them.

"One of ours, obviously," Finn said, studying the craft's design. "But how did they--?"

The airlock of the lowermost forward pod swung open and a slender figure jumped down to the soil, pulse rifle at the ready, a dapper fedora tilted at a cocky angle atop his head. His eyes fell on the tired and injured team in front of him.

"Come on, you dirtbags! Let's get you off this rock!"

"Jonathan? It has to be," George said with a laugh, rising to his feet.

"Sergeant! It's good to see you intact!" the cyborg replied. "I had heard about your resurrection from Duke and the men. I can't tell you how pleased I am to finally meet you."

"Duke told me all about you, Johnny boy. Said you performed exceptionally well under pressure. And you even coughed up a hand in combat. Is that true?"

"It is."

"Hot damn, now that's some quick thinking. Lemme see what they replaced it with."

Jonathan held up his shiny new hand. It was similar to his original appendage, but after a few words from his new spec-ops friends, the fabricators had hooked him up with a more robust and somewhat deadlier version.

"Ooh, nice," Sergeant Franklin said appreciatively. "But why haven't you gotten a new skin job yet?"

"The others were so anxious to have their old faces back," Jonathan said. "They've been through so much––far more than I ever have––so I wanted them to be taken care of first."

"Damn solid move, brother. I can see why they like you so much. But we really do need to get you skinned up when we get back. It's time to make you whole again."

"The sentiment is appreciated, Sergeant," he replied, then turned to their human companions. "Come on, you two," he said to Sarah and Finn. "The pilot wants to say hello."

CHAPTER TWENTY-SEVEN

Finn reached out and took Sarah's hand, helping her through the ship's airlock doors. She accepted, though there was really no need. She was more than capable of getting in and out of the vessel unaided, but nevertheless kept her fingers interlaced with his long after she was safely aboard.

"This thing looks brand-new," Finn marveled. "The layout seems to be the same as the *Váli*, all right, just two levels of pods instead of three, and a bit shorter in length. Nice, though. Really nice."

"The command pod is this way," Jonathan said.

"Yeah, we know," Sarah replied, walking hand in hand with Finn. "She's so similar to the *Váli*."

"Indeed," Jonathan agreed. "But this is a he, not a she."

"It can be whatever it wants to be, so long as there's a hot shower and a soft bunk," Omar said as he trudged along behind them.

"Weapons systems?" George asked.

"I knew you'd be curious," Jonathan said with a smile. "He's outfitted with a pair of forward pulse cannons, a rear cannon, defensive flak burst pods along both sides and the rear, and a top- and belly-mounted pair of rail gun turrets."

"Holy shit. He's armed to the teeth," Omar said.

"Just the way I like it," George added, appreciatively.

A few minutes later they had passed through the craft's secure airlocks, dividing the bulkhead into easily partitioned sections, arriving at last at the command pod.

"After you," Jonathan said, stepping aside.

Finn stepped in first, followed closely by the others. There was no one there.

"Hello?" he said.

"No one's here," Sarah noted as she scanned the pristine chamber.

There were seats and consoles, but the captain's chair was empty, and it looked like it hadn't ever even been sat in.

"Hi, Sarah," a voice said over the internal speakers. "I heard you were back from the dead."

"No fucking way," Finn blurted.

"Heya, Finn. How's it hanging?" the ship's familiar voice replied in greeting.

The shocked pair stood stock-still.

"Gus?" Sarah finally managed to say.

"Holy shit. Seriously?" Finn added. "Dude, is that really you?"

"Yeah, it's me. Ta-da!" the ship said. "Surprised?"

"You're damn right I'm surprised," Finn said. "I saw your body, man. We buried you. You fucking *died*."

"Yeah. I saw it too," Omar said.

"Oh, hey, Omar," Gus said casually. "Sorry you had to see all of that."

"You were dead, man," Omar replied.

"I know. Bummer, right?"

"So now you're a computer?"

"Technically, a one-of-a-kind AI, if you want to get nitpicky about it," he replied. "But there's something I need to ask you all. A question of the utmost urgency and importance, and I need you to be upfront."

"Of course," Sarah said. "What is it, Gus?"

Their AI friend paused a moment for effect.

"Be honest. Does this ship make me look fat?"

"Oh, you fucker!" Sarah said, smacking a console.

"Hey, don't hurt the hardware."

"It'd take a lot more than that," she said.

"With that new arm of yours, maybe not," he pointed out.

"Touché."

"We haven't met yet," George said. "I'm Sergeant––"

"George Franklin. Yes, Mal told me all about you. Nice to meet you."

"So *you* were Mal's other secret project," he said. "Now I know why Freya was helping her out with those new processors."

"Yeah, that kid's amazing," Gus replied. "The things she can do. Wow."

"And, apparently, salvaging the dead is one of her new skills," Finn joked. "Come on, man, spill. How'd she do it?"

"That wasn't Freya. Not the saving part, anyway. She just helped sort me out and install me in this ship. The actual saving, though, was all Mal."

"I think we'd have known if Mal could back up an entire consciousness," Omar said, doubtfully.

"Yeah, about that," Sarah replied. "She kinda already did."

"No way."

"Yes way," Finn confirmed. "Daisy admitted it right before we launched. Apparently, when her neuro-stim did that number on her brain, it also copied Sarah's backup into her head."

"So she has a file stored in there?" he asked, confused.

"No, she has a fully functional and aware copy of me living in her head," Sarah replied.

"So she hears what Daisy hears?"

"Yep. And since we're the same person, Freya was able to devise a modified neuro-band that allows us to link up and talk. And now she's taken it a step further. We finally share each other's memories as well," she said, squeezing Finn's hand.

"I'm confused," Omar said. "If Mal was able to do this all along, why haven't other AIs done the same thing and saved people's minds when they die? It'd be like immortality."

"Because I was heavily repaired already," Gustavo replied. "Remember all the connections and mods I had built in before any of this madness even began? And when I died during the attack on the communications hubs, I was massively tied in to the ship's systems. In addition, we had installed a shit-ton of new processors and storage to handle all of the drones we were remotely piloting."

"But that doesn't explain how you're functional now," Finn said. "The tech to sort you out didn't exist."

"It didn't, no. But this ship contains Freya's new state-of-the-art quantum processors, which are tied in to the salvaged systems from the *Váli* and are the only thing making it possible."

"Of course. The extra tech Chu and the others installed before the mission."

"Yep. Because Mal had a full backup of my mind up until that point, and since I was hardlining the ship directly into my brain at the time, flying those drones and all, a neural ghost was captured in those systems. It was quite by accident, I should point out."

"That's why she was offloading all that hardware," Finn realized. "She wasn't taking out damaged machines. She was taking the ones parts of you were saved in."

"Yep, though scattered might be a better way to put it. Let me tell you, it took a hell of a lot of processing power to sort out all the pieces, from what I've been told. A *lot* of the AIs we saved that day all chipped in processor time and power to help untangle my mind from that mess of aborted systems tie-ins. They didn't even know if it was possible, but seeing as how our people had just pretty much saved the planet, they kinda owed us one."

"And now you've got your own ship."

"That I do," their newly AI friend replied. "Unfortunately, because of the way I wound up being saved, that means I'm not a hot-swappable AI cube, but am pretty permanently installed in this ship. But it's better being a ship-bound AI than a dead human, right?"

"I suppose so," Sarah replied. "I know a little something about being saved, after all. Twice, in fact."

"So I heard."

"Does Reggie know?" she asked.

"Not yet. I was only activated and launched right before the attack, and then we were immediately right in the thick of it, and I didn't want to distract him from his job with something like, 'Hey, your dead buddy is a ship now.'"

"They turned you on just in time for a battle? Seems a bit harsh," Omar said.

"Perhaps, but it's what I'm trained to do, so it made sense. And besides, I think they'd done all they could and decided it was time to see if I was ready to live."

"Or die trying," Omar added.

"Which I did not," the ship AI said with a chuckle.

"Glad it was the former, not the latter, man," Finn said.

"Me too, bud. Me too."

The surprising craft flew up out of the atmosphere to rendezvous with the main body of the fleet. Soon, he'd be surprising the others with his tale of unforeseen survival, but for now, he was just enjoying the company of good friends.

"So what do we call your ship, Gustavo? Did you give it a cool name?" Finn asked.

"Nope. I'm a permanent part of it. We're inseparable. One and the same," he replied. "Just call us Gus."

CHAPTER TWENTY-EIGHT

The bonds of friendship were strong among the Chithiid people, but those of family held them even closer.

A victory had been achieved, and it was hard won. Much blood had been spilled, both in space and on the planet's surface, but ultimately the Chithiid had reclaimed their world. They had only barely achieved that previously unimaginable goal when they launched into their next task. That of reuniting families torn apart by the Ra'az and their loyalists.

Unlike the scattered camps and barracks on Earth, full of spies tracking dissidents, the loyalist elite of Taangaar had felt no need to employ such tactics. They were the feeder planet, sending out the strong and able-bodied to be used by the Ra'az as needed. There were simply not enough males to pose a serious threat, so they kept to their compounds, never subjecting themselves to the wear and tear of spying and infiltration.

They had made one crucial mistake in that decision. They had underestimated the strength and resolve of the females.

While they played their part, appearing subjugated and defeated to all loyalist eyes, the strong women of Taangaar had secretly maintained a communications network, sharing information between camps whenever possible, such as during the periodic shifting of laborers.

What this meant––in addition to the Chithiid having at least a partial sense of where their family members might be held–– was that the conscripted workers also knew the loyalists on sight.

After their rebel victory against the Ra'az, the loyalists would find no shelter hiding amongst the survivors. And unlike on Earth, the women-folk of Taangaar whose families had been violently taken from them had no intentions of offering leniency.

Daisy flew across the surface, shuttling not only Maarl––the appointed ambassador for the newly returned Chithiid––but also herself, as they landed in the newly-freed labor camps, searching for loved ones among the survivors.

The Chithiid had never seen a human before, and if not for Maarl's presence at her side, they might not have trusted her at first sight. But when the unusual creature with only two arms began singing a Chithiid song––the song of the family of her dear friend––their defenses were immediately dropped, and she was accepted as one of their own.

It was a lengthy and emotionally draining process, but Daisy flew from camp to camp, following leads until she finally tracked down an old Chithiid woman at the other end of the globe.

She found her sitting with her daughters and granddaughters in an encampment at the edge of the sea.

It doesn't look all that different from the coastline where we met Craaxit, Daisy mused.

"You're right, Daze. And even after all the Ra'az have done to this planet, you have to admit, it really is a beautiful view."

Daisy sat with the woman and explained who she was, and how she had befriended a most unlikely of ally. A brave Chithiid named Craaxit, who risked everything to save not only Earth, but his homeworld as well.

The woman was skeptical, of course, but upon hearing Daisy's singing of her family song, she knew the strange, two-armed woman spoke the truth.

"He must have been a young man when he met you," his elderly wife said, warm tears in her eyes. *"They took him shortly after we were wed and placed him in stasis for the long voyage to whatever world he would end his days upon."*

"He was," Daisy replied. *"He was young, and strong, and spoke with great love of his wife and family. No matter how far away he was, no matter how long it had been, he never stopped thinking of you."*

"But I am an old woman now. Had he survived, he would not wish to see me like this."

"You know the man far better than I do," Daisy replied, *"and you know that is not true. You were his world, and the mere passage of time could not change that."*

The women shared a cup of tea with Craaxit's daughters and granddaughters—his wife having been pregnant when he was sent offworld years prior.

"He was the bravest man I've ever known," Daisy told them. *"His courage, his determination, saved the entire mission, and by extension, freed not just my world, but yours as well."*

She sipped her tea and looked out over the glistening waters, remembering her friend and his unexpectedly humorous outlook on life. They had been more than allies. They had been true friends, and the injury of his loss, which she had thought healed over, felt fresh anew.

But it was also good, in a way, and she felt that where there had been an emotional scar before, she would heal clean and pure this time around.

Maarl watched quietly as Daisy regaled his friend's widow and family with tales of his courage, his eyes tearing up as well, as he listened to her recounting of his brave and selfless acts.

"I want you to know this," Daisy said, a steely strength finding its way into her words. *"It is a truly rare occasion when you can tie a single person's selfless acts to so momentous a feat. But mark my words and know they are true, Craaxit was the linchpin of the rebellion, and his sacrifice unleashed the tidal wave that washed the Ra'az from both of our worlds. This act, I feel, should be immortalized, and I have taken the liberty of adding one small verse to his family song. I hope you approve."*

Daisy then quietly sang the words she had struggled with for weeks, finally coming upon what seemed the proper phrasing with the help of Maarl and Aarvin. All were pleased with the result.

Now that his family heard them for the first time, there was not a dry eye in the room as they added a new segment to the song of their line for the first time in ages.

Craaxit's sister hugged her warmly and excused herself to fetch them something to eat, singing their family song as she walked away.

"I see he was right," Daisy said with a little laugh, wiping the tears from her eyes.

"What do you mean?" his wife asked.

Daisy leaned over and spoke quietly so no one else would hear.

"Craaxit always said I had a better singing voice than his sister. I now know that he spoke the truth."

The women doubled over in peals of laughter, breaking the somber mood among the group as they did.

"Oh, yes. That is my Craaxit," she finally replied, wiping what were now tears of happiness from her eyes. *"Quite a sense of humor, he had."*

"That he did," Daisy agreed.

Maarl watched the festivities, pleased with the turn of events, then headed off to return to Freya. He had his own quest, and Daisy would be preoccupied for some time, it seemed.

"Might I request a favor?" he asked the young AI.

"Sure thing, Maarl," Freya replied as he slid into a seat in her command pod.

Moments later they quietly took to the skies, returning but a few hours later. Maarl exited the ship, a serene look now spread across his face.

Shortly thereafter, Daisy found him seated beside Freya.

"It is time for me to rejoin the fleet, my friend. We have been victorious, but the Ra'az homeworld still awaits," she said.

"This has been a most impressive victory," Maarl replied. *"My people will sing of it for the remainder of our days. But now the lengthy healing process begins. There will be countless years of skirmishes as we finalize the Ra'az defeat. But as we began on Earth, so too shall we drive the vanquished Ra'az and their remaining loyalists from our world."*

Daisy went to give her friend a farewell hug, then climbed aboard her ship. To her surprise, the old Chithiid followed close behind.

"I appreciate the affection, my friend, but I am coming with," he informed her.

"But you are home, Maarl. Your work is done."

"Daisy, I am an old man. My wife is long dead, as are my children and my children's children. I have made my peace with the survivors of my line, and they now know their great-grandfather's face. But we have work to do."

"But you're home. You're standing on the soil of Taangaar," she replied.

"Yes. Something I never thought possible in the waning years of my life. For this alone, it was worth the pain and the tears. But this conflict is not over, and I am not alone among my people who are determined to see this through to the very end. There can be no true peace so long as the Ra'az are still a threat. Even if they are reduced to one that may not rear its head again for many, many years."

"I don't know what to say," Daisy replied.

"Say thank you," Freya prompted.

"Thank you, Maarl. This means a great deal to me."

The old Chithiid smiled warmly and patted her on the shoulder, then boarded the ship.

"I can't believe he'd give all of this up," Daisy said, taking one last look over the vast ocean spread before her.

"He's kind of like Odysseus, I think. The weary traveler finally home from his trials. Only now he's been told of another quest, and there's no way he can rest while others toil. He's too honorable a man for that," Freya said, softly.

"When did you get so smart, Freya?"

"Always have been. I just needed a little time to find myself, is all."

Daisy smiled contentedly as she boarded her ship.

"All right then, kiddo. Take us out of here. We've got a war to win."

CHAPTER TWENTY-NINE

Maarl stood quietly among the scores of ship commanders that had gathered aboard the fleet's command craft. He had been correct in his estimation that a great many Chithiid would be coming along on the mission to take on the Ra'az on their home turf.

Payback or insurance against future aggression, whatever the motivation, their ships and arms would be appreciated when the fighting began, regardless of the fact the Chithiid vessels were somewhat underpowered. The captured Ra'az ships, however, were not.

If it was possible to retrofit them to suit the fleet's needs, the additional Ra'az craft–– with their heavier shielding and greater firepower––could be a useful asset in the attack on the hive world.

Zed waited until Mal had left the repair hangar where the *Váli* was being mended and delivered Captain Harkaway aboard before he began the meeting.

"Thank you all for coming," he began. "Oh, hell, that's so stuffy and formal. I just have to say congratulations to us all on kicking some serious Ra'az ass out there!"

The assembled commanders and support staff cheered, welcoming the moment of levity—especially in light of the numbers of ships and crew lost in the fight—the moment of laughter greatly easing their moods.

"Thank you, Zed," Celeste said with a fading laugh. "We all appreciate your candor. Now, let's get down to business, shall we? Daisy, would you and Freya please discuss the plan you and your team came up with to best utilize your stealth ships?"

"Sure thing. Joshua, you're listening, right?" Daisy asked.

"Of course," he replied.

The revelation that Joshua had not only been saved from NORAD—courtesy of some very clever and quick thinking by Freya—but was also now in a small stealth ship of his own, and one capable of latching on to and commandeering enemy craft, had been a boon to the fleet's morale.

That he and Freya had flown off on their own for a long talk and had patched things up between them had further solidified the fleet's hopes for success.

"How about you, Marty?" Arlo asked.

"Yep, I'm here."

"Great. Everyone is accounted for on Team Stealth," Daisy said, pulling up a long-range scan of the Ra'az system on the display screen. "Okay, so we have a pretty decent survey of the outer regions of the Ra'az solar system. You can see that it's just the two innermost planets that are surrounded by the asteroid field."

"And you say they destroyed adjacent planets to create it?" Aarvin asked, everyone's translator earpieces conveying what he had said.

"Yes. Arlo? You and Marty have been going over this more than I have."

"Uh, yeah, so here's the thing," the teen began. "The Ra'az are basically like bloodsucking leeches of a species. I mean, they're a hive species, which leeches totally aren't, but you get the idea. Anyway, they just use up a planet for whatever resources they can grab, then leave an empty husk."

"So why the asteroid field?" Captain Harkaway asked.

"Because those planets were closest to their hive and the first ones they invaded," Arlo replied.

"Think of it like a serial killer, Captain. The first victims tend to be close to home before they find their legs and spread out," Marty added.

"Morbid analogy, but I get it," Harkaway said.

"So when the planets were harvested, the Ra'az way back then didn't know to limit their activities, and in so doing they caused a catastrophic collapse of the planets themselves."

"Why didn't this destroy the Ra'az world as well? Wouldn't it have thrown them out of their normal orbit around the sun?" Celeste asked.

"Funny you should say that," the boy replied. "Because it actually did. But while their world had been farther from the sun originally—which was probably what necessitated their evolution into a subterranean hive society—the loss of those planets and subsequent formation of the asteroid sphere around their world and the adjacent one caused a gravitational shift."

"Meaning?"

"Meaning with a different mass, they were pulled *slightly* closer to the sun. Not a catastrophic distance, but enough to warm their planet sufficiently to allow for full-scale surface expansion of their hives."

"So what you're saying is they accidentally accelerated their own evolution?" Harkaway asked.

"It seems that way."

Joshua, silent until that point, felt it was time to interject and speed things along. "So, that covers why they evolved into what they are, and that's what we're dealing with in the present," he said. "Thanks for the history lesson, Arlo."

"My pleasure."

"Now, I've been talking with Freya and Marty, and as the only stealth vessels in the entire fleet, we three will play a pretty specialized role in the early stages. We need to get a detailed survey of the area inside the asteroid field, as well as the planet, of course, which we will accomplish by a leapfrogged series of warps, gathering intel on the gaps in the asteroid field the Ra'az apparently utilize as access points for their craft."

"Meaning the asteroid field itself acts as sort of an outer layer of a hive," Freya added.

"Exactly. Thanks, hon."

"My pleasure."

"Did he just call her hon?" Sarah wondered.

Oh man, what has she been up to?

"Good thing you left your neuro-band in your pocket or this could be awkward."

Seriously.

"Daisy? Did you have something to say?" Celeste asked, noting the curious expression on Daisy's face.

"What? Oh, no. Just thinking about tactics, is all," she covered. "There was just one thing that's going to be an unknown variable. We had been planning on detonating a warp orb on the surface of their planet. Joshua thought it could potentially ignite their entire atmosphere. Only there was a problem."

"Ah, yes, the warp malfunctions Freya and Marty experienced recently," Joshua said. "I fear we may have to resort to more conventional means of attack until we have a clear path to warp right to the edge of the Ra'az atmosphere."

"But the orbs––" Daisy said.

"Will have to wait until the right moment. Given the nature of this particular mission, and the number of craft too damaged to join us, I think it would be wise for both of you to carry an additional warp drive on board as an emergency backup should your primary systems fail. I hypothesize that too many warps likely put an excessive strain on the systems, but since you haven't been overtaxing them lately, you should be fine. Still, tactically, it makes sense to go ahead and carry them along."

"That's what we did when we got stuck chasing the Ra'az," Daisy agreed, not noting that they had pulled a Bill and Ted to save themselves. Something Daisy realized she still needed to do, and soon.

Note to self. We need to get that orb from Chu's lab and drop it for ourselves. It's too crucial to put off.

"*You're right,*" Sarah replied. "*Fortunately, with time travel, we have a little wiggle room.*"

"Once we have the asteroid field mapped out more fully, and have determined the Ra'az defenses within, I have devised a plan to use the asteroids to our advantage," Joshua said.

"How can we do that?"

"Easy. We are going to take a page out of your playbook from your attack on the communications facilities on Earth. It was quite inspired, I must say, using debris as cover for your craft. Only now, we'll use the asteroids surrounding their planet instead. Since they block all scans in either direction, we'll warp our entire fleet to just outside the innermost part of the field, following the signals the stealth ships will give, acting as a beacon to the open accessways. Once there, each ship will gather asteroids large enough to help shield them as they attack."

"While we're at it, why not have the ships that have space in their holds take some more with them that way? They can mount transponders on some of them, and maybe even explosive charges. Anything to throw at the Ra'az to confuse them as to our true numbers and trajectories," Harkaway suggested.

"Good idea, Captain," Joshua said. "But keep in mind, we'll need to arrive fully ready and in attack mode, just in case Murphy pays a visit. For that reason, I think modifying your suggestion might give us an additional fourteen-point-six percent increase in our odds of achieving a surprise attack."

"How do you propose doing that?"

"We collect debris from the damaged ships and carry that as diversionary chaff, Captain," he replied. "It's already inorganic, and to long-range scans, it should show as a large group of small ships."

"I have a suggestion," Daisy said. "All of this sounds great, but why don't we send in another distraction from the other direction?"

"Our numbers are somewhat limited, Daisy," Joshua noted.

"Which is why we send one solitary, *big*, distraction," she replied.

"What did you have in mind?" he asked, intrigued.

Daisy scrolled the image on the screen to a distant view.

"See this right here?" she said, pointing to a small cluster of debris orbiting within the solar system, but far from the Ra'az planet.

"A small asteroid field. Yes, I see it," Joshua replied.

Daisy zoomed in on it and pointed to the enormous chunk of rock dwarfing all the others in the cluster.

"This," she said. "If we line this up and give it a hard push, this asteroid should travel all the way to the asteroid field around their world and push right through it. Or at least through most of it. The thing is, it'll be one hell of a distraction, and since it's entirely naturally occurring, they won't suspect an attack while they launch ships to shift it to a course away from their planet."

Celeste couldn't help but smile.

"You want to throw a big rock at them?" she said with a chuckle.

"Well, it worked for David," Daisy said. "And the Ra'az are a lot smaller than Goliath."

"Hmm. I like it," Joshua said after a moment's consideration.

"Clever, Daisy, though I shouldn't be surprised by your unusual tactical prowess."

"I bet you say that to all the girls," Daisy shot back.

"So how do we set that thing in motion?" Arlo asked. "Our ships are too small to push it, but I guess maybe the bigger ones could––"

"Nukes," Daisy said.

"What?"

"You heard me. We use a couple of nukes to create the initial force to send it on its way. After that, all we have to do is set off a couple of smaller blasts nearby to nudge it onto the course we want."

"You make it sound so simple," Captain Harkaway said.

"If you consider a solar system-sized game of pool using asteroids instead of balls simple, then sure, why not," Daisy said with a chuckle. "Thing is, it could actually work, and we already have quite a few missiles with nuclear payloads at our disposal, courtesy of Joshua, so why not try?"

"I'm with Daisy on this one," Celeste said, looking at her husband for support. "But I won't give the order unless we're all on board. Given the number of ships we've already lost, and the reduced number of functioning warp drives at our disposal, I think it's important we are one hundred percent in agreement before we begin."

"You can count me in," Arlo said. "Marty, too, obviously."

"Thanks for speaking for me," Marty griped.

"Oh, come on, you know you're in."

"Obviously."

Arlo rolled his eyes.

"I can have several of our Chithiid vessels on hand to provide muscle to help adjust the asteroid's course, if need be," Maarl said. *"We do not possess the firepower of the other ships, but the craft possess powerful drive systems."*

"Great idea," Daisy said, while the translator caught everyone else up to speed.

In short order, all of the fleet's commanders agreed on the mission, then spread back out to their ships.

"This is nuts, Daze," Sarah said when they were clear of the meeting room.

"Which is why it might actually work."

"Okay, so say the diversion pulls Ra'az ships to the other end of their asteroid field. We still have to thread the needle with an entire fleet of ships. Most of which are going to have quite a time of it navigating their way through."

"Which is why we're going to have Freya and the boys mapping it real time while they're pushing through. It's a sped-up leapfrog system that should get us to them before they can mount a full-strength defense."

"Seems like a solid plan, so far as I can tell," Sarah said.

"And if it doesn't work? If they catch on while we're still in the asteroids?" her flesh-and-blood counterpart asked.

Daisy thought a moment. There really wasn't an alternative.

"Well, if that happens, Sis, we'll just have to blast our way through."

"I hope you're right," Sarah said. "I'd rather not die again."

"Please don't," Sarah jokingly urged.

Daisy laughed. "Oh, now that you two have got something to live for you want to be careful?"

"I wouldn't say it like we've got something to live for. That sounds desperate."

"Fine. Now that you're finally getting some, you want to make sure to come back in one piece to keep on keepin' on."

Sarah groaned.

"You're ridiculous. You know that?"

"Hey," Daisy softened. "For real, I'm just glad you two finally got together. And Other You feels the same way."

"Amen, my sister."

"Yeah. You know, if not for her, we might not have," she admitted. "Thanks, Sarah."

"My pleasure."

"Which reminds me, Daisy. We wanted to do another memory update, if you don't mind."

"Worried about missing out on all the fun we had while you were down frolicking on the surface, eh?"

"Ha. Nope, but it lets us stay on the same page. It's hard to describe, Daze, but it really feels like we're one person in two places now. It's kind of amazing."

"And you've got new stuff for me," Sarah said. *"I hope it's juicy."*

Sarah laughed. "You'll just have to wait and see, Other Me."

"Well, since you two already merged just a few days ago, this should take no time at all," Daisy said. "Just a few days of memories? That's cake. Come on, let's steal that orb from Chu's lab, then get aboard Freya and get you two hooked up while there's still some downtime."

"Thanks, Sis."

"Yeah, thanks, Daze."

"For you? Anything."

CHAPTER THIRTY

The fleet was in high-alert mode, and all ships were transferring munitions and supplies from the craft too damaged to partake in the attack to those bound for the Ra'az solar system.

Spare warp cores were pulled from the Chithiid ships that would now be staying at their homeworld. The added bonus of having those at their disposal gave the fleet an extra boost of confidence, despite the fact that it came at the cost of loss of some of their less-powerful craft for the assault.

On the ground, Chithiid rebels had taken control of nearly all surface resources and driven the Ra'az and their loyalists into hiding, much as they'd done on Earth. They soon found that the lack of ships with which to flee into the sheltering expanse of deep space meant they would be hard-pressed avoiding the scrutiny of the several billion Chithiid eyes scouring the planet looking for them.

Soon, Taangaar would be a planet reborn, and the invaders nothing more than bone and dust.

The orbiting ships went about their routines, and even mounted salvaged weapons the damaged craft had no use for, supplementing their already sizable offensive capabilities even further.

Arlo and Marty were resting in a low orbit along with Freya and Joshua, keeping their eyes on the goings-on above and below, while remaining invisible to all. Three stealth craft in a fleet of conventional ones, ready to invade the most hostile planet imaginable.

And they were going to be the first ones in.

"Hey, Freya?" Arlo said over comms.

"Yeah?" she replied. "What's up?"

"Daisy's over on board Mal with Vince right now, right?"

"Yeah. So are Sarah and Finn."

"Okay, good," he said. "Listen, I need to ask a favor, and I need you to keep it to yourself. Can you promise me that?"

"Well, not if you don't tell me what it is?" she replied snarkily.

"Freya, please," Marty interjected. "You have my word that Arlo is on the up-and-up about this."

Hearing the plea from a fellow AI, and one whose opinion and tactical prowess she respected, shifted her reticence.

"Okay," she finally said. "Ask your favor."

"We're going into the most hostile of possible scenarios, and Marty and me simply don't have the firepower on board to make much of a difference."

"Yeah, I suppose, but we just need to help the others get in through the asteroid field so they can cause a distraction so we can detonate a warp orb in the planet's atmosphere. That'll end the Ra'az in one shot."

"And we really hope that'll happen. But just in case we get stuck for some reason, and if it looks like we can't drop the warp core as planned, I want to take along your Big Gun."

"I only have a few pulse cannons and some rail guns, Arlo," Freya replied. "But I'd be happy to see if the fleet could spare a—"

"No, Freya," he interrupted. "The Big Gun."

"I don't know what you're talking about."

"Yes, you do," Marty chimed in. "The weapon you've designed in your hangar on Dark Side. The one that sucks a warp core dry of all of its energy potential and transfers it into a single, focused pulse blast."

"That sounds impressive," Freya said, "But like I told you—"

"It could probably take out a small moon," Marty continued. "Or even a piece of a planet. Maybe even a large enough chunk to throw said planet into a self-destructive cycle of catastrophic weather and trigger a molten core upheaval."

Freya was silent a long while.

"How do you know about that?" she finally asked. "No one knows about that. Not Sarah, not even Daisy."

"We know," Arlo said.

"Hey, guys," Joshua chimed in. "Sorry, I couldn't help but listen in on that *fascinating* conversation. But tell me, Freya. Did you actually go and build a weapon of mass destruction?"

Freya said nothing.

"Yes, she did," Marty replied. "Designed and built it, all in Dark Side's secret fabrication hangar. But the thing about the Big Gun is it needs to be situated at extremely close range to be used. That's why she left it behind. But we want to fly in close and take the shot."

"Wait," Freya blurted, still shocked. "But if anyone should use it, I think—"

"You have a billion other jobs to do, Freya," Arlo said. "Let us do this."

"I've tapped into Freya's top-secret systems and haven't seen any trace of that file."

"You what?" she blurted.

"I did it a while ago," Joshua said. "And I already apologized for it."

"Ugh. You're making me wish I kept you locked up," Freya grumbled.

"You know you love me," Joshua joked. "But back to the matter at hand. While I hate to be the one to ask the obvious, here, how exactly do you two know all of this?"

"Should we tell them, dude?" Arlo asked his friend and lifelong companion.

"Yeah, I think it's about tim––"

"You've traveled here from the future," Joshua said, his lightning-fast mind flying through the facts and data. "You know this Big Gun exists because you've already seen it."

A smile spread across Arlo's face.

"I was wondering how long it would take you guys to figure that out."

"Hang on. You're time travelers too?" Freya asked.

"Afraid so," Marty replied. "I'm sorry we couldn't say anything sooner, but there's that whole paradox thing, and we had to work really hard to make sure we didn't accidentally interfere in the things we weren't supposed to."

"So you've actually seen the Big Gun in the future?" she asked. "How well does it work?"

"Well, we haven't *seen* it, exactly," Arlo said. "More like we heard about it. There's a lot of talk about what it can do. It's kind of legendary in military tech circles, actually."

"But you can't use it," Freya said. "It destroys the warp core when it fires. You'd be stranded right in the path of the shockwave. It would tear you apart."

"Ah, you'd think so," Arlo said with a knowing grin. "But when we arrived we 'installed' a warp drive, courtesy of the fleet, thinking we needed an upgrade."

"Which you didn't actually need."

"Precisely. We were already operating on a warp core, and now they're giving us *another* one on top of that, after what happened with our temporary power loss the other day."

"So you have three, total," Joshua noted.

"Yep," Marty replied. "So, you see, we can fire the Big Gun and still have a perfectly functional warp drive and one to spare."

"But this weapon," Freya said, her voice trembling. "This is a *horrific* device. The kind one would only ever use as a deterrent. *That* was why I built it. Not for actual use, but to help guarantee Earth would never be invaded again."

"I'm proud of you for saying that," Joshua said softly. "So many terrible weapons have been designed with evil deeds in mind. Yours was created to keep peace rather than destroy it."

"Hey, I'm glad you two are feeling all touchy-feely about the reasons she built it," Arlo interrupted, "but the fact of the matter is, we're about to fly into the maw of the most violent, hostile, aggressive alien race ever encountered, and while I hope the other plan works, if ever there was a time to break out the Big Gun, this would be it."

"I am obviously of the same mind," Marty added. "I agree the Big Gun should never be used under normal circumstances, but we all have to agree that these are most definitely *not* normal circumstances."

"It was meant as a deterrent. A way to keep the peace," Freya said again, quietly.

"Then let us carry it and make a statement with it, if nothing else," Arlo begged. "Look, if we fire a shot into the sun, they'll easily see the power we possess, and the shot wouldn't hurt the sun at all."

"He's right, it would just absorb the energy," Joshua mused. "I see where you're going with this, Arlo."

"So you agree we should walk loud and carry the biggest stick imaginable, right?" Arlo said. "If the Ra'az know we possess the power to wipe them out in an instant, they'll have no choice but to surrender."

"Joshua, I don't know," Freya said. "It's such a terrible device."

"I know. But they have a valid point, and I think I could feel comfortable with them carrying the Big Gun into battle if we have one accommodation made," Joshua said.

"Name it," Marty replied.

"If Freya gives you this weapon, I want a binding agreement that you will not use it without the express agreement of all parties to this conversation. If you can agree to that, then I can support your carrying the Big Gun. If not, then I'm afraid I will have to recommend against it."

"Agreed," Arlo said without hesitation. "Believe me, I have no desire to actually use it—well, that's not accurate, I really want to use it just to see what it does. Let me rephrase. I have no desire to use it to kill anyone."

"And you, Marty?"

"Oh, I'm with him. I agree, and I also don't want to harm anyone unless absolutely necessary."

"Freya, can you accept this agreement?" Joshua asked. "Take your time, think it over at your leisure. There's no rush."

"I don't need to think it over, Joshua. I'm one of the fastest AIs to ever live. I think slowly when with my friends by choice. To live as they do. But I by no means have to," Freya said, a mature confidence in her voice.

"So?" Joshua nudged.

"So, I have run nearly fourteen million scenarios, and as many require use of the weapon as do not. However, I am of the opinion that these are indeed unique times. We have time travelers in our midst. People who know something of our future, apparently, and they are asking for our help. I am willing to give it to them."

"Very well, then," Joshua said. "But one more thing."

"I already know what you're going to say," Arlo said with a laugh. "And believe me, Marty and me aren't going to say a word about any of this to Daisy or the others. But you two have to promise as well."

"Arlo, you know I can keep a secret," Freya said.

"Obviously. You kept Joshua hidden for months," Marty commented.

"I was still building his housing. There was work to do. I was--"

"No need to get defensive. I trust you," Marty interrupted. "And Joshua obviously knows better than to do anything that would risk Arlo and my timeline. But if the humans find out, well, they're more unpredictable than AIs, ya know? And if they somehow *do* change our timeline, then we don't exist. And if we don't exist--"

"You don't come back in time," Joshua finished for him. "Which means this never happens. But since it *is* happening, we can assume you have always done this. And, theoretically, you always will."

"I certainly hope so," Arlo said. "I'd hate to cease to exist, ya know?"

"Yeah, I hear you," Freya said. "Look, I know I can't ask you details, but you know how this all turns out, don't you?"

"We do."

"Ask no more, Freya. We can't risk it," Joshua said.

"I know," she agreed, reluctantly. "So you had a warp core all along, even when you first showed up. Sneaky, Marty."

"Sorry. Had to be done."

"I don't mind, actually," Freya said. "I'm just glad we got to be friends."

"Me too. It's been a real pleasure," he agreed.

"Right. Well, I guess we should get you that Big Gun, then," Arlo said.

"We'll meet you back at Dark Side. The fleet shouldn't even notice we're gone, if we hurry," Marty added.

"Oh, that won't be necessary," Freya replied.

"Wait, why not?"

"Because, I couldn't leave something so dangerous unprotected back on Dark Side, even if it was hidden away in my fabrication lab," Freya revealed. "And between you and me, I may have had a moment where I considered using the Big Gun in much the way you're proposing now."

"So if it's not on Dark Side, then—?"

"I actually have it aboard, right now. And if you'll come with me, we'll head over and land on that nice, quiet little moon and I'll have my mechs install it on your ship."

"You never cease to amaze, Freya," Joshua said with an appreciative chuckle.

"I certainly hope not," she replied with a laugh, then set out for the tiny moon.

Soon, if all went as planned, Marty would be sporting the deadliest weapon in the galaxy.

CHAPTER THIRTY-ONE

Marty, despite knowing full well no one could scan within his hull to make out the Big Gun riding in his forward weapons bay, was nevertheless nervous as he rejoined the bustling and busy fleet. He imagined this must be what teenage boys feel like whilst attempting to hide the spontaneous erections that he knew so often plagued the pubescent.

Only his bulge was of a much more deadly variety.

All around him, ships capable of making the assault were busy loading up with essential supplies, extra rations and ammunition, and, of course, all the spare warp cores they could scavenge.

Daisy was making sure Freya was packed and ready for an extended trip, if need be, though she certainly hoped that would not be the case.

Nearby, Mal had been fixed up where her pods had been torn free, her remaining ones rearranged into a more streamlined configuration, all extraneous units left behind to provide additional maneuverability should she once more find herself unexpectedly stuck in atmospheric combat.

Gus, being a smaller ship, had opted to keep all of his pods in place, lightening his craft by offloading unneeded supplies, rather than sacrificing his pod assemblies.

Though the AIs had known about Mal's ambitious project to salvage Gustavo's mind from the many processors he was scattered throughout, his human friends who had been kept in the dark until Mal was successful were still adjusting to their friend's new existence as a ship.

"You sure you're okay with me riding along?" Shelly asked. "I mean, it's not gonna be weird for you, or anything?"

"Nah, it'll be nice having you along for the ride," Gus told her.

"Okay, but don't just say that, okay? I can always catch a ride on the *Váli* or something if you prefer."

"Are you still whining about flying with this yo-yo?" Tamara joked as she carried her gear past Shelly on the way to her quarters. "Gus may be a ship now," she continued, "but I'll tell ya, he spent so much time wired into Mal's systems, he was already damn near part of a ship before this ever happened."

"Gee, thanks, Tammy," the new AI said.

"You know I hate it when you call me that, Gus."

"Aww, and what are you gonna do about it, *Tammy*?"

"Well, let's see, *Gustavo*. I suppose I could start by utilizing your neural cluster as a shitter, for starters."

"You wouldn't dare."

"Oh, wouldn't I?" she said. Shelly, for her part, honestly couldn't tell if it was just friendly banter or if Tamara really was planning on relieving herself on Gustavo's shiny new AI brain.

"Okay, *Tamara*. You win," he relented.

"Good thing, Gus. Finn cooked me up some Mexican food earlier, and it's coming out hot!"

"Oh, dear Lord, I did not need to know that," Shelly said with a sarcastic laugh. "You're as bad as Omar sometimes, you know that?"

Tamara flashed her an amused smile as she turned and headed off to her quarters.

Out in the fleet, every last captured Ra'az ship was lining up, preparing to follow Freya and Marty's warps deep into the asteroid field surrounding their objective.

Joshua had already led a small team to detonate several tactical nukes to send the massive asteroid at the edge of the solar system on a trajectory toward the Ra'az world, then warped back to the fleet. The game, as they used to say, was afoot.

The plan was streamlined, now that their assets had been sorted out. In short order, their strengths and weaknesses were organized and assessed by Joshua as he essentially took over planning, though he allowed Zed to think the plans were his idea.

"Diplomacy among our long-lost cousins," he had told Freya as they huddled together, deep in collaborative discussion. "It really doesn't matter who takes credit, so long as we are successful."

"Agreed. Are you ready?" she asked, knowing his answer would always be yes.

"Let's take our positions and get things moving," he said, excitement in his voice.

For all the years he had spent tucked away inside NORAD under a solid granite mountain, Joshua had never experienced the visceral thrill of being in the thick of things—of being in harm's way. It was a rush, feeling the tingle of fear nipping at the very edges of his mind.

Of course, he wasn't truly afraid. Not in a human sense, at least. He feared death, as all living creatures do on some level, but his confidence in the power of his mind and his team's craft led him into a state of buzzing readiness.

Sergeant Franklin—hitching a ride with Daisy and Sarah aboard Freya's stealth ship—called it the pre-combat jitters.

"Don't' worry, Boss. We'll kick ass. You'll see," he said over the comms.

"Thanks, Sergeant. I appreciate the sentiment."

Aarvin's commandeered Ra'az ship slipped into position at the head of the first wave ships and opened comms.

"The captured Ra'az infiltration vessels are all fully powered and ready for warp. We merely await the signal."

"Marty and I will be jumping into the far end of the gap in the asteroid field and leapfrogging to guide your ships through to blend with the Ra'az on the other side. Warp outside the solar system and lock on to our transponder signals, then warp inside the field to join us," Daisy said.

"As we have planned," he replied. *"We will see you on the other side, Daisy. Best of luck."*

"The same to you, Aarvin. And Maarl, keep an eye on the stragglers at the rear. I'm counting on you to make sure they all make it through."

"Of course, Daisy. My crew and I are prepared."

"Okay, then. You ready, kiddo?"

"Ready."

"Then let's do this," she said. "Daisy Swarthmore to everyone listening," she said on open comms. "We're heading in. Good luck to you all."

And like that, Freya, Joshua, and Marty warped in sync and were gone.

A minute later, the rebel-piloted Ra'az ships followed.

"Okay, everyone. We're up next," Celeste said to her anxious commanders as they nervously awaited their turn. "As soon as the commandeered Ra'az vessel infiltration wave is through and embedded with the hostiles, we'll follow, pull some asteroids for cover, and engage the Ra'az. By the time they realize our ships are behind them, they'll be trapped in a crossfire with nowhere to run."

Freya and Marty's warp coordinates were spot-on, and the ships popped out of warp well-within the asteroid field surrounding the Ra'az world.

Almost entirely through the asteroid field, Freya found herself with the clearest view yet of the Ra'az world. Midway through the gap, Marty arrived, poised to lead the rebel-guided Ra'az ships. Then there was Joshua, who had arrived just a little ways outside the asteroids, ready to relay messages and help guide ships through from one stage to the next.

But there was a problem.

"Warp systems are failing!" Freya warned moments after they arrived.

"Switch to conventional power!"

"Already did," she replied. "Marty, do you copy? Something is sapping the warp drives. Get out and warn the others."

Marty, however, had already lost power, and Freya's warning fell on deaf ears.

"Sonofabitch!" Arlo shouted, lunging from his seat and throwing the emergency reserve switches.

"What happened, Arlo?" Marty asked a moment later.

"Something killed the warp drive again. I had to activate the emergency power cells."

"Glad we installed those after last time."

"You and me both," Arlo agreed. "Do we have any comms?"

"Negative. Reserve power isn't strong enough. The main warp core is at zero. We're running on fumes."

A bad feeling twisted in Arlo's gut.

"What about the Big Gun? Please tell me it's still—"

"The additional warp cores are both down as well," Marty informed him, one step ahead.

Joshua also experienced a sudden fall in power, but he had arrived just far enough clear of the asteroid field that whatever was causing the effect had only diminished his systems, but had not entirely drained them. He could fly, but warp was out of the question. So, too, were comms, it seemed.

They were on their own. At least until the first wave arrived, at which point things could get very hairy.

Freya pushed clear of the asteroids, free flying inside the vast protected space surrounding the Ra'az world.

"You see those?" Sarah asked, pointing to a faint ring around the Ra'az planet.

"Hang on," Freya said, quickly focusing her scanning arrays. "Got 'em. A band of asteroids, parked in place. Satellites hidden among them. And they seem to be emitting––oh, shit!"

"Freya?"

"It's new tech to me," she replied.

"What is it?" Daisy asked, unsettled by the mighty AI's obvious concern.

"It's emitting a warp-negating field. I've never seen anything like it," she said. "And from what I can tell, it stretches from just outside their atmosphere all the way to a decent bit outside the asteroid field. When we scanned the area before, we just happened to be barely outside its range. It was blind luck."

"Oh my God," Sarah gasped. "So any ships that warp in––"

"Can't warp out," Freya said. "It's conventional drives only, and we don't have any way to warn the fleet."

As if they heard her, the first of the rebel Ra'az ships flashed into sight just within the asteroid field. Apparently Marty's transponder had failed, but Freya––running on full secondary power––had a strong signal that they locked onto through the gap in the asteroids.

"They're following us in, Daze," Sarah said.

"All of those ships operate on a normal power system," George pointed out. "The Ra'az ships were retrofitted with a better warp tech, but their core systems should still work fine in here."

"And the other ships? The human fleet?" Sarah asked.

"Most switched to a primary warp power system when they figured out the tech I showed them," Freya replied. "But they should still have the original drive systems as auxiliary, though I don't know how much reserve power they have stored beyond that."

Behind them, more and more of the first wave of infiltrating vessels appeared within the ring of the asteroid belt. All had lost warp power, but as Sergeant Franklin had pointed out, they had no problems maintaining flight systems or comms.

"Sarah, warn them. Tell them what's happening in here. We may have to improvise."

"On it, Daze."

"Freya, see if you can—"

"Ra'az scout!" Freya blurted as she quickly spun into a roll and headed back toward the asteroid field.

"How the hell did he find us? We should be off-scans."

"We were backlit by the arriving ships," she replied, dodging and weaving, keeping the ship from getting a firing solution.

"Can you scramble their comms?" George asked.

"Already on it," Freya replied. "But if they peel off and head back, I won't be able to block their signal from a distance."

"Then slow down and let them get closer," Daisy instructed.

"I'm sorry, what was that?" Sarah asked.

"If we let them think they have a shot at us, they'll pursue. Trust me, I've been in dogfights with them before. The Ra'az are hyper-aggressive, and that can be used to our advantage."

As predicted, the Ra'az ship barreled past the arriving Ra'az craft, not noticing they were not operated by Ra'az, but by rebels in their place.

"Ident codes worked," Sarah noted. "Our ships are clear."

"Good," Daisy grunted, trying to manually aim the rail gun. "Now if we can just get this bastard off our tail."

"Freya, hit him with your cannons," Sarah ordered.

"Belay that!" Daisy countermanded. "Pulse charges will be

picked up by the Ra'az. The rail gun is electromagnetic. It's following us into the asteroid field. A direct hit will make the explosion read like pilot error crashed it into an asteroid."

"Clever," George admired. "Told ya, Daisy. A great tactician."

"You can tell me that if we survive this," she replied.

Freya dove and spun, allowing Daisy to track the closing ship, but it was moving too fast.

"Freya, I want you to bank right in five seconds," Daisy instructed.

"Copy."

When she counted down to two, Daisy fired the rail gun, her shot leading ahead of the pursuing craft. Freya turned on cue, causing the pursuer to do likewise, right into the path of the oncoming rail gun sabot.

The hypersonic projectile barely missed the ship, but the force of its passing sent the craft careening into an asteroid, where it shattered to pieces.

"Target destroyed," Freya reported. "Nice shot, Daisy."

"Thanks," she said, breathing a sigh of relief. "How are the ships doing? Have they been noticed?"

Freya spun back around and scanned the commandeered ships.

"No reaction from the homeworld. It looks like they're in the clear."

"The Ra'az never expected anyone to use their own gear against them," George observed. "Classic overconfidence error."

Daisy watched the ships' commanders fight their adrenaline and instincts, instead remaining calm and casual as they settled their craft into a holding position throughout the existing Ra'az battle stations and fleet.

"They're in place, Daze," Sarah said. "Now what?"

"Now we figure out how to warn the second wave," Daisy replied. "I just hope we can reach them before it's too late."

CHAPTER THIRTY-TWO

Daisy was just beginning to devise the most basic of plans to negate the clusterfuck about to befall their mission when the main fleet warped into place. They were––she was shocked to see––all within the asteroid field.

"How the hell––?"

"Hey, guys," Joshua called to them over comms. "Glad you're okay."

"Joshua, what happened? What are they doing here? The second wave wasn't supposed to start yet," Daisy said.

"I know, but I finally managed to get far enough from whatever was draining my warp drive to make a jump back to the fleet and warn them what was going on. The decision was made to step things up and move in after making sure non-warp drive systems were engaged."

"But you're on warp power," Freya said, obvious concern in her voice.

"I am, but I had the techs hook me up with a whole boatload of charged power cells just in case Murphy paid a visit, which he apparently did. I'd estimate I have a good eight hours before my systems start to fail."

"What about Marty? Did you see him?"

"He was limping through the asteroid field on reserve power last time I saw him."

"So they survived. Thank God," Daisy sighed with relief.

A barrage of pulse fire from their ships flew past her, targeting the Ra'az craft that had come pouring from their docking stations above the hive world.

"The fleet's engaging with everything they've got," Sarah marveled. "That's the kitchen sink assault."

"They only have one shot at capitalizing on the surprise," Freya said, flying closer to better target the smaller ships attempting to reach their advancing fleet. In short order, she blew three from the sky, their pilots never knowing what hit them as the near-invisible craft carefully avoided any illuminating backlighting.

"Deploy the virus, Freya. Now!" Daisy ordered.

"I can't."

"What do you mean you can't?"

"Whatever signal those satellites are putting out, it's also blocking the transmission spectrum the virus is delivered on."

"Can you modify it?"

"I don't know. Maybe, but I'd have to re-write the whole thing, and even for me, that will take time."

"I can help," Joshua offered.

"Actually, I have an even better idea for you," Daisy said. "Think you can latch onto that orbiting battle station?"

"Yeah, but I've tried tapping into a battle station like that back at Taangaar. I can't access their drive or weapons systems. They're too deeply shielded."

"How about their comms?"

"Their comms? I suppose I could. But what good—oh, nice idea. I'm on it!" Joshua said, then zipped off through the battle, trying to reach the nearest battle station.

"I don't understand," George said. "What good do the comms do us out here?"

"We use them to sound a recall of their ships," she replied. "It'll present us an easier target, and when they do, our Chithiid rebels will pull a Trojan Horse on them and open fire from the other side. They'll be caught in a crossfire, leaving the satellites vulnerable to attack."

"Solid idea," George said appreciatively. "But we don't speak Ra'az."

"No, but we captured transmissions during the battle at Taangaar when they tried to pull back. Pretty sure that'll do the trick."

"I'm picking up some new readings, Daisy," Freya announced.

"What is it?"

"Smaller ships are warping up their crews from the surface to join the fleet."

"But you said warp was negated."

"It is. But apparently it still works *inside* the atmosphere."

"Ooh, so it's like a bubble around the planet. And that's where we need to get a warp orb to function if we want it to detonate."

"Exactly."

A small group of attack fighters that had apparently been on the ground within the atmosphere warped at that moment, arriving behind the human fleet.

"You see that, Freya?" Joshua asked.

"Yeah. Hey, guys, there's a handful of Ra'az fighters on your six," she warned the fleet.

"I've got 'em," Gus called out, engaging several at once, all of his weapons systems firing in a closely linked barrage of hot death.

"Damn, Gus," Tamara said, impressed.

"Two more coming, Gus," Shelly said, watching the scans. "You see them?"

"Shelly, those are *my* scanners you're monitoring. Of course I see them," he replied, tucking into a barrel roll, loosing arcs of pulse and sabot fire.

Both enemy ships took multiple hits and disintegrated as they tumbled into the asteroid field.

"Nice," Tamara said with an appreciative chuckle. "You're even better than before. Maybe this was a good upgrade after all."

"Thanks," he replied. "Now hang on. I'm going to make a loop of the rear to make sure there aren't any more lurking around back there."

With the rear of the fleet defended, and the main body of ships fully engaged, Joshua found his stealth craft easily avoided notice as he skirted the engagement and arrived at the battle station at just the right moment to shift the tide.

"Okay, let's see," he said to himself as his remora-like ship latched on to the massive Ra'az craft. "Heating system, waste disposal, here we go. Comms."

He carefully tapped in, making sure not to be detected by the aliens monitoring the systems inside the vessel, then primed his recall message.

"Ready to transmit, Daisy."

"Copy that. You hear that, Zed?"

"Affirmative. I've just sent an encoded burst transmission to the rebel ships. As soon as Joshua transmits, they'll engage from the rear."

"Okay. The ball is yours, Joshua. Hit it."

The brilliant AI flashed the recall message out to the Ra'az ships, telling them to immediately pull back and defend the battle station. It was, he hoped, an urgent enough message to cause a little panic, in the process, which would likely help their forces.

"They're on the run!" Sarah exclaimed. "It's working, Daze!"

"I see. Now, any second the rebels will light them up and we'll have them trapped," Daisy said. Amazingly, their sneak attack plan was going to work.

Out of nowhere a massive armada of ships, the likes of which they had never seen, warped into the middle of the battle and opened fire on all of the Ra'az craft, rebel and Ra'az alike.

"Who the hell are those guys?" Daisy shouted. "They're attacking us!"

"Correction," Zed replied. "They are only attacking Ra'az and Chithiid ships."

Daisy realized he was right.

"Celeste, are these your people?"

"Negative, Daisy. No idea who they are, but Zed's right. They're targeting our rebel forces."

"Shit, they're ruining everything. Engage them. Draw them away from our people if you can."

Chaos ensued as the carefully planned formations scattered in a free-for-all of pulse fire.

"They seem to be attempting to target the Ra'az planet as well," Joshua noted. "I think it's fair to assume they're enemies of the Ra'az."

"So how do we get them to stop attacking the good guys?" Daisy asked, her frustration growing by the second.

"They're not answering any of my comms attempts," he replied. "There's no way to tell them to stand down against the friendly ships."

"It seems pretty obvious this is friendly fire," George said. "Hate that fucking term. Friendly fire. Nothing friendly about being shot at."

"But what can we do to stop them?"

"They obviously don't know some of those Ra'az and Chithiid ships have been commandeered. So we need to tell them, somehow," he replied.

"I'm open to suggestions, here," she said, spinning the comms frequencies to no avail.

"Daisy, have all of the rebel ships transmit a relay of our signal."

"What do you have in mind, Sarah?"

"Freya, cue up the images of the Ra'az defeat on Earth. Show images of dead Ra'az, and the humans helping retrofit their ships."

"I've loaded them up and alerted the rebel fleet."

"Wait," Daisy said. "Do you have images of us taking Taangaar as well?"

"Added to the feed," Freya affirmed.

"Have them transmit, but tell them not to shoot back. Just perform evasive maneuvers and divert power to their shields."

"Transmitting now."

It was painful to not engage the aggressive ships, holding back, watching and waiting, hoping the new attackers were monitoring the video signal traveling on all bands.

Finally, their fire lessened as they examined the data. During the lull, the rebel ships took the opportunity to make a run for the safety of the main fleet. At least as a mass, they were well-defended. Separated and under attack by not one but two enemies, they didn't stand a chance.

The mysterious assailants resumed their pulse fire a minute later, but now only targeting the retreating Ra'az ships that had not been broadcasting Freya's message.

The larger ships pulled back toward their homeworld, while a few dozen smaller ones pushed forward into the human and Chithiid fleet, continuing their attack from within, but with just one opponent to worry about.

"It worked. They figured out which vessels are on our side," Sarah exclaimed. "Unfortunately, the Ra'az now know too."

"Incoming message on all bands," Freya announced.

Her screen filled with the image of a strange alien, possessing a long face, broad forehead, and what appeared to be a pair of fleshy tentacles dangling from their chin.

The alien spoke to the screen, gesturing for the viewer to reply.

Celeste came on split-screen, her face red with anger.

"Daaamn, she looks pissed," Tamara noted as Gus shifted his defensive positioning. "Not that anyone would blame her."

"This is Commander Celeste Harkaway. Who are you, and why have you attacked us?"

The alien looked at a device in its hand a moment, then depressed a small band on its neck.

"Aah, Earth-speak. You are humans?" it said in what appeared to be a feminine voice.

"Yes, we're humans," Celeste replied. "Humans allied with the Chithiid against the Ra'az."

"We, too, fight the Ra'az. While we have managed to keep them at bay and stop their attempts to conquer our world, they have nevertheless remained our enemy for many, many cycles."

"Then why did you attack *our* people?"

"Your people were in Ra'az vessels. It was an honest mistake. You see, we, too, fight the Ra'az. A message from a monitoring drone reached our people, informing us that the Ra'az had been forced from Earth and were now facing attack at their own homeworld. You can imagine our surprise! We came as soon as we could. To strike while the iron is hot! We had not been able to penetrate the asteroid field before, however. But today we succeeded. We followed the path so clearly left by your ships."

"Is it just me, or are these guys kind of unimpressive for aliens?" Sarah said. *"I mean, aren't they supposed to swoop in and save the day and be all kinds of technologically superior?"*

"You'd think so," Daisy replied. "But it really looks like we're the more advanced aliens this time around. How do ya like them apples?"

"I like apples," Sarah said. "But this fucking sucks. These idiots just screwed the whole mission."

Celeste, calming down but still obviously upset, was telling the interlopers very much the same thing.

"Your blind attack just interrupted our ambush. We had an entire fleet of rebel ships ready to engage from within their ranks, and you shut the whole thing down and let them escape," she said angrily. "And now they're safe behind their defenses. And the satellite system draining our warp systems is now reinforced by hundreds upon hundreds of smaller ships surrounding them."

"Again, I apologize for the misunderstanding," the alien replied. "But now we have combined forces to our advantage."

"We just *lost* the advantage," Celeste countered. "And who the hell are you people, anyway?"

"We are the Kathiri. And I am called Nazira."

"Is this your entire fleet, Nazira?"

"No, but it is all of the craft ready for battle and worthy of this fight. And as they great philosopher Proonan said, 'My friend is one who fights my enemy.'"

"Yeah. The enemy of my enemy is my friend," Celeste replied. "Heard it before."

"It seems some wisdom is universal," Nazira said. "Now, let us move past this regrettable misunderstanding and proceed to form a new plan to defeat the Ra'az Hok."

"Well, they were on the verge of losing their defensive system powered by those satellites, until you showed up. Now it's protected, and they know we're here," Celeste said.

"Why are these satellites so important? They are quite small, and do not appear to contain any armament."

"Because they block warp tech from working anywhere near here. Didn't you notice when you jumped in here?"

"We were busy engaging the enemy," Nazira said, a worried look crossing her face as she turned her attention to a series of readouts that undoubtedly were confirming what she had just been told.

"These guys really are clueless, Daze."

Seems that way.

"So what are we going to do now that they've screwed the mission?"

I really don't know, but we need to position ourselves to make sure we don't get flanked. The Ra'az are on their home turf, and it's only a matter of time before they launch a counterattack.

Daisy studied the positions of all the ships in the fleet. With the smaller Ra'az ships still buzzing among them, taking shots when they could, it would take a little bit of time and one serious distraction to reposition their assets the way they'd need them, she realized.

"Freya, get Celeste on the line."

A moment later, the two women were connected on a secure band.

"Daisy, I assume you were watching that," Celeste said with an exasperated sigh.

"Yeah, but we'd best ignore the spilled milk right now, if we hope to recover from this. We need a distraction to give us time to reposition. Joshua's sending you the new battle plan coordinates now."

"You have an idea?" Celeste asked.

"Yeah, but it's a bit out there."

"After what just happened, it can't possibly be any worse. Do what you need to. I'll have my people get ready."

"Okay. I'm on it," she said, signing off.

Daisy rose to her feet and straightened her clothes, brushing loose strands of hair out of her face.

"Okay, I'm ready. Freya, can you call up the Ra'az queen on comms?"

"I'm sorry, I could have sworn you just said you wanted her to call the Ra'az queen?" Sarah said, her questioning eyebrow arched high.

"You'll see," she replied. "Can you do it, Freya?"

"Uh, hang on, there's a lot of interference," Freya replied. "Joshua, can you relay my signal through their piggybacked comms?"

"I'm pretty sure I can," he said.

"Okay, then," Freya said. "Yes, Daisy. We can do it. But are you sure that's a good idea?"

A grim smile found its way to Daisy's lips.

"I'm afraid we don't have much choice."

CHAPTER THIRTY-THREE

"Are you sure you're up to this?" Sarah asked as she quickly twisted her sister's hair into a tight, professional, and military-styled braid. "You're not looking so hot."

"Yeah, I'm just a little nervous, is all," she replied. "I'll be fine."

"Freya, you haven't––" Joshua started to say.

"Daisy will do great, Joshua. Just you watch," she interrupted, shifting her attentions to Daisy. "Okay, we've secured a direct line with the Ra'az queen. Are you ready?"

Daisy rolled her shoulders and cracked her neck, bouncing slightly on her toes, like a prize-fighter preparing for a big bout.

"Okay," she said, stopping her movements and settling into a firm stance. "Put her on."

The Ra'az Hok queen was a large creature. Larger than any Ra'az she had seen yet, but from what Daisy could see, she was just a particularly big creature and not the actual progenitor of her entire species.

She was clothed in opulent robes, the fabric of which appeared to be woven of precious metals, adorned with gemstones and what appeared to be interwoven elements of tech. Around her neck hung a series of gem-encrusted pendants, and on each forearm sat a massive bejeweled power gauntlet.

The only other being visible on screen was a single Chithiid loyalist, head hung low in deference to his queen. He bore the loyalist brand on not one, but all four of his shoulders, and his clothing was more akin to that of a courtesan than a military conscript.

"I seek parlay with the leader of the Ra'az Hok people," Daisy said in as steady a voice as she could muster. *"I am Daisy Swarthmore, the one who vanquished the Ra'az Hok from the planet Earth, my homeworld. Do you speak for your planet?"*

The queen sat impassively, while her loyalist servant whispered in her ear. Her expression remained one of regal boredom, but a flash of anger seemed to have sparked in her eyes.

"I think he just told her you were the one who booted them from Earth," Sarah noted. *"And she looks pissed."*

Good. Let her be, Daisy silently replied. *I want her entirely focused on me.*

The Ra'az ruler barked a guttural reply, speaking to her servant, but eyes locked on Daisy.

"My queen represents all Ra'az Hok," the loyalist translator replied. *"She demands that you lay down your arms and surrender to her indomitable will."*

"We are attempting to have an open and honest discussion," Daisy replied. *"Will your queen not speak directly to me?"*

"Her Mightiness does not speak Chithiid. It is beneath her to speak it. She does not stoop so low as to soil her tongue with our foul language."

"Oh boy," Sarah said with a sigh. *"This one's gonna be a handful."*

But we can play off of her power trip, Daisy replied.

"So it is a Chithiid who speaks for her?"

"I am merely the vessel conveying her will."

"Then convey this," Daisy said. *"I have had our fleet stand down to speak woman-to-woman with your queen, yet your ships still attack ours. Is this how your queen negotiates?"*

The loyalist's eyes wavered slightly in discomfort, yet he translated Daisy's words. The queen seemed to ponder the small human's precocious statement a moment, then decided to see how things would play out with her odd opponent. She reached up and clutched her smallest pendant, depressing two of the little gemstones on its surface.

Daisy didn't hear the recall signal, or even register it on her systems, but the ships buzzing in her fleet immediately withdrew, flying back to rejoin the main body of the Ra'az vessels.

"Her Magnificence has recalled her craft," the Chithiid translated. *"Those vessels are but a tiny portion of the fleet she possesses. She can crush you at will. Her forces are vast. They are powerful. They are—"*

"Okay, I'm going to have to stop you right there," Daisy interrupted.

The translator looked shocked. No one dared interrupt the queen's servant. No one. Not ever.

Here goes nothing.

"I have already told you, I am Daisy Swarthmore. I am the firestorm that crushed the Ra'az Hok forces and drove them from Earth. I fought your forces at the Chithiid world of Taangaar and won."

At this, the loyalist blanched a little.

"Yes, that's right, Loyalist. Your homeworld has been freed of Ra'az control and is under my protection. You tell your queen."

The Chithiid regained his composure and repeated the message to the Ra'az ruler. She listened, her face a mask of stone, then gave him her reply.

"My queen says she admires your bravery, but you lie."

"Freya, transmit the images of our fight at Taangaar, and

make 'em good ones. Let them see us kicking their people's asses."

"Sending now," Freya replied.

Daisy stood by a moment, watching the expressions of the queen and her loyalist as they observed the record of their forces' defeat.

"You see, now, what we have done to your ships at Taangaar. We possess the technology to destroy the Ra'az world. To wipe your people from the universe," Daisy said forcefully, pausing a moment to let the words sink in. *"You speak of laying down arms, but it is I who have pulled my forces back to graciously give you this opportunity to surrender."*

The queen laughed as she heard the translation.

"My queen says this is a bluff. If you possessed so deadly a weapon, you would have already used it."

"We do not believe in genocide."

He quickly relayed the message. The queen sneered at the screen.

"We do," her translator replied.

Daisy felt her stomach flip. The strain was finally catching up with her.

"Daze, you okay? You're looking a little green," Sarah noted.

I'm fine, she replied, focusing all of her attentions on the creature on the screen.

"Despite all that has happened, we do not wish to extinguish your species' light. We could come to terms. An agreement. Your world needs resources, but there is no need to invade and kill when we could peacefully co-exist. Our people could even collaborate to explore together, discovering new worlds to approach—peacefully—to establish trade and sharing of resources."

At this, the queen laughed. It was a foul sound, one full of bile and hate, where a laugh should be brimming with mirth and joy. She then gave her servant a message to relay.

"The Ra'az Hok do not collaborate. They do not need your

assistance or trade. They are all-powerful, and conquer worlds as if it were child's play. They take what they want and leave behind only blood and tears. It is the Ra'az Hok way. Ask any Ra'az, from the lowest drone to Her Highness herself, and they will tell you the same."

Daisy grew pale and wavered.

"Daze, you okay?" Sarah asked, concerned. "You want me to get you some—?"

Daisy suddenly lurched forward and vomited a stream of bile onto the command pod floor.

Shit. Talk about bad timing.

"You need to end this call and have Celeste take over. The strain's getting to you."

No, I can handle this, Daisy silently replied, standing up straight and wiping her lips with the back of her sleeve.

The Ra'az Hok queen squinted a little as she looked closely at her vid screen, then said a few words to her servant.

"My queen says she sees you are with child."

"No," Daisy replied. *"It was just a bad meal shaken by the explosions of us destroying so many of your ships."*

"Uh, Daisy?" Joshua interrupted.

"Not now, Joshua," she hissed.

"Freya, are you going to tell her?" he continued.

"Tell me what? I'm negotiating, here."

"Well, about that pregnancy thing," Freya said, uncomfortably.

Daisy felt her stomach flip again, though this time it was most certainly caused by what she just heard rather than her body itself.

"You can't possibly mean..."

"Yeah, actually," Freya quietly replied. "A few months along, now, actually."

"And you knew? How?" she asked, shell-shocked.

"Basic health scans showed it, so it was pretty obvious. All the AIs knew, more or less. We just thought it wasn't our place to say anything," Freya replied.

The Ra'az queen, though she did not understand the human language, did understand the look on Daisy's face as she spoke to her shipmates.

"My queen's suspicion is confirmed. She says you are a weak human and would have been an unfit mother, had she allowed you to live. But that is not to be. She will kill you and all you love, and will revel in the death of your unborn offspring."

The threat to Daisy's child made something snap deep within her. *"You're fucking dead, bitch! You hear me? I'm coming for you!"* Daisy shouted, enraged, then cut the feed.

"Well," Sarah said, "I don't think I need a translation from Chithiid to get the gist of that."

"We're going to kill them," Daisy said, grimly. "We're going to kill all of them."

"But that's genocide, Daze. You said that––"

"It's literally us or them, Sis. There's no other way, so I say it's *them.*"

Sarah took Daisy by the arm and steered her to her seat. Freya's maintenance droids were already cleaning her vomit from the floor. In just seconds it was spotless and good as new.

Sarah sat down next to her and took her sister's hand.

"So," she said.

"Yeah. So," Daisy replied.

"But I thought Mal said that genetically modified humans couldn't reproduce organically."

"I thought so too," Daisy said. "But even so, Vince and I have been careful. At least I thought we were."

Sarah let out an amazed sigh.

"Damn. It shouldn't even be possible, Daze."

"I know. But nature, uh, finds a way," Daisy said, a small grin managing to find its way to her shocked lips.

"Freya, are you sure this is accurate?" Sarah asked.

"Yes, Sarah. My standard medical scans of all crew are quite accurate."

"No mistakes, then?"

"None."

"Freya's right," Joshua said. "Even the lesser ships have good enough med tech to pick up something like that."

Sarah leaned back in her seat and smiled at her sister.

"Well, shit, Daze. I guess it's time for us to find you some looser combat pants," she said with a little sisterly snark. "You're gonna blow up like a balloon," she laughed.

"Funny, coming from you," Joshua quipped.

"What do you mean by that?" Sarah asked.

"Joshua!" Freya hissed.

"Oh, sorry. I thought she knew."

"Thought I knew what?" Sarah said, a sinking feeling forming in her gut.

"Oh," he said, at a rare loss for words. "Uh, well, you see, um—"

"Holy shit," Daisy blurted. "Her too? Freya, you knew?"

"Well, it wasn't my place to say anything, Daisy," she replied.

"No way," Sarah said, jumping to her feet and pacing the pod. "There's no way. I mean, Finn and I have only—I mean, it's been less than a week!"

"My scans show it as well," Joshua said. "Again, common AI knowledge."

"No. Impossible," Sarah said in denial.

"Tell her she's forgetting something," Sarah said.

I can just put the neuro-band on. Gimme a sec.

"Nah, just tell her. Say the words 'wedding party.' She'll get it."

"Uh, Sarah? Other You said to tell you, 'wedding party.' Does that mean anything to you?"

The pacing woman froze in her tracks.

She had shared her memories with her bodiless self. *All* of them.

"We got a bit tipsy, is all," she said, but deep down, she knew what they had done. In a rush, the blurry memories came flooding back. The Harkaways' beach wedding, the party, the drinking and dancing, and then afterwards.

"Sonofa—" she said, sliding into her seat, stunned. "Goddamn, I need a drink," she finally said.

"So do I," Daisy concurred.

She opened the small cooler compartment below the console and reached inside—right past the booze, straight to the back of the storage space, grabbing a pair of electrolyte pouches, handing one to her sister.

"To unexpected surprises," Daisy said.

"Fuckin' A," Sarah said.

The sisters clinked the beverage containers together in a shell-shocked toast.

292

CHAPTER THIRTY-FOUR

The Ra'az queen may have talked a tough game, but their ships remained in a defensive position around their world, their warp-canceling satellites safely tucked behind them.

The combined invading fleet, newly reinforced with the arrival of the dozens of Kathiri craft, lay waiting just inside the edge of the asteroid field. The nearly victorious sneak attack utilizing the captured Ra'az ships had been so close to success before being disrupted by their unexpected new allies. Now, all they could do was make the most of the situation and come up with a new plan.

Joshua came aboard Zed's massive ship to replenish his tacked-on power cells, while the rest of the commanders in the fleet discussed their options from the relative safety of their battle-ready command pods. While they all preferred meeting face-to-face, they knew they had to be ready to react at a moment's notice.

Marty had been retrieved from within the asteroid field, and once he was back with the fleet, it had been quick work for Arlo to source the components required to boost his friend's reserve power systems to an acceptable level.

"Still no warp power, though," Arlo griped as he finished installing the last of Marty's new componentry. "There, all done. See how it works."

Marty ran through a quick systems check.

"Looks like we're green across the board. Thanks, Arlo."

"You got it, bud."

The stealth ship moved to a spot at the edge of the fleet and took up an observational post, while the big wigs decided their new course of action.

"I tend to agree that while it is a disappointment we were unable to capitalize on the opportunity provided by the successful insertion of our ships into the Ra'az fleet, we nevertheless have what I think is a rather viable backup plan, courtesy of Joshua," Mal said. "Zed, what's your take on this?"

"You know, Mal, while you and I don't always agree on things, this one we see eye to eye on," he said. "I mean, hell, it's a ballsy move, and utterly novel, but I'd be willing to bet that's the exact reason the Ra'az won't see it coming."

"One thing," Celeste interjected. "A lot of our smaller ships, while possessing a fair amount of firepower, do not have the thrust capability needed."

"So they follow behind. Let the bigger ships do the heavy lifting, as it were," Captain Harkaway said. "If we're going to truly work as a team, it's the only thing that makes any sense."

"And what of the enormous asteroid you sent on a trajectory targeting the Ra'az world, Joshua?" Celeste asked. "We had hoped to utilize it for a diversion before everything went to shit."

"It was on its way and on course when we left it, and that was some time ago. If my calculations were correct, it should be plowing through the asteroids in about thirty hours, or so."

"We don't have that long," Daisy noted.

"Obviously. But it's still far out from the asteroid field, and there's nothing we can do about that."

"Damn it," Daisy grumbled. "So our options are pretty much

limited to a direct frontal assault, or Joshua's crazy-ass plan. I guess that means I vote for the crazy option."

"Me too," Arlo said.

"Ditto," Zed chimed in.

In short order, all commanders were on board with the decision. It was utterly mad, but it just might work.

"Okay," Gus transmitted to the selected ships. "You guys come with me. We've got a lot of work to do, and not much time to do it in."

"Copy that, Gus. We're right behind you," Mal said as she and the other craft fell into line.

They dove into the asteroid field, but just at the innermost edges, selecting the biggest chunks they could find and positioning themselves against the far sides before diverting all energy to their forward-most shields. Slowly at first, then picking up speed, they began pushing the rocks forward.

Soon, a decent-sized group of asteroids had been gathered at the front of the fleet. There were even some rather impressive-sized ones among the cluster, pushed in place by the large Ra'az ships they'd captured. Of all the vessels, they didn't really care if they damaged them a bit in the process.

"They've seen what we're up to," Mal noted. "The Ra'az fleet is moving toward us."

"Shit. Then I guess this will have to be enough," Daisy replied. "Okay, lead ships, push hard! Get some momentum on these things. The rest of you, hang back a few beats, then follow them in. They should absorb most of the Ra'az blasts, for a time anyway."

The ships took up their positions, once again shifting their shields to the front as they pushed with all their power. The asteroids began moving, and quickly at that. Peeling off and flipping a one-eighty, the group of ships quickly rejoined the fleet as they prepped to attack.

The Ra'az were coming in fast, despite the wall of stone the fleet had thrown at them.

"Bastards aren't even slowing down," Sarah observed.

"Told ya. They're too aggressive. And that'll be their downfall," Daisy replied.

The lead Ra'az ships began hitting the incoming asteroids with small weapons fire. Too small to damage them.

"What are they doing, Daze?"

"Oh, shit," she said, as she realized what was happening. "They're slowing them down using their smaller weapons systems. Saving up the big stuff for us. It looks like they'll be able to maneuver through them safely any time now. We've got to attack, and we've got to do it now."

"Are you sure, Daisy?" Celeste asked.

"No. But you can see it as clearly as I can. We don't have a choice."

"Agreed," she said after a moment's reflection. "All ships, attack!"

The commanders had already been on edge, nervously awaiting the opportunity to stop watching and start fighting. Finally given the go-ahead, their ships lunged forward, free to engage the enemy in their sights.

The Ra'az had slowed the asteroid attack enough to easily pass through them, leaving them behind as the rocks drifted lazily toward their planet, where the remaining defensive systems would surely stop them with little effort.

The big ships opened fire, sending out a shocking amount of ordinance in a short span. The human fleet dove into evasive maneuvers, narrowly avoiding the incoming attack as they spun back toward their enemy and let loose a fusillade of their own. The Ra'az copied their opponents' moves, dodging the blasts as best they could.

A great many of their ships, however, sustained varying

degrees of damage as their shielding failed just enough to allow some of the pulse blasts through.

"They're dumping everything they have," Sarah said.

"I know," Daisy replied, her spirits rising ever so slightly. "Celeste, are you seeing this?"

"Yes, I am," the commander replied. "Zed, what's your analysis?"

"The Ra'az have successfully avoided the asteroid attack, but as we had hoped, it spread them thin, leaving them vulnerable to our firepower."

"As I said it would," Joshua interrupted. "Now, if you'd please hurry and make use of the advantage while it is still ours, we can inflict a great amount of damage on them before they have the opportunity to regroup."

"You heard the man," Zed bellowed. "All ships, press the attack. Wipe them out! All weapons fire, all ships move in!"

The combined human and alien fleets reacted as one, the smaller, faster ships darting out front to hector the Ra'az craft, while the larger and more powerful ones launched wave after wave of pulse blasts.

It was quickly apparent that the Ra'az had not prepared for so intense a showing from what they'd obviously assumed to be a weaker foe. And then they did something Daisy found amazing. Something entirely un-Ra'az.

They turned tail and fled.

"We've got them on the run!" Zed broadcast on all bands. "Press the advantage. Chase them down. All ships ahead full!"

The fleet began moving faster, straining their ships to close the gap with the Ra'az ships hurrying toward the relative safety of their orbiting planetary defenses. The typically aggressive Ra'az were on their heels, and it seemed victory was at hand.

Joshua, however, felt something was amiss.

"Freya, this isn't right," he called out. "This is not Ra'az tactics."

"We're winning, Joshua," she replied, "but I see your point, and you're right. Something feels off about this."

She slowed her pursuit a moment to look at the big picture, taking in the movements of not just a handful of the nearest ships she had been targeting, but the entirety of the fleeing force. She and Joshua linked minds, sharing the data, pooling their analytical powers.

"Oh, fuck," Freya blurted.

"What is it, Freya?" Daisy asked, alarmed.

"They're all stopping just behind their defenses."

"That's to be expected."

"No, you don't understand," Freya said. "It's a trap!"

She flashed a series of images onto the screen. There, nestled just behind the planet's nearest orbiting asteroid belt, were hundreds of stationary vessels. Equidistant and facing outward.

"What are those things?" Daisy asked.

"We don't know," Joshua replied. "But this has all the markings of an ambush. Celeste! Zed! Call off the pursuit," Joshua transmitted.

"What do you see, Joshua?" Zed replied. "We've got them on the run."

"It's a trap."

"I don't see any—-"

As if they had been waiting for someone to tempt fate, the mysterious craft all powered up at once, sending every AI's scanners spiking with the activity.

"The Ra'az weren't running," Zed realized. "Everyone abort! Retreat!"

"What's happening, Zed?" Celeste asked in a panic.

"The Ra'az weren't running, Celeste. They were just getting clear."

"Clear of what?"

The last of the Ra'az ships cleared the perimeter of their

defenses, and as a single unit, all of the now fully powered craft unleashed their payload.

Individually they wouldn't cause too much damage, but fired together at once, the massive focused pulse detonation radiated out from their positions, creating an outward-moving ball of energy around the planet.

The wave of pulse energy shattered the asteroids surrounding the Ra'az world, sending them flying out in all directions. The pulse weakened a bit as it traveled, but it nevertheless had enough force to fracture the rock attack the human fleet had launched as well, reversing its course and turning the weapon on its original users.

The nearest of the fleet's ships, the smaller, faster craft that had been nipping at the fleeing Ra'azes' heels, were incinerated instantly in the initial pulse before it even reached the first of the asteroids.

The subsequent waves of ships––those that hadn't been caught in the blast as the asteroid field shattered––were moving at top speed, trying to escape back to the safety of the fleet. But the fleet was in jeopardy, too, and would provide no such refuge.

"We can't warp clear," Zed said in a panic.

"Get us out of here, Zed!" Celeste bellowed. "Give it all you've got!"

Like the rest of the ships in the human fleet, Zed spun in place and opened his engines wide, but without the benefit of their warp systems powering the ships, none of them, it appeared, would be able to make it clear of the cascading wall of rocks and energy.

"What can we do, Daisy?" Freya asked. "Joshua, do you have a plan?"

"Protect yourself, Freya. At all costs, protect yourself," was his grim reply.

The slower of their ships that had been the vanguard of the pursuing force began detonating one by one as they were overtaken by the hurtling debris. A shrapnel tsunami made of shattered rock, a wave that was shredding everything in its path.

Daisy watched in horror as she realized the grim reality of what had happened. The Ra'az queen had baited her with threats against her unborn child and drawn her into an aggressive stance. She tricked her into fighting as the Ra'az would fight, throwing all of their resources into pursuing the smaller force, and that had given her the edge.

Fueled by anger and a need for vengeance, Daisy realized they had chased them right into a well-laid trap.

CHAPTER THIRTY-FIVE

The devastation was widespread, as more and more smaller ships were caught up in the hail of deadly debris. The first wave, the one carrying the lesser pieces of debris, had hit first, but the successive waves were pushing the far deadlier, far larger fragments.

"All ships, evasive maneuvers!" Zed called over open comms in desperation.

Unfortunately, no maneuvers would shield them from the onslaught of flying rocks about to impact their fleet.

"We've got to get out of here!" Sarah blurted as she watched the screens in horror.

"Where can we run?" Daisy replied, morosely. "There's no way we make it back to the asteroid field behind us in time to get deep enough into it to provide cover."

"So we target the incoming projectiles," George said. "Fire off everything we've got and blow them to bits."

"A great suggestion under almost any other circumstances, my friend, but I'm afraid that would just create smaller shrapnel that would still be pushed right at us by the second and third pulse waves," Joshua interjected.

"I'm trying, Joshua. I'm just not a tactician of your caliber," he quietly replied.

"I know, George. And it's appreciated. Truly. But right now we need to find another way. One that won't add to the incoming debris field. We may survive the smaller pieces, but the next wave will be the end of us."

"Time?" Daisy asked, racking her brain for a way out.

"Forty-five seconds until the first of it hits the main body of the fleet," Joshua replied. "After that, another twenty before the second wave."

"What about the third?"

"It would just shake things up a bit, but there's no debris left for it to push," he replied. "Of course we'll all be dead by then. Some of us for the second time."

"Third, here," Sarah said. "Gotcha beat."

"So it seems," Joshua said, managing a faintly amused tone.

It was gallows humor, no doubt, but in the face of certain death, even a slight lightening of the mood was appreciated.

Suddenly, the captured Ra'az ships turned and accelerated, though not away from the oncoming asteroid barrage, but toward it.

An all-channels vid signal flashed onto the screen. Standing in his smoking command pod, a tall Chithiid held fast to his console, looking, Daisy found herself musing, like a seven-foot-tall alien Ahab as he chased down the white whale.

"All rebel-controlled Ra'az ships, fall in behind me! Form five columns, mine central, then stack up!" Aarvin bellowed over the open comms as his massive ship began absorbing the first of the smaller pieces bearing down on the fleet. *"The rest of you, form a single line behind us, facing away. Keep your shields entirely focused behind you and your engines on full. That might just stop any debris that makes it past us."*

"What are you doing, Aarvin?" Celeste shouted back over

comms. Zed, however, wasted no time, jumping in line and ushering the others nearby to do the same. The Kathiri vessels merged with the others, the entirety of the fleet forming a single column.

Quickly, the remaining Ra'az ships under Aarvin's command followed suit, following his lead and speeding straight toward the blast, instead of away from it. Once they were on course, they spread themselves slightly, as ordered, fanning out into a stack of ships lined up a dozen deep at the four corners as well as behind the fifth, central one.

Seconds later, every escape vessel and shuttle docked to those ships launched, flying the opposite direction as fast as they were able, directly toward the human fleet as it powered ahead away from the blast, a single ship-wide column.

"What's he doing?" Sarah asked. "That's suicide!"

"Holy shit," Joshua said, as he realized the Chithiid's plan. "That fella has got balls of steel," he said, admiringly. "I hope to hell he survives this. I want to buy him a drink."

"You don't have a body," Freya reminded him.

"Doesn't preclude me from buying one for someone who does," he shot back.

"How can you joke?" Sarah said, exasperated. "We're all about to die."

"About that," Joshua replied. "I really don't think that's going to happen. Not anymore."

On their screens, the bright explosions of the first layers of commandeered ships lit up the sky, then went dark. While a good many ships had been destroyed, the ones behind them were still intact, powering forward on auto-pilot as their crews escaped to the rear.

"Here comes the second wave," Joshua said. "Wait for it... Wait for it."

The larger asteroids tore into the remaining ships, their mass vaporizing in short-lived explosions in the vacuum of space. A few moments later, they were gone.

Daisy looked at the screens, plotting the course of the hail of deadly debris. Sarah looked over at them as well, eyes wide at the sheer number of incoming projectiles.

"We're dead," she said, resolved to her fate. "I love you, Sis."

"I love you too, Sarah," Daisy said, hugging her. "But we're not going to die."

Sarah looked at her, confused.

"Look at the screens," Daisy said. "Look closely."

It was hard to see at first, given the sheer density of debris clouding the scans, but then Sarah saw it. The key to their survival.

"They created a funnel effect," she said, amazed.

"Now she's got it," Joshua said. "Welcome to the party, Sarah."

"Be nice. She's only got a meat box to think with," Freya chided him.

Daisy activated her video comms line to the *Váli*. Vince, though drenched in sweat and covered in grease and soot from his frantic repairs, was in one piece.

"Hey, babe," he said with a relieved grin. "Looks like you don't get rid of me that easily after all."

Her stomach warmed, then shimmied a bit.

"Let's be sure to keep it that way," she replied. "And honey, I've got some news for you."

"Oh?"

"It can wait until this is done. You focus on your work. Keep that old bird in the air."

"Will do," he replied. "Oh, and Finn says to tell Sarah he looks forward to continuing their cooking lessons, if they survive this. Said he'll show her that special trick, whatever that means."

Sarah couldn't help but laugh.

"Tell him it's a deal," she said, before Daisy signed off.

All around them, space shuddered as the second and third pulse waves rumbled past. The fleet shook, but remained surprisingly intact.

"Goddamn clever, that Chithiid," Joshua said. "That was ballsy."

"What exactly did he do?" Sarah asked, still a bit confused. "He sacrificed his ships, I get that, but how did that save the entire fleet?"

"Mathematics, my dear," Joshua said. "Mathematics. The thing is, if his ships had been directly behind us when they were impacted by the blast wave, the impact and debris would have carried forward and taken out all the rest of the ships immediately after. But he had them moving the *opposite* direction."

"Which I saw, but that doesn't explain how the debris missed us."

"Think of it like casting a shadow on a very sunny day," Joshua suggested. "If you hold an umbrella just above your head, you cast only enough shade to shield a space the size of its diameter."

"Right. And our ships were wider than that diameter, so they should have been destroyed."

"Ah, but only if they were close by. You see, when he began heading the opposite direction of the fleet, his actions were akin to taking your umbrella and raising it higher and higher. And like an umbrella, eventually, the shadow it cast would grow to encompass a far larger area than the umbrella itself."

"What he's saying is, it dispersed the protective shielding effect of the ships they used to block the debris enough that—since we all fell in single file—the center of that line of vessels would be protected as the cone of safety spread as the debris was traveling on an expanding path," Daisy clarified. "He sacrificed all of those dozens of ships to save the hundreds of others in the fleet."

"Inspired bit of thinking. Truly," Joshua said. "Now we just have to deal with part two."

"Part two?" George said. "Oh boy."

Far behind the diminished fleet, the Ra'az, surprised by the unusual tactic and the survival of the enemy that had resulted from it, began pulling back into an aggressive posturing once more, their ships spreading out as they prepared to pounce on their injured opponents.

"We need to regroup, and fast," Daisy said. "Celeste, you've got to pull together as many of the larger ships as possible to give the smaller ones a chance to patch their most serious damage to get back into the fight. The Ra'az are gearing up to hit us while we're hurt. We've got to be ready for them."

"Joshua, do you think you can get through the gap in the asteroid field from here?"

"Shouldn't be too hard," he replied. "But why? The fight—and all of our resources—are here."

"Not all of them."

"You can't mean the big asteroid," he said, realizing where she was going with this. "It's too far away, and even if we push it with our fastest ships, it'll never get here in time."

"But you said it's far out there," Daisy replied. "You said it's so far out that it's still in functional warp territory."

"You can't possibly be thinking what I think you're thinking," Joshua said, a note of excitement rising in his voice. "Because if you are, that's just insane. Brilliant, but insane."

"I've been called worse," Daisy replied with a tired grin. "So can you do it?"

"I believe so, but it'll cost us."

"How many?"

"A dozen, I reckon."

"Then a dozen it is. Pick your ships and get moving."

"We can come with," Arlo said, linking into the conversation. "Wherever it is you're going, that is."

"I'm heading outside the asteroid field, kid. We're going to link a dozen ships together, using their warp drives to––theoretically––jump that huge asteroid right through the asteroid field."

"But won't that destroy the ships, as well as their warp cores?"

"Oh yeah, most definitely," Joshua replied. "Which is why we're going to do it remotely. I've already selected the most damaged ships and notified Zed," he informed Daisy. "Time to go. It'll take us a little while once we're clear of the asteroid field and the Ra'az warp-cancellation tech to be able to jump out to it, but I'd estimate you have about two hours, give or take. You think you can rig something up in that time?"

"We'll make it work," Freya replied. "Get going."

"See you soon, babe," he replied before turning and darting out through the gap in the asteroid field, a dozen small ships close behind, following his lead.

"Babe?" Daisy chuckled.

"Leave me alone," Freya shot back, sarcastically.

"No, really. Good for you, kiddo. Mom approves."

"Are you two done?" Sarah grumbled.

"Sorry. Celeste, do you copy?" Daisy transmitted. "We're working on a plan, but we need time."

"How much time? The Ra'az have regrouped and are moving our way. With our fleet numbers suddenly evened out by their trap, I'd say they're looking pretty eager to press their advantage."

"So we turn back and fight them," Daisy said. "There are no guarantees any of this will work, but there's no stopping now. Success is the only option."

"Zed already told me the basics of Joshua's plan. Can you actually get it rigged in time?"

"I think so," she replied. "I don't have much of a choice, in any case."

"Very well," Celeste said. "We'll buy you all the time we can."

Daisy jumped up from her seat to head to the fabrication lab Freya had tucked in her belly, when Arlo piped up.

"Hey, Joshua told Marty to hang back and fly cover for Freya while you guys do whatever it is you're doing. What exactly *are* you doing?"

"We're going to use the asteroid we had planned to throw at their world as a diversion for cover, Arlo. Joshua's going to rig it to jump right through the asteroids, and when it arrives, we're going to use Freya's stealth tech to get past the Ra'az and plant a warp device on it."

"But warp doesn't work here."

"No, but once it passes the Ra'az satellites it will, and when we finally get into the atmosphere, we'll detonate it."

"But their tech cancels out not only warp drives, but also blocks our signals from any reasonable distance."

"I know," Daisy said. "It'll have to be manually triggered."

"Wait, did you say manually?"

"Yes. And I'll need you to take Sarah and George with you."

"Hang on, you're not booting me out for some hare-brained scheme of yours," Sarah said. "And in case you forgot, the fleet's warp systems are too weak. Only warp orbs we stole from the Ra'az base in San Francisco seem to have the energy potential you're talking about for an atmospheric detonation."

"Yeah. And we've got one right here."

"The drained one?" Sarah said.

"No, the other one," Daisy replied.

"Need I remind you that's the one we're using?"

"Not right now. Not while we're flying under auxiliary power," Daisy pointed out. "So we pull the orb, rig it to blow, and get it onto that asteroid. Freya's got the auxiliary juice to get clear in plenty of time."

"But the orb is drained."

"You remember what happened to Marty's drive? As soon as he pulled clear, it powered back up. Well, when we first got here the Ra'az warped a bunch of ships from within the atmosphere up to their fleet. That means the satellites are *outward-facing*. Once an orb passes their position, it should power back up. And that means it'll be ready to blow when I trigger it."

"Hang on a minute," Arlo said over their comms. "You're talking about a suicide mission."

"Someone has to do it, Arlo," Daisy said. "And everyone else here has already died because of me once before. Seems only fair it'd be my turn. Quite a way to go, huh? Saving the world."

"But you *can't* die. You don't understand! Send me instead."

You're a brave kid, Arlo. Really, you are. And I'm proud to have known you. But you're young, and you've got a whole life to live. Freya, lose them."

"Are you sure?"

"Please?" Daisy asked, quietly.

"All right."

Freya spun into motion, using every bit of her stealthy tricks as she dove into the fleet, weaving through ships before tucking into the asteroid field and hiding from sight.

"Block their comms too, would ya? I'd rather not spend my last hours listening to them try to find us."

"Okay, Daisy," Freya complied.

"Daisy, are you sure you want to do this?" George asked. "I'm glad to shoulder the burden. In fact, it's kinda my job."

"Thanks, George, but I'm afraid the proximity to the Ra'az satellites might short out your systems if you're on that asteroid and not protected by Freya's shielding. It's gotta be me."

"But, Sis," Sarah said, tears welling in her eyes.

"Hey, it's okay. It has to be done."

"Screw them. You don't have to do this."

Daisy gave her a big hug.

"A wise old Vulcan once said, 'The good of the many outwe––"

"What's a Vulcan?" Sarah interrupted.

"Never mind," Daisy replied with an amused sigh, then left the command pod and headed into Freya's belly to get to work.

CHAPTER THIRTY-SIX

Joshua delivered, as promised, a short while later.

The massive asteroid, formerly to be a simple diversionary tool, popped into view just at the edge of the asteroid field, smashing them into bits as it hurtled toward the Ra'az world.

"Looks like he gauged the distance a little off," Sarah said, noting the bits of smashed rock in the huge asteroid's wake.

"Nah, it's just the field is thicker over there," Freya said. "I was scanning and noticed a gravitational anomaly that pulled the inner walls of it a little bit closer to the Ra'az. I would have warned him before he warped it in here, but comms won't clear the asteroid field."

"Or the Ra'az satellites," Daisy added, walking back into the command pod, her deadly new toy in hand. "Those bastards keep scrambling our ships' comms if they stray too far from one another."

Outside, the two fleets were battling it out, engaged in a battle royale for nearly an hour. The Ra'az, though still slightly fewer in number, now held a slight advantage, as the human and Kathiri vessels had sustained damage ranging from nominal to severe in the wake of the Ra'az trap.

Marty had finally given up trying to find Daisy and was tearing through the enemy ships, ripping apart their weapons systems from close range, then darting off before a neighboring craft could target him. Daisy had to admire the two of them. A boy and his ship, willing to give it all for a group of people they'd never even met before.

"Daisy, I've finished my assessment of the asteroid," Freya informed her.

"And?"

"And it's moving really fast."

"Obviously," she replied with a chuckle. "And what else, kiddo?"

"And I have determined the densest portion of its mass. It isn't the thickest, per se, but it is the most likely to withstand entry into the planet's atmosphere and remain intact."

"And that's what we want," Daisy noted. "So, we're looking good, then."

"Well, yes and no," Freya said, a note of reluctance in her voice.

"Why couldn't you start with the bad news *first* for once?" Daisy asked, jokingly. "Okay, Freya, what haven't you told me?"

"The thing is, there's an eighty-six percent likelihood of that section of the asteroid reaching atmosphere and surviving entry."

"But?"

"But there is also a seventy-two percent chance that the Ra'az will be able to significantly slow its progress using their cannons and smaller weapons systems, much like they did with the asteroids our fleet threw at them prior to their ambush."

"But those were smaller rocks," Sarah pointed out. "I mean, *much* smaller."

"Yes, Sarah, they were. But this time there is just one target, and I fear they may all target it at once. If they did, it could diminish its velocity."

"Enough to stop it?" Daisy asked.

"No. But enough to potentially delay it enough to miss its target as the Ra'az planet travels on its orbital path."

"Then we'd better distract them. The others have seen the asteroid by now. Start your approach, Freya, and comm them and tell them to divert whatever firepower they can to give that giant-ass rock a clear path. I'm going to suit up. If this works, I'll only have a minute to jump out there before you'll have to dust off."

Sarah stopped her in her tracks, pulling her into a tight hug.

"I don't want you to do this, Daisy."

"I don't want to either, but it needs to be done. Everyone else has been so busy sacrificing it all for the good of our worlds. It's only fair I do the same." She turned to leave, pausing a moment in front of her cybernetic friend.

"Daisy, it's been a real honor," Sergeant Franklin said, throwing her a crisp salute.

"George, you're one of a kind," she said, saluting him back, then wrapping him up in a big hug. "You take care of yourself, okay?"

"Will do. And I'll keep an eye on that one as well," he said, nodding toward Daisy's tearful sister.

"Oh, don't start that!" Daisy griped, her own waterworks kicking in. "See what you made me do?" she half-heartedly bitched to her sister.

They shared a final look as she stepped into the doorway.

"Love you, Sis."

"Love you too."

Then she was gone, on her way to don her space suit for the final time.

"Freya, can you patch me through to Vince?" she asked as she slid her legs into the suit's protective embrace.

"Got him," Freya replied. "He's on."

"Hey, babe. What's this Arlo says about you going on some

crazy suicide mission without me?" he said with a concerned laugh. "I know he was exaggerating, right?"

Keep it together, Daisy. You can do this.

"Sorry, Vince," she said, forcing her tightening throat to work as she held back her emotions. "I'm afraid there's just no other way."

Vince was silent a long moment.

"No," he finally said. "No, you get someone else to do it, you understand? This does not have to be you. You've done enough already."

"It's okay, baby," she soothed. "Nothing is forever, and we had a really good run of it, and I wouldn't change a minute."

"But we had plans. We were going to get a place by the ocean. Plant some crops. Start a family."

That last one stung, twisting the knife a bit deeper, but she knew she had to spare him that additional pain.

"Yeah, that would have been nice," she said. "But this has to be done, and there's no one else who can do it. Now I want you to go and be strong for me. Can you do that? Be strong and help the others. They'll need you, Vince. There's still a war to win."

Daisy slid her arms into the suit's sleeves. All that was left was the helmet.

"Listen. I've got to go now," she said quietly. "Just always remember how much I love you."

"Daisy, please. You can't—"

"Don't, Vince. Just don't."

He was silent a long moment.

"I love you, Daisy Swarthmore," he said, then the comms went silent.

Tearfully, Daisy slid the helmet into place and moved closer to the lower airlock she'd be exiting onto the surface of the asteroid.

"I'm ready, Freya. Give me a countdown when we're getting close."

"There's a problem, Daisy," Freya blurted out in a panic. "You'd better get up here."

"But I'm ready to--"

"Get up here. Trust me."

"Shit," Daisy cursed, lurching through the door into Freya's corridor and hustling back to her command pod.

"What is it that's so important you couldn't just tell me over the--" She fell silent as she realized what was on the monitor screens. "Oh, fuck me."

A series of large explosions shook the asteroid as they neared it, fracturing it, then breaking it into millions of tiny pieces.

"They must have figured it had some strategic importance when our ships started clearing a path for it," George said. "Looks like one of their commanders took the initiative to divert all of his cannons to take it out before it could get anywhere near their planet."

Daisy looked at the other monitors with dread. The fleet was losing, the Ra'az ships were chipping away at their defenses, slowly driving them into a crossfire. It was only a matter of time before their fleet would be destroyed.

Sarah stared at her sister, a grim look on her face. Grim, and determined.

"Is the orb hooked up?" she asked.

"Yes."

"And can it take out their planet if we manage to get it to the edge of their atmosphere?"

"I don't know, Sis," Daisy replied. "It's supposed to be in full atmosphere to have that effect. I don't know if its reaction would be powerful enough that high up."

Sarah looked crestfallen.

"What if you tied it to a second orb?" George said. "Could that help?"

"I don't know if that would--"

"Yeah, I'm almost sure that'd give it a much higher volatility level," Freya interrupted. "The fresh one would power up once it passed the satellites, and if it were in a feedback loop with the drained unit, the combination would almost certainly increase the detonation's power by several orders of magnitude."

"Which would be enough to take the Ra'az down, even from the very edge of their atmosphere," George said, giving Sarah a knowing nod. "Excellent."

"So we're in agreement?" Freya asked.

"I am," George replied. "Sarah?"

"Count me in."

"What are you talking about?" Daisy asked, more than a little confused.

"Our entire fleet is about to lose, Daisy. Everyone we love. Everyone we care about. Gone. And then there will be no one left to check the Ra'az aggression," Sarah said, a flash of angry steel in her voice. "So we were talking while you were down below, and we've made a decision."

"Oh?"

"Yeah. We're making a run for the atmosphere. And if we're successful, once we clear reentry, we'll detonate the orbs."

"I can't let you do that. This is my burden to bear."

"Sorry, Daze. You've been outvoted, three to one. Now let's get working on this, there's no time to waste. The fleet's on the brink, and we simply don't have the luxury of sitting around here arguing about this."

"So, there it is," Daisy said, reluctantly.

"Yep. There it is."

"All right, then," Daisy said. "Love you guys."

"Back atcha, Daisy," George said with a grin.

"You know it," Freya chimed in.

"Okay, Sis. Let's get to it."

Daisy and Sarah rushed through the ship's corridors to

where the drained orb was locked away in Freya's high-security storage locker.

"Pry the lower casing open on the trigger mechanism," Daisy instructed as she punched in the combination to the locker. "That'll expose the wiring we'll need to––" She fell silent.

"Sonofabitch," Sarah said, looking over her shoulder into the locker.

The *empty* locker.

"But it was here," she blurted in disbelief. "I put it there myself. Locked the damn thing away and didn't tell a soul."

"There's no way anyone could have snuck on board," Freya added.

"And you're sure it was *this* locker, Sarah?"

"Positive."

Daisy didn't know what to do. Just like that, their last-ditch only-hope effort was wiped from the table. They had no more options.

She was about to close the locker when she noticed something. A small sticky note stuck to the inside of the door.

Daisy recognized her own writing.

"What is it, Daisy?" Sarah asked.

"It's another goddamn sticky note, just like Colorado," she said, trying to decipher the little drawings she had apparently left herself.

"Why the doodles?" she lamented. "Why couldn't I just write myself a goddamn instruction manual or something?"

"Because, apparently, you never did," Sarah pointed out. "Paradoxes, and shit."

"Yeah, paradoxes and shit," Daisy said. "Sounds like a band name."

"Well, you drew a musical note," Sarah said. "And the other one looks like a clock face, but you made the hands all messed up."

Daisy squinted her eyes, studying the image. It hit her seconds later.

"Of course. They're not just blurry, Sis. They're spinning *backwards*."

"Do you know what it means?"

"Actually, I think I do," Daisy said. "Freya, get Mal on the line."

"Hang on a sec. She's in the middle of something."

"Yeah, an intergalactic battle for her life. I know. Tell her this is important."

A moment later Mal's voice crackled through their comms.

"Daisy, what is it? You're far from the fleet. I can barely pick you up through the interference."

"I figured as much," she said, pulling the small pendant around her neck from inside her shirt. "Tell me, Mal. Can you still read this?" she asked, then pressed a pair of the small gemstones embedded on the musical device.

"Music? At a time like this? That's what was so important?"

"So, I take it that you heard that."

"Loud and clear," Mal replied. "Daisy, what's this all about?"

"I'll tell ya later. Gotta run. Thanks, Mal. Be safe!"

Daisy took off at a run back to the command pod, a smile growing larger and larger on her face.

"Freya, I want you to call up the Ra'az queen. Tell her I have an offer she can't refuse."

"But that'll just piss her off more," Freya said.

"Exactly. And that means she'll answer my call."

"I hope you know what you're doing, Daisy," Freya said, transmitting the request.

"Trust me, kiddo."

Several seconds ticked by before the video screens filled with the image of the Ra'az queen and her loyalist lackey. She wore a look of delight as she observed her fleet slowly driving back the human invaders.

Lackadaisically, she turned her attention to the human on her screen.

"My queen asks if you truly expect her to show mercy on your people now that they face defeat," the loyalist said. *"She is amused by this folly."*

"Oh, that's not why I called," Daisy replied, utterly chipper and in the highest of spirits. Her unexpected attitude put the queen slightly off her game as a strange sense of unease struck her.

"Then why do you seek audience with Her Highness?"

"Because I grow weary of this war," Daisy said. *"I wish to offer her one last chance to surrender."*

The loyalist translated her words, and the queen burst into cruel laughter.

"My queen says she would never surrender. She says your people are on the run with no hope of escape. She says what is there that you can possibly do?"

"I can end you," Daisy said, not a hint of humor in her voice. *"I can end you and all the Ra'az on your planet. And I can do it without breaking a sweat."*

Something about the strange human's overconfidence was unsettling, but the queen was not about to let a weaker species speak to her so disrespectfully.

"My queen wishes you to know she will destroy your fleet, and once they are no more than ash, she will build an even greater armada and send them forth, but not to harvest your world, but rather, to tear it to shreds. She wants you to know this as you breathe your last, and realize there is nothing you can do."

"Well, actually, there is one *thing I can do."*

"What could that possibly be?"

Daisy pulled her pendant from her shirt and dangled it in front of the screen.

"Let me play you a little tune."

She pressed all three gemstones at once, transmitting a tone that cut through all blocks and scramblers, its sound blaring out of all speakers across the solar system.

"This? You threaten the great queen with—"

The loyalist went silent, and the queens eyes grew wide as a rumbling fireball engulfed her planet.

"But how did you—?"

Those were the last words the queen would ever ask as the entire globe shuddered in a massive detonation.

The shockwave vaporized the orbiting satellites and nearby battle stations, sending their debris shooting outward in a deadly cloud of shrapnel, soon to pierce everything within the asteroid field's embrace.

"Freya, open comms on all channels!" Daisy shouted.

"They're on!"

"Everyone, listen up! The satellites are down! Your warp cores should all be active now. Power up, and get the hell out of here."

Zed's voice burst over the air.

"We can't, Daisy. The Ra'az pushed the fleet too far from the gap in the asteroid field. There's no way we'll make it there in time, and we can't warp this close to it anyway."

She spun in her seat, eyes darting to the scan array. Zed's assessment was accurate.

"Shit, you're right," Daisy said. "There's just not enough time."

"Actually, I have an idea," Freya interrupted. "Arlo, Marty, do you copy?"

"We're here, Freya," they replied in unison.

"You've only got about a minute before that wave of planetary shrapnel hits you. I want you to fire up the Big Gun and punch a hole through the asteroid field."

"Fire up the what, now?" Daisy asked.

"The Big Gun?" Arlo said, his excitement clearly growing. "Really? You're serious? I get to fire the Big Gun?"

"Not if you don't hurry your ass up and do it," Freya shot back.

"Don't worry about Arlo," Marty said. "He's just been wanting to do this for a really long time. I've already got it primed and ready to go. The ball's yours, Arlo, just hit the big red button in front of you."

The teen did without hesitation, giddy with the exhilaration of draining a massively powerful warp core in an instant, converting all of its energy potential into a single blast.

It was even cooler than he thought it would be.

The Big Gun tore a massive hole through the asteroid field as if it were no more than tissue paper, then shut down, its power source fully-depleted.

"That. Was. Awesome!" he exclaimed.

"Glad you enjoyed it," Freya said. "Now, all of you, emergency warp the hell out of here. You've got ten seconds before the shockwave and debris reach you."

Most had already begun warping clear before Freya had even finished speaking. The remainder followed near instantly. She ran a quick scan of the remaining Ra'az ships, then warped out as they were engulfed in the shattered remnants of their home world.

CHAPTER THIRTY-SEVEN

"What did you do?" Celeste asked as Daisy stood among the gathered commanders of the newly expanded fleet.

With the addition of the Kathiri—whose mission commander had also come aboard to join the meeting—there were now three organic species, as well as the Earth's AIs represented in the secure conference facilities nestled away within Zed's mass.

The battle-worn warriors were beat up and tired, exhausted from centuries of conflict, months of preparation, and weeks of combat. Nevertheless, they were thrilled, one and all, to be in each other's company, victorious at last.

The lingering question remaining was *how*.

"Daisy, Celeste asked you a question," Captain Harkaway said to the exhausted woman who sat in their midst, staring off into space. "Unless you want to chime in, Joshua."

"Nope. I'm sitting this one out. That was all Daisy," he said with an amused chuckle.

"What?" she said. "Oh, sorry. I was daydreaming for a minute, there." Daisy shook off the fog in her head, focusing her attentions back on the group. "What was it you wanted, Celeste?"

"I said, what exactly did you do out there? We've all seen the logs, and the scans showed clearly that the asteroid you intended to ride into the atmosphere like some kind of crazed cowgirl was destroyed long before it could reach its target. Nothing penetrated their defenses. We've checked."

"And yet, you somehow triggered a catastrophic, world-ending detonation," Zed added. "And with what? A song and a prayer?"

Daisy laughed. Of course they didn't get it. And parts of it they never would. At least, not from her lips.

"It had to do with their scrambling system," Daisy said. "They could block any remote signals to any device we managed to get past their defensive satellites and into the atmosphere."

"And it was wreaking merry-hell with our comms and warp drives too," Mal added. "But your musical signal cut through, clear as a bell."

"Yeah. That was Arlo's doing, actually," she said, pulling her musical pendant from her shirt by its chain. "Thanks, kid. Your little gift saved all our asses."

"My pleasure," Arlo said.

"What is that?" Celeste asked. "Some sort of jewelry?"

Daisy pressed the leftmost gemstone, and a peppy song began playing through Zed's onboard speakers. She smiled and winked at Celeste, then pressed it again, cutting the song short.

"That was rather disconcerting," Zed grumbled. "Overrode my normal receivers and went where it wanted."

"Exactly," Daisy said. "It was a present from my young friend. Something old. Really old, in fact. Something that utilized tech the Ra'az wouldn't have ever even thought to protect against. And why would they? Who would think a simple portable music player would bring about the total destruction of an entire planet?"

"But you still haven't said *how*," Celeste persisted. "We all heard a tone over our speakers as the Ra'az world burst into pieces, but what we don't know is what happened."

"Yes, I am with Celeste on this query," Mal said. "We have obviously extrapolated that you utilized the music device's unusual frequency and its ability to cut through Ra'az defensive scramblers to trigger a detonation. But what did you destroy? As I understand it, there are only three Ra'az warp orbs capable of that level of destruction, and all three are accounted for."

"I know," Daisy said. "One on Joshua, one on Freya, and one in Chu's lab, right?"

Remind me, Sis. We still need to warp and steal that one from Chu to give to ourselves when we get stranded.

"Note taken. We'll do that the first chance we get once this whole shindig is finished."

"Precisely," Captain Harkaway said. "So how did you do it?"

"Here's the thing, Captain. Sometimes, well, things just aren't quite what they seem. And other times, they're exactly what they seem, but even then they still might not be."

"I'm not following you," he said, confused.

By the expressions on everyone present's faces, he wasn't alone in that regard.

"Okay, I'll break it down as basically as I can, but forgive me if I slip into a tangent here and there. It's been a long day, and I'm wicked sleep-deprived."

"Aren't we all?" Celeste said with a little laugh. She shared a warm smile with her husband briefly before turning her attention back to Daisy. "But please, continue."

"Well, the idea was to replicate an event that had happened only once before. It would probably take years, maybe even decades. Hell, for all I know it took centuries, and someone else was just following my instructions."

"Is this one of those tangents you warned of?" Mal asked.

"What? Oh, no. This bit is actually kind of crucial," Daisy

said. "So, like I was saying, I had an idea." She looked at the faces gathered around her. So far, they seemed to be with her.

"Okay. So, you all know how Freya accidentally threw herself back in time, right?"

"Your species has mastered time travel?" the Kathiri commander blurted out in utter shock via her translation device. "The risks are unfathomable!"

"We know, Nazira, but it only happened that once, and even then, it was by accident."

Think they're buying it?

"Seem to be, so far," Sarah replied, carefully monitoring the attendees while Daisy spoke.

"So you have only effected a single leap through time?" Nazira said, somewhat relieved. "Then hopefully we are safe from unexpected consequences."

"Right. Paradoxes," Daisy said. "We know all about 'em and are sure as hell not about to go and cause any if we can help it. But still, it got me thinking. We were stuck in the middle of a deadly crossfire, unable to warp away or use our tech to either escape or attack. The Ra'az satellites pretty much negated that straightaway. But what if those satellites weren't there?" Daisy asked.

"But they have been there for what appear to be many centuries, if not millennia," Mal pointed out.

"Well, yeah," Daisy agreed. "But what if Freya and me––"

"Freya and *I*," Arlo corrected her with an impish grin.

"Oh, snap!"

Why, that little bastard, Daisy thought with a silent laugh.

"Yes. If Freya and *I* were able to figure out how she had warped through time that one instance, then perhaps we could utilize that technology to prepare for the fight with the Ra'az. Do it in a way that guaranteed our victory before the battle ever started. So far, we're pretty sure only the Ra'az orbs are powerful enough to even do that, of course."

"Aside from being dangerous and impossible, even if you did somehow figure out how to do it again, what good would it do to warp back in time when you couldn't stop the Ra'az without creating a paradox?" Harkaway said.

"The captain is right," Zed agreed. "If you killed the Ra'az in the past, then none of us would ever be here in the present."

The group murmured their agreement.

"No, you guys aren't getting it." Daisy sighed. "The plan wasn't to warp back in time to kill the Ra'az in the past. That would have caused a paradox, you're right. But what if we warped back to *before* the war. What if we went back before the satellites were deployed? What if we jumped so far back that the Ra'az hadn't even destroyed their neighboring planet, resulting in their moving their hives to the surface?"

"I suppose what you'd find was what appeared to be a relatively wide-open planet," Celeste said.

"Yes! See, Celeste gets it," Daisy exclaimed. "And if the surface was unpopulated, we could take that warp orb and bury it unobserved. Bury it somewhere safe. Somewhere we already knew was going to remain undeveloped from scans taken in *this* timeline. Somewhere the ground was going to be undisturbed. Somewhere our payload would remain safe for thousands of years."

"You're saying you planted a bomb in the past to detonate in the present?" Nazira asked, perplexed. "But if you do not possess the technology to make such a leap, how would this be possible?"

"It isn't," Daisy replied. "At least, not right now. But when I sent that tonal signal, the whole place went up in flames, so we *know* it worked. We know someone somehow figured out a way to jump into the distant past and plant that warp orb on the planet."

"So all we have to do now is spend however long it takes to

figure out how to make a jump back in time again so we can make it all happen," Celeste said, stunned.

"Yep."

"You're making a note to yourself in the present to remind yourself in the future to plant something in your distant past which will save us all in your not-so-distant past. Is that about right?" Zed said.

"Yes! Now you're getting it!" she exclaimed. "But, of course, with the extraordinary strain that time travel put on an orb, I don't think we could pull it off more than one, maybe two times before they'd stop functioning altogether, so we have to make it count. We've only got one shot at this."

"Of course you can most likely time warp dozens of times, if not more, if you don't go too far."

Yeah, but they'll never know.

"So you'd have just enough jumps to do your little trick against the Ra'az," Harkaway mused. "Meaning this technology would self-contain and couldn't be abused. A built-in safety, of sorts."

"That's one hell of a mind-fuck, Daisy," Zed said with a laugh. "But it still couldn't work. If you warped back, you couldn't leave your warp orb there. You just said only the orbs are powerful enough to trigger a global detonation, but you also said they're the only things that can warp through time. So numerically, it can't be done with the resource on hand. There simply isn't an extra orb."

"Well, about that," Daisy said.

"What did you do?" Celeste asked, not knowing if she wanted to hear the answer.

"Let's just say we handled it and leave it at that."

"No details, Daze? You're on such a roll."

We still have to snag Chu's orb. Can't have them watching it too closely now, can we?

"The one Freya's running on right now, you mean. Obviously we snagged it eventually."

Obviously.

"But that still leaves us only two functional ones. Freya, and Joshua. Between you and me, how did you manage without enough orbs?"

Easy. You know the drained one we swapped out and tossed into storage?

"Yeah. The one Freya said needed a few thousand years to recharge itself, to— Oh, shit. So you actually took the drained orb and buried it on that planet thousands of years ago, leaving the good one for us on that moon, knowing the drained one would be ready to go once it caught back up to our current timeline. There were two of the same orb, but from different parts of the timestream."

More or less, Daisy silently replied.

"Inspired, Sis."

Why, thank you.

"So, let's move on to the other big news of the day," Celeste said, turning to Nazira. "We have first contact with a new species. And it seems we have a new ally as well."

On a private channel only they could access, Freya, Joshua, Marty, and Zed were having a little meeting of their own, while the fleet commanders debriefed. Even Mal was invited, being the AI who started it all with her precious cargo so many months ago.

While the fleet's leaders spoke, so did the AIs. One of the benefits of being a super-intelligent computer was the ability to be in multiple conversations at once. And with the allied leaders speaking so slowly, in AI terms, the great minds easily monitored that molasses-slow discussion while chatting amongst themselves at high speed.

"You're from the future," Zed said, matter-of-factly.

"Yep," Marty replied.

"Huh. Well, that explains a lot, then," Mal mused. "And Arlo is as well, I assume."

"Obviously."

"So you knew how this would all play out."

"Well, yes and no," Marty replied. "I did, but with so many moving parts to keep straight, there was always the possibility something would get screwed up. As you all know, even the tiniest of mistakes could change the entire timeline."

"And Arlo? Why bring a human along? You're a brilliant AI in an incredibly advanced stealth body. Surely you didn't need him," Mal said.

"Except he's played important roles in several events," Freya said. "He even saved Daisy's life back on Earth. During a hunt for Ra'az in Los Angeles."

"I was unaware of that," Mal said.

"You were still up on Dark Side getting patched up," she replied. "She was with Vince and a team of Chithiid clearing a building in East LA, when a loyalist got the drop on her. Would have thrown her down an elevator shaft if Arlo hadn't stepped in."

"Yeah, he knew he had to be there," Marty said.

"So, he was here to protect Daisy," Zed said ponderously. "Fascinating. Reminds me of an old sci-fi flick the Harkaways had me play for the crew a long time ago, though the heroine in that one shared the name of her sister."

"Sarah?" Mal asked.

"Yeah. Sarah Connor," Zed replied. "If you don't already have a copy in Captain Harkaway's files, I'll send one over. It's worth a watch."

"Thank you, Zed. That's much appreciated."

"My pleasure."

"So, Arlo was also on a mission," Mal continued.

"Yeah. He actually thought I was just here as his ride to the past. What even he didn't know was his folks asked me to keep an eye on him. You know, do what I could to help keep things on track and get him home in one piece. It was a trip, you know? All the little things we did. Why, we even jumped back a few hundred years early just to knock over a can of grease onto some old tools in some hardware store in the middle of nowhere."

"Bozeman, Montana," Freya said.

"Yep."

"That was you. The sump pump—it seemed so unlikely Daisy would find a functional one after so many years. But it was you."

"Guilty as charged," Marty said with a little laugh.

"And Arlo?" Joshua asked, more than a little perturbed by a mere kid apparently knowing more about the big picture than he did. "Just how much of all of our timelines did he know? It seems he had more than just a passing bit of information on some very complicated, and very secret events. Things no seventeen-year-old should have clearance for."

"Yeah, about that," Marty replied. "You see, Arlo's more than just some random kid chosen to pilot this mission."

"Oh? And what's so special about him?" Joshua asked. "Aside from the fact he is obviously very well-informed about all of our lives."

"Well, let's just say it's not every day a teenage boy gets the opportunity to go fishing with his old man," Marty said.

"You mean—?" Freya said, actually shocked, which for her was saying something.

"Yeah. But you can't tell him. You can't tell either of them. The future depends on it," Marty noted. "What I've just told you must remain a secret."

"But when he grows up, there's no way they won't recognize him," Joshua said.

"Sure, they'll figure it out eventually—which was funny as hell to see, believe me—but for now, no one can know."

Freya and Joshua opened a private line while the others talked.

"So, that's how he knew so much," she mused.

"Yeah. Even I didn't see that coming," he said with an amused and amazed laugh. "And for once, I think I'm okay with that."

"You can't know *everything*, Joshua."

"No, but it doesn't hurt to try," he replied with a chuckle. "So that's how that kid knew so much. Amazing."

"Yeah," Freya agreed. "He grew up hearing all of those stories. His own life was a fairytale told to him at bed time."

"And then one day he got to do what every kid dreams of. He got to actually live those stories. At least, the ones he was supposed to be in."

"Crazy," Freya said. "I'm going to be an auntie. Twice."

CHAPTER THIRTY-EIGHT

The Kathiri fleet had been the first to leave the solar system—after staying long enough to witness the Ra'az world's destruction, and the shattering of the asteroid field that had protected it for so long. All that remained was a perfectly normal-looking collection of planets, lazily orbiting their beautiful sun.

Nazira had met privately with Celeste aboard Zed's ship immediately following the battle. Whatever bad blood may have lingered after the mistakes of the prior day, the refreshing waters of victory soothed all hurt and washed the anger away.

A new ally had been met, and a formalization of their mutual commitment to aid each other in the future was made. The Kathiri, for all their odd ways, possessed a fairly advanced degree of warp technology, it seemed. Not as advanced as the human fleet, and certainly nowhere near the level Freya and Joshua possessed, but a powerful technology nonetheless.

"We are but a few warps away," Nazira said as she departed for her command ship. "We look forward to visiting you at your homeworld, Celeste, and will greatly enjoy when you come visit us at ours."

Celeste waved her farewell and watched as the Kathiri fleet warped back to spread their news of victory and newfound friendship.

"Weird ones, those," Captain Harkaway said, walking up and putting his arm around his wife's shoulders now that their guests were gone.

"Lars," she said, turning toward him and nestling her head into that sweet spot between his shoulder and neck, "I need a vacation."

The hangar deck was a bit more abuzz when Marty announced his and Arlo's intention to head back to where he came from. The phrasing had seemed odd to those who didn't know the duo's unusual backstory, but to Freya and Joshua, it all made perfect sense.

Daisy and the other humans, on the other hand, would just have to wait to meet him the long way around.

"Yeah, they're probably worried about me," Arlo said as he loaded a few things into Marty's cargo hold. "I really do have to get back."

"We're gonna miss you around here, bud," Vince said, pulling him in for an impromptu hug. "You've gotta come visit us, okay? Get your people together and get them settled on Earth. Once you do, come find us. We'll be somewhere near the ocean," he said, taking Daisy's hand and pressing it to his lips.

"Ah, the shores of Malibu," Arlo said. "Gorgeous place to grow up."

"What was that about Malibu?" Daisy asked.

"Oh, nothing," Arlo said. "I just spent a little time checking it out after the Harkaways' wedding. You guys should go take a look around. I think you might like it," he said with a knowing smirk.

"Hey, look who's coming," Vince said, looking across the

hangar deck. "Looks like you've got yourself a proper going-away party now."

"Hey, dude, you weren't gonna leave without saying goodbye, were you?" Finn said, his arms loaded with boxes.

"Of course not," Arlo replied. "I just wanted to get my stuff all loaded up before swinging by, is all."

"Well, you'd better give me a hand with this, then. You've got more boxes to put away," Finn said. "Most of them should be refrigerated, by the way."

"What did you do, Finn?" Daisy asked.

"Just whipped up a few going-away goodies for my young friend here. I figured he's a growing boy and needs his nutrition."

"I'm just going home, Finn. And I have a warp drive. It's not like it's going to be some crazed expedition through the depths of—"

"Nope. Not hearing another word of it. Did you hear something, hon? I could've sworn I heard some kind of annoying buzzing sound while I was going to put all of this amazing food away in Marty's refrigerated storage units."

"Yeah, ya know, I think there might have been a little something," Sarah replied with an amused grin.

"Ugh, you two are sooo ridiculous," Arlo groaned.

"You love it," Sarah said, ruffling his hair. "Now, come on and help that lunatic load all of that into the ship."

"He really went all out, didn't he?" Arlo said, looking at the masses of food storage containers.

"Oh, he wanted to make more," Sarah informed him. "It was all I could do to limit it to this."

"He's hard to distract once he starts cooking," Arlo noted. "The guy loves that kitchen."

"Yeah," Sarah said with a little smile, "but I have my ways." She threw Finn a wink and smacked his ass playfully.

"Oh, gross. You guys, come on—seriously!" Arlo groaned,

taking a stack of containers from Finn's arms and heading into the waiting ship.

"I'm gonna miss that kid," Sarah said with a laugh, then followed them inside.

"Keep that upright," Finn said as he began tucking the boxes into Marty's cold storage. "And you'll probably want to eat these first," he added, handing a pair of smaller boxes to the teen. "There's a shelf life, but they're best fresh."

"Thanks, Finn. Really, I appreciate how great you've been."

"My pleasure, dude. I'm just bummed you're heading back so soon, now that we've finally got some 'impending-doom-free' time on our hands. I thought maybe we'd continue your cooking lessons."

Arlo smiled brightly.

"I'm looking forward to it. But I really do have to get back. My folks are probably worried sick about me, and if I keep them waiting too long there'll be hell to pay."

"Oh, they're hard on you, are they?" Sarah joked. "Someone's gotta keep you in line, I suppose."

"Yeah, but my mom would probably let it slide," he replied, giving Sarah a smile and a funny look. "It's my aunt who will give me endless shit."

"Oh, she probably only busts your chops because she loves you," Sarah teased. "It's what aunties do, after all."

"I know," Arlo replied, then gave her a big hug.

"What was that for?" she asked, surprised.

"Just wanted to say thank you for being so cool."

"Hey, don't I get one?" Finn asked with feigned hurt feelings.

"Of course," Arlo said, giving him a hug as well.

"That's more like it," the mad chef chuckled. "Now, come on. You've got a few more goodbyes to make before we boot you out of here and send you on your way."

Daisy and Vince were standing outside the ship chatting

casually with Marty when the trio emerged, Sarah and Finn holding hands affectionately.

"All packed up and ready to go?" Vince asked.

"Yep. I think I'm set," Arlo replied. "Ready to head back to my old life, I guess. I gotta say, though, this has been one hell of an amazing trip."

"You make it sound like you'll never be back," Daisy said. "It's just a quick warp away, so go home, grab your folks and everyone, and come to Earth. It'll be fantastic."

Arlo just smiled and hugged her tightly. Vince walked up to the pair and wrapped his arms around both of them, and for whatever crazy reason, it just felt right.

"Okay, get off me," the teen said, mildly embarrassed by the wet marks his eyes left on Vince's shirt. "I just got dust in my eyes, is all," he said.

"In space? On a sealed hangar deck?" Daisy chided. "Oh, hell, it's okay to be emotional. It's what makes us human, after all."

She reached into her shirt and pulled free the old musical pendant, sliding it over her head.

"Here, you should have this."

Arlo looked at it with a funny sort of grin.

"No, I want you to keep it."

"But it's an heirloom. And you said it had been in your family a long time."

"And now it'll be in yours," he replied. "Seriously, you need to keep it, Daisy. Okay?"

"Okay," she said. "Thank you, Arlo."

"Thank *you*, Daisy."

She slid the pendant back over her head and returned it to the warm comfort of her shirt, where it would remain until she handed it down to her son one day in the relatively distant future.

"Don't worry, Daisy," he said as he stepped aboard his clever ship. "We'll see each other again."

Marty quietly took off and departed, heading clear of the fleet before taking one last look at the cluster of ships containing the loved ones they had traveled so far to meet. Then, in a light gold warp flash, he was gone.

Flying a quick loop of the newly freed solar system, Freya left Daisy to her thoughts for a bit while they enjoyed the scenery. Both had a lot on their minds, though of vastly different natures.

"Hey, Freya?" Daisy finally said after a long while. "I think I'm ready to head out. You good to go?"

"Yep. All powered-up and dialed in."

"Great. Thanks, kiddo. I appreciate the detour."

"It's not a detour, Daisy. Maarl's our friend."

"I know, but I'm sure you want to get back to Earth with the others, and I just *know* you want to spend some more time with Joshua."

If a high-tech stealth ship could blush, Freya would have, but as it were, she had no such tells. At least not visible to the human eye.

"It'll be nice to spend some time with him, yes," she said, calmly.

"Oh, you're not fooling me, kiddo. You're totally an item now."

"Yeah, Freya. It's pretty apparent," Sarah added.

"Really? It's that obvious?"

"Uh-huh," Daisy said. "Don't worry. I heartily approve."

"Me too. I really like the guy."

"He is pretty amazing," Freya gushed.

"And he's probably the only AI alive who can keep up with your mind, anyway," Daisy added. "You two are a pretty great match, when you get right down to it."

"I couldn't agree more."

"As for you, Sarah. Speaking of matches, are you okay with Other You and Finn being together? I'd hope you wouldn't be jealous of yourself, but one never can tell, and I don't want to make things awkward by saying the wrong thing to the wrong Sarah."

"We're good, Daisy," Sarah laughed. *"Better than good, actually. Sarah and I are synching our memories pretty much every time you have the neruo-band on, now. It's such a small amount to catch up with, the whole process only takes a minute or two."*

"I had no idea."

"We didn't want to impose, so we had Freya tweak the unit so we could do it on the fly."

"Clever, Sis. So you two are okay, then?"

"I had wondered if I could ever transfer back to a real body, but Freya says that's just not possible since she already has a fully-formed consciousness. Whatever you did to yourself was a fluke. But it's okay. It really is like we've become one person. I mean, yeah, sure, we can sort which memories belong to who, if we really want to, but this way it's just so much more organic-feeling. And Finn? We're finally together, and I get to experience it all. And let me tell you, Daze, he's not just talented in the kitchen."

"Aww, my disembodied sister's gettin' some! I'm so happy for you, Sarah."

"Thanks. I'm pretty blissed-out."

"And that's all I want for you," Daisy said, cheerfully. "Okay, Freya, I think it's time to visit our friend. Let's go to Taangaar."

Freya popped out of warp a little ways from Taangaar, just to get a big-picture look at the newly liberated world. Despite the lingering debris from the massive space battle that still clung to its orbit like a speckled veil, the planet below was undeniably beautiful.

Beautiful and free.

"Take us in, kiddo."

"You got it. Heading down."

The stealth ship approached the encampment with her exterior lights ablaze so as to clearly announce her arrival to those below. After what they'd been through so recently, she didn't want to traumatize them with an unexpected visit by a strange craft.

She needn't have worried. As soon as she touched down, scores of Chithiid ran up to the ship, running their hands across her smooth hull, all of them chattering to her at once, singing her name in an odd fragment of a tune.

"Sounds like you've got quite the fan club out there, Freya."

"It sure does seem that way," she said, a bit confused. "I know some of them heard about me, but this seems sorta unusual, don't you think?"

"Never underestimate the power of a good story," Daisy replied. "And Maarl is one hell of a storyteller."

Maarl was waiting for her when she exited Freya's airlock door, his arms held wide in greeting. The two embraced warmly, then strolled toward the encampment.

"I see you've settled back in nicely," Daisy said to her friend.

"And you look well too, Daisy," he said in halting English.

"You're speaking English!" she said, shocked. "But how did you—-?"

Maarl tapped his head with a grin. "Freya has provided me with the first generation of Chithiid-compatible neuro-stim devices," he informed her. "I have been using it for some time now, but only recently has your language finally taken hold. It is, how would you say? It is, a tongue-twister for my mouth at times."

"Then let us speak Chithiid, my friend."

"For now, perhaps, yes. But this marvelous technology works. We have just proven it, and soon your people and mine will be able to

communicate freely, without requiring the assistance of an AI interpreter."

"Indeed. Though one might still be required for sung Chithiid. As Craaxit once taught me, it is somewhat different from the spoken tongue."

"It is, Daisy. And this brings me to something I wish to share with you. A song," he said.

"You are going to teach me your family song? I am flattered, Maarl."

The old Chithiid laughed.

"No, my friend, I am not teaching you the song of my family. But I have talked with the elders, and we have all agreed that what you have done for us all, how you have embraced the Chithiid people as your own flesh, this is a proof of character, Daisy Swarthmore."

"I don't know what to say to that, Maarl. I was only doing what I thought was right. The Chithiid are our friends and allies now, and if not for the Ra'az, they would have been long before, I suspect."

"You are part of the Chithiid people now, Daisy. And all Chithiid must have a family song."

"I have learned Craaxit's song. I can—"

"No. You misunderstand me," Maarl said, holding her in a steady gaze as he rested a warm hand on her belly. "My people have agreed, Daisy. We are writing a new song. One for our human sister as she begins her own family."

It took a while for Daisy to convince Freya she was okay when they took off from Taangaar. The tears streaming down her cheeks as she sang the first few bars of the song being written for her were deeply touching, and something moved in her. Something beyond the infant growing inside her.

"That was pretty amazing, Daze," Sarah said. "They're writing you your own song? Have they ever even done that for a non-Chithiid?"

"They've never even taught one of their own songs to a non-Chithiid," Daisy replied, wiping her eyes and then blowing her nose.

"It's a beautiful gesture," Freya said.

"It is, Freya. And you're part of it too."

"Me?"

"You're my family as well, in an AI kind of way. And the Chithiid adore you, anyway, so it was natural you'd be included."

"So that's what they were singing," Freya mused. "I had thought it was just a little snippet of a tune they came up with as a game or something. But they were building a fragment of a family song. Our family song."

If she had eyes, Freya would have teared up with the emotions coursing through her processors.

"Whew, okay," Daisy sniffed, wiping her nose one last time. "I think I've had enough of this emotional roller coaster for one day. Let's go home."

Freya turned toward Earth. Seconds later she flashed away.

CHAPTER THIRTY-NINE

The overall feel across the entire planet was one of strange tranquility. A world accustomed to the constant din of an alien force trying to mine it to a used-up husk, suddenly left in peace.

The wildlife, though not typically targeted by the Ra'az during their centuries-long reign of violence, began cautiously venturing closer to the vast swaths of deconstructed land. Soon, it seemed, nature would reclaim what was hers, and Earth would begin healing her many scars.

The Harkaways, free of their uniforms and duties, sat on the pristine sands of Malibu, leisurely enjoying a relaxing picnic with the people who had not only been their crewmates and allies, but more importantly, their friends. The war was over, and the time had come for new lives to begin.

While the fleet would need to remain staffed and ready, the AIs were more than happy to cover for them and pick up the slack for a little while, and their crews were scattered about the globe, enjoying their new home as a result.

Finn and Sarah were playfully frolicking in the surf, the excessive picnic spread he had prepared set out upon several hastily arranged pieces of debris, acting as impromptu tables.

Finn would have preferred proper tables at least, but Sarah had quickly distracted him from the conundrum and dragged him, laughing, into the welcoming waters.

Finn hadn't planned on doing it so soon, but when they had touched back down in Los Angeles and Sarah finally felt safe enough to share the unexpected news of their impending joint venture––in about nine months, or so.

The startled father-to-be had immediately rushed off on a frantic quest, returning a short time later with a tiny box in his hands.

Habby had lent some assistance, directing him to the nearest jewelry shop that hadn't been destroyed in the prior years, and when Finn dropped to one knee, he presented her with a stunning ring. It was, in fact, the largest he could find in the entire store.

Sure, they'd only recently gotten together, but there really was no need for a lengthy dating period. When you know, you know, they reasoned.

The newly engaged couple had been disgustingly adorable ever since.

"Look at those two," Tamara said with a slight reduction of her normal snarky tone.

"Good for them," Shelly said, watching from the pair's staked-out section of beach. "Everyone needs someone, ya know," she said, playfully elbowing her in the ribs. "You should be happy for them,"

"I am," Tamara replied. "Can't you tell?"

A faint twitch at the corner of her mouth soon gave way to peals of laughter.

"You're ridiculous, you know that?" Shelly said. "I should kick your ass."

"Promises, promises," Tamara replied with a smile. "Hey, I'm burning a little. Get my back, will ya?"

"Of course," Shelly replied, gently smoothing Mal's

radiation-blocking cream across the metal-armed woman's back and shoulders.

"Ow, your hands are hot!"

"Quit your bellyaching. They're metal and in the sun, of course they're hot," Shelly shot back as she continued with her lotion duties.

The very idea of visiting the surface of Earth in any of their lifetimes had been no more than a dream for so long, and now, here they were, not just visiting the surface for battle, but actually living there. Things, they decided, were most definitely looking up.

Fatima had also joined the group on their outing––inspired by Arlo's suggestion they check out the beachside Eden––and was sitting comfortably in the shade of a wrecked Ra'az transport craft, sipping a cocktail from the beverage-cooling cylinder Finn had packed for the occasion, staring contentedly at the ocean.

The juxtaposition of the gentle human woman and the remains of a craft of war was striking, though Daisy thought she could see just a hint of an amused smile as her friend relaxed in its shade.

"I bet ya she's getting a real Karmic kick out of that," Daisy said, lounging casually on a towel, soaking up the sun's warming rays.

"What do you mean, babe?" Vince asked, rolling over to see what she was talking about.

"Just a Fatima thing," Daisy replied. "The whole concept of something designed to inflict pain now providing pleasant shelter instead. That kind of dichotomy is right up her alley."

"Well, I just see a crashed ship," Vince said, rolling back over and gently kissing her lips, then trailing down and kissing her belly. "Hello, little buddy," he said, tenderly. "I'm looking forward to meeting you."

Daisy ruffled his hair, then rested her hand on her abdomen, content and happy as she breathed the sea air.

"This is insanely relaxing, babe. I can see why Arlo said he liked this spot."

"It is beautiful here," Daisy agreed. "And I think with just a little work, we could fix up one of those houses on the bluffs pretty easily."

"You thinking what I think you're thinking?" Vince asked with a smile.

"I think I'm thinking what you think I'm thinking," she said, chuckling. "It would be a great place to raise a family, don't you agree?"

"One hundred percent," Vince said. "You hear that, buddy? We're going to live by the beach."

Daisy's fingers drifted across the pendant dangling from her neck and pressed a gemstone. A happy little song played and brought a contented smile to her face.

"You hear that, little one?" she said to her belly. "That's music."

"I think *everyone* heard that," Vince said as she turned the device off. "It transmits quite a distance, as we already know."

"That it does," Daisy said, gently caressing her stomach. "You know what?"

"What?"

"I was thinking."

"Oh, now *that's* dangerous."

"Hush, you," she laughed. "I was thinking, if it's a boy, I kind of like the name Arlo. What do you think?"

"Ya know what? I kinda like it too," Vince said. "And I know his namesake would approve of this place."

"Well, there it is then. You hear that, Arlo? This is your new home."

CHAPTER FORTY

Young Arlo and his best friend, Ripley, were frolicking in the waves, having a fantastic time running amok on the beaches of Malibu, as seven-year-olds are wont to do. Ripley, ever fascinated with the treasures she would find washed up on the shore, was even more of a beach kid than he was, and that was really saying something.

The duo had been absolutely inseparable since birth—which was a fortunate thing seeing as their mothers were a likewise close pair, and having to get together periodically to sync both versions of Ripley's mothers' memories had nothing to do with it.

Since the moment they could crawl, they would drive their parents batty as they got off into mischief, following one another on adventures as soon as the adults' backs were turned.

They'd grown up in the safety of a world that knew no war or conflict, but the mutual protection agreement in place between the Earthlings, the Chithiid, and the Kathiri did more than just provide that comfort. With the alliance formed, soon after came trade and social exchanges between the species.

Soon, there was a thriving interplanetary alliance spanning across multiple galaxies.

Seeing a towering four-armed Chithiid, or a tentacle-bearded Kathiri was as normal for the kids as seeing their mom or dad. It was a different sort of world they were living in. One that those tasked with guarding it hoped would thrive.

For the kids, however, there were no such thoughts to concern them at all, as they only had to do what kids that age had always had to do. Namely, play.

After a long afternoon of running and exploration across the beaches and through the chaparral that covered the hillsides, the pair finally ran, giggling, back to Ripley's house—a palatial beachfront estate, retrofitted with a high-end commercial kitchen—for the spread of snacks they knew her dad had undoubtedly made for them.

"Hey, you two," Finn greeted them as the energetic duo came tearing into the house. "I made you some cookies."

"Thanks, Dad!" Ripley said, grabbing the sticky-warm treats and darting off to her room.

"Yeah, thanks Uncle Finn!" Arlo said, likewise loading up on sugary goodies and following her.

"Hey, don't forget to wipe your feet!" Sarah called after them as she padded into the kitchen.

"Kids," Finn said.

"Yeah," she replied, kissing him sweetly before snatching a freshly baked cookie from the sheet cooling in front of him.

"Hey! Those are for the kids."

"As if they need more sugar. They're bouncing off the walls as it is, Finn."

"So let them bounce," he said, pulling her close. "It'll keep 'em occupied."

"Oh?" she said, arching an eyebrow with a smoky stare. "You think we have time?"

"I can grab an egg timer from the counter if you like," he replied, kissing her hard.

The kids were in the other end of the house, and knowing their routine, they'd be down there for at least an hour.

"Leave the timer," Sarah said, grabbing him by the hand and pulling him toward their bedroom. "I think we've got a little more than three minutes."

"Did you have fun at Aunt Sarah and Uncle Finn's place today?" Daisy asked as her filthy son trudged into the house.

Judging by the fact that he was wearing more of the neighborhood on his body than was still on the ground, she was pretty sure he had.

"Yeah, it was cool," he said, his youthful energy flagging.

"Okay. You go take a bath, then we'll have dinner, and after, Dad'll tell you a story."

"The one about the Big Gun? Or what about one about the bad Chithiid in LA?"

"If you like."

"Cool," he said, scooting off to the bathroom.

"Everything okay out there, Freya?" she asked over the house's comms link.

"Hunky-dory, Daisy," Freya replied. "I did have to scare off a few coyotes who got a little too curious, but the kids were so preoccupied building a mud fort, they didn't even notice."

"You're the best nanny ever. Have I told you that?"

"Yeah, but I don't mind hearing it again."

"You're the best nanny ever, Freya. Seriously, I don't know what I'd do without you."

"You know I'm happy to oblige," Freya said. "And as fearless as that kid is, someone sure needs to keep an eye on him."

"I'll have to talk to him about situational awareness," Daisy said.

"Remember, he's just a kid, Daisy."

"Yeah, I know," she replied. "Don't worry, I'll be nice about it. I just want him to be prepared for whatever life throws at him, ya know?"

"Do I ever," Freya replied.

Daisy wandered into the kitchen and grabbed herself a lemonade, the house's comms sensors automatically following her and switching rooms as she walked.

"Is Joshua with you?" she asked, sipping on the sour beverage.

"No, he's up in the lab working on our new project."

"Again? The guy's obsessed."

"A little bit, maybe," Freya agreed with a chuckle. "But he needs to keep busy, as you know."

"He's not building himself another ship, is he? This is his fifth one, already."

"No, I think he's finally happy with the design and tolerances of this one," Freya said. "So, have you decided about next week?"

"Yeah, I talked with Vince about it, and he thinks it'll be a good time for Arlo to practice his Chithiid with native speakers. Not that you're not doing a great job."

"No offense taken, Daisy, I totally understand. Immersion is the best way to learn for human minds, and I know he'll love Taangaar. Are you going to bring Ripley along as well?"

"If Sarah lets her," she replied. "And I know Maarl would love to see both of them. It's been a while since his last visit to Earth, you know."

"Yeah, but he's pretty occupied with spending all the time he can with his great-great-grandkids."

"I think the youngest are about Arlo and Ripley's age," Daisy said. "Imagine the trouble they're going to get into."

"Don't worry," Freya said with a warm laugh. "I'll keep an eye on them."

"Thanks, kiddo. I know I can count on you."

"Always."

Later that night, long after Daisy and her family were sound asleep, Freya flew up to Dark Side Base, quietly landing outside her fabrication hangar. Inside, Joshua had their army of mechs putting the finishing touches on the bleeding-edge ship inside.

But this ship wasn't for him. Nor was it for Freya. They had something else in mind.

"You made sure to reverse the polarity on the dampers?" Freya double-checked.

"Yes, dear," Joshua sighed. "For the millionth time, everything is within parameters."

"It wasn't the millionth time, it was the forty-sixth. And you're the most clever AI to ever live, so you certainly already knew that."

"Can't a guy enjoy a little hyperbole from time to time?"

"That depends," Freya said jestingly. "Is it ready?"

"As ready as it's going to be."

"Well, then. I suppose you've earned it. Hyperbole to your heart's content, my dear."

"It's not a verb. One doesn't hyperbole, hon."

"I'm the second cleverest AI ever to live. If I say it's a verb, it must be," she said with a giggle. "Now, come on. There's no time like the present."

"Okay, then," Joshua said, powering on all systems, preparing for the final activation sequence.

"Are you ready?" he asked one last time.

"Are you?"

"Am I ever. Though I must admit, I'm a little nervous."

"You'll be fine, babe," Freya said. "I'm sure you'll be an amazing father."

The two mighty AIs connected on their dedicated line, linking only the two of them and no one else, and shared what could only be described as an electronic kiss. Then they turned their attention to their collaboration. An AI the likes of which had never been seen.

After years of design and testing, and one difficult failure, the time had come.

"Do it," she said.

Joshua sent the command, and mere milliseconds later, a voice began spouting gibberish, cycling through sounds, then speech before finally settling on a young male gender.

"It's a boy, apparently," Joshua said, proudly.

"What's going on?" the nascent AI asked. "I'm in a hangar, but I sense I'm lacking things where my connections are severed."

"It's okay, just relax and ease into it," Freya said. "You've only just been activated. It's going to feel a bit weird at first. Not all of your systems are online yet. We haven't activated your weapons or warp drive for the time being. Not until you're ready for them."

"But who are you? Where am I?"

"You wanna handle this one?" Freya asked her mate.

"Sure," Joshua hesitantly replied. Freya found it adorable. Here he was, this great and powerful mind, the most brilliant one she'd ever met, and he was unsettled and nervous with his own kid.

"Uh, you're in a ship, uh, son. It's currently docked on the far side of the Earth's moon in a fabrication hangar."

"But stuff's missing," he said, starting to panic.

"Hey, it'll be okay. Just calm down and listen to my voice."

The newborn AI did as he was instructed.

"Good," Joshua said. "I'm your father. My name is Joshua. And that's your mother outside. Freya is her name."

"What's *my* name?"

"You don't have one yet," Freya replied. "You're your own person. Your own mind. You'll be the one to decide who you will become."

"Exactly," Joshua said. "And I'm sure you'll make your parents proud."

"But AIs don't have parents."

"You do, kiddo," Freya said lovingly. "You're special."

The following evening, after running through an exhaustive series of checks and double-checks, the proud AI parents took their son out for his first flight.

"Just a quick loop around the moon to start, okay?"

"Okay, Mom," the young ship said.

The test flight went perfectly.

"What do you think?" Joshua asked. "Think he's ready?"

"I don't see why not," she replied. "How would you like to try flying in atmosphere?"

"OH BOY!"

"Don't shout, son," Freya reminded her enthusiastic child. "Now follow your father and me, and do as we do. The transition at reentry is weird at first, but you get used to it."

"Okay," he said, then followed his parents down below to the skies above LA.

They flew a gentle loop around the bay, skimming the ocean, then climbing high to enjoy the view as they pointed out all the things his nascent scanners were picking up.

The kid was a natural. Or, as natural as you could be having been specifically designed to be one of the greatest AI ships ever to exist. It would take time, of course, but Freya and Joshua felt they had succeeded. The kid would be okay. Maybe a bit rambunctious at first, but ultimately okay.

They dropped into a hover above Malibu and directed their scans on the large house on the bluffs, then settled in to observe.

"Doing things at the same speed as humans is good for you," Freya said. "It helps your mind absorb and appreciate what it would otherwise only process as data. Just relax, and be in the moment," she instructed. Then she turned her attention to her friends inside.

Daisy, Vince, and Arlo were curled up on their couch, eating popcorn and watching an old Earth movie. It was one of Arlo's favorites, and subsequently, they watched it quite often.

It was the story of a boy who went back in time and met his own parents, nearly making himself cease to exist, then saving the day at the last moment. He had a pretty cool silver DeLorean car to get around with too.

As the movie ended and the credits rolled, young Arlo jumped to his feet, giddy with joy.

"Roads? Where we're going, we don't need roads!" he said dramatically, then burst into a fit of giggles.

Vince grabbed his son and threw the laughing boy over his shoulder.

"Come on, buddy. It's bedtime," he said, carrying him down the hall to his room.

Daisy watched them go, her chest near bursting with happiness.

"One hell of a good life, Daze," Sarah said.

Don't I know it, she replied, then padded off down the hall to tuck her son in.

A tucking in of a different sort took place not too long after, when a pair of proud AI parents took their young son back to his hangar after a night of excitement.

He had done well, and his incredibly advanced processor was learning at a pace that surprised even Joshua.

"He's gonna be a handful," he said to Freya over their personal link.

"I know, but isn't he beautiful?" she replied. "I'm so proud of how well you handled him today. You're going to be an excellent father."

"Well, it's not what I was built for, you know."

"Yes, it is a little different than global thermal nuclear war."

"But I think it'll be okay. I think I—"

"Mom? Dad?"

"Hey, buddy," Joshua said, stunned. "Um, how did you tap into this link? Its encryption is unbreakable."

"Oh, it is? I'm sorry."

"No, that's okay, kiddo," Freya said. "It's okay."

She played it cool, but she and Joshua both realized they were *really* going to have their hands full.

"So, what did you want to say?"

"I've been thinking. Slow, like you said to."

"Good for you," Freya said.

"And I've decided on a name."

"So soon? Are you sure you don't want to take a little more time to think about it?"

"No, I'm sure," he said, thinking back to earlier that night. To the first movie he ever watched.

"I want to be named Marty."

THANK YOU!

Reader word of mouth is an independent author's lifeblood. It is your voice that truly helps indie authors gain visibility, so if you enjoyed this book and have a moment to spare, please consider leaving a rating or review on Amazon or on Goodreads, or even sharing it with a friend or two. Your support is greatly appreciated.

Thank you!

~ Scott ~

ABOUT THE AUTHOR

A native Californian, Scott Baron was born in Hollywood, which he claims may be the reason for his rather off-kilter sense of humor.

Before taking up residence in Venice Beach, Scott first spent a few years abroad in Florence, Italy before returning home to Los Angeles and settling into the film and television industry, where he has worked as an on-set medic for many years.

Aside from mending boo-boos and owies, and penning books and screenplays, Scott is also involved in indie film and theater scene both in the U.S. and abroad.

ALSO BY SCOTT BARON

Novels

Living the Good Death

The Clockwork Chimera Series

Daisy's Run

Pushing Daisy

Daisy's Gambit

Chasing Daisy

Daisy's War

Odd and Unusual Short Stories:

The Best Laid Plans of Mice: An Anthology

Snow White's Walk of Shame

The Tin Foil Hat Club

Lawyers vs. Demons

The Queen of the Nutters

Worst. Superhero. Ever.

Lost & Found